FIREWEED

Other Novels by Mildred Walker
Available in Bison Book Editions

THE CURLEW'S CRY

WINTER WHEAT

FIREWEED

MILDRED WALKER

Introduction to the Bison Book Edition
by Annick Smith

University of Nebraska Press
Lincoln and London

First Bison Book printing: 1994
Most recent printing indicated by the last digit below:
10   9   8   7   6   5   4   3   2   1

Library of Congress Cataloging-in-Publication Data
Walker, Mildred, 1905–
Fireweed / Mildred Walker; introduction to the Bison Book edition by
Annick Smith.
p.   cm.
ISBN 0-8032-9758-0 (pbk.)
1. Lumber trade—Michigan—Upper Peninsula—Fiction. 2. Young
women—Michigan—Upper Peninsula—Fiction. 3. Marriage—Michi-
gan—Upper Peninsula—Fiction. 4. Upper Peninsula (Mich.)—Fiction. I.
Title.
PS3545.A524F57   1934   93-44130
813'.52.dc20   CIP

Reprinted by arrangement with Mildred Walker Schemm.

This novel was granted first prize in the Avery Hopwood and Jule Hopwood
Awards Contest for 1933 at the University of Michigan.

∞

To my mother and father

Introduction to the Bison Book Edition
LEARNING TO STAY PUT
by Annick Smith

Fireweed is a common wild flowering plant. It grows all over the United States, except in the East, where Mildred Walker was raised in Baptist parsonages around Philadelphia. The weed is stalky, rising from one to seven feet and holding many lance-shaped leaves. Its blossoms are pink, or magenta, sometimes a lilac hue, the tall raceme blooming from the bottom up, seed-pods forming at the base while the pointed top still flowers. When Mildred Walker came to Michigan as a young doctor's bride, she must have been impressed by fireweed—a glory in the open woods, pink on prairies, or clustered along stream-banks where it thrives in the damp, rich earth.

Fireweed grows best in disturbed ground, in burned-over tracts, or ghost towns gone to seed. There is fireweed on the mound of clay earth that we dug up to make a hole for the basement of our ranch house in Montana. And there is an abundance of fireweed scattered over Michigan's upper peninsula. Which is where we come to see it again and again in this novel.

The sixty years since Mildred Walker wrote *Fireweed,* the first of her thirteen published novels, have transformed American life and American possibilities, yet the north woods around Lake Superior remain a frozen land wild enough for wolves. The peninsula has changed since 1927, when Mildred arrived in the milltown of Big Bay, near Ishpeming, an honors graduate from Wells College in Aurora, New York. But the region remains essentially wild. It is one of America's many backwaters where the old ways survive like the hardy weed.

"Michigan," writes Walker in the book's opening lines, "sprawls on the map like a hand and the upper peninsula hangs above it, always a little out of reach." You can find the headwaters of the Mississippi River in the tangled woods and swamps near Ishpeming, and you can fish Hemingway's Big Two-Hearted River. You can ski in resorts and rent pleasure boats, but mostly you will find shabby small towns where logging and iron mining have brought work to generations of immigrants from Scandinavia, Poland, Austria, Finland, French Canada.

Once there were great forests of white pine, said to be the province of Paul Bunyon. Then the more resilient hardwoods; finally the iron boom. Now, in a land depleted of its natural resources, you will find mostly tourists and the old-timers who fish and hunt as the displaced Indians used to do, hanging on to meager livelihoods in a place they cannot or will not leave. It's like Appalachia or Maine, Louisiana or Montana.

Why do some stay, and some go? What is it that holds a person to place when it makes no economic sense? I have lived in a logging community in western Montana for some thirty years, where most jobs revolve around a lumber mill in a company town. *Fireweed* is placed in a remote milltown just like it, at the edge of privately-owned woods. The characters and situations are familiar: loggers and millworkers, bosses and unions, shutdowns and lay-offs. It's the boom and bust history of American settlement as it moved westward.

Working people who harvest natural resources have always balanced their attachment to place against the certainty that the logs will run out, or the iron, the oil, the gold. They will never be rich like the urban stockholders they work for. Their children will move out, following jobs in whatever city is most burgeoning, most close, most gilded with promise.

Mildred Walker did not stay in Big Bay. After three years doctoring the loggers and millworkers who lived along the shores of Lake Superior, her surgeon husband, Ferdinand Schemm, became infected with radiation poisoning from defective x-ray equipment. Eventually he would lose all the fingers of his left hand to gangrene. Dr. Schemm went back to medical school at the University of Michigan in Ann Arbor to do an internship and residency in internal medicine, which did not depend on the skill of his hands.

Mildred and her baby daughter came with him. Although pregnant with her second child, she went to graduate school and studied creative writing. While at Ann Arbor she wrote *Fireweed,* which won the university's Avery Hopwood and Jule Hopwood Award for 1933 and was published by Harcourt, Brace the following year. With the money from this successful novel, the Schemm family moved to Great Falls, Montana, and a land more dependent on farming and ranching, the renewable resources of grass and wheat.

Imagination, observation, and empathy are a writer's renewable resources. Mildred Walker was well-endowed with all three. After her husband died in 1955, she taught at her alma mater, Wells College, until 1968. Retiring to Vermont, and then Missoula, Montana, to be with her daughter, she continued to write into her eighties, when her eyes and health dimmed and she moved to a retirement community near her son's home in Portland.

Walker wrote four novels set in the West: she imagined the lives of missionaries, Indians, and mountain men in *If a Lion Could Talk* (1970); chronicled a turn-of-the century ranchwoman's view of the end of the romance of the West in *The Curlew's Cry* (1956); and described a contemporary ranch family's life on the northern plains in her best-selling *Winter Wheat* (1941). Her two novels about doctors and their wives (*Medical Meeting* and *Dr. Norton's Wife*) include a good deal of first-hand material, but do not reveal the heart and soul of the author.

None of Walker's novels is strictly autobiographical, but *Fireweed,* written out of the isolation of new motherhood in a strange Midwestern wilderness, reveals perhaps more than she would approve. Its main character is a teen-age mother with verve, good looks, wit and ambition. The girl is younger than the author, less educated, blond rather than dark-haired, working-class instead of middle class, and the child of immigrants. Despite a simplicity and innocence of vision that dates it, her story is more than a curious bit of Americana. Its inherent conflicts have not gone away.

Thomas Jefferson's democratic dream was predicated on yeoman, small-town communities, an educated populace, a land of equality. We wonder if that dream is done for. Dying rural towns were landmarks during the Dust Bowl days of the thirties, and in the more prosperous nineties they continue to die. We drive down deserted Main Streets on side roads all over America and see that the red brick facades and white bungalows have become rest homes for the elderly, havens for the unemployable poor, or watering holes for wealthy professionals escaping urban complexity. Those who have stayed put are often rigid, backward looking, xenophobic in their distrust of the larger culture.

Still, from the vantage point of cities and suburbs gone to anger, strife, and anomie, the possibilities of community—of living deeply in places connected to the natural world—beckon us back to more rooted lives. If there is hope for Jefferson's dream, it lies with the young generations—the teen-age mother in this novel, the out-of-work young father—young people who are inventive and determined enough to figure out ways to endure on the land they call home.

Fireweed is about Celie Henderson and Joe Linsen, children of immigrant loggers, Swede and Norwegian, the girl seventeen, the boy twenty. They live along Lake Superior in an area known as "the sticks" in a milltown called Flat Point. In winter, writes Walker, the town "is blocked off from the world by snow except for a single plowed road. On the edge of the great lake, ice-blocks wall it around like a prison camp, and the life around the mill is thrown in on itself."

Life thrown in on itself is the perfect subject for a traditional novel. In fictional Flat Point, life is walled in by weather, but also by work, by class, by ethnic group, by sex. Walker tells the story mostly through Celie's consciousness; but also through black-haired Joe's. Celie is a beauty who buys silk dance dresses from the Sears catalog, wears only opera pumps, and knows that her real life lies amid the glitter of Milwaukee or Detroit. Joe is a canoeist, hunter, and fisherman who finds freedom, independence, and pleasure in his work in the woods and in the wilderness. The two are sweethearts, then young marrieds, then parents. Which of them will prevail?

Arthur Farley makes the story a triangle. He is a musician who has been hanging around honky-tonks in Detroit, playing piano; and he is the nephew of the mill-owner boss. His uncle brings him to Flat Point to learn the lumber business and manage the mill. Young Farley, as he is called by the men who work for him and who must constantly save his ignorant bacon, takes his meals at Celie's mother's boarding-house, and is attracted to Celie. He plays piano at a spring dance attended by lumbermen and camp followers, women with babies, the Indian wife of a fox-farmer, and he is homesick—"sick of this godforsaken town on the edge of the lake, of looking out over the lake, of eating with mill-hands."

If this were a television melodrama, we would know what happens next, but it's not and we don't. *Fireweed* is no bodice-ripper romance because Mildred Walker is more akin to Balzac than to Margaret Mitchell. Her social drama is proper and discreet, as she was and is. It details the needs and conflicts of people who are decent, but torn nevertheless, as she must have been—a minister's daughter from the East, college-educated, lonely, bearing her first child among strangers, the rough Finns and Swedes and Canucks who were her husband's patients.

Mildred Walker's daughter, the poet Ripley Schemm Hugo, was born in Ishpeming and is portrayed in *Fireweed* as the baby Rose Marie. Ripley is a friend of mine in Montana, and as we talked about the genesis of this novel, she said something that was key to my understanding. "Mother agreed to come to the peninsula and marry my father on one condition," Ripley said, smiling. "She would come if he promised she would never have to do any washing."

Women not wealthy enough to have servants did washing in the thirties, and hung it out by hand. They washed and shopped and cooked and sewed and made babies for their men. Such women asked for no other life; and if they did, they were thought queer and so dreamed their dreams in secret. To be independent, to aspire to be a writer, was to be outside the orderly *kafee-kalaser* society of proper wives. A trapped fictional girl like Celie Henderson Linsen might spend her days washing, but not Dr. Schemm's ambitious young wife.

In Michigan, Mildred Walker saw immediately that an isolated milltown was a prison for its young women, especially the bright ones who yearned to escape. This is why, as Celie becomes initiated into the roles of wife and mother, her moods swing wildly. Sometimes she is happy and buzzing with energy, then she sees leaves falling from the maple in the yard, or thinks of the fireweed in the ghost town where she and Joe made first love—where she got pregnant—and instantly she is bitter, despairing.

These swift changes of mood, the quick passions and slow acceptances of a life that has chosen Celie more than she has chosen it, recur so often the reader wonders what the writer is doing. But the writer is writing truly about adolescence, about child brides. I was married at nineteen, a mother at twenty, and bore my second son a week after my twenty-second birthday, and though I was city-bred and a university student, I can see myself in Celie, as Mildred Walker must have seen herself, too.

Young women seem to have more choices now than they did in the thirties, when Mildred Walker started her career, or in the fifties, when I was coming of age. But we have more teen-age mothers than ever these days, and most of them are poor. The situation of a young woman making do with very little, learning to nest, is a universal human condition. And that is the situation Mildred Walker draws most vividly.

Here, for example, is Celie on the first day in her new home, a company-owned shack at the edge of town, which she and Joe have redecorated:

> The paper label on the new green and ivory kettle smelled a little when she put the pan on to heat. She made the coffee. It was queer moving about the kitchen to get supper. She kept going places for things where they were in her mother's kitchen. Even the floor felt strange under her feet; the raised sill into the front room, the step down to the woodshed. The feeling of its being hers was new and stirring.

Then here she is less than a year later, with a new baby:

> The kitchen had lost its shiny new look. The paint, like the sauce pan, like Celie herself perhaps, was too cheap a grade to last. Rose Marie cried. . . . Celie nursed her impersonally, with her eye on the alarm clock on the top of the stove. . . . The baby was doing well, almost three months she was, and big and pink-cheeked. It was queer Celie couldn't realize the baby belonged to her yet; Joe did.

Motherhood is not so automatic as we would like to think. It takes time and practice, and a willingness to be someone you have never been. Although Celie often feels smothered in the

milltown, yearning for a better life going on somewhere else, it
is in nature—the lake, the wild woods—that she comes to rec-
ognize, again and again, what she values most. She loves her
husband; she will love her children.

> Rose Marie drooped sideways, her lips still parted just as they had
> left off nursing. Celie . . . went out to the open shed door . . . She
> held Rose Marie more tightly to keep her warm. . . . The lake from
> up here at the end of town looked covered over with a white veil.
> The sky toward Canada was pink; as it arched up, it turned to a light
> blue that made it seem higher. Celie looked up a minute, and then
> back to the lake and to the wooden buildings that stood between the
> mill and the last house. . . . A tiny sense of possession grew within
> her. For the first time since Rose Marie was born she felt free of the
> hard bitterness in her mind.

I will not give away more of the story for you who are about to
read it. I say only that *Fireweed* is a novel about yearning and
resignation, about daily life, death, hope, and the hard limits of
choice. It's an old-fashioned read with characters you like and
trust, although sometimes they seem a bit smaller than life. In it
you will find a world as sharp and linear as the lovely woodcuts
of pines, smokestacks, and cloud-dotted shores that illustrate
the four divisions of the book. And if parts of the novel seem
dated as a black and white movie featuring Gary Cooper and
Claire Trevor, with lines like, ''Gee, Cele, you're swell,'' never
mind. You will be entranced by the story's simplicity and truth-
telling. You will stay up all night to see how it comes out.

Americans are addicted wanderers in a country run out of
frontiers. We have cut down most of our forests, mined our
mountains, pumped a great deal of oil, and we wonder what the
hell we can do next to make a quick buck from the land. Maybe,
like Celie and Joe Linsen in the Depression era of closed mills
and no jobs, we should learn how to make do where we are—

canoe the lakes, fish the rivers, hunt the deer, tend our own gardens, and replenish what we have taken.

In the open ending of this tale, Celie, like so many of our mothers, will try to live through her children. She will teach them to leave and not come back. Luckily, we know more than Celie could imagine. We can expect more.

As the century turns, we know we'll be connected to a global world through electronics and airplanes, information and travel. And we also know that we can be connected to a community, a place in the natural world where we can choose to put down roots. It is possible for our generation to invent a future in which we teach our young to take care of what remains. We may send our fledglings from the nest hoping that someday they will find their various, devious, and sweet ways home.

Part I

THE tall white pine, smooth and white-fibered, first brought men to that piece of Michigan that juts out into Lake Superior. It is a state in itself, that higher piece, divided from the greater part of the state by the Strait of Mackinac. Michigan sprawls on the map like a hand and the upper peninsula hangs above it, always a little out of reach.

It was still the west when the lumberjacks of Maine and New Hampshire shouldered their belongings and tramped towards it. They had heard of white pine for the taking, close to the rivers and lakes, forests of it, miles upon miles, in the virgin timber lands of upper Michigan. Since the Indian days, only the French Canadian had blazed trails through these green solitudes. Only a few fishermen had tried the shore. They had left their nets to dry on the bright, white sand; left them to rot with the years, sometimes, and gone to know the cruelty of the clear, blue lake.

It was called frontier when the tales of Paul Bunyan were in the making across the shanty stoves of the lumber camps. Men wrestled with the strength of the tall, green giants; sinews of flesh with sinews of timber. Men's hands were covered with pitch, and barked and calloused from shoving the logs along. All day, the resin ran from the trees like blood. The white fibers strained and twisted and gave. Each day's sun found a wider clearing in the forest's gloom. At night, the lumberjacks went back to their shacks hungry as the wolves that watched their camp fires. Dark came down in the woods and the silent snowflakes dropped, dropped, dropped. They had stumps to cover and green boughs heaped in funeral piles.

Lumber . . . more lumber, for the new towns of the west; for ships and trains and new saloons! The saws worked faster. The logs piled up. The sunny clearing in the forest grew. But there is an end to all things, even the riches of the north country. The white pine fell, tree after tree, acre after acre, in one great massacre. The logs slipped well over the deep packed snows to the river bank. Day after day of winter, the saws kept working, the logs piled up.

Winter came to an end in the country north of the straits. The ice cracked, the rivers flowed free, only to be clogged by that great avalanche of logs, bobbing, bumping, floating down to the mills in the great spring drives. Doughty men rode the logs down the river. The lumberjacks tramped in from the camps to the nearest center, hungry for whisky, for women, for spending. Millions were made by men who moved down to the populous places of the state, or on to the further west where there was still white pine for the taking. The lumberjacks followed wherever there was ready pay at the end of the long winter's run. The tales of Bunyan reached to Oregon and Washington.

A lull came over the upper peninsula, an intermission in the drama of the north country. The sound of the saws was stilled. The hardwoods grew taller. Ground pine and alders and jack pine covered over the scars of the forest. Then again came the cry: lumber, more lumber; hardwood now, for fashionable mansions and polished bars, for chairs and chiffoniers. Back came the lumberjacks, for the hardwoods after the pine. The saws were at work again, but their way was harder now; maple and hickory and oak are tougher than the soft pine fibers. The men had to sit down on the old pine stumps to get their breath. Sweat flowed freely even when the breath floated white in the winter air. Many a walking boss coming upon the stumps of the white pine, left by that greedy and wasteful generation, whistled enviously. The lumberjacks were back, but they were mostly foreigners now. Paul Bunyan had to hold his own with the giants of Swedish and German and Finnish lore. Cursing in strange dialects was heard through the woods as the saws grated against a knot in the timber's heart or the skidder logs were snagged on a root.

The trains took the great logs. The mills came closer to the woods in the piece of upper Michigan men called the sticks. Towns grew around the mills and only the crazy or those fresh from the old country worked out in the camps anymore. A sensible Swede who had been here awhile, or a good German who liked a garden, found him a wife and lived in the mill town now. A few of the old sort, Black Jack Morris and Oliver Adams, who lumbered the white pine off the same piece thirty years before, could still pull a saw with twice the skill of the greenhorn "furriners." The lumber camp was in their blood, but their generation had gone with the white pine and the blazes of the old trappers' trails.

These latter years, things are different in the north country. The walking boss drives out to the very beginning of the fresh cutting in a Ford car. There are engines and pulleys to lift the great logs. The radio blares the latest Broadway hit in the heart of the woods. The lumber shacks are freight cars run in on tracks. The hungry wolves gaze wondering at the holes men make and slink farther north. Only cold and danger and the smell of the woods and the fall of the white snow and the bound of a deer are the same.

Timber is growing scarce. But men have steel now for trains and skyscrapers and even for chiffoniers and chairs. The veins of iron in the country beyond the straits have done their share. The beehive furnaces have melted that iron to steel. The country of the sticks looks less majestic, shorn of so many of its tall trees; naked in places except for jack pine and alders and paper poplars. Bad fires have cut a wide swath, too. Rich men, up for the hunting, talk of buying up a hundred acres and plowing it under, but at the end of the hunting season, they drive back in their big cars, content with the country if a buck is strung along the side, and leave the burned-over land of the upper peninsula to squirrels and beavers and deer and fox, and, here and there, a town. Where the roots of the tall trees are charred into the earth, a wild weed springs up. A pretty weed, it is, with a spire of violet pink blossoms, fragile-looking but sturdy at the roots. One old lumberjack said he'd seen it on the roadsides in Maine; fireweed, they called it there.

Real towns have grown up; three, five—not big as towns are counted below the straits, but large enough to hold a lumber baron's fortune in their real estate or the railway station for the ore cars, headed south and west and east. Back in, or up along the lake edge, here and there, a mill still saws the logs the trains bring in; not sufficient in itself these days, but subsidized by some great industry. The towns still squat around the saw mill; Pointe Platte, Grand River and Sacuenay, surviving eighteen, twenty years, some of them.

Pointe Platte, as it was on the old maps, Flat Point now, lies close to Superior, there where the shore juts out in a wide curve and then swings in again to make a bay. It was a man's town, first, with only a mill and a bunk house. Then the camp cook brought his wife; a big Swede, Sven Svenson, brought a blue-eyed woman he called Hanna. The lumber company built a street of houses up from the mill. One day, a baby was born in the Point. Men came to work in the mill who had never worked in the woods: millwrights and saw-filers, men who knew trades. Good Swedish names, Henderson, Bernsen, and Findarson: good German names, Schmitz and Schultz and Heinrich, were carried on and intermingled. French Canadians and Finns came drifting in and families from older towns where the lumber was running thin. Another street spread up the hill with twenty box-like, flimsy houses.

Now, a second generation has grown up in this small town. The Hendersons have a daughter, Celie; Lin Linsen has a son, Joe. There is a school and a company hospital and a Catholic church. Life is different, shorn of its need for pioneers. It is neither so hard nor so bare, lived closer to the few large towns, connected by flivvers and radios to the current of things. The "giants of the earth," the tall trees, are almost run out. The new generation, like the fireweed, spreads over the country of the sticks in their place.

The life, lived here between the great lake and the thinning timber lands, so close to town and yet so far, is a curious passionate growth, an epic struggle, unseen, unsung. All summer, and through the fall, there comes the persistent low music of the wind and the lake going on above the noise of the town, never quite drowned out, yet altered by it, taking from it some human cadence of tragedy and courage. Winter comes, and the music of the wind rises until it shrieks above the town like an ancient curse, malevolent and unearthly. The town is blocked off from the world by snow except for a single plowed road. On the edge of the great lake, ice-blocks wall it around like a prison camp and the life around the mill is thrown in on itself.

But, today, the snow in Flat Point was melting. The high walls of snow that lined the board walks down the three streets of the town were streaked with dirt and rounded and humpy like stone walls. The walks were slippery. In places, the heavy gold-seal boots of the men on their way to the mill had tramped the snow bare to the boards.

Celie Henderson's high-heeled opera pumps dug soft little holes in the softer snow of the walks and left no trace where there was still ice to slide along. March is a bad month underfoot in the towns along Lake Superior. But still it was March, and Celie Henderson had kicked her galoshes off in the woodshed with the first mild weather and was not to be snared into wearing them unless fresh snow fell. Celie Henderson always wore opera pumps. When the lumberjacks went clumping past with three pairs of woolen socks in their shoe-packs, and Celie's mother, thrifty Mrs. Ole Henderson, wore thick stockings of her own knitting, Celie pulled on chiffon hose that might be half or all rayon but still were sheer, and slipped into her opera pumps.

"You spend half the money you make on your shoes," Mrs. Henderson complained, but Celie would smooth the light braids around her head and laugh.

"Two ninety-five isn't so much. That's all these cost!" Celie would point her toe in its short-vamped patent leather pump and shiny black heel. It was a pretty foot.

This morning, Celie's patent leather pumps carried her swiftly down to the rambling barn of a company store shortly after seven-thirty. They trod lightly on the long board steps of the store stoop. Celie went eagerly enough. Her introduction to life was there in the barny room with its foodstuffs and merchandise. All the world of Flat Point traded there. Even those who sent large orders to "Sears and Monkey Wards" to beat the company's profit had, at least, bread and eggs and occasional pork chops to buy. Anyone might lean over the counter and smile into Celie's young face. Men from the city who came up to hunt at deer season stopped in to buy provisions and often paid Celie compliments. Someday, they might need an extra girl in the office next door, who knew? Pretty Celie Henderson was there to watch her chances.

Already, this morning, Baldy, the stoop-shouldered old Finn, was bringing out the boxes of potatoes and turnips. Mr. Simpson, who ran the store for the company, was unlocking the candy counter and bread case. Mrs. Munsen was flicking a feather duster carelessly over the yard goods and toilet articles on the other side of the store in a superior way. Celie was supposed to stay over by the canned goods and vegetables, but sometimes she wandered over to Mrs. Munsen's side. Anybody could tell that was more her line than cornmeal and malt and prunes.

" 'Lo, Baldy . . . Mis' Munsen."

She hung her coat and hat out where the girls from the office hung theirs. There was a wavy surfaced mirror on the wall. Celie powdered her nose and fluffed the hair out under her braid. She looked critically at her face. She was always too sleepy to see much in her mirror at home. She did have a "Garbo" look. Funny Joe didn't like Greta in the movies. He couldn't see that they were anything alike, either. "Doesn't have half the looks you have, Celie," he always said.

Celie twitched her belt in a practiced way. She could give an air to a $1.98 model by a simple twitch of her belt and a shrug of her shoulders. Satisfied, she walked smartly out on her high-heeled pumps to spend the next ten hours reaching and weighing and tying and charging up accounts on the company's charge slips.

Celie Henderson was quick. Old Mr. Quinn, the butcher, from down at the end with the meats, liked to hear her sharp, quick footsteps flying up and down back of the long counter. He looked up sometimes to see her light hair braided round like the girls back home in Sweden. She called him "butch," like the others, but with such a way to her, the name was a jolly thing. His clear blue eyes twinkled to hear her.

Celie had blue eyes. Real Swede eyes, her father said. They could grow dark with pity when she waited on Mrs. Daily the day after her man was crushed to death by a log down at the pond, or anger when one of the traveling Jew salesmen, who brought their samples periodically, "got smart." Or they could turn light blue like a child's when a little edge of fear crept into them. Celie Henderson had pretty eyes.

She was seventeen and had her height, a straight five feet six of it, with only a slight curve at the breast and hip. She could reach for the cereals on the next to the top shelf with easy grace while Mrs. Munsen was off to get a pole to hook them down.

"Bad walkin'," said Mr. Simpson, clinking his keys officially, "hope you had your gold-seal boots on, Celie."

Celie laughed and the sound of Celie's laughter in the store made old Mr. Quinn forget the sharp pain in his heart when he hefted the half of a side of beef onto the block.

"And how!" She extended her slim high-heeled foot to view.

Mrs. Konski wanted rice and yellow soap and onions. Celie rattled a paper bag open and poured the rice. The morning rush had commenced. The mill whistle blew the lunch hour at eleven-thirty, and eight o'clock was late to shop if you planned to have a pot roast or an Irish stew on for your man's dinner.

At eleven, there was a lull. Celie walked out to the front window by the cash register. Buddy Hefflin ran it. He lost a leg down at the mill and the company gave him the job on the stool in the cramped little box. Buddy Hefflin didn't care with Celie Henderson to look at. He hoarded any bits of gossip that he picked up on his trips to the office with his money-till to have the chance of talking to her. He had a sober Finnish face, but when he hissed mysteriously, "Hi, Celie!" his left eye squinted comically.

"Yea, Buddy, what's the hot dope?" Celie answered, leaning over the corner of the cigarette and tobacco case.

"The big gun's nephew is coming here. Goin' to learn the ropes and keep an eye on things for his uncle, they say." Buddy's face cracked into a humorous leer. "Won't he have a sweet time, though?"

Celie was interested. Anyone from the world beyond the straits was interesting. Anyone who belonged to the big shot was exciting. The big shot was Mr. Farley, administrative head of the Lake Superior Lumber Co. His word was law in Flat Point. He determined alike whether to repair the roof on house number 20 or run a night-shift at the mill.

"Yeah, an' d'you wanta know more?"

"Wait a sec, Buddy, there's little Bobby Irwin with a slip of paper."

Celie took a kerosene can from the small boy who stood in front of the counter and went back to a gloomy supply room to fill it from the large tank. Celie did it in a rush. She was afraid of rats in there, and Mr. Simpson always told her when he caught one or brought it out by the tail to make her scream.

". . . and two loaves of bread, and a pound of cheese, Bobby." She read from the crumpled slip in the little boy's fist.

Little Bobby Irwin rubbed the back of his hand across his nose. He had a snuffly cold and the Irwins had no time or money for handkerchiefs. He wore a sweater of his sister's pinned together with a safety-pin, and his cap with eartabs was too large, but he was a proud figure in his own four-year-old eyes. He was going to carry a gallon of kerosene, and groceries besides, all the way up home by himself.

"C'mon, Ginger, hi! Blast you, get out of that meat market!" Bobby called to his hound dog. He made his voice loud like his big brother's. He picked up the can and trudged out of the store.

Celie came back to the end of the counter, near Buddy.

Buddy pretended absorption in "figgers."

Celie hit him neatly with a gumdrop from the candy counter.

Buddy popped it into his mouth and took up where he left off.

"What's more, the big shot's sending his nephew up here cause the fellow wants to be a musician and Mr. Farley wants he should go in the lumber business."

"A musician!" said Celie who knew no men who were able-bodied who made music, saving Sabonich, the Austrian, who played the accordion.

"Yeah, played the piano in a night club in Detroit till his uncle made him quit."

"Celie, Celie, there's Mrs. Larsen waitin'!" Mrs. Munsen called over rebukingly from the dry goods department. "I'm busy." She was showing Mrs. Henry the newest thing in baby nighties since her last baby was born two years ago.

"They get new things all the time," she assured Mrs. Henry just as though they both didn't know that the coming Henry baby would wear throughout the clothes of the last three Henry children.

Celie recommended the Sunset brand of sliced peaches to Mrs. Larsen and Jolly Boy peanut butter. She made out the slip and put it into the little container that carried it with a squeaky whine to Buddy's booth. Then she got out new crape paper to flute for the display table.

She ought to meet him when he came into the store, first off, the big shot's nephew. She would wear her bright red dress this afternoon and tomorrow, just in case.

Celie went home for lunch at quarter after so's to be back in time to arrange the vegetables and count the bread that came on the one and only noon train through Flat Point. Her high heels made new holes in the snow on the way back up the street. The snow was melting fast under the warm sun. The walls of snow grew dirtier and lower. The sound of dripping water came from every roof. Even the three-foot-long icicle on the edge of Pop Slichter's roof was dwindling, but still hung dagger-like and shining in the sun.

The Hendersons' house was no different from the Bernsens' on one side and the Melsingers' on the other, unless the white sash curtains in the Hendersons' windows were starched a little stiffer and cleaner than any others on the street. There was a red geranium in a coffee can on the sill.

Celie went around back to the storm shed. She knew before she opened the door the hot steamy smell that would meet her. Mrs. Henderson took in boarders: three young fellows in the mill who'd rather pay a dollar more a week and get clean Swedish cooking than eat at the company boarding house. Mrs. Henderson and Ole were quick to turn a penny when they could. Celie hated it, hated the pile of dishes she helped with at noon and in the evening, hated the heavy meals they had to have every day . . . meat and potatoes and pie and coffee, or meat and rice and cake and coffee, day after day.

At first glance, there was no resemblance between Celie and Mrs. Henderson. The older woman's skin was of a leathery texture, reddened to an even color where Celie's was pink and white and smooth. The line from cheekbone to jaw was sterner. Her iron gray hair was scanty now and brushed back to a firm knot in the back. There was no quick flash of expression save only in her eyes, and her mouth was a thin line that closed tightly. Her body was lean and bony and her dresses were as she had made them when she came from Sweden to another mill-town like Flat Point, twenty odd years ago.

Christina Henderson wasted few words. She only looked up a second as Celie came in. She was busy dishing up. Celie hung up her hat and coat and took the dishes on the table. She and Ole ate their dinner with the boarders. Christina was busy in the kitchen most of the time.

At eleven-thirty the mill whistle shrilled forth and the men came up the hill in a steady stream. Celie looked out of the window at them unseeingly. Somebody new was coming to Flat Point, a musician who had played in a night-club, like that one she'd seen in the film Bebe Daniels was in.

The three boarders came in together.

" 'Lo, mornin', Mis' Henderson, Celie." They were three Swedes, tall, hungry fellows . . . a half peck of potatoes lasted only a day and a half at the Hendersons'. Two of them were blond, but one was black-haired. He was Joe. His mother was a French woman and he was only second generation Swede. He had blue eyes, though, that went at once for Celie and rested on her while he ate. Joe Linsen was in love with Celie Henderson.

Celie broke the large slice of home-made bread daintily in two before she buttered it, with a self-conscious glance around.

"Joe, Sam, he say you goin' to run the limey engine next month, yeah?" Hans Mottberg held his well-filled knife in the air to ask.

"I guess," said Joe, shortly, his eyes on Celie. He hadn't meant to tell her till evening when they went for a ride. She looked up quickly. Then she went on eating. Celie ate mostly in silence at her mother's table with the boarders. Mrs. Henderson had set ideas as to what was right and proper for her daughter.

"I don't want you makin' yourself common, Celie," she had ordered.

"Well, Joe," said Ole Henderson, "that isn't the mill game, but you like machines—I guess you got what you wanted." Ole Henderson worked on the pond. He worked on contract instead of day wages, and made more than most of the men in Flat Point. It was a dangerous job, and had to pay more.

"I don't like it, Ole," Christina Henderson had been saying for five years, now.

"It's all right, Christina, I do it awhile. We got the girl to bring up and something to lay by, then I be millwright again or maybe buy a little farm. Don't worry. I'm careful of my skin," Ole always answered.

Christina Henderson would go back to her work grimly. Whatever fears she had she shut her lips tightly upon, in the habit of a lifetime. What else to do?

Joe knew Celie was dainty. She liked the way movie fellows did things. Joe held them up to scorn when they went to the show together. "Look at 'em . . . cake-walkers, Celie, nothing but!"

"Oh, Joe, not Jack Gilbert, not him!"

But when Ole and the others got up from the table they always helped themselves liberally to toothpicks from the glass hat on the center of the table. Joe didn't. He had seen Celie's look of scorn once. She had fancy notions like that, but that was right, Joe thought to himself. He and Celie weren't always going to live in a mill-town.

"Can I walk down with you, Celie?" Joe took out a cigarette. Celie hated chewing tobacco.

"No, Joe, I got to change my dress."

"Well, s'long, then, see you tonight." His smile was

broad. He had a handsome face, not carved of hardwood like Ole Henderson's or Stumpf's, the walking-boss, or old Pat Weil's who'd come out back in the white pine days, but handsome in a softwood way, cedar or poplar or spruce, maybe. He was tall, six feet two, and his plaid shirt bent back a little from his belt, and his long arms swung as he walked in a free sort of way.

Celie cleared the dishes off and stacked them, then she flew up the steep stairs to the backroom. Not many girls in Flat Point had a room to themselves, but Ole and Christina Henderson had only one child. They'd lost two before her. Maybe they pampered her a little. She slipped into her red silk.

"You won't have anything if you wear the best you've got to the store, Celie," Mrs. Henderson commented.

"Oh, well, I thought, then, I wouldn't have to bother tonight."

Christina Henderson liked red herself. She said no more. Her own dress was a gray printed flannel. She wore it all day, but changed her apron in the afternoon.

At the store, the new shipments were in. Celie liked arranging them on the shelves. Ten more cans of peas, two dozen boxes of dried codfish, a hundred and fifty loaves of bread. Celie flashed up and down behind the counter. Afternoons were busy in the store.

By two-thirty the mail was out. Housework in Flat Point was done. Women came drifting in with their babies. They stopped to talk to Celie and Mrs. Munsen.

19

Flat Point had changed in the fifteen years the town had stood. In the old days, provisions came in by boat. Women baked their own bread and visited each other in the afternoons for coffee instead of collecting at the store. Now it was common gossip that Tad Norton's wife fed her family out of the can, and plenty more besides her. Only the old people baked their own bread. Times were different.

"Celie, the new Sears catalogue's out." Selma Lichtenberg was Celie's age and just married. She spread the new catalogue on the counter. "There's a purple silk in here for $3.98 I think I'll get and you oughta see the console table!"

Celie was excited, too. The new mail order catalogue was Vogue and Paris itself to the female portion of the Point. But all afternoon, Celie knew whenever the latch of the store door was jerked up. No one in city clothes drifted in. Maybe he'd come tomorrow. She could see him asking for cigarettes and herself waiting on him.

At five-thirty, Celie was sweeping out behind the counter. She hated to get the dust in her red dress. She swept down by Buddy Hefflin's cage.

"Say, what you all decked out for, Celie? You musta expected the big shot's nephew."

A tell-tale red flushed over Celie's face.

"If that isn't a joke, he ain't coming till next week."

"Oh, don't be so silly, Buddy. I'm going out with Joe," retorted Celie crossly. "You think you're so smart." She brushed lightly back down to the butcher's end and put the broom in the corner. That could do.

The old Ford bobbled from rut to rut and slid between the newly frozen holes the sun had thawed in the road that morning. Joe and Celie were driving into town, thirty-five miles from Flat Point.

"Think we better go all the way, Celie?"

"Why not? We can get there for the late show."

"All right. I thought, maybe we could just drive."

Celie was silent. She watched the road streaking ahead between the dark trees on either side. There were cleared places at intervals, places where you could see through to the lake in the day time. Halfway there was the town of Mead. Twenty-five years ago it had been just such a town as Flat Point, deserted now, but with the tumble-down old houses still standing, two streets of them along with the framework of a store and part of a mill. It always looked spooky in the moonlight. Tonight, the deserted buildings crouched together in the shadows.

Trees came down to the road again and stretches of low jack pines. There was the place where Crazy Bill lived, who everyone said was rich from selling moon to the lumberjacks. Ten miles from town where the road drew into the lake again, the hunting shacks and cottages of folks from Clarion began. Celie always looked at them curiously. Sometimes, there were lights in one or two and big cars out in front. She would like to have a cottage on the lake to come to, and live in town, really.

"What's the matter, Celie?" Joe pulled her over to him.

"Nothing, only, I guess I'm getting sick of the Point."

"Well, wait awhile, Celie, we'll be getting out of there one of these days. I was talking to a man who sells radios and he says there's a big field in the mechanical side. Might even get to a bigger place than Clarion, Celie, Milwaukee, maybe."

Celie squeezed his arm a little. Joe was a bright fellow. They'd get there.

They were almost into town now. Mamma thought it was awful to get back so late, with Joe getting up at five-thirty; but you couldn't stay at home all the time.

"Kiss me, Celie, 'fore we get way in?"

Celie kissed him.

"You were nice, Joe, to come in to a movie tonight."

"Aw, that's all right, Celie." Lord! she was a swell kid.

Joe bought two red hots when they came out of the movie at eleven-thirty. They got in the car and started back.

"Sleepy, Cele?"

"Sorta."

"Curl up and go to sleep so I can wake you up to drive when I get sleepy."

It was an old arrangement. Joe never waked her. He liked to feel her cuddled up against his shoulder. Sometimes, her hair blew against his face. That made up for feeling half-dead in the morning.

The dim headlights of the old Ford cut a path of light back over the dark road, flashing for a second on a pane of glass in the old store at Mead or gleaming on a white birch. Once they caught a deer, stationary for a second before it bounded off into the deeper darkness.

2

A WEEK later, Celie brought the Sears catalogue home with her at noontime. There was a dress in there, with puffed sleeves and a long flared skirt that went longer in back. She could see herself in it. It came in six colors: "poppy-red, black, turquoise blue, foam-green and down-yellow." Celie walked up the street thoughtfully trying to decide. She'd show it to Mamma and see what she thought. The book said "all silk, no rayon." Mamma would like that—"remarkable at $4.95."

She was a little later than usual. The whistle had blown already. Mamma would have dished up. She flung into the kitchen and stopped by the door. The dining-room was in plain view of the back door. At the table sat a stranger in a city suit. He was thin and pale beside Joe and Ole and the other two. Mrs. Henderson came back into the kitchen. Celie noticed she'd baked some of her ice-box rolls specially.

"That's Mr. Farley's nephew, Celie; he's going to take his meals here."

"He is!" Celie whispered. She dropped the catalogue under the sink and went in to dinner.

Ole Henderson looked up and announced briefly between mouthfuls,

"My daughter, Mr. Farley, Celie."

Celie flushed a little and smiled across the table at him.

"Pleased to meet you."

Mr. Farley's nephew rose and bowed. Hans Mottberg and Sam looked a little embarrassed at such a gesture. They ate more busily. Joe looked at Celie. There were fried pork steaks and rice with brown gravy and rolls and canned corn and cream pie for dinner.

"This your first time up in the sticks, Mr. Farley?" Ole Henderson asked in the patronizing manner of one who had tried the city and found it wanting, tried the sticks and made a living there.

"Yes, it is," answered young Farley, passing cigarettes around the table. Only Joe smoked them, but Swedes are thrifty. They each took one.

"Of course, it isn't what it used to be; timber's going some," Ole continued. "Compn'y'll have to begin and buy pretty soon."

Young Farley listened politely. Sam and Hans finished and left the table. Joe sat smoking his cigarette.

Celie was eating her pie daintily. Ole filled his pipe and tipped back from the table. They lingered so long Christina Henderson came in with her plate.

"Here, Mis' Henderson, you sit here." Joe rose. He had to get back. He didn't care so much for the way Celie watched this Farley. He opened the door reluctantly.

"Well, see you again, Mr. Farley. 'By, Celie, Mis' Henderson."

Celie tipped back to see the kitchen clock. It was quarter past. She jumped up and smiled across the table. "Good-by."

Young Farley rose. "I must be going, too. Do you go toward the mill?"

"I work in the store," said Celie.

"Fine, we'll go together."

Celie decided not to take the Sears catalogue back this noon. She'd say she'd forgotten it.

Mr. Farley helped her on with her lapin jacket. She stooped for a second at the sideboard mirror to pat her brown beret farther back on her head. She pulled on her cotton gloves that she usually forgot.

" 'By, Mamma."

"I'll be walking down with you," said Ole Henderson.

The three walked down the street. Ole tramping on the snow at the side with his big boots that had seen five winters and as many summers. Young Farley still in his city oxfords, black with a slight point to the toe.

Celie in her patent leather opera pumps, her old ones that had cracks across the toes.

"D'you come alone, Mr. Farley, or your uncle with you?"

"Yes, but he'll be on tomorrow. He had to come round by Chicago."

"Goin' to be in the office?" Ole went on between puffs on his pipe.

"Yes, I guess so, eventually. At first, I'm going to be down at the mill with Mr. Lorenson."

"Yard boss," explained Ole briefly. "Well, hope you like it here." Ole Henderson's face was solemn and without expression. He turned down the steep hill to the pond. But his eyes were bright with amusement. Sandy Mac caught up to him halfway down the path.

"That the big boss' nephew?" he queried, jerking his thumb back.

Ole knocked out his pipe against a freight car, then he commented, "Mmm-hmm, little Jack Pine." And the comment went around the yard.

On the long porch of the big building that was both store and company office, young Farley looked at Celie. "How's for showing me the town tonight?"

Celie laughed softly. "There's not much to show; three streets and the lake, that's all 'sides the mill."

"There are other towns. I've got a little bus up here," said Farley. "Well, see you at supper."

Celie ran into the store. She knew that Buddy had been watching out the window, but it didn't matter.

26

She walked rapidly back to the closet to hang up her things and the next minute was counting out clothespins for Mrs. Landers.

Supper was a strained meal at Ole Henderson's. And after it, Joe sat smoking, waiting for Celie to finish the dishes. Ole was whittling till his digestion settled. Sam and Hans had the radio going and were sitting close by it to listen. Young Farley sat down a few minutes and then sprang up restlessly.

"Here, let me get you a real program. That's nothing." He put his hand on the knob of the radio and turned it around. The crooning voice of Al Jolson filled the red plaster walls of Ole Henderson's house. Christina Henderson wrung out her dish towels and hung them back of the stove, her face expressionless. Celie took fancy steps between the table and sink and hummed with the music. She was so excited she forgot to dry the coffee pot and dried the drain dish instead. Then she flew upstairs to put on her red dress.

In her room, one electric light bulb that hung from the ceiling was tied over the dresser to a nail. It had a rose crape paper shade that in important moments Celie ripped off. Her clear fair skin could stand the hard glare of the electric light bulb. Her blonde hair shone in the crinkled mirror. The red dress had a cowl neck that pulled down to a low V in front and was far enough off at the sides to show the slight bluish hollows by her collar bone. Celie had red earrings, bought at Clarion at the Five and Ten, to match the slimsy

27

silk. She screwed them into her ears and shook her head to see them move. She added some powder and a drop of perfume, a sample that a salesman at the store had given her. It was potent and a faint breath of it hung permanently in the slanting roofed room. Purple orchid, it was called.

Celie ran down the stairs that ended abruptly in a passage way between the parlor and bathroom. There were hooks on the wall facing the stairs. Celie took down her lapin jacket and went into the parlor. Sam and Hans had left now. They seldom hung around long after meals. Ole was reading the paper. Mrs. Henderson sat crocheting. Joe had gone out to the stoop. His low persistent whistle cut clearly across the radio singer's

"Who could ask for more . . . in sleepy valley?"

Young Farley sat in the chair by the radio, a moody expression on his face, humming with it. He looked up as Celie came in.

"Good li'l piece," he commented, nodding toward the radio. "Ready?"

Celie's eyes sparkled. "We're going to ride, Mother, Mr. Farley and I."

"Don't be too late," Mrs. Henderson answered. She was not awed even by the nephew of Mr. Farley who could discharge Ole at a minute's notice if he would. Christina Henderson was a fatalist, through twenty years of living in lumber towns. The big bosses came and went, along with the rest. It didn't pay to be scared of them, or worry about your job. She wasn't like Mrs. Lyman who never cut her curtains to fit the windows, but always saved the extra in a big hem, for fear Matt Lyman would get his time, or the mill would shut down.

The storm door was still on the front of the house. Mr. Farley pushed it open and the keen, clear air of early spring rushed into the stove-heated house.

"Oh, it's swell out tonight," Celie began and noticed Joe sitting on the stoop as he often did nights, waiting for her to come and sit with him or go to the show or walk down to the lake and back. "Oh, Joe, you here?"

"Goin' out, Celie?"

"Mmm-hmm, Mr. Farley wants me to show him the town."

" 'Nite, Linsen," said young Farley, his hand on Celie's elbow. At the end of Henderson's walk was a bright blue Ford roadster, very new, very conspicuous next to Joe's old open Ford touring car.

"What a slick car, Mr. Farley!"

"The old man had to come across with some kind of a bus if he expected me to come off up here to the sticks."

"Didn't you want to come?"

"Hell, no. Would you? Why a week ago tonight I had a job with one of the best orchestras in Detroit."

"I heard you were a musician. What did you play?"

"Piano at the Tricorne Club. It's a night club, a first rate one; you'd love it."

"I bet I would." Celie was very conscious, as she drove down the street, of the glances cast her way. She didn't care. What if they did say she was shining up to the big boss' nephew. He'd asked her. She and Joe weren't engaged yet, anyhow.

The three streets of dwellings all ended on the main street that ran along the crest of the hill overlooking the lake. The store and company offices, the boarding house and movie house all loomed up like square kites, each with its tail of little story and a half houses dragging up the street behind it. Down by the lake sprawled the mill buildings. The four great stacks smoked red against the night. The smell of new lumber drifted up to them from the yard.

"And that's the way out of this dump," commented young Farley, pointing to the station. "I know that."

As they drove past the boarding house, music from a dozen radios jangled against each other.

"It's kinda gay at night when you go past here," said Celie. "And there's the Town Hall where we dance. It's got a real good floor. You ought to play for us."

They drove on past the Catholic church and the scattered shacks belonging to people who didn't work for the comp'ny, past Crazy Bill's and Ma Talbot's house and the place where the lumberjack got killed in a poker game, on the road toward Clarion.

THE old frame building of the Carlson House was four stories high. It stood at the end of Clarion's main street well up from the lake but not too high to bear the full brunt of the north winds. Its wooden front was highly decorated with jig-saw work and the old sign, The Carlson House, was ornamented with elaborate scrolls. Sixty years had taken the gilt from the letters and left them yellow, but few people had to bother to read the sign. Everybody north of the straits knew the Carlson House, and its broiled lake trout was known as far south as Milwaukee and Chicago.

Mike Farley scarcely noticed the new red non-tippable ash trays in the old lobby, or the fire of birch logs. He did glance uneasily a second at the large oil painting of a man with a revolver shooting straight at him as he entered the door. Some said it was a famous painting. It had an uncomfortable way of following you with the eyes wherever you sat to read the paper.

Mike Farley, who was the Detroit boss of the operation at Flat Point, thirty-five miles up the lake, was well-known. He bought the best cigars and tipped for all manner of other little extras, such as ginger ale at two or three in the morning.

The old Carlson House had seen some hard ones in the day when the gilt was new on the sign, old lumber barons who gambled with vast timber and iron holdings in the dingy rooms upstairs and decided the track of a new railroad over a whisky straight. Some of the fortunes that now maintained places along the North Shore of Lake Michigan and supported a second or third generation in Paris had begun here. But those men were part of the country and had the virtues of an unexplored country along with the vices. Now old man Carlson was eighty-five and sat dozing near the fire these cold spring nights while Red Topping was at the desk. Carlson woke out of his light naps to see a succession of drummers with a new line of Ready to Wear for the fashion shops or automobile salesmen from lower Michigan . . . a new race and a worse in his eyes. He looked up now under his white eyebrows and touched his forehead to Mike Farley.

" 'Lo, Cap'n," Mike greeted him gruffly, then he stepped up to the desk.

"Twenty-three as usual?" Mike had a way with hotel clerks. He usually got what he wanted.

He was a big man, grown a little slumped from much sitting in club cars and behind large flat top desks, though there was less of the latter than he wished. He had been perhaps good-looking in his youth, dark and tall like young Arthur, his nephew. Now he was a trifle too florid and heavily jowled.

There was only a trunk elevator in the Carlson House. Mike walked heavily up the red carpeted stairs behind the desk clerk. The Carlson House would not take on a bell boy until the tourist season was under way.

In room twenty-three, he took off his coat and threw it with his hat and bag on the big brass bed. Then he took out a cigar and sat down by the window. He got out some papers from his pocket and laid them on the hotel Bible. He poked the cuspidor out from under the table with his toe. Mike Farley knew this room well. He had had it on his honeymoon twenty-six years ago, that was also his spring business trip north. He had been in the office then, a kind of a salesman for the Consolidated Cabinet Company. He chose not to remember that when he came up now. That was a good long while back. Ruth Farley had grown too busy to go north with him on his quarterly visits to Flat Point even if he had asked her and he, well he managed.

Before dinner, he put through a call to the office at Flat Point. It pleased him to sense the flurry the announcement of his arrival always caused. A call gave DesMains, the superintendent, a chance to wear a white shirt and clean off his desk a bit. He would still be a little uncomfortable and red-faced. Mike Farley felt twice the power here in the telephone booth at the Carlson House that he did in Detroit with his secretary to put through the call for him.

"Hello, hello, Farley speaking. Yes, I'll be out in the morning. Get Arthur for me, will you, and have him drive you down here for dinner with me tonight. Yes."

Farley walked out of the booth and seated himself in one of the large leather chairs in front of the big north window. He chewed his cigar and looked unseeingly across the lake. He was too busy with his own thoughts to take in the brown red of the ore-docks jutting boldly out into the cold gray of Lake Superior.

Unless he found new timber lands quickly Flat Point was done for in ten years' time. That didn't suit his plans. It would take more than ten years to squeeze his way in as one of the partners of the firm. He could best do it through his management of the operation at Flat Point. If that could be made to show the largest profit of any of the lumber mills supplying lumber for the Detroit yards his advance was assured.

But Mike Farley, sitting alone over his dead cigar in the front window of the Carlson House, counted his own losing tricks. He was no shrewd lumber man. He had made plenty of slips in judgment. Trouble was, he had started out as an office boy in the Detroit office, back when the company made cases for sewing machines only. He had to trust other men's judgment on timber lands and the operation of the mill.

Getting Art in there to learn the lumber business was an inspiration. . . . He distrusted DesMains. Now he had Art there.

It was just as well, too, to get Art away from the jazz orchestra he was in—he was Flora's boy and Flora always was a fool—but the boy was all right—might even have the makings of a lumberman in him. Mike Farley pursed his lips over his cigar; he always had been soft about Art ever since he was a little tike; anyone might think he was his own son! He'd like to see him taking DesMains' place. There'd be no trouble then getting his own ideas carried out, no danger of any smart criticisms coming in to the Detroit office either, Farley reflected. Good thing for the boy, too. It wasn't often that Mike Farley's own purposes served a generous end as well. The rôle of philanthropic uncle gave him an odd satisfaction.

His mind worked out the details of the plan. There was a big place out on the bluffs above the lake, Hilton's Folly, it was called, that the first owner of the mill had built. Hilton had sunk his money in it and then committed suicide fifteen years ago. It was a swell place, stable and tennis court . . . That would appeal to the boy! Farley threw away his cigar and grasped the ends of the chair with fat blunt fingers.

He stood up and looked for a second out the window at the lake, in the March twilight. A few lights had flashed on along the main street. But the buildings looked small and shabby after the siege of winter. Cold place, Clarion, Flat Point was colder still. He'd have a hard time selling the idea of life here to the boy.

The waiter brought orders for three to Mr. Farley's table; for Mike Farley himself, for the thin sulky looking young man who slumped into his seat, for the big figure of a man fitted uncomfortably into a stiff collar and ready-made suit of clothes.

Mike Farley looked across the table at the mill superintendent. He was too stubborn a man, DesMains, too sure he was right.

"It's good to sit in a hotel again after Mrs. Henderson's table, I'll say," commented Arthur with a lazy smile.

"Mis' Henderson sets a good table," said DesMains firmly. "I ate there one winter."

Farley brushed his nephew's comment aside and drew a line on the cloth with his knife. "But it's a great chance you have, Art, to be right under DesMains here. He'll teach you the lumber game as no one else can." His tone was both full of praise for DesMains and firmness for his nephew.

"Takes time, Farley, and he won't learn it unless he likes it," said DesMains mildly.

"He'll like it all right," said Farley with a confidence he scarcely felt.

"He's down at the yard, now, and around the mill. Work in the camps is beginning to slack up. That'll let him get a good idea of things before he comes up to the office."

Arthur Farley looked bored. He looked at DesMains, at the way his coat sleeves wrinkled over his arm, at the brass collar button showing plainly between the rounded edges of his old-fashioned collar, his ruddy color . . . not a bad sort, he didn't care about ousting him in spite of the old man. The intricacies of the lumber game were as complicated as Chinese to him, and as dull.

"Three pie à la modes," ordered Farley with a broad

smile for the waitress—a pretty girl, he thought, well filled out; new one since the little black-haired girl he'd taken a fancy to the last time he'd been up.

DesMains ate his pie à la mode silently. He scraped up the last morsel with his fork.

"Too bad the snow didn't last longer. We'd've got them logs out faster. Ground's getting awful soft in the woods."

4

IT WAS April. Along the edge of the Point a faint green showed against the somber shade of the firs. It was invisible close by, except as greening twigs of poplar, still leafless. Across the cut-over land between the stumps and tangled swamp thicket gleamed red patches that near to were only the new skin on the shoots of the alder bushes. Day after tomorrow was Easter Sunday. Celie had sold Mrs. Schultz three packages of Easter egg dye and a dozen altogether. Mrs. Maloney took home the altar cloth of the little Catholic church to do up fresh. Mrs. Lampier prayed her baby would be born then. If she did the washing Saturday maybe she could bring on the pains a week ahead. You could sometimes with the fifth baby. The butcher got in stewing chickens at twenty-seven cents a pound. The Post Office had an extra mail bag full of parcel post packages these days; new hats and dresses and shoes from the mail order houses.

Celie Henderson ran into the side door of the Post Office that was back of the company store as soon as she had the bread checked off.

"Did it come, Lu?"

"Yep, there's something for you."

Celie went back to the coat closet and opened the package eagerly. She had ordered "foam green." She took it in for Lu, the Post Office girl, to see.

"Look, Lu, it looks like spring, don't it?"

She went back to the store with a rich feeling in her heart. The slippers would come on tomorrow's train, sure. Moiré opera pumps . . . you bought 'em white and had 'em dyed to match . . . no extra charge. Celie's mind was too full of her new Easter things to be scared even of rats when she went back to the storeroom for lumberjack socks, size twelve.

"Celie, you wanta break the sprouts off those potatoes down cellar sometime today. Folks ain't buying 'em with the sprouts a foot high," Mr. Simpson said as he came by.

"Can't Baldy do it?" asked Celie, her carefully reddened lips pouting a little.

"He's got the new shipments to open and the back to clean up. I'll be down after a bit to give you a hand."

In the lull around ten-thirty, Celie went down to the dark root cellar under the store. She could see the green sprouts of the potatoes way up to the top of the bin walls. The cellar was too warm with the new pipeless furnace installed. She seated herself on the end of a packing box and began breaking off the sprouts. She'd do a bushel and that was all.

Only two electric light bulbs hung from twisted cords in the whole long ceiling of the cellar. In summer, light came through the half windows, but now the windows were covered with packing paper and walled off by the snow that was still piled in frozen banks against them. Celie sat under one of the hanging bulbs and all the light seemed to center on the light hair smoothly coiled around her head.

She hummed lightly. Mr. Farley said it was a pity she couldn't get a job singing at the Tricorne Club or maybe, dancing. She saw herself there, Mr. Farley watching her all the time—smiling at her while he played the piano. She would wear a green dress with green opera pumps to match. Celie broke sprouts rapidly for a few minutes.

Some practical streak in her Swedish nature told her it wasn't so simply done. Still, she could dance. Everyone always wanted to dance with her. Maybe, if she could get ahead a little . . . Ole and Christina would never help her. They remembered their first few days in Chicago just after they came over. They had been close to starving, Celie guessed. Christina Henderson had no use for cities.

"Smoke, soot, grime, high rents. You're always washing."

"Only rich folks get to go fishing there," Ole said.

Celie heard feet tramping overhead. There must be more in the store than they could wait on easily. She pushed her half-filled basket away with her day-dreams and ran upstairs, blinking in the bright light of the store.

"Hi, butch," she called and Mr. Quinn looked up from ladling sauerkraut for Mrs. Heinzler to wave his spoon.

"Hello, Minnie, what's yours? Pastry flour again, I bet, for your angel-food cake!" Minnie Hepburn liked fancy cooking and hated plain. She sold cakes to Mr. DesMain's wife and the Doctor for seventy-five cents a cake.

Celie reached for pickles and a can of sardines. Celie Henderson could tell what most folks had for dinner.

It was quarter after eleven. Fifteen minutes more and she could go up home to try on her new dress. She looked up to see Joe coming over to the counter. Celie smiled. "Hello, Joe."

"H'lo." Joe admired her with his eyes even now when she'd been cutting him for that Farley fellow. "Luckies, Celie, two packages."

She got them for him. "You're up the hill early, aren't you?"

"Yeah, I'm goin' on the limey this afternoon."

"Oh, then you won't be home for lunch anymore, will you?"

"No, you and Farley can walk back together."

Celie straightened the cigarettes in the case.

"Celie, how's for taking the canoe out of the shed tonight with me?"

"Oh, Joe, it's too early."

"We took it out last year this time. I'm not going to spill you in. Maybe your city friend would."

Celie laughed at him delightedly, her blue eyes twinkling, the too red lips spreading widely. "Joe, you're jealous! But I can't go with you, honest, Joe. I said Mr. Farley could bring me home."

"I could tell you something about him would maybe make you change your mind."

"Oh, I know that. Dad said it was cause young Farley told on him that Luke got his time, but everybody knows Luke's no good."

"Yeah, but spying is a pretty poor job for a man. Folks say he's trying to worm in DesMains' place but he don't know the first thing about the mill."

"He's going to play the piano tonight at the dance. Come on'n go, Joe."

"And stand and watch you and him all evening? Not me, thanks."

"Oh, come on, Joe, I want a dance with you."

"I'd rather take the canoe out."

Joe lit his cigarette and turned away from the counter. Celie leaned back against the shelves of canned goods and watched him. Of course, it would be fun taking out the canoe the first time this year, but she could wear her new dress and, anyway, Mr. Farley had asked her to drive afterwards.

Arthur Farley sat on the platform at the end of the Town Hall playing the piano. Willie Denard crooned on a battered saxophone. Sabonich, the stocky little Austrian, sat holding his accordion during this number. He didn't care much for the way folks clapped for this fellow's playing, still it wasn't bad. Sabonich liked any kind of noise.

Arthur Farley looked moodily out on the crowd. Some difference, this and the crowd at the Tricorne Club. He was homesick. The smell of liquor and perspiration and cheap perfume suffocated him. His eyes roved over the walls and ceiling of the hall, ornamented with chips of glass sprinkled generously into the plaster. He speculated on how it had been done. The door to the women's coat room was crowded with the girls of the town, two mothers with small babies moved their blanketed bundles in time to the music. Pearl, the squaw, who was Hels Helsen's woman, stood stolidly, hands folded over her round front, watching the dancers from narrow black eyes. Big Tim, the lumberman at the Cross Roads was there with three camp-followers. The tall one with the henna hair was the famous Lizzie he'd heard about already. She wore a green lace dress that revealed a too flat chest and bony shoulders.

Arthur Farley half closed his eyes. The moving figures blurred in front of him. Even these greasy keys

42

felt good under his fingers. He shifted on the hard straight chair. His shoulders were lame from grading lumber all day in the yard and his feet ached. He was sick of this godforsaken town on the edge of the lake, of looking out over the lake, of eating with mill-hands.

The music poured steadily from the old piano. He nodded at Denard and repeated the chorus. The very notes on the music sheet in front of him seemed to mock him. He thought of the Tricorne Club, of the sleek women . . . of Charlotte. Charlotte had called him a "sucker" for coming up here in the first place. He'd told her it was too good an opening, the old man had his heart set on it. He'd had no idea his uncle meant him to camp out here for life. What if Charlotte could see him here tonight? She would twit him on his youth. He hated her for reminding him that she was thirty-three against his twenty-three years. He'd told her over and over again that what he admired in a woman was that very sophistication.

Celie Henderson danced up to the platform as the chorus ended.

"You're great, Mr. Farley. Gee, that's music!" Her cheeks were very pink. Her blue eyes danced with excitement. She wore her new green dress that fitted her body tightly, like a sheath. She was dancing with Al Ralston, the time-keeper from the office.

"How about a dance with me then, Celie?" Arthur stepped down from the platform. The crowd stamped and clapped for more, but Sabonich grabbed up his accordion and began, glad for the chance to perform alone again. More of the older people crowded out on the floor. This jazz! But they could all dance to the old accordion.

Arthur took Celie's arm possessively from the time-keeper. "Don't know whether I can dance to this or not," he said. Celie laughed gayly at the joke of it. Why, anyone could dance. Fat Mrs. Nerla and Guy Bates bumped against them so that he held Celie tight to keep her from being dashed against the next couple.

"Lord, what a dog-fight!" he growled.

But Celie laughed again. "It's better if you just jig around," she explained. She was shaking her head at Guy Bates.

"You keep off my feet, Guy!"

"Can't help it, Celie, they just go that way."

Arthur was swept along by her laughter. He took little steps in a small circle. He was aware of the hollow in her back under the sleazy new green silk. Her green moire slippers followed little twists and turnings of his instinctively. Tiny beads of perspiration stood out on her lips. She hunched her shoulder to wipe them off and jerked back suddenly.

"Oh, my goodness! did I smear my lipstick?"

Arthur laughed at her. "Just a trifle at the corner," he told her and made elaborate work of wiping an imaginary smear off with his handkerchief. Sabonich blew a whistle for a square-dance.

"Let's get out of this. I've played enough anyway. Let's take a ride."

Celie looked around the room doubtfully for Joe. He wasn't there. He'd taken the canoe down, after all, when there were lots of other nights. "I'll get my coat." She pushed her way through the crowd around the door of the women's coat room.

"I see you got a new beau, Celie!"

"Out with the big town boy, eh?"

"Remember you're your Ma's own girl when you get in the car, Celie!"

Celie laughed good-naturedly. "Oh, come off!" Over the green silk the lapin jacket became an evening wrap by the way Celie held it tightly across her and looked out over its turned-up collar. It was a way bred either of instinct or the movies. After the stifling heat of the dance hall, the cold air was intoxicating. Celie leaned her head back against the open top. The stars were very high above Flat Point.

"Want the top up? It's pretty cold driving."

"Oh, no, it's swell this way," answered Celie, stuffing her hands in her cuffs. She felt the cold air rushing against her skirt, but admitting the cold was not in her code.

"It's early yet, only ten. What d'ye say we drive in to the hotel in Clarion and have a bite?"

Celie was thrilled. "You bet."

They drove fast; faster than she and Joe could go.

The road seemed strange; the familiar landmarks whizzed by so swiftly.

"I'll give you a card to Mr. Benson at the Tricorne Club. Maybe you could get in on one of the acts," Arthur was saying when they drove into Clarion.

Celie had never been in the Carlson House before. She pulled her jacket a little tighter as she went into the lobby.

"Oh, Joe, Mr. Farley, I mean, that picture over there of the man with the gun scared me."

"Queer old thing."

The lobby wasn't as splendid as Celie had thought it would be and the dining room was closed so they had to go down the street, after all. They found a Greek place that had high booths to eat in and wonderful sundaes. A "banana split" and a "tin roof," Arthur ordered and Celie peeked around the booth at the other people. A radio was playing. Celie clasped her hands on the table. The Tricorne Club must be something like this.

Celie stayed awake all the way home. Mr. Farley put his arm around her and kissed her once. That was all right. It was swell of him to drive way in to town like that.

"You're a nice kid, Celie. I'd like to take you back to Chicago and show you around a bit. You'd go over big," he said suddenly.

Celie was thrilled. Did that mean he was going to ask her to? She leaned her head back again and looked up into the dark. They were whirling by Mead now; they were halfway home. In the car, the lights were so bright on the road, the little light on the dash so cozy, there was nothing desolate about the road at all, tonight.

5

IT WAS May. All the snow had melted in Flat Point. There was nothing to soften the ugly box-like corners of the roofs of the company houses. The tin cans of the winter's meals were heaped far up above the barrels back of each house and sprawled over on the ground. Dwindling wood piles were littered with a stray mitten, an old double boiler, a discarded tire covered over all winter by the merciful blanket of snow. Ragged children, no longer snug in their winter caps and jackets, looked a little peaked in the bright spring light.

Celie came listlessly up the street from the store as the eleven-thirty whistle blew. At the top of the street where the woods began again, over back of the tiny cemetery, there was a bright, joyous green, but up the treeless street there was only newly discovered poverty and ugliness.

Celie's lapin jacket was open and the worn edges showed. Her head was bare and the soft breeze of May blew the short hair around her face gently. But her blue eyes were sparkless. She didn't want to go home to lunch this noon, to eat dinner with Sam and Hans.

Arthur, Mr. Farley, that is, had gone home yesterday. He said he'd be back in a month, prob'ly. She had waited for him to come into the store during the morning to say good-by. But he hadn't. She watched the smoke of the noon train disappearing around the bend of the lake and knew he was on it.

"Guess the big boy's nephy got sick of the sticks, eh, Celie?" Buddy had called over to her. "I seen him go down to the station just now."

When he had been in town everything was more exciting. It was as though there were a visible contact between Detroit, the world beyond the straits, and Flat Point. Celie had thought of herself as going away with him sometime. She had shut her mind to Joe's coolness nights when he came in to supper. She had smiled across the table at Mr. Farley instead. He gave her a card one day to Mr. Benson of the Tricorne Club. It was stuck into her mirror, now. Celie looked at it doubtfully when she was combing her hair. She looked into the mirror closely and tried to find more of a Garbo look. She wished she had more of her mother's guttural Swedish accent. Her voice was high like all the voices of the young people in the Point, with the questioning "eh?" at the end of their sentences. Spring made her restless. She wanted more spring clothes. Her green moiré opera pumps had a dirty mark around the base of the tapering heels, already. The "foam green" silk wasn't going to wear any time. It was pulling at the shoulder seams. Celie's shoulders were broader than the average size sixteen.

She dried the dishes after lunch silently. Christina was already paring potatoes for supper. She hung up her towel and pulled on her jacket.

"I gotta hurry back today," she said as she went out the kitchen door. She walked swiftly back down the street, past the store and on down the path the men took to the mill. She went along between the high piles of lumber. They towered above her like the tall buildings on a city street; blocks and blocks of them, with a road between wide enough for trucks to pass. The lumber was piled for seasoning and had stood there all winter. The sun slanted in between the boards and fell on Celie in a barred pattern.

Beyond the last tall building was the lake. Celie ran now. There was so little time before she had to be back. She knew the shore around the Point by heart, all the way out to the lighthouse and around to the cliffs on the other end. She had gone as far as she had time for. She sat down on the piney bluffs above the shore. A little later, there would be blueberries here. Now the ground was greening over. Ground pine and new winter-green leaves gleamed shiny against the brown pine needles of other seasons.

Celie leaned back on her hands, her head resting on hunched shoulders. Lake Superior was a sharp blue, deeper than the sky. Far out a man sat in a flat boat. He seemed stationary, a figure painted in a picture. Joe's

49

father, prob'ly; he was a queer, silent Swede for you, always taking half days off to fish. No wonder Joe wasn't scared to canoe on the lake. He'd rowed his father's boat since he was little, in storms and all. A sudden wind arose in the top of a giant pine tree, one of the few survivors of the white pine massacre, but it was May and the wind lost itself in a gentle sigh before it could gather volume. Celie wanted to be alone. She wanted to get away from Flat Point. She wanted anything but what she had.

It rested her to come off down here and look across the lake. The blue stretching out and out as far as she could see had no connection with the town behind. Celie forgot even to think of new clothes. A sunny stillness filled her. There was no room for discontent. The great lake lapped softly against the sand. It was shallow there along the edge as the shallows of Celie's mind, but it flowed out to deeps far below the sun's reach.

"Time changes, time changes, time . . ." the words were there in the lap of the water for the sky to hear and the twisted trees that had once been straight and young.

Celie got up and hurried back up the path. In the soft sawdust road between the piles she turned her ankle sharply and a heel came off. She limped along until she came on Silas Pederson and Tony, the little Austrian, piling lumber on a new plank building.

"Oh, Silas, could you pound this in for me? I'm late now." Silas took the slipper from her with a slow smile.

"Sure Mike, Celie. What you doin' by the lake?"

"Nothin' . . . just walkin'. Thanks, I'll do you a turn someday."

She was off up the hill. Mr. Simpson always knew when you were back late. Why had she gone down there, anyway? She was a crazy one, right.

Celie felt better coming up the street in the evening. The light was softer on the naked little houses. The men were on their way up from the mill. Each box-like dwelling had a waiting look. The air was sweet in spite of the smell of fried potatoes that came from Mrs. Larsen's kitchen and Norah Maloney's and the one on the corner.

" 'Lo," Violet Freedman's husband passed her with an admiring glance.

"Hi," answered Celie.

There was no use, tonight, looking up the street to see if the blue Ford was out in front of their house. She could look down the tracks to see if the limey engine was in. Joe would think she was being nice to him again only because Mr. Farley was gone. That wasn't it. It was natural for her to take up with Arthur. Joe knew she wanted to get across the straits someday. It was natural for her to be interested in anybody from Detroit. She wondered if Joe would ask her to go out tonight. She'd have to go some place, it was so springy out.

Celie crossed over to see Selma Lichtenberg. She was

on the stoop waiting for Norm to get home. Selma used to work down at the mill before she was married, six or seven of the girls did, pasting labels. It must seem nice to her now, Celie thought, being home.

"Supper all ready, Selma?"

"You bet, and I tried a recipe for cake that came in the baking powder can, four layers. Gee, it turned out good."

"No wonder you're out waiting for Norm to come," jibed Celie.

"I was just out here reading the last installment. It's wonderful, and honest, Celie, the way that girl feels about Malcolm makes me think all the time of me an' Norm."

"I didn't get a chance to read it today at the store. We were awful busy."

Most of the younger women in the Point were following *The Love Trap,* a serial running in the *Clarion Daily.* They were as apt to discuss the latest complications in the life of Violet Vance as in their own. It had run all winter and was now nearing its tense and tumultuous ending.

"Well, so long." Celie felt her interest lag tonight, even in *The Love Trap.*

Suddenly a piercing steam whistle flung itself far out on the lake and into every dwelling at the Point. Celie stopped to look out toward the fringe of tall firs where the tracks led in from the woods. There came the log train, car after car, chained in a melancholy procession behind the dinky little engine at the head. Joe was there in the engine. Impulsively, Celie waved. Two figures on the engine waved back.

Celie felt better. Maybe Joe didn't know who it was, but maybe he did.

There were rice fritters with the sausage and a fresh cake. Joe always liked rice fritters, Celie thought to herself as she set the table.

"Celie, mind you don't put such a chunk of butter on the table at once. It's awful the way them men spoon it up," called Christina Henderson from the kitchen.

Celie turned the radio on and opened the door to the spring air. It was beginning to stay light a long while these days. Joe was late coming up from the yard.

Hans and Sam and Ole Henderson were already sitting at the table.

"I'll fire up, Mamma, you sit down." Celie wanted to wait tonight till Joe came. She put wood in the stove and turned the last batch of fritters on the griddle.

"They're goin' to lay off the night shift tomorrow," said Ole. "Won't need it till next winter."

"I guess the Svensons set by a good bit workin' both shifts," commented Christina enviously.

"They'll likely lay off and fish awhile this summer to make up for it," grunted Hans.

Celie heard Joe's step on the front stoop.

"Evenin'." He looked toward the kitchen and saw Celie in the doorway. His gaze rested steadily on her for a second, but he sat down without speaking to her.

Celie came in with a plate of fritters.

"I kept 'em hot for you, Joe." Then she wished she hadn't said it.

"You needn't 'a' bothered," muttered Joe in a very low voice. "We got held up today, hot box on the engine." Joe turned to Ole. His voice shut her out. "Thought I'd be later than I was."

If the others were aware of Celie's silence, they gave no sign of it. Hans and Sam left when they finished. Christina picked up the dishes. Ole tipped back in his chair and took out his pipe.

"Like runnin' the limey, Joe?"

" 'S not bad. Makes a long day, but I like being out so much. Good in the woods, too. The camp's moved out near K40, now, over by Snake Creek. Makes it a shorter run in for the logs. Almost forgot, Mis' Henderson, I got you some arbutus I saw. Funny thing, I put my lunch box down almost on top of it."

Joe brought a large bunch of arbutus out of his jumper pocket.

"Thank you, Joe." Christina took it from him and put it in a pickle glass she had painted red. The sweet fragrance rose in the small crowded rooms. Christina Henderson smelled it eagerly. "Seems sweeter every year, don't it?"

Celie finished her cake and got up from the table. Joe was mad or he'd have brought the arbutus to her. She knew for sure, now. She stacked the dishes and went outside with the scrapings. A splinter of a new moon

54

hung over the woodshed. It was pale in the light sky. Joe couldn't stay mad long, but she wasn't sure. Inside, he was talking to Ole as though she weren't there. Maybe he'd come out and offer to dry dishes for her.

She washed the dishes silently, aware of the voices in the next room. Christina Henderson mixed bread for the next day and set it to rise on the shelf over the stove. Then she took her crocheting and went to sit by the dining room table.

Celie shut the cupboards noisily on the last dish and hung up her cloths. She came through the dining room and stopped a minute at the radio. Then she dropped it guiltily. Joe would think she was remembering Mr. Farley. She ran upstairs to comb her hair over.

When she came down, Ole and Joe were playing cribbage. She sat down to read the installment of *The Love Trap*. Suddenly, she got up impatiently.

"I'm goin' out on the stoop, it's so nice out."

Christina Henderson looked up from her crocheting. "You better wear your jacket." Ole and Joe went on playing.

Lots of folks were out on the street; they were so glad the winter was over. Hiney Richter was trying to get his old Buick to work. Mrs. Maloney went into the house on the corner where the woman was expecting. Pat Olney was taking down his storm windows. Celie's gaze wandered on down the street. At the end, below the hill, rose the roof of the mill and the four black stacks, then the lake. She thought of the night she had showed Mr. Farley the town. Gee, she wanted to get away. She had ten dollars saved up now. If she didn't spend any of it, maybe by fall she could go to Detroit.

"You seem lonely, Celie." Joe came out and stood by the door. "I s'pose you miss Mr. Farley."

"Joe!" Celie's voice was scornful. "You sound spiteful as a woman."

"I saw you wave, tonight."

"I wish I hadn't, now, if you thought it was just because Mr. Farley had gone."

"Wasn't it?" Joe asked abruptly.

"Oh, Joe, you know better."

Joe lighted a new cigarette.

"I didn't take the canoe out that night, Celie. It was too early, I guess. Want to help do it tonight?"

"You bet, Joe, I'll get my old clothes on, I won't be a minute."

"It oughta be good on the lake a night like this," said Joe.

6

THE July sun in Flat Point warmed even the long board steps of the company store. It was Sunday and the store was closed. Chuck Rebeaux could lie full length on the step with his hat over his eyes and sleep. Nobody going up and down, in and out, today.

Chuck Rebeaux was a French Canadian. He had been a lumberjack and tramped out to the woods with his stuff strapped to his back a year ago and no thought in his head of the tree that would fall on his arm. It was just as well, though; now he helped the cookie in the kitchen car, and often got a snack between meals. Last night, he had tramped in to get drunk at Crazy Bill's. He had slept it off, but it was comfortable to doze a little more. He shifted his weight and tipped his hat farther back on his head.

A car rattled past, a girl and a fellow. Nice to get into town now and again, 'nd see girls. He used to take girls out once in a while, up in Canada and then he'd gone into the woods. Goin' to stop some time when he got ahead a little 'nd find a girl. Chuck Rebeaux felt for his plug of tobacco in the pocket of his Soo woolens where his pay had been. He dozed again.

Celie and Joe rattled on. Joe had taken the top off of the Ford this spring. The sun beat down on Celie's fair hair and the green dress, on Joe's clean white shirt and bright blue tie. But Joe drove fast enough to keep a breeze stirring.

"Hope you don't mind the rattles, Celie." Joe was still sensitive about the new blue car of Mr. Farley's.

"Oh, Joe, I'd rather ride in this and you know it."

Celie was happy. Things were just as they had been before Mr. Farley's coming, but different. She waved every evening when the log train came in and always kept a plate of supper hot for Joe. She hadn't changed any about wanting to get to the world across the straits. She and Joe felt alike about that.

"We'll get ahead a little, Celie, and then we'll get married and go, you wait!"

Joe was happy. He strode down to the yard in the morning whistling and climbed into the cabin of the little engine. All day in the woods, he switched and backed and stopped and ran ahead again, but his thoughts traveled straight ahead with Celie. He'd talk to Mr. Farley, not that light-weight nephew, but the old man himself, the next time he came up; he'd go right up to him with his mill clothes on and say,

"How's chances of getting a job in the Detroit plant?" It would be a good way to get down to the city. Often at night he came home with a sprig of balsam stuck in his cap. And he was sure of Celie, now.

"Someday, Celie, we'll drive away like this and keep right on going, down over the straits and into another state, maybe."

"Oh, Joe, I wish we could do it soon. It's all right in summer, but I hate it in winter something fierce."

"I'll see, Celie, we might. Would you marry me, Celie, if I had a job all ready in the city?"

"We'd need a little something ahead."

"I don't know, if we had something coming in regular that we could count on, we could manage. Look at my father and mother and your father and mother. They came over here from the old country, blind, you might say, didn't know what they'd find or how they'd get along. . . ."

"Yes, but we're different, Joe. We have to have

things. Times are different, too. If you're going to get anywhere, nowadays, you have to start out right," Celie proclaimed in a worldly-wise tone, her eyes fixed wistfully on the winding road ahead.

Joe was silent. He thought of some of the old-timers in the Point. Of Ole and Mrs. Henderson, of Stumpf, the walking boss, of an old fellow down at the yard who was a sawyer. They'd come to the Point when they had to get there by boat and wait for supplies the same way. They'd seen hard living, almost pioneer times, but there was something about them that made you feel like keeping your mouth shut and going along.

Still, it was as Celie said, too. They were different. The old folks were satisfied with mighty little. He and Celie were young. The country was settled now; nobody wanted to be a pioneer and scrimp along these days; money so easy and plenty of jobs. They wanted part of whatever was going.

"Joe, you see, don't you?"

"You bet, Celie." Gee, she was swell.

"Look, Celie, we'll be too early for the show even when we've had our supper. How about stopping awhile. We've got lots to talk about."

"All right."

Joe slowed down. They were going by Mead. "It's pretty over there. I came down here last hunting season, Celie. Let's drive in."

He drove down a level grassy path that had once been the main street of the old mill town and stopped

59

by a deserted house built above the lake. Joe got out
over the side and came around to help Celie out. Here,
where no one could see him he didn't feel foolish. He
even bowed over her hand a little, like the fellow
would in the movie. Celie giggled.

"Joe, you!"

They walked down the old street a ways. Joe couldn't
let go of her hand. A curious lightheartedness fell over
them. The whole town was theirs. Their laughter stirred
an echo against the wall of the old mill. Joe called to
hear the echo answer. Every nook and corner of the
tumbledown buildings was penetrated by sun and wind.
Sweet fern grew between the boards of the porches.
Moss tinted the leaky roofs.

"Nothing spooky about this place in the daytime, is
there? Look, Joe, that's a cute house. Let's sit over
there."

Against the end of one of the porches someone had
once built a home-made trellis and woodbine still grew
over it in a thicket.

"Want to bet someone was just married and his wife
wanted that business built?" said Joe.

"It's pretty. I wish we had one by our stoop at home."

They sat down in the grass at the end of the porch.

"Someone must have loved living here. Look at that
view of the lake."

"Maybe they hated it like you do."

"No, they wouldn't have bothered with the trellis. I
wouldn't do a thing in a house at the Point. Just as

you get it fixed up you're in danger of losing it," stormed Celie.

"You wouldn't have to fix up your house, anyway. All you'd have to do would be to live there and the place would look all right," said Joe a little clumsily.

Celie smiled down at her dress and the green pumps to match. She wished she'd worn them first with Joe instead of Mr. Farley.

"Think of the people that would be falling out of their houses to see who the beautiful lady going down the street is!"

"Joe, you're such a silly!" But with his words, Joe had peopled the houses. Celie looked around at the vacant windows in the house opposite, quickly.

The houses had been empty so long, rain and snow and sun and wind had taken every homely mark of human life away. The houses were as much a part of the place as the rocky hills on the other side of the road, as impersonal and well-weathered.

"Joe, I didn't mean to show you this, but look at it." Celie put a crumpled note into his hand. Joe read it slowly.

"DEAR MISS HENDERSON,

"My nephew has told me about you and how attractive and quick you are. I am in need of a maid to take with me to the Cape this summer. I thought perhaps you would be glad of the opening. My nephew says you are anxious to leave your present home. If you find it pleasant and prove satisfactory, you might make this a permanent place. Please let me hear from you at once.

"Ruth B. Farley

"(Mrs. Michael Farley)"

"I squnched the note up when I first read it I was so mad," Celie confessed. "I don't know why. I suppose it's a good chance to get away."

"And work for some-a his folks!" Joe boiled. "You're as good as him."

"I felt awful when I got it, but, now, way out here, it seems all right."

Joe's eyes flashed dangerously. "He's a scrawny jack pine, for sure, just as your father said. Celie, don't cry!" Alarm was in his voice. "Why, Celie!" Celie was mopping her eyes with a tiny ball of scented handkerchief and laughing as she cried.

"I don't know, Joe; I'm a baby, I guess. Only, it hurt after I'd gone out with him and all, but maybe I should take the chance."

Joe gathered her into his arms. He kissed the back of her neck. Celie didn't stop him.

"Oh, Celie, Celie." He held her tightly. She was sweet. The sky was very blue and the lake a shade brighter. Joe could look out at the lake over Celie's head. He bent and kissed her again. "Do you think I could let you go down there to Detroit, Celie? Why, those weeks when you were so taken up with him, that Farley, I didn't care whether I lost my job or not. I even stopped working on the radio I was building up in my room. Now, why, Celie, it won't take any time for us to get ahead, together." Joe stopped planning.

Celie looked up from his shoulder where she had hid her face. Her eyes were wet. Joe looked straight into them and at her full red lips. He kissed her, her eyes and then her lips. He had only kissed her before hurriedly, shyly, before Celie would bob her head away and look at her face in her mirror. Now he kissed her with all the strength of his loving her these three years back. His arms slipped farther around her. He wanted to bruise those soft lips a little . . . he wanted . . .

Celie gave herself up to his kiss. A loneliness and a hurt were wiped away by his very fierceness. It was good to have Joe care so, to have him love her so.

"Oh, Celie," he breathed. He pulled her down in the grass with him. His hands caressed her, felt for her slight breasts, her firm, slim body. He burrowed his head against her, in the hollow of her neck. He wanted to hide in her. His driven hands felt along her hips, fearfully, fiercely; found the sash of the green dress. His hands could not be still, they could not have enough of her, get near enough to her.

"You're beautiful, Celie," Joe's breath came hotly through her dress on her body.

"Why, Joe!" Celie spoke in a small, amazed voice. "I didn't know you cared so . . ."

"Gee, Celie!" Joe held her more tightly. His head rested hard against her breast now. It hurt a little.

Celie's arms went around him. Her hands felt his shoulders timidly. He was so big, so hard-muscled. She felt suddenly that she had held him so before. He raised his head and kissed her again on the lips. His whole weight was against her. She slid further down on the grass and wondered that she could bear him so lightly on her.

So great was the stillness Celie could hear the bees humming around an old tree stump, and the baffled whirring of the wind caught in the grass. A woodpecker bored noisily near them. Grasshoppers strummed a tune of heat. Joe's head lay on Celie's arm. She brushed his hair back from his hot forehead. A great new tenderness for him came over her. It was sweet to lie there hidden in the tall grass of the old village. A strange contentment stole over Celie. Joe seemed too content to stir. Celie was alive in every sense to all that breathed and moved in the hot summer day. She looked around her with heavy-lidded eyes. Across the grassy ground that had once been a street the building had burned. There was still the slight depression of an old cellar. Now it was filled with fireweed. Tall stalks of violety pink flowers moved slightly in the breeze, delicate, tiny blossoms each set off like a jewel on a separate stem.

Slowly, time was blotting out the signs of habitation with the magenta masses of fireweed. Celie gazed at the softly waving spires . . . some time the whole town would be lost, hidden by witch grass and weeds. Once people had lived here; people like her and Joe had loved each other under the gabled roofs of the tumbledown board houses. Sometime, Flat Point would be like that, tumbledown and deserted, covered over with fireweed, even the mill and the store. Celie shivered. A fear rose in her mind.

"Joe, Joe," she whispered loudly. "We've got to go, quick. I want to get away from here. It's scary, Joe. I don't like it. Oh, Joe, we shouldn't ought to have."

Joe raised on one elbow. He smoothed back his hair.

"Celie dear, it's all right. Don't be afraid. He hid her head against his shoulder. But his fierceness was gone. He was just Joe Linsen again. He couldn't comfort her. The fear persisted. Celie pulled away from him and got up, quickly. She looked at the wrinkles in the green dress anxiously. There was a deep smear of grass stain across the toe of her slipper. She started back to the car silently.

Joe acquiesced with her mood. He straightened his tie and slipped in behind the wheel. The car rattled down the grassy road back to the main highway. Celie couldn't keep from a hurried glance back at the ghost of a town.

The fireweed moved in the wind. A humming bird clung by his bill to a single flower and swayed with the motion of the tall stalks.

7

TUESDAY of that week, Celie came out of the store at five-thirty. She walked so slowly up the hill her high heels tapped out no rhythm on the board sidewalks. She wore an old yellow gingham dress that she had discarded last summer. It was too long-waisted, too short in the skirt for the new styles. She had got it out this morning because it suited some sternly self-accusing impulse. She had not slept well these nights. The rooms under the sloping roofs of the company houses were hot in summer and cold in winter. Her face was paler than usual.

Mrs. Hacula was looking out of her window as Celie passed. "I declare, that Henderson girl gets prettier all the time, don't she? You'd think she'd be married by now."

"She's likely waitin' for young Farley to come back to see if he'll have her. She's got big ideas, Celie Henderson has," answered her daughter, Urna.

Celie went into the house. They were having sauerkraut for supper, sauerkraut and wieners. Christina Henderson sat in the sitting room crocheting.

"Celie, it's an easy supper. I thought I'd just finish this while I'm at it. You look tired, child."

"I am. It's the heat, I guess." Celie stooped at the sideboard to smooth her hair. "It's quarter of, I'll get things on."

Out in the kitchen, the savory flavor made Celie hungry, after all. There was something comforting and hearty in the smell. In the bowl of apple sauce on the kitchen table, the freshly ironed clothes on the racks back of the stove. Celie felt reassured. Everything was the same. She moved around getting supper on. Ole and Joe came in together tonight. Hans and Sam had gone fishing right after the mill whistle blew. Joe came out to wash up. He came over by her with the pail for water.

" 'Lo, Celie," he said low by her side. It seemed all a dream, his calling her beautiful the other night. She sliced bread on the table by the kitchen window. She could watch Joe going up to the corner pump. He stooped to take the little Pederson boy pickaback on the way. He was getting as brown as the bark of a tree. She watched his shoulders in the blue shirt, patched across the back. She remembered how bony they had felt to her hand . . . she piled the bread on a plate hurriedly and came away from the window.

They sat down to supper. Celie caught Joe's eyes on her and looked at her plate. She had kept away from Joe since Sunday. She said she had to go down to Selma's for a spread pattern after supper last night, and when she came back Joe was on the lake fishing with his father. Tonight she would see him, after supper. She flushed. The talk went on.

"DesMains was telling me today the call they had for lumber meant running a night shift all next winter," Ole announced with satisfaction.

"I like it when the mill runs nights," said Christina.

"You like the idea of someone working while you sleep, eh, wife?"

Christina laughed. "No, no, but it don't seem so lonely, then."

Christina Henderson had always had a friendly feeling for the black millstacks. They meant security. She liked to see them sending up their red smoke at night. She had seen towns close down before now; then everyone had to move. There was the time at Earheart when the fire got the timber; and the mill at Boss Lake that had to close down because it went broke. Moving was no good. Some women thought the next place would be nearer town or have warmer houses . . . not her. She was satisfied where she was.

Celie carried the dishes off the table. She had never thought of her mother being lonely.

"Can I give you a hand with the wiping, Celie?" asked Joe.

Perversely, Celie answered, "No, you smoke your pipe." She had meant to say yes and was hurt when Joe went out to the stoop with Ole.

Christina Henderson came out to fold up the ironing. She did washings for the men who boarded with her. Freshly ironed clothes hung on the rack back of the stove everyday but Sunday. Celie looked up from her dishpan. She and her mother seldom talked as they did the housework together.

"Can't work and talk too," Christina would say.

"Do you like it here, Mamma?" Celie said abruptly, tonight. She had never asked her before. She had no idea.

Christina Henderson's brick red face, leathery in texture, stood out boldly in the light of the swinging electric bulb. She shrugged her shoulders.

"Ole gets good pay. It might be worse."

Celie put away the dishes. So many things might be better, too.

She went out to the stoop and sat down by Joe.

"Wanta drive?"

"No, I wanta talk, Joe."

Joe was filling his pipe. "We could do both."

Celie sat moodily on the corner of the stoop. It was still very light at eight o'clock and would be till ten, these nights. But the light had a strangely luminous quality, a greenish tinge that softened all it touched. From the end of the street came the moaning cry of the foxes at the fox farm. Across the street, Wood Judson was painting his old flat-boat. The street swarmed with children. You could not see the lake unless you walked out to the sidewalk. There were no trees. When Flat Point was built, the first step was to clear off a bare space and then start in. The trees began a little back of the fox farm. Celie stared dully across at Wood Judson.

"What's the matter, Cele?" Joe's voice was low and tender. It broke up the cold wall around her mind.

"Joe, I've been thinking about Sunday. You know . . ." Now that she had brought herself to mention it, she could talk clearly. "It was wrong. I should have known better."

"Celie, don't go blaming yourself and spoil it all."

"We were both wrong, Joe. I've been thinking and I want to get married. I couldn't ever look at anybody else after that . . . I want to get married right away."

Joe stared at her. In the eerie late light, Celie's hair and skin were touched to a gleaming that had no property of color. The organdie collar of her dress was as softly silver as the wing of a moth flying by in the dusk. Her beauty made Joe dumb.

Celie looked at him quickly. "Joe, you still want to marry me, don't you?

"Why, Celie, you know that, but I don't want you to marry me because of . . . if you don't really care."

Celie looked away from him, down the street. A shadow of Christina's grimness tightened the full curve of her lips. "I thought maybe next Sunday, Joe, we could drive into Clarion. I don't want anyone to know till we're married." Her voice was brisk.

"What about Ole and your mother?"

"They can know afterwards. They like you, Joe."

Joe dug in the bowl of his pipe with a match.

"Celie, I haven't got a job away, yet. It would mean goin' to live right in the Point." He was dubious. This wasn't the way folks got married.

"We can go away next spring."

The enormity of the decision sank into Joe's mind.

"Celie, is it because you're afraid about, about my loving you that way, what might happen?"

"A little bit, but, anyway, Joe, I wouldn't feel right unless we got married."

Joe was silent. Celie rested her chin on her fists. The luminous quality of the sky had disappeared. Joe could hardly make out her features. She was any woman sitting on a stoop looking at the sky.

"Let's walk down to the lake, Celie."

He took her arm. They walked down the street below the mill to the lake. It was cool there. The lake swished silkily against the shore. A breeze blew Celie's hair against her face. The night was wrapped in a mantle of gentleness, no passion, no resentment, no striving, only gentleness rested softly on the water. Celie stood still on the shore. She thought how the spires of fireweed must blow in the dark, how lonely the empty houses must look. She shivered.

"Celie," Joe felt her shiver. "Celie, we'll get away from here, don't you worry."

Celie slipped her arm in his.

Joe squared his shoulders. He felt better.

8

CELIE and Joe came out of the Swedish minister's house at Clarion and got in the car. Celie wore her green dress, newly pressed. A smirch of the grass stain still showed on one toe of the green slippers. It was just six. Celie had been very quiet all the way down. She was quiet now.

"I thought we might as well have supper here before we go back," said Joe.

"All right," said Celie. She was trying hard to feel that she was married . . . to Joe Linsen . . . Celie Henderson Linsen. It sounded Swedish enough.

Joe drove up to the Carlson House. After all, one wasn't married every day. He went round to let her out.

"You go in; I'll park the car."

Celie stood on the long porch and watched Joe drive the car in between the other two parked out in front. When Joe came, they went into the lobby together. Celie looked quickly to see the man in the painting pointing his gun straight at them as they entered. Joe noticed it too.

"That's a sweet welcome to a place!" He had never been in the Carlson House before or any other hotel. He wondered if you wrote in the big book at the desk. He guessed not just for dinner. Suddenly, an idea struck him. He would speak to Celie about it later. Past the desk he saw a sign, "Dining Room," over a door.

"Is supper ready?" he asked the boy at the desk.

"Five to eight," answered the boy, looking Joe over. He was used to seeing tall Swedes from the woods around town, in to spend their roll.

Celie was pleased at going to the Carlson House for supper. It was nice of Joe. She was glad she had worn her white kid gloves, even though they were short and there was such a gap to her sleeves.

There was a head waitress in the summer months at the Carlson House. She was large, with ratted masses of taffy-colored hair and calculating pale blue eyes. She rested them now on Celie and Joe and led them over to the side table on the left hand side. They would look more like the real thing from that distance. She had to keep her mind on the general effect of her dining room. Trade had been good this summer; local folks as well as tourists and the usual run of business transients. Burdmans, a Finnish family, were over at the large round table. They looked native but still they were coming over regular Sunday nights before the show; they had to have the table they wanted. He looked like the miner he'd been all his life, but Red Topping told her old man Burdman's son had made a neat little pile in stocks this year. Red Topping had made money himself in stocks; maybe she ought to go out with him now and then. The head waitress paused in her thoughts to smile at the gentlemen at the conspicuous table on the right. All her mind needed to be concentrated in that smile. The head waitress, Mattie, knew her material.

"Let's get lake trout, Celie, eh? Why, people come miles to taste one of them broiled here, someone was telling me," said Joe to Celie.

"Isn't that the little Henderson girl that works in the store, Art?" Mr. Farley was up with his nephew.

Young Farley looked around.

"Yeah, with Joe Linsen." He would catch her eye in a minute. She was one of the bright spots about that place. He'd have to bring her in to dinner, sometime. She'd get a big kick out of it, the way she did when they drove in after that dance.

"Pretty, isn't she?" Mr. Farley commented, looking her over carefully. "Some of those Swedish girls are, you know. Don't wear well. Funny thing how quickly they get old. Well, you know, like her mother, Ole Henderson's wife."

Arthur Farley smoked his cigarette thoughtfully. Last night he'd been with Charlotte. She really was in love with him in spite of her free ways with Mollisson. If he should wangle a good job out of the thing and got that Hilton Folly place to live in, maybe she'd come up. He turned to his uncle with a keener gleam of interest in his eyes than Farley had ever seen in them.

"How do things stand, do you mean you really are dissatisfied with DesMains?"

"Well, Art, I wouldn't trust him any farther than I could see him. Too blamed independent. Thinks he can run the mill without any help from me and that won't go. Nash feels that way about him, too. I tell you, Art, there's your chance."

"How do Nash and McNalty and the rest at Detroit

feel about me?" He distrusted his uncle's confidence
sometimes.

"Nash is for you; says when you're fitted to run
things to give you a tryout. What Nash says goes with
the rest."

It wasn't often that old Farley admitted that his own
word wasn't law. Arthur Farley had seen his uncle in
a different light these last few weeks he'd put in at the
Detroit office. He had even heard one of the men there,
one of the unimportant younger men, call him "old Bag
of Wind." "Old Bag of Wind's back, I see," he'd said
one morning when he didn't know young Farley was
there.

Arthur Farley had never thought much about him
until recently. His uncle had always been the successful
one of the family; rich Uncle Mike, who gave him
money when he needed it. Now he had plenty of op-
portunity to know him. He didn't like the familiar way
the head waitress spoke to the old man; or the way all
of them, the bell boy and the man at the desk, treated
him like one of themselves. Young Arthur Farley
would never have that easy way of the born traveling
salesman himself. He didn't like it in his uncle.

His thoughts came back to his own problems . . . to
Charlotte in her black velvet negligee waiting to go out
and do her act at the Tricorne.

"McNalty and Nash thought your report was pretty
good. We decided to let Lukas go on your say-so."
Arthur liked his uncle better when he was talking busi-

ness. "The thing for you to do these next few months is to learn lumber. Stick close to DesMains; learn his stuff and if you get anything on him, don't forget it." Farley wiped his mouth vigorously with the napkin. "Let's go."

As they went past Joe and Celie's table, Arthur stopped.

"Hello! Mrs. Henderson's patrons seem to be leaving her for the Carlson House," he said brightly. "How are you, Celie?"

Joe pushed back his chair and stood up.

"This is my wife, Mrs. Linsen. We got married today."

Celie reddened.

"No kidding?" Arthur looked at them incredulously. "Well, say, congratulations." He nodded to Joe, but turned back to Celie. "I thought you were coming to the city, Celie! I'll have to tell Uncle Mike the news!" He went on out to the lobby.

Celie's ice-cream tasted suddenly flat and warmish to her. Joe beamed.

"Did you hear me say, 'my wife,' Celie? Guess he got something he wasn't expectin'. Say, Celie, how would you like to spend the night here. I ought to've thought of it before. We could telephone the doctor's office and then they could send over to tell your mother."

"I haven't got any clothes here or anything."

"You could manage, maybe, with what you have.

Wouldn't you rather than just going home plain, to-night?"

"I guess so."

When they came out into the lobby, after dinner, Joe went up to the desk. Celie stood by the stairway. She looked around the lobby over toward the corner where the hotel radio stood. Arthur Farley was sitting close by, humming with it, probably. Something in the cut of his hair, his clothes, some air of the city about him excited her. Why hadn't she waited? Why hadn't she gone to the city as a maid even and tried it out? She felt left behind. A wave of sickness rushed over her that blotted out even Joe for a minute.

Joe came across from the desk. His coat bulged over his arm muscles as though the sleeves bound him too tightly. The blue was too bright against the red browned neck and face. He had a jaunty set to his shoulders, his black hair fell away from the side part crisply, but it was too long. He looked just what he was, a tall Swede from the sticks who'd just gotten married. He smiled at her from way across the room.

Suddenly, she was embarrassed. All those people seeing Joe walk across to her. She felt the angle of her hat, instinctively, the curl of hair against her cheek. She tried to look carelessly across the room away from Joe. But her eyes came back to him. There was something in Joe she couldn't resist. He stood by her now.

"All set, Celie. They have some smart rule here about no bag—no room. I paid 'em in advance and showed the funny boy at the desk our license. Guess not many have all their papers with 'em. Let's go to the show . . . or do you want to go up t' the room first, Celie?" He was a little proud.

"Oh, yes, Joe," Celie answered eagerly, "the powder's all off my nose."

Celie went upstairs to room 38 in the Carlson House. She had never been in a hotel bedroom before. It seemed a model of convenience and elegance. The thick red carpet was soft under the thin soles of the green moiré slippers. The white iron bed had splendid brass knobs to distinguish it from the iron beds common in the Point. The windows looked out across Lake Superior. Celie opened a window and the night air blew coolly across from Canada. It was the same wind that bore softly in through the windows in the Point, but here it was mysterious and strangely exciting.

Celie added more rouge and deepened the color of her lips. Her eyes were very bright in the mirror.

She and Joe were going to have swell times.

9

CELIE and Joe were the only ones down in the dining-room for breakfast at quarter of seven. They had the thirty-five-mile ride ahead of them.

"You'll be awfully late, Joe."

"Yeah, well, let 'em wait. I don't get married every

day. I guess Tim can take the limey out for once alone. You'll get there in time to stop by and see your mother. D'ye think she'll say much?"

"Mamma never says much. She'll be mad, at first."

"I don't believe Ole'll take on about it. He's all right."

Celie nodded. "What about your dad, Joe?"

"He's a queer one about things, living alone an' all—he'll never say anything."

"I hate to see everybody at the store, though."

"What do you care, Celie. It's nobody's business but our own."

"I know, but . . . I sorta wish we could take a trip." Celie looked down at her plate wistfully.

"Gee, we didn't plan ahead much, you know, Cele."

"Oh, Joe, as if I didn't know I . . . I kinda put you up to doing it."

"You know darn well I wanted to all the time . . ."

A silence spread between them. It was the first time they had mentioned the suddenness of their wedding.

"Well, we'd better go." Joe rose.

The road back to the Point was as though they had never traveled it. It stretched ahead portentous, unknown. Celie did not look at the summer cottages as enviously as usual. She had a sense of sharing something with the owners of these. Living in Clarion overnight gave one a feeling. They said little. Celie watched the roadside.

There was sunshine in the morning and warmth.

Grasshoppers sounded close to the road. The feeling of heat later in the day came to them across the open stretches but cooled away at the wooded places; heat that was always so brief the country of the sticks drank it up greedily, taking it down to the roots of its short flowering life.

The road followed around Lake Superior.

"There's the color of your eyes again, Cele, out there in the lake," Joe said.

They were up to Mead before they knew it.

"Funny, the forest fires never hit that place," said Joe carelessly.

"Yes," Celie answered. She looked to make sure. The house with the trellis was out of sight of the road. The town looked ghostly to her now in the early morning, the fallen roofs, the sag of the larger building, witch grass and weeds, milkweed and mullen stalks right in the old street of the town. Fireweed . . . almost like a garden flower it was . . . growing wild everywhere. A place that had been; a place to keep away from.

"Where d'ye s'pose the people are, Joe, that used to live there?"

"Oh, they've got other jobs. They don't care anything about Mead any more. You know the Finkels; they lived there, and old Quinn, the butch."

They were glad when Mead was out of sight.

At the sharp turn where Lathe Riggs had once smashed up, a log lay across the road too far to get around. Joe stopped suddenly.

"I guess I better haul it out of the way. Look at that, Cele." He turned it over with his foot. "Beavers, damn plucky workers, trying to lug it down to the creek and they got tired out. Here, you, I'll give you a break." Joe kicked the log down the bank.

The squatters' huts began soon, the ne'er do well fringe of the town. Crazy Bill's, the top of the little Catholic church, the bunk house, the store, the four stacks of the mill, the quick turn around the store corner, their street, Ole Henderson's house.

Cele got out, conscious of the Haculas at the window. She went up the walk and jumped quickly up the first step that was always too high for the width of her skirts. She pulled at the screen door. It was locked and Celie and Joe had to stand on the stoop, the target of all the eyes of the street.

There was the sound of Christina Henderson's slippered feet on the linoleum of the kitchen floor.

"Hello, Mamma," Celie said.

"I thought you'd decided not to work today, maybe." Christina was just the same. "Hello, Joe. Folks are some surprised around here."

Joe stood awkwardly at the door. "Well, I'll be getting down to the yard. I s'pose I'll get a razzing there if the boys have heard of it."

" 'By, Joe." Celie walked around the parlor table aimlessly. "I guess I'll go up and change my dress." At the doorway to the stairs, she hesitated.

"Mamma, I wondered about Joe. Shall I bring him

here to live?" Christina Henderson started to answer tartly, I s'posed you had that all planned. She said instead,

"If you want, Celie. You took a queer way to do, going off and sending us word through the doctor's office. You must've known before in order to get your license."

"I was afraid you'd want us to wait," Celie answered.

"Wait!" Christina made a tck of impatience. "When you know as much as I do about things you'll know it pays to get a little something together first." She turned toward the kitchen. Celie went on upstairs.

On the foot of her iron bed lay two new quilts and a crocheted afghan. There was a wrinkled roll of paper on top. Celie opened it. Six sterling silver spoons that Christina had brought from the old country.

Queer, sudden tears filled Celie's eyes. She unfastened her dress quickly and slipped it over her head. Her red sweater and the plaid silk butterfly skirt would do today. She fastened the skirt on her way down. The accordion pleating whirled out from her waist as she went.

"Thank you for the things, Mamma."

"Well, you might's well have them. I meant to give 'em to you when you was married." Christina's face showed no slightest change of expression, but her voice had in it a droop of sadness. She had hoped for other things for Celie, that Celie, maybe, would marry someone who could give her a real house, not just one rented from the mill, things she had never put into words, that

Celie would live on a street with a white cement walk and trees, in a place big enough to have a postman deliver the letters she would write her. Christina brought out the potatoes to pare. She was tired out today. The washing must have been bigger than usual.

Ole was easy about it, as Joe had said. He overtook Celie on her way up from the store at noon.

"So you're married, Celie! Well, Joe'll be a good provider."

That was all he thought of, Celie told herself.

A pity not to have a big wedding, wine and cakes in the house and drinking healths. Young folks were queer the way they did things, Ole thought to himself.

Selma called out as they passed, "Smarty, you, Celie! No wonder you didn't come down to get the last three installments of *The Love Trap*."

Celie laughed. She had laughed all day at everyone who had chaffed her on the news, a high thin laugh. They turned in at their walk. Mr. Farley's car was standing outside. He would be eating there as usual. She didn't want him there any more, with his city ways, making Joe seem country; being nice to her and kissing her and then going home to tell his aunt she'd make a good maid . . . that kind he was. She came in a little defiantly. Arthur Farley sat in the big plush chair Christina had bought with soap coupons. He looked up from his paper and whistled the wedding march.

"So you pulled a fast one, Celie!"

83

Celie could think of nothing to say. "I don't know," she answered and went on out to the kitchen.

"Miss Munsen asked me would I rather have a kitchen or a hit and miss shower."

"You better say kitchen," said Christina, pounding the potatoes to fluff with a wooden masher Ole had whittled for her. "Ole says Joe can have some of that last beer he made when they shivaree you tonight."

Celie had forgotten that. "D'ye think they will?"

"Why not? Just cause you got married on the quiet isn't any reason."

"Getting married in a mill town is the worst," said Celie sulkily. Anyway, Joe'd be there. He seemed a tower of strength. He'd think it was all fun. She hated it. She didn't know quite why.

"You forgot the vinegar, Celie. Ole'll want it on his sauerkraut. It's never tart enough for him."

Anyway, she hoped Arthur Farley wouldn't be around.

Through supper, that night, Ole Henderson was jovial. Sam and Hans chaffed Joe. Arthur Farley looked on with an amused smile. Celie's cheeks were pink beyond the rouge. Christina Henderson got out fruit cake, the white one she made last Christmas and the black one from Thanksgiving. There was raisin wine on the table. Ole was having his celebration, after all.

"May all your troubles . . . little ones," said Hans Mottberg when Ole urged him to toast the bride and groom. Joe smiled at it all. It was fair enough.

After supper, he dried dishes while Celie washed. "I spoke to DesMains about a house of our own today, Cele. He said the only one there was empty was up by the fox farm, that bungalow the Berwyns had. I thought maybe after we were through we'd go up and have a look at it."

"You're to stay here tonight, Joe, Mamma said. We'll need furniture and all if we get a house." She said it dubiously. It was the first time they had broached the subject of finances. "I have fifteen dollars saved up," she added timidly.

"I have twenty-nine," said Joe shamefacedly.

"We oughta look in the catalogue tonight," said Celie. "Selma Lichtenberg and Norm, they got their things there."

"I could make a kitchen table as good as that," suggested Joe, looking at the one of the Hendersons' thoughtfully. "I'll see Wilhelm at the yard about lumber tomorrow."

"Let's look at it out here, Joe." Celie hated to have Arthur Farley see them. Folks in the city went to stores to buy stuff.

They pulled the table over under the bulb and spread open the catalogue. Celie felt as though she were someone else; someone in a book, one of the girls, Selma or Rose Nelson, looking at furniture. But, suddenly, a kitchen range in green and ivory caught her eye. "Look at this, Joe! 'Beautiful Jewel wood range only $37.50.'"

Joe was silent a second.

"We wouldn't have much left," he said slowly. "Later we could get it. I heard the Tobins were moving out and they had an oil stove to sell for five dollars. It has a little oven you can bake in, too. Mrs. Tobin was tellin' me it does good work."

"Why, Joe, you been to see it already?"

Joe reddened, caught in the act. "A man's s'posed to provide a house for his wife," he muttered in a low voice.

Celie was touched. Joe took more responsibility than she did. She hadn't even thought about a house until today.

A loud banging broke in upon them, directly outside the kitchen window. Cat-calls and whistles, a cow-bell, honking of automobiles, shrill, childish voices and a steady beat of a wooden mallet on an empty boiler.

"Hi!" Ole Henderson shouted, jumping up from his paper. "Celie, Joe! you wondered if they'd shivaree you." He filled his pipe with tobacco standing in the kitchen doorway. A satisfied grin was on his lean wrinkled face. He had seen many mill-town weddings . . . that was the way, give 'em a shivaree and start 'em out right.

Christina was turning the heel of a stocking. She smiled too. She hadn't liked it, this running off secretly and getting married, almost as if . . . she forebore to shape the thought even to herself. Celie was a smart girl. Joe, he was a good fellow; there wasn't anything like that in it. She looked out through the kitchen past

Ole, at Celie's slim figure bent over the table. In her short plaid skirt, she looked like a child still. Christina took a good deal of secret satisfaction in Celie's prettiness. She had never minded ironing a little dress a day to keep her nice when she was a child, and now she ironed the lavender and peach and green georgette dance sets and spread them out on Celie's bed without a word. Celie's ways weren't hers. Girls were different nowadays. Back in her time women were scarcer in the mill-towns. They didn't have time to be foolish. The shivaree outside made the wedding seem more regular. She'd go see if there were enough doughnuts to pass out for the children. If she'd only known ahead of time!

"Lord, what a racket!" Arthur Farley laughed. "So this is a shivaree! Do they keep it up all night?"

"Oh, no, you let 'em do it awhile then you go out and buy 'em off with something to drink or eat. If you don't, they storm till you do come out," Ole explained. He climbed down through the trap door in the kitchen floor to the root cellar for his beer.

The din irritated Celie. She tried to seem oblivious to it. She felt it made her immeasurably less in Arthur Farley's eyes. It would make a good story when he got back down to the city.

"Here's a bedroom set, Joe, for $19.50. It says: 'Ornamental rose silk boudoir lamp comes free.' "

"I sh'd think you could manage for now with a bed and a box you covered over," put in Christina. She had come out to look at the doughnuts.

"I want to have things nice," answered Celie, "only, I s'pose really we ought to buy things for the sitting room first."

"You can take the stuff in your bedroom for a while, Celie, and then save for your other furniture."

"That'd be a real help, Mis' Henderson. Celie, then we could buy that over-stuffed davenport and console table you wanted."

Some of the children had combs and were scratching on the screens. The thin scraping sound penetrated even through the deep booming of the boiler. "I've got to go out and see this," Celie heard Farley say in the other room. "This is an idea for the next wedding I go to."

Celie hated him and his superior city ways.

"Oh, give 'em the beer and make 'em stop, Joe!"

Joe went out on the stoop and the noise subsided. In a minute, it began again.

"Where's your bride? Haven't you got her there? We want to see the bride!" yelled the crowd good-naturedly.

Joe came in for Celie. Celie grew stubborn. "I won't go a step. They can't make me."

"Oh, come on, Celie," Joe urged.

"I won't. They're a pack of silly fools." She became engrossed in the catalogue. She had heard shivarees before and helped make the noise, but this was different. She was as different from the Celie of a week ago as Flat Point from Clarion. Joe went back on the stoop.

"Celie says she's shy." At that the noise broke out

again, louder and more strident. Ole clapped his thigh.

"You better go, Celie girl; they've come to see ye and they're going to do it."

"Where is she? We'll carry her out!" Celie heard someone shout.

"Not so fast, not so fast," came Joe's voice. There was a scuffle on the board step. Ole went to the door. The crowd cheered loudly.

" 'At a way, Joe; fight for your woman!"

Anger flared up in Celie; anger at the day in Mead with Joe in the first place, and the feeling of wrong and the fear that had hurried her into marriage, this shivaree that seemed to tie her ever so securely to Flat Point, and above all, at Arthur Farley's watching it. She slapped the catalogue shut and flounced to the door in her tight red sweater and pleated skirt. She pushed by Ole.

"Well, here I am, you silly fools!" Her voice was shrill with anger. It broke on the fools. There was Selma Lichtenberg's husband, Norm, and Sabonich and Mary Kelly and a lot of children; why, they were just the people she saw every day in the store. She felt foolish. She wanted to run and hide in the house. She turned toward the door. The crowd was quieted for the moment, a little abashed. Christina handed out a pan of doughnuts.

"Here, Celie, you give 'em out."

Celie was glad of something to do.

"Here, all you kids, have a doughnut," Joe announced.

89

The children shrieked and rushed toward the stoop.

"Kids over seventy, Lym!" Joe called out to old Lym Nelson who edged in with the children.

"If she makes doughnuts you won't starve, boy," shouted Norm Lichtenberg.

"Bring your cups and have some beer." Ole handed bottles out to Joe. Joe popped the tops and poured.

"Woops! She's going over. Quick, try your nose in this." Ole went on handing out bottles. Celie gave out the last doughnut. She didn't mind them any more. She even laughed at Heine Peters who drank so fast he was coughing.

"Well, as good life as your ma's doughnuts and your pa's beer!" Lym Nelson quavered out.

"Glad to get you young things started right," called Norm. The rest yelled advice to them; a few of the children experimented with the big boilers left behind. The shivaree was over.

Celie and Joe went back in the house.

"Some tame compared to when we was young, eh, Christina? They used to stay half the night, and drunk, say." Ole laughed thinking of it.

There was a knock at the door and Lin Linsen, Joe's father, came in. He was as tall as Joe, but with a shock of thick, careless tow-hair. His light beard had a day's growth and gave a burly look to his thin face, which, shaven, was almost ascetic. He had a sheepish air about him. He had worn his one suitcoat with his khaki shirt and trousers and added a tie in honor of the occasion.

"I didn't come off the lake in time to shivaree ye, but I thought I'd come over now," he said, looking at Celie.

" 'Lo, Lin," Ole said. Christina smiled at him in her silent, old-country way with her husband's friends. Joe looked at him with no comment. He was the old man. They understood each other without words. Celie smiled uncertainly. She had always been shy of Lin Linsen as a child. He was such a silent, lonely sort of man, always going fishing or mending his nets down along the sand. Now she looked at him critically with his mill clothes and uncombed hair. He wasn't much like Joe.

"Let's have a glass around ourselves." Ole filled five glasses. "Here's to you!" Celie lifted her glass to her lips and noticed suddenly over the rim that she and Joe were standing across from her father and mother in the same position. She and Joe were married. Someday, they'd be like Ole and Christina, only they wouldn't be living here; they'd be gone to the city before that time. A tiny fear of the future clung in her mind, as small as a bead on the rim of her glass that sparkled and disappeared.

"Thanks for the beer, Mr. Henderson."

"Better start out right, Joe, no Mr. Henderson."

Joe looked embarrassed.

"Better go on calling me Ole, like you do at the yard, Joe."

Lin Linsen, warmed with the glass of beer in him, came over to Celie. "Joe got him a swell girl, I'll say that."

Celie looked up at him. She was startled to see how different he looked when you saw his eyes. They were bright blue, like Joe's. Her own fell a little shyly. She didn't want him to look like Joe.

"Going to kiss the bride, Dad?" Joe asked. "Then I got a right to kiss Christina."

Celie lifted her face and kissed Lin Linsen. She had always thought of him as an old man. Now, as she touched his firm lips, she felt with a little shock that he was not so old. She looked in his eyes again and saw how like he was to Joe, only he always wore mill clothes.

"I sure hope Joe makes you happy, Celie. Don't let him get crazy about the lake like me." He smiled.

"Kiss your old dad, Celie." Ole put his arm around her.

Some Old World instinct for ceremony stirred in them, gave their awkward embraces a kind of grace and meaning. Christina's eyes were wet.

"Here, I won't know whether she's my bride or not." Joe put his arm around her. Celie's face was very pink. She felt really married. She was glad no one had said anything about her getting mad at the shivaree. She wasn't any longer.

Part II

THE scarlet leaves of the hardwoods flung a brief defiance at the somber green of the firs. A young maple outside the last low company house flared bright red like a signal flag. It stood alone, as gangly on its slender trunk as a new faun. Some bustling wind had blown its seed from the tall maples beyond the town.

Celie Henderson was nailing up her kitchen sash curtains. She looked out of the newly washed pane of glass at the tree. Its leaves were red; as red as her old red silk. The houses down the street had no trees, only their neighbors' windows to look at out the side windows. It was nice to be the last house in town even if there was no running water and the fox farm so near.

The curtains were green dotted to match the handles on her new saucepans and the egg beater and mixing spoon that came in the shower. Christina offered her an iron skillet of hers, but she liked the look of a shiny new one best. It didn't cost so much, only ten cents at the Five and Dime and big enough for her and Joe. Celie had hurried up the street from the store just as the whistle blew. This would be their first night in their own house. The company had given the paint and she and Joe had done the work. Now it was ready and very clean.

"It'll take some paint to get a place ready for a Swede after those French Canadians," Christina had said.

Celie was proud of the house. Joe's table in the kitchen covered with green oilcloth and the two chairs and an oil stove were all the movable furniture of the kitchen. There were two shelves and hooks for the dishes. Joe was going to make a cupboard himself. The front room had the davenport and another chair. Celie had given up the console table in favor of a chair and small table. They bought a lamp in Clarion, a wonderful affair with a gilt base and a crusted shade with a parrot on it. It gave a rose light and was connected by a long cord to the bulb that hung from the center of the ceiling. Arthur Farley had given them a big mirror with a scroll sunk in the glass. It was handsome. Celie wanted drapes, but for now the white sash curtains would do; drapes would hardly pay; they would probably have large windows when they moved to town.

Off the parlor was the bedroom. It looked so like hers always had, it didn't seem new at all.

Christina was even more proud of the house than Celie. "You've got some beautiful things, Cele," she said after her tour of inspection. Celie had ideas about other things.

"Of course, it needs another chair," she said deprecatingly when she took Selma or Rose or Mis' Simpson through, or "I don't know how we'll do without a bathroom," until Christina said,

"Why, Celie, if you could see how we started!"

"Yes," said Celie, "but we're different."

It was growing dark early now, at the end of September. By the time Celie had finished her curtains, the brave flare of red outside the window was lost in the dusk. The woods beyond the small cemetery had bunched in a dark huddle. It was time to put the potatoes on. The paper label on the new green and ivory kettle smelled a little when she put the pan on to heat. She made the coffee. It was queer moving about the kitchen to get supper. She kept going places for things where they were in her mother's kitchen. Even the floor felt strange under her feet; the raised sill into the front room, the step down to the woodshed. The feeling of its being hers was new and stirring. It was no wonder folks got married and went to housekeeping all the time. She even forgot the news she had to tell Joe for sure. Oh, well, he'd take it all right.

She put down the tumblers quickly and ran to the door when the scream of the limey whistle came out of the woods. The engine where Joe rode looked tiny in front of the high-piled logs. Joe would be looking. She couldn't see him in the dusk, but maybe he could see her. She waved her apron. There was no stoop on the front of their house, yet, just three steps down. She stood on the top step in the doorway with the rose lights of the parlor behind her. The train was long tonight. She watched till the last car went past. She was strangely thrilled by the slow-moving procession of logs, like a toy train against the dark space of the lake. Being up here in a new house at the top of the town gave her a lonesome feeling and yet it was kind of exciting, too.

The short stack on the engine belched out a smell of smoke that mingled with the flavor of suppers cooking, the heavy, rotting smell of the fall woods, the crisp breath of the night itself. Celie had never spent much time standing still alone. Suddenly the lonesomeness bore down on her. The woods looked cold and dark. She turned back in and hurriedly put her pork chops on to fry. She'd made the coffee too soon, but Joe liked it strong.

Joe strode up the length of the long hill from the lake, tirelessly. The day in the woods never tired him much. He was strong and easy-going. He never got angry at the boys in the woods, or impatient when the train broke down. He would only laugh and say, "What d'ye know?" to the world in general. His big hands rolled a cigarette deftly as he came up the street.

He whistled tonight. Nice to come back to their own house. Nice to see Celie waving from there. He hadn't expected her to marry him for a long while yet—maybe not at all. But she had; it was right enough with him. Well, times were good; he ought to get a job in town easy. He'd get a day off pretty soon and go in to Clarion.

He went around to the shed door. He made his step a little heavier than usual as though he had always come home up here. He pushed the door open.

" 'Lo, Celie."

She was standing in front of the stove. He put his arm around her and kissed her.

"Looks pretty neat around here, don't it, Cele?"

"It's real nice. Are you hungry?"

Joe's face was cold against hers. He smelled of the woods. He was hearty and strong. It made her feel good to have him here.

"I set the pail outside, Joe; if you want to get some water, I'll dish up."

"Putting me to work, aren't you?"

He took the pail and went down to the corner. The house pumps didn't give drinking water, but there were pumps at the intersection of the streets. Carl Ulrich was filling his pail when Joe came up.

"Y'look like a married man, Joe," Carl chuckled.

Joe laughed and made a pass at his pail with his foot. Old Carl had come when the town was built, started lumbering up in Maine and drifted out here. He lived alone in a house of his own.

"I notice you have to get water if you aren't married, though, Carl!" said Joe. He went back up the street with his pail, whistling. He wondered if Celie would hear it. It was a good night. The stars were out already and bright; wouldn't be too cold to go canoeing. Maybe Celie'd like to paddle along the lake awhile.

"Smells good, Celie, 'n' there's your water."

Celie was flushed from getting supper. She had spread lace paper doilies on the green oil-cloth table.

"Looks like a party," said Joe appreciatively.

They sat down to their first meal.

"I guess the oilstove and that little air-tight stove won't be enough to keep the house warm. We better start saving for a wood range, right off," said Joe, looking around their domain.

"I'd like one better, anyway. I know I could bake better on it."

"This pie's all right for me and then some!"

After the pie, they still sat at the table. The kitchen was warmer than the front room and less formal.

"D'ye want some more coffee, Joe?"

"You have some, too, and I will."

Celie poured two cups.

"Joe, I guess it was just as well we got married."

"You bet it was, Celie. I never felt so good about anything in my life as tonight. And we look pretty snug to me."

"I mean for the other reason, Joe. I'm going to. I s'pose it'll be about next spring."

Joe looked at Celie. She was looking in her coffee cup. It came to him, suddenly, that he hardly knew her. She looked less than seventeen, sitting there across the table. Joe was twenty. He wanted to protect her from something, from having a baby.

"Wouldn't that get you!" was all he could think of to say. He felt for his pipe.

"I haven't told Mamma or anybody. I'd rather not till later."

"Come on with your dishwater. I'm going to wipe."

Joe wanted to do something to help.

Celie waited. She wanted to talk it all over. There was nobody but Joe to talk to.

"I wish you could have your new job and we could be moved by then," Celie said wistfully.

"Sure we can," declared Joe cheerfully.

2

A LATE snow fell steadily in Flat Point. Celie Linsen could see it outside her bedroom window. It showed white against the woodshed. She lay still and watched it. Her mind was a bare clean space, swept free of thoughts. The flakes made a little whirlpool at the corner of the roof. They went faster and faster until one stuck to another and careened off in space beyond the window. The snow fell steadily; there must be six inches by now. It had started just after the baby was born. They had turned off the light in the room.

"There, now you can sleep," they said.

The log train came slowly through the snowy dusk. The great logs were powdered and the visor on Joe's cap was covered white as he leaned out the windows of the limey engine and worried about Celie. The baby was born at four that morning. He'd stayed home all the day before, like all the men in the Point did when their wives had a baby, all those that cared, that is. He'd gotten dressed as though for Sunday, his white shirt and blue tie. It tired him out to be around the house all day. He'd swept the house out and gone to tell the doctor and Christina and Mrs. Maloney, and kept up the fire in the range. He'd gone for water and down to the store because they needed bread. Then there'd been all night. The snow had helped a little. Snow in April! Christina said to go over and stay with Ole, but he hadn't wanted to. Instead he piled wood in the shed and cleaned his gun and looked at the paper.

Celie'd had her baby here, after all, when she'd wanted to be away by then. But it was better to stay here till after that. There wasn't any job that would pay much more than three-fifty a day to start and living in the Point was so much cheaper than anywheres else. But they'd go now, soon as the baby was old enough.

Then Mrs. Maloney came and told him he had a daughter. Mrs. Maloney was a good nurse. Roy Larsen had her for his wife, but she was too hearty for his liking. She grinned all over at him and looked as though she had one on him when she told him.

He'd gone in to see Celie a minute.

"I'm going to work. I'll be back soon," was all he could think of to say. She hadn't seemed to care what he did. Maybe she thought he should have stayed home another day. But he couldn't have stood the house and the women. He was ashamed of how glad he was to get to the woods. While they stopped for lunch he went off by himself and got some arbutus. He had it hid in his lunch pail now. He felt better; women had babies all the time, it was nothing so awful.

Mrs. Maloney had gone. Christina had set out Joe's

supper and then gone too. The house was warm and still when Joe opened the door softly.

"Celie," he called.

"Yes." Celie's voice sounded flat.

3

CELIE sat still after Joe had gone. In a few minutes, Rose Marie would cry and she would have to take her up. Her coffee cooled in the cup. The oatmeal turned solid in the dish. Celie had been busy ever since five o'clock when she measured out the coffee and stirred the cereal into the boiling water. The bright electric bulb glared at the unreal lightness of the spring morning. She had forgotten to turn out the light; electricity didn't cost anything in the Point. The house was so still with Rose Marie sleeping and Joe gone it was eerie and lonesome. Celie never ate till Joe had gone. She put up his lunch pail while he ate and slicing summer sausage with the large onion to put between the bread for his sandwiches left her unhungry.

Her hair was still down her back in a light braid. It was rumpled and soft around her face. She looked less than eighteen in the faded kimono over her bright cotton pajamas. The heels of her slippers were caught on the rung of her chair, her elbows rested on the table. Celie Henderson Linsen was looking past the young maple and the squat roof of the fox farm, past the woods outside her window at her own life.

She had thought she hated it before now, before she married Joe, but she knew now that really she had liked it. There had always been something ahead; some excitement at the store, a new catalogue, a date with Joe or someone, or a trip to Clarion or the Soo. Now there was nothing, not even the excitement of the store each morning. She missed the store, having to be dressed up and smart every day, seeing new people all the time, not knowing just what would happen next. Her gaze came back to the small kitchen. The smoke of the piece of bacon she had burned hung heavily against the walls. The chairs already needed a new coat of paint. The green and ivory saucepan was badly nicked. She should have taken the iron skillet Christina offered her. The kitchen had lost its shiny new look. The paint, like the saucepan, like Celie herself perhaps, was too cheap a grade to last. Rose Marie cried. Celie drank her cold coffee and went into the bedroom.

It slowed her up so in the morning to have to nurse the baby. It made her so late with her dishes. It was a good thing Joe didn't come home for lunch. Joe said if Celie didn't eat more for lunch he'd start coming. Celie had lost weight since the baby was born.

Celie came back to the seat by the kitchen window. Rose Marie kept up a plaintive cry until she felt herself cuddled against Celie's breast. Celie nursed her impersonally, with her eye on the alarm clock on the top of the stove. Rose Marie was a sturdy one that would nurse an hour if she had the chance. Celie had letters from the state on how to take care of her. The mill doctor gave them to her. The baby was doing well, almost three months she was, and big and pink-cheeked. It was queer Celie couldn't realize the baby belonged to her yet; Joe did. He liked Sundays when he could see her bathed. He wanted her to get big enough for him to play with.

The baby nursed noisily. Celie watched the flash of mahogany red against the wire cage at the fox farm. A lumberjack came by the window. That was the way at the end of town, you never even saw anybody. It had been all right at first, with Joe talking about getting a job in town. He hadn't said so much about it lately, not since that day he'd gone into Clarion just after the baby was born. He'd gotten all dressed up and left right after breakfast. She'd been so excited and made a butterscotch pie for supper to celebrate. Joe didn't get back till after dark; then he'd come in quietly.

"Clarion isn't much of a place, Celie, you'd be surprised. I don't think you'd want to live there, anyway. Milwaukee, maybe; that'd be a lot better."

Celie watched him from the stove where she was frying potatoes. She knew then, without any more words, that Joe had not found a job. She asked no more questions. She was, of a sudden, like Christina, burying things down inside of her to think over later. But she tacked down the linoleum that had come loose under the sink. She was going to let it go, thinking they'd be moving and all, but now that they were staying awhile, she fixed it. Nights, Joe tinkered with his radio and explained it to Celie. Celie tried to listen, but her mind kept wandering to a baby carriage she'd seen in the new catalogue for $14.50 and a coat for herself. She wondered what it would be like living in Milwaukee.

Rose Marie drooped sideways, her lips still parted just as they had left off nursing. Celie stood up to take her back to bed, but instead, she went out to the open shed door. It faced the lake and the left corner of the fox farm. The day was cool still at six o'clock. Celie's bare ankles were cold and her neck. She held Rose Marie more tightly to keep her warm.

The lake from up here at the end of town looked covered over with a white veil. The sky towards Canada was pink; as it arched up, it turned to a light blue that made it seem higher. Celie looked up a minute, and then back to the lake and to the wooden buildings that stood between the mill and the last house. She could see the back side of the store from here, the door where she had swept out so many times. The man moving around must be old Quinn, the butch. He always gave her the best cuts now, and sometimes slipped in an extra chop. Old Quinn was a cute one, right . . . Out here, there was space. Celie had always lived as close to her next door neighbor as if she had lived in the city. It was a new feeling to be alone. It was almost a pleasure.

Rose Marie began to grow heavy in her arms. Celie

shifted her head up on her shoulder more. It bobbed over against her neck. A tiny sense of possession grew within her. Rose Marie was hers. The little house was behind her. For the first time since Rose Marie was born she felt free of the hard bitterness in her mind. It had started the day Mr. Farley brought his bride to live in the old house on the bluffs. Their being there with maids and a greenhouse and all seemed like a personal taunt. Celie had seen Mrs. Farley in the store once in a fur coat and hat that had a different look from any Celie had. She was smart-looking as she came in with Arthur.

". . . if we have that many for the week-end, darling, we'll need another case of ginger ale," she was saying. There was a hint of laughter always in her words that Celie hated, as though she were laughing at the place and the people. Arthur introduced Celie to his wife. Celie said, "Pleased to meet you." Mrs. Farley had only said "hello" with that laughter in her voice. "Art tells me maybe I could get you to help out with the waiting on table one of these days when I'm having company." Celie didn't even smile.

"I'm going to be pretty busy. I'm having a baby in the spring." Celie took her groceries and went on out before they could answer. Out on the store steps, her cheeks burned. She didn't know why she had said it. Anyone could see that she was expecting even if the whole town didn't talk about it. Some fierce instinct of self-protection had driven her to prove to herself that she didn't mind, she who a year ago would have hung over the counter taking in every detail of Mrs. Farley's city clothes. Ever since, she had pretended not to be much interested when Selma Lichtenberg or Hattie Reay told her some gossip about the gay life that flourished at Farley's. How they had finger bowls and a different size glass for every kind of drink, and how Mrs. Farley wore velvet pajamas in the evening. Secretly, she was pleased when Joe muttered over his pipe that "Farley, the son of a gun, was riding for a fall sure. Why, he wants logs brought in faster'n they can saw 'em up. He oughta stay in the city where he can play his piano." The bright blue Ford streaking past was always a taunt to her, saddled here in the Point like all the rest of the women, with a man in the Mill and a family. She wanted to prove some way that she was different.

Now, on this May morning, Celie kissed the top of Rose Marie's head. She tucked the blanket around her and turned back into the kitchen. She would get a good dinner for Joe tonight. His lunch pail wasn't much.

That afternoon, when Celie was fixing the pot roast for supper, Christina came by. She always sat down in the parlor and eyed each item with keenest appreciation.

"Celie, Mis' Bernsen asked me to bring you over to her house for coffee, so I stopped by."

Celie had never been to one of the older women's *kaffee-kalaser*. Being married and having a child made her eligible in their eyes, Celie realized.

"All right, soon's I dress Rose Marie."

Mrs. Henderson took out her knitting. Even in her daughter's house she felt too great a reticence to go into the bedroom without invitation. Besides, she had been a little put out with Celie for this baby so soon. Some of the neighbors had talked. 'Course there was nothing in it, but just for the sake of Mrs. Hacula's tongue, she wished Celie could have waited a month or two longer.

"You wanta hold your broom sideways when you sweep these wide cracks, Celie," she called in.

"I know; they hold the dust like everything."

Celie was dressing Rose Marie in her best dress with the ruffled bonnet and knit jacket she'd got in the baby shower. When she had her ready, she put her in Christina's arms. Christina held a child safely but awkwardly; her long, stiffly jointed arms were not intended to bend in so short a curve.

"She's getting pretty, Celie. I b'lieve she'll have your hair 'n' eyes."

Celie, with the baby off her mind, got herself into the green dress. It had had a rest for so many months it seemed as nice as new again. She shaped her lips carefully and powdered her nose. It was good to dress up in the afternoon, it pepped you up. Celie had been housebound now for nearly a month except for hurried trips to the store. Feeding Rose Marie every three hours split the day into four parts too small to do much with. One Sunday afternoon toward the end of April, Joe had stayed home to mind the baby while Celie drove the car out the road a ways.

"Go on, Cele, it'll do you good," Joe said, feeling vaguely that being home so much had something to do with Celie's thinness.

She had gone, driving the rickety old Ford out around the curve of the lake. The air was damply cold by four o'clock. The snow had taken on a greenish tinge beneath the shadows of the trees and jagged cakes of ice still edged the shore. A snow-shoe rabbit hopped across the road, a striking white against the coming brown-green world of spring. The woods and lake were like a naked child that waited, shivering for the warmth of summer sun. The maple branches showed green buds. The alders bristled red against the pale spring greens. But winter was still in the earth, deep, deep down in the very roots. The old Ford slid along the icy ridges.

At first, it was good to be away from the little house and Rose Marie, to feel the cold air and the motion of the car, but the woods chilled Celie. The sky was fading into gray. She turned around at the first place where the road widened and drove back. Joe was sitting in the kitchen with his boots on the range. He was holding the baby while he read the Sunday paper. His pipe dangled a few inches above the baby's head. But the room was warm and smelled of Joe's pipe and the Sunday roast.

"Oh, Joe, you mustn't hold her. The letters say to put her down after each feeding, an' you'll burn her hair with your pipe." But she felt affection for him, for the circle of warmth and light they made against the bleak loneliness of the woods and lake.

Celie and Christina went down the street together. At the corner, they met Mrs. Flauberg and Mrs. Wilhelm. The women peeked at Rose Marie.

"Isn't she a sweet one! My! an' big, too. Mis' Henderson was tellin' me she weighed a good seven pounds."

"Gott!" said Mrs. Wilhelm enviously. "I remember my first one and how proud I was."

Celie had not felt proud. She was silent now.

As they passed Mrs. Sabonich and Mrs. Ole coming up from the store they tried not to seem too superior. The Finnish women lived on a lower social scale and seldom got through their work in time for social gatherings in the afternoon.

At Mrs. Bernsen's, there were more to admire Rose Marie.

"Just put her on my bed, Celie, right in the center. Enjoy your luck while you got it. My young 'un's on his feet now, an' say! I wish he was back where I could leave him on a bed and know where he was."

Celie looked around her curiously at these women she had known all her life. She had waited on them in the store, but she had never really looked at them before. She had never thought of herself . . . Celie Henderson, Celie Henderson Linsen, of course, as one of them. They were all of them young, her mother was the oldest there and she was only forty something. None of them used lipstick any more, except Celie, or bothered about their hands. Celie glanced at Norma Halberg's red fingers pulling the yarn through the rug she was hooking; at Mrs. Wilhelm's that were short and stubby and scarred with the paring-knife. Their clothes, too, were scrupulously neat but the way they wore them! Even Nora, who was only a few years older than Celie, looked like a mill-towner, Celie told herself.

"They say she's been on the stage, an' he met her in the dance hall where he played the piano," Mrs. Bernsen declared. "She came in here the other day to ask me to make cakes for a party they were having. She wanted three chocolate angel foods that afternoon and you'd think she was stopping at a bakery."

"Did you tell her you'd do it?" asked Mrs. Wilhelm breathlessly.

"I said, 'Mis' Farley, one's all I'd dare bake at a time in my oven and two's the most I can make 'tween now and six o'clock,' " Mrs. Bernsen answered proudly.

"An' she said, 'well, that's all right. Mr. Farley and I aren't dining until quarter to eight it's so far from town.' Well, I said, I have to feed my own man at six."

The women nodded approval over this recital. Celie wondered suddenly if young Mrs. Farley wasn't lonesome out there in the big house on the bluff. Not that she would ever do anything about it, she wouldn't, but she just wondered.

Mrs. Bernsen spread a red and white cloth, beautifully laundered, over the round dining room table and set out cups. No one offered to help. Mrs. Bernsen might think her snooping. She poured the strong black coffee and brought a plate of cake.

"With all of them eggs to use up, I made two nice daffy-down-dilly cakes," she explained, passing the light golden slices. Celie found herself forgetting to listen, so absorbed was she in watching. She wondered passionately if these women had ever wanted to move away from mill-towns the way she did, if they had hated the bareness and ugliness and cheapness of it. Only her father and Olaf Bernsen made more than Joe did . . . three-fifty a day.

"I got that table cloth in Stockholm the year before I came over here . . ." Mrs. Bernsen was saying.

"Did you live in Stockholm, Mis' Bernsen?" Celie asked wonderingly.

"Yeah, I live there. It's a nice city. We go back some day to show the kids, but not to stay."

"Do you like it better here?" Celie asked incredulously.

"Oh, yeah, we're young. We wanted to go to a new country where there's some chance."

Chance! Celie thought to herself.

"For the children 'n' all. An' Chris, he work in the match factory there; never feel well, no color. Now, say, he could eat a whole plate of cake if he got the chance."

She laughed and the other women laughed too, till the small boxlike room rang with hearty housewives' laughter, the over and above of strenuous living,—something bright and cheery as a red linen table cloth.

"It isn't the same when you go back," said Mrs. Wilhelm. "I take the baby back to see my mother just last winter, to Germany, you know? Say, they've had awful times there since the war. Oh!" Mrs. Wilhelm's round face seemed rounder when her mouth shaped a round *O* of tribulation.

They're foreigners, Celie told herself. They think it's good living here 'cause of what they had in the old country. They don't want anything different.

"That tastes the best of anything I've ate for two months," said Nellie Hann, licking the crumbs from her finger tips. "You know how it is."

"I tell Nellie that's just like her mother. I couldn't keep a thing down for the first three months of one of my five," Mrs. Halberg interpolated, "but then it was over with."

Celie looked at Nellie Hann who was pregnant for the fourth time. She was still in her twenties. The group turned to the subject of permanent interest to all of them, that was sure to come up at every gathering over coffee cups: babies and the getting of babies.

Nellie would have looked rather more smart than the rest of them, Celie decided, if she hadn't been so colorless and tired. Her sweater and skirt were a green that set off her dull red hair. She was no foreigner; she'd been born right in the Point.

"Where did you leave Johnny, Nellie?"

"Selma wanted to keep him for me and the other kids are playin' outside. You know, I don't believe from somethin' she said the other day, that Selma kin have any." Nellie's voice sank to a dramatic whisper. "Isn't that awful an' her an' Norm are crazy about children, too."

"Ach! that's too bad, ah!" Sincere pity at the idea of barrenness was in the women's faces. For all that the babies came too fast, and were always underfoot, they were part of their lives. Celie thought swiftly of Rose Marie in her bonnet and sacque. It would be awful not to be able to have any. Mrs. Wilhelm roused out of her pity.

"She mustn't give up yet. I know a woman that only had one every five years, but say, when she got through!"

The hearty laughter filled the house again, to be cut in two by the shriek of the mill whistle rising imperative and mournful over the lake and the little village.

"Oh, my goodness! an' my potatoes ain't pared." Nellie Hann sprang up from her chair. Celie rushed in to pick up Rose Marie. She must get home and nurse her before Joe got there or his dinner'd be late.

"Come over soon, Celie," Christina said. "We miss you so your father says you'd better come back and take your meals at our house." She laughed as she went out. It was a good joke. Part of being married was having your own house and cook stove and table. Celie thought she had never seen her mother so jolly. This

115

was the woman-world her mother lived in, a society you weren't a part of until the mystery of having a husband and a baby were yours. Celie went up the street with Rose Marie in her arms feeling that there was something in the life in the Point to take hold of, something warm and solid like Rose Marie in her arms. When girls got together for birthday parties or showers there was always talk of clothes and movies and going into Clarion, restless talk of things to buy and places to go. This was settled talk that made you feel part of the town.

As Celie reached the end of the walk, the limey whistle came shuddering out of the woods. Rose Marie jumped in Celie's arms. Celie stopped to wave.

"That's Daddy, Rose Marie, that's Joe."

That night after the dishes were done, Joe stood about uneasily. He went out to the woodshed door and looked down over the housetops to the lake. Celie came out to take in the diapers blowing on the line.

"Say, Celie, what d'ye say we drop the baby over at Ole's and take the canoe down. It's about time for it."

" 'Member last year, Joe?"

"Do I? You went to a dance instead."

"An' you didn't take the canoe out."

"Yeah, waited like a softie."

"Look what you got though!" She looked at him archly over the pile of clean diapers. He swung her to him with a long strong arm and kissed her.

"Oh, Joe, I feel so good tonight."

"It's like not being married again, isn't it, Cele, only nicer?" They clung together.

"And I'm not an old married woman, Joe . . ."

"You? Say, Cele, you're as young as . . ." his eye fell on the new moon that hung over the corner of the fox farm fence, "as that moon up there, girl, that's what."

Celie laughed and kissed him again. "Let's go, Joe. I'll wrap up Rose Marie. Gee, it's wild goin' as late as this, Joe."

"Who wants to be tame?" Joe asked of the backs of the houses in the Point.

Celie rushed in to get into a skirt and old shirt. On a sudden impulse she looked at her hair, braided round her head. It looked too foreign, too matronly. She tumbled it down, seized the shears and started cutting just at the shoulder. It was hard cutting through the thick rope of hair. Her impulse gave out.

"Joe," she called in a small frightened voice. "Joe."

Joe came into the bedroom.

"Celie, you fool." He eyed her sternly. "You . . ."

Celie burst into tears. "Why, Celie, what's the matter; you crazy, sweet little fool. What on earth?"

"I wan . . . wanted to stay young, Joe. I get so scared sometimes that I'll be all settled down like Christina an' the others, an' my hair looked so kinda old-fashioned."

"Celie, you dumbbell, it looked swell."

"Doesn't it look swell this way?" Celie raised her

shorn head from his shoulder. The fair hair hung softly about her face. "See, Joe, I'll pin it back this way, and curl up the ends, see?"

"Mmm, it's all right, kinda like that Garbo woman. Say, if you're coming, bobbed cat!"

As they sat in the canoe, sliding swiftly through the dark cold water, Celie reached up and felt the soft brush of hair in her neck.

"It feels funny, Joe."

"Yeah, but good. She only needs another coat of paint to be as good as ever."

"I meant my hair," said Celie, apologetically.

4

CELIE always remembered afterwards the still pallor of heat that hung over that day in August. At five o'clock the edge of the sill was hot when she closed the windows and the sun surged boldly across her parlor rug threatening to fade its bright rose pattern. These days that lasted far into the night, the heat never seemed to leave before a new day had begun. The box-like house at the top of the town was suffocating in its four dimensions. Celie took Rose Marie to the shore along the lake, afternoons. Sometimes Selma or Helmi or Christina went with her. Sometimes she slipped down alone. Celie didn't mind being alone the way she used to. She was so busy most of the time between feedings; it was nice just to sit and look out over the lake or play with the sand. Christina said she must learn to knit, but Celie thought Christina could keep Rose Marie in sweaters. She thought perhaps her hands grew whiter moving through the white sand.

Today, as usual, she laid Rose Marie on a blanket in her diaper and sun-bonnet, like the doctor told her, and watched her breathe in sun with her sleeping. It was funny how beastly the sun felt in the little house, how desperately hot and dragged out it made you and how good it felt down here along the lake, with the old white pines to scare up a breeze, and the moving blue-green coolness of the water to look at.

Celie wore her bathing suit, a brief red affair, and stretched out flat on the sand beside Rose Marie. When it was time to feed her, she climbed up the bluff a ways and sat on the piney ground against a tree. Nobody ever seemed to come down there; the children of the point played around the old dock. Rose Marie's eyes moved around as she nursed, sometimes they watched the pattern of sun that filtered down through the pine boughs or the white foam of the lake, Celie was sure. That day in August, after she finished nursing, Celie tickled her with a pine needle and of a sudden Rose Marie laughed, a bubbling sort of gurgle that ended in a tiny ecstatic shriek. It was her first laugh. Celie could scarcely believe it. A new, proud sense of possession stirred in her. She wondered what Joe would say! She held Rose Marie up over her shoulder to settle her meal and hugged her a little. She wanted to make her laugh again, but she took her back to her blanket.

The lake lapping against the rocks and on the sand made gurgling sounds of laughter, too; miniature laughter like Rose Marie's. The day was all bright colors and sharp edges. The white clouds were blown out full and floated in the shining blue of the sky like soap suds. The lake was a deeper blue. It sparkled joyously in the depth of each ripple, rolling up until it broke in a final ecstasy of joy against the shore. Some of the tiny drops of spray reached way to Rose Marie's blanket. Celie moved her back to the dry sand and cocked a newspaper over her head to keep off the sun. Then she ran down into the water. It was too blue and shining to resist. Sometimes she waited until Joe came back and they went in together, but today she would go in twice.

Celie caught her breath. Lake Superior is ever mindful of the far north beyond her other shore and of the cold depths that lie beneath the reach of men and boats. All summer the sun drops down in that liquid blue from the burning arch of sky above, but it is never enough. No single summer's sun can fill such depth of hungry cold. Celie jumped high to keep warm and then plunged into the water all over. She ran back out dripping to look at Rose Marie. She shook her short hair in the air and wiped the water out of her eyes with her hands. The joy of the day, fiercely hot, and shining, entered into her. She was part of the lake and sand and sun; not one whit of Celie Henderson Linsen remained. The tiny breeze that rustled the top of the twisted pine tree danced with her. Rose Marie was a bubble of mist, catching the sun in the short hair that curled damply on her head and in the tiny lashes against her cheeks. Celie ran back into the water again.

None of the children of the Point learned to swim well, but few had any least fear of the water. They jumped and plunged near the shore like water spaniels, then rushed out to dry in the sun before they tried it again. But Joe could swim and sometimes when they went in in the evening he would leave Celie on the dock and swim off toward the north with long powerful strokes a hundred rods before he came back to her.

Celie was shaking her hair dry a second time when Norm Lichtenberg came running towards her.

She shook the hair back out of her eyes. "Whatever is the matter, Norm?"

"Celie, Ole was hurt pretty bad at the pond . . . they took him over to the hospital. I went up to your house and when you weren't there, Selma said you maybe were down here." He was winded from his run up from the mill and back to the lake.

Celie couldn't take his words in for a minute, her mind had stretched so wide to compass the world of space and light and movement. Then her thoughts came together and focused. The news sobered her, squeezing out the sensuous joy of the day and leaving her limp and terrified.

"Norm, is he going to die?"

"I don't know, Celie. Come on, I'll take the baby up to Selma and you can go right over to the hospital."

"Norm, see if you can get Joe, will you?"

Celie slipped on her raincoat and followed Norm up the road. The whole way was unreal; between the city blocks of piled lumber, past the station and the mill, past the pond where Ole had been hurt. She went by the store in a kind of numb fear. There was a little group gathered outside the porch of the hospital. They stepped back as Celie came by. Norm went on with the baby. Celie heard another part of herself say,

"Tell Selma I'll be there to feed her at six." Rose Marie had almost vanished from her life.

She was blinded for a minute as she came in from the outdoors. Only the smell of medicines and carefully lowered voices came to her consciousness, then a sound that rent her frame more than the pains of childbirth: hoarse, labored sounds . . . Ole groaning. The sounds brought her to life. She saw everything in the bare shiny white room at once.

"Celie." Christina sat motionless in the chair at the doctor's desk. It was by the door and Christina had sunk into the nearest one. Her face showed no emotion, only her eyes had a steady hopelessness in them. Her shoulders sagged, her hands rested on her aproned knees and at the groans the fingers tightened. Behind her hung the doctor's framed diploma which the hopeless droop of her shoulders put to naught.

"Mamma," answered Celie. She sat down in the chair next to her. "Maybe he'll only lose his leg like Arvid Lehtenen did, you 'member?"

Christina shook her head. When you couldn't see where a man was hurt except in his face—you could tell. She had not lived in a mill-town for twenty-five years for nothing. She knew Ole would not live. Already she had remembered everything in their lives together up to this morning, and even sitting here in the doctor's office was familiar to her. It was as she had always known it would be.

The nurse, shiny in her stiff white uniform, came in. She held the door open for them and Christina and Celie went through to the back room, the kitchen of one of the box houses turned into a room for surgical dressings.

Even the shock and the agony of pain could not take the heartiness that was Ole Henderson away. He was hardwood, sound to the core, that could only be felled by a gigantic onslaught. The doctor held a glass of whisky to his lips. His eyes, even at such a time, appraised the quality. Sweat stood out on his face. His fingers twitched, but he could not move them.

"Well, Ole," said Christina in a low voice that meant more than endearment.

"Yea, Tina," said Ole Henderson, thickly, using the name he had wooed her by in the old country.

Celie was different from these. She bent and put her lips on Ole's blue cold ones. The short hair she had not stopped to pin back, fell on his gray face and a few drops of the lake water mingled with the cold sweat. She burst into tears and the doctor pulled her gently away. She went out into the next room and buried her head on her knees.

They did not risk moving Ole from the emergency couch to a bed in the ward upstairs. He had been crushed under a giant log and was bleeding internally. They could only keep him warm and wait. Outside on the steps of the hospital, the little knot of people changed from time to time, but Stumpf and O'Mara and little Jock never left.

"The mill kin go to hell, for a' me," grunted the short Scotchman and spat.

"De Point not be's so good now," declared Zenti, whom Ole Henderson had always called Dago Red.

Stumpf, the walking boss, could only shake his head. He had seen many bad signs this year; the thousand foot of kiln-dried lumber that was spoiled, the coming shortage of good timber, the new jazz player of a boss, his losing at poker three times in a row, but none so black as Ole Henderson's going.

"Say, ain't it lucky the Doc, he ain't on a binge?" whispered Mrs. Hacula to Mrs. Vogel.

"That's the worst of a mill doctor; there's usually something wrong with him or why would he come off up here. But they say he had a wonderful city practice till he took to drink, that's one thing."

"I'd like to promise him a dozen bottles of my best

124

wine or even some of Tim's moon if he'd just be sober when my time comes next month." The women at the corner of the hospital porch giggled.

"If there's one thing'll make him sober it's the sight of Ole Henderson hurt," growled Nels Nelson, who had overheard them, and the women were silenced by his sternness.

The mill whistle shrilled its five-thirty release. The men swarmed up the three streets of the town. Even glum and silent men like Toiva, the Finn, who never talked before he had his supper coffee, talked about Ole Henderson's hurt. At six, the light of the log train cut its way through the darkness of the woods. The jammer whistle blared across the Point. Ole Henderson winced as it pierced even the blanket of unconsciousness that was slowly blotting out the agony in his back and down his legs.

Norm Lichtenberg met Joe as he stepped out of the engine box.

"And say, Joe, your baby cried something fierce and Selma didn't know what to do; she didn't want to call Celie from the hospital so she took the baby to Mis' Bierbauer's, you know, she's got a new baby, and she nursed her."

Joe's tranquil face was sobered as he went into the hospital. Celie had stopped crying and sat by the door into the surgery room, crumpling her handkerchief in a ball. She was still in her bathing suit and raincoat. Her feet in the red bathing sandals were twisted around the chair leg. Even her hair seemed to have dried in dejected uncombed strands that she had to keep pushing back from her face.

"Celie, you poor kid." Joe was suddenly the man of the family. He went in to see Ole with his arm still around Celie.

"I hear they got you down a bit, old man!" he greeted Ole in the tone of the healthy man to the injured, unconsciously patronizing.

But Ole was past sending a barbed retort. When his eyes opened wearily they rested on Christina who sat by him. Only once had she touched him, wiping the sweat from his head with her large rough hand. Joe and Celie sat down by Christina. The doctor stood watching, his sad, weak, brilliant face intent on the almost carved features of Ole Henderson, Swede.

At seven, he nodded to Christina. "I'm sorry, Mrs. Henderson." He had treated the high born of Chicago in his day and knew how to give comfort, but he knew better than to offer it here or to suggest rest. He put away a few things on the table while Christina got stiffly to her feet.

"Tank you, dey bring Ole to the house tonight, maybe." She spoke more brokenly than usual, with effort.

Celie and Joe walked home with her, through the little knot that expressed its sympathy as it could; Stumpf by pulling his felt hat further down on his head, little Jock with a loud spat.

Celie's grief seemed suddenly centered in the pain of her distended breasts. She put up her hands to them. They were oozing steadily.

"Why, Joe, Rose Marie . . . I never fed her . . ." Horror that she could forget her was on her face. But at the thought of her, warm and living, a little comfort crept into Celie's being. She put her hand on her mother's arm protectively.

"You come home with us, Mamma."

"No," said Christina, but she in turn felt warmed a little in her loneliness by the thought of Celie . . . only a little; Celie and Joe and Rose Marie were other generations.

It was two weeks before Celie remembered to tell Joe of Rose Marie's first laugh.

Part III

IN SEPTEMBER, Joe went on the night shift at the mill, learning to be a saw filer. Young Farley stopped by one day to leave word for him. Celie looked out the window to see the bright blue car in the road. She smoothed her hair into place and opened the door. The sight of young Farley still gave her a feeling of excitement.

"Come in," she smiled.

Young Farley came just to the doorway. He looked at the snug, bare little house. Fifteen months of living had subdued the newness of the furniture. The sun had faded the vivid green and purple lamp shade. Christina had braided a rug from Ole's old woolen trousers and shirts. It had the place of honor in front of the davenport. The mirror young Farley had given them hung over Joe's homemade radio. Celie had put some bright leaves in a pitcher on the table. She had just finished sweeping the room. She watched his glance, proudly. Young Farley's eyes came quickly back to Celie.

"Well, marriage agrees with you, Celie."

"You seem to like it all right yourself." She was the old Celie back of the counter at the company store.

He had grown heavier and more ruddy. He looked less like a piano-player at the Tricorne and more like the boss of an operation, a boss in the moving-pictures, perhaps. The mill had done more for him than it had received in return. He laughed.

"Say, Cele, why don't you help out waiting on table

for Charlotte. She likes your looks, and you know how I feel about you."

Celie stood very straight in her doorway.

"I'm too busy here, Mr. Farley."

Young Farley sensed he had made a mistake. He had no intention of offending her. He had just come all the way up from the office to see Celie.

They needed a dependable man on the night shift for filer. He had thought of Joe, himself. It pleased him when he thought of things. Once an idea occurred to him he backed it in the face of any opposition from Stumpf or Weil, the head office man, to the very teeth of his uncle and the Detroit office. Authority was growing on him.

Thinking of Joe made him think of Celie. He had taken a notion suddenly to go and see her. In a way that drove Edelfart, the neat little Norwegian in his office, to muttering, young Farley went out and jumped into his car, calling out, "I'll go up there now and tell him."

"At ten in the morning!" muttered Edelfart aloud.

Now, looking at Celie with the morning sun on her, in her house dress that was too short, she made him a little confused about his errand.

"Celie, what I stopped in for was to tell you I've decided to give Joe a chance on the night shift, learning saw filing. It's a good job and that'll get him out of the woods."

"I'll tell Joe," Celie said. "There's Rose Marie crying, Arthur—I mean Mr. Farley—I've got to go."

No word of thanks, no time even to flirt a bit. Young Farley got into his car in a hesitant mood. He was getting too damned sensitive, that was all. Folks in the town didn't like him so well, but that was natural, he was from the outside. The old man wanted him to do more managing . . . these people couldn't be managed, dumb Swedes and Finns . . .

Joe didn't care much about leaving the limey at first. He liked the trips through the woods even at the slow pace of the log train. He tipped back in his chair with his feet on the stove while Celie cleared away the supper dishes.

"Y'know, Cele, you can't even smoke a cigarette when you're down at the mill. Y'gotta check in and out to be sure you ain't stealin' time on the comp'ny. That's why old Hiram Block pulled out and took to running that garage of his so he could be independent."

"Yes, Joe, but you gotta think of your future," Celie said solemnly.

"Yes," said Joe slowly, "that's right, Cele, and I been thinkin' of it right along. If I was to leave here and get a job away, running the limey's as good as anything. If I take this job in the mill and be a saw filer I'd have as good a job as your dad, almost, Cele, and I could go from here to a mill anywhere in the country and be a saw filer."

Celie scalded the coffee pot, silently. Here was the

thing that had been down in their minds all this time; that she had been waiting to talk about. Her hands trembled a little in her excitement.

"You'd always have to live in mill-towns, then, Joe." Her words sounded loudly in the little kitchen.

"Yeah, but there's worse places, Cele, than livin' on this lake where the fishing's good and there's hunting and it's so healthy for the kid. Sometimes when I'm running the limey, Cele . . . you get a lot of thinkin' done on that job . . ."

Cele thought guiltily how she had blamed Joe in her mind for being so happy-go-lucky, not getting another job as he said he would. And, here, Joe had been thinking all this time.

". . . you know, Celie, I'm getting to like it here."

Celie looked at him quickly. He was getting to look like his father more and more. Folks even said Lin Linsen was a little cracked, and he did look half crazy when he'd stop in to see them and tell them about the trout he'd caught. His blue eyes would flash and his white hair would lop down over his forehead the way Joe's black hair did. Other times he was silent, a good enough worker when he worked, but he didn't have a spark of ambition. Whenever he wanted, he'd lay off. He'd be out in the woods half the time when the hunting-season came. Folks always said Joe was so different; he must have got his ambition from his mother who'd died when he was a little fellow. It scared Celie to catch the resemblance in Joe. She was silent. She scoured the sink busily, then she burst out,

"I thought you didn't want to live here all your life either, Joe, an' you haven't worked on your radio for ever so long." She didn't look at him but her voice was accusing and a little shrill.

Joe puffed at his pipe.

"Yeah, but, Cele, what would you have in the city that you don't have here?"

Celie raised her eyes from the sink.

"Oh, Joe, maybe this house is your idea, but it isn't mine. Maybe you like living on the edge of the woods and going to a show where they haven't even got talkies. Maybe you want Rose Marie to grow up with the Bouveard kids and learn to swear like a lumberjack, Joe Linsen, but I don't."

Celie's voice was more than shrill. It had in it a half sob that went into the walls of the box-like house and became part of their timber. In some other day when the Point was bare of people and the winds blew through the deserted buildings that tone would sound forth to become part of the age-old moan of Superior as it washes the shore. Celie and Joe were suddenly two tiny figures in a drama as old as the country of the sticks and older.

"Well, what would you do?"

"I'd take this night job and then in the daytime you could go into Clarion and hunt a job. I bet you didn't half look, Joe."

At the suspicion in her tone, Joe's face grew sullen.

"Say, I work when I work. When would you say I'd sleep?"

"Oh, Joe, you weren't so worried about your sleep when we used to go to dances."

A bitterness rose between the two, tiny at first, but real. Little Rose Marie sucked in that bitterness with her mother's milk as, perhaps, Celie had drawn it in from Christina.

But without more words, Joe went to work on the night shift. Like his father, he was born for the outdoors. In the white pine days he would have been in the lumber camp, but times had changed in the upper peninsula and he was Celie's man. He hated working down at the mill under the too shiny, too yellow light. The fine white particles of sawdust, everyplace, seemed to get in his throat. The saws even scared him a little, though he did not admit this fear himself. The sound of the file against the saw made shivers at the back of his neck. The first few days he grew frantic for a cigarette. He kept feeling in his pocket for the package. When he came back up the hill from the mill, he saw the limey pulling out. He felt cramped . . . tied. He began to think about himself and his lot as he had never done before. He had to look sharp at this new job and keep his eyes on the fine edge of the saws. He frowned a little and narrowed his eyes to watch more closely. A tiny line grew in his forehead that was new to his face.

The first day, he came home with no appetite. Celie was just up and his dinner was her breakfast. She cooked

136

eggs and ham and potato cakes and coffee. She ate a slice of bread with her coffee and that was all. Joe wouldn't eat either.

"Now you ought to get to bed, Joe," Celie said. "I'll fix it for you. Wait till I get Rose Marie out, first."

Joe laid down as he was. He stretched his arms up under the pillows. The under side of Celie's pillow was still warm. A queer half light came in the windows around the edge of the shades. He could hear Rose Marie making tiny squeals in the kitchen. Celie tip-toed around, but every now and then she would forget and her high heels would come down sharply on the floor. He turned over and put his face in the pillow. Just as he fell into a half sleep Rose Marie's tin rattle jangled to the floor. He woke with a start, tense from head to foot. He was at the mill again and had dropped one of the big saws with a great clatter. He got up and pulled on his boots.

Celie was bathing Rose Marie on the kitchen table by the sunny window. She looked up in surprise.

"Why, Joe, you must go on back to bed." She spoke as she might to a child. Her mind was on Rose Marie's weight.

"I thought you'd say I ought to be on my way in to Clarion to hunt a white collar job."

"Oh, Joe, you know better!" Celie flushed.

"Well, I don't feel like it, anyway. And I can't sleep. I'm going over to the fox farm and see Hels." A burst of cold air came in as he opened the door.

"Go on, then, quick, Joe. Rose Marie'll catch her death."

Joe sauntered over to the shack where Hels Helsen was cooking horse meat for the foxes. The half rancid smell filled the small shack. Joe sat down on his heels by the open door.

"Hi, Joe, ain't you working no more?"

"Oh, I'm on the night shift, filin'." Joe lit a cigarette.

His face in the strong light was strangely discontented. His heavy black hair fell over his forehead. His eyes were tired and rested moodily on the mash simmering in the rusted iron kettle. It was still a boy's face, a little sullen, impatient at being tied to an old man's job.

Hels was a short, stocky man in a plaid jumper, stagged trousers and boots. His face and hands had been grimy so long that the grime was a pigment in his skin. He had been out in bad weather a good part of his life. The rough wind across the lake, the snow blowing into drifts and the cold rain of early spring had roughened his face and taught him to carry his head down between his shoulders, as though he had a wry neck.

He had made snowshoes in the old days, learned the trade from an Indian at the Soo. He'd had a fling at the mill, he could tinker with machinery like a millwright, but he had no knack for steady work. Then he bought a few acres of ground at the top of town and a pair of fox a few years back. Once he sold a keg of moonshine to a lumberjack for the price of another fox. Now he had eighteen. Two white ones had come from Alaska and had cost him "plenty," as he told the curious. The love he had never lavished on the half-breed woman that lived with him fell to this pair of Alaskan fox. He gave the mash another stir and added a slab to the fire.

"C'm here," he grunted to Joe and stalked ahead on his stocky legs to the wire cage that fenced in the white fox. He pounded on the ground near their burrow with a stick until the sly, nervous creatures appeared. He watched them, not allowing himself a smile, but the satisfied stance of his squat figure as he stood surveying them was in itself a smile.

They sniffed the air with their pointed noses raised, stood motionless, trailing their plumy tails.

"Look at 'em brushes," muttered Hels. "Wait'll I get a litter off'n 'em." Joe leaned against the wire and watched the foxes. Raising fox was all right. It was a job, like any other, but he'd rather trap 'em; beat 'em at their own game, the sly devils. He oughta have some traps out like he used to as a boy; might even get a beaver. There was a law against it, like there was everything else, whisky an' fishing for trout in the fall and livin' where a man wanted to.

Hels gave him a jab in the ribs with his elbow.

"What d'ye say, huh? Got some powerful stuff." He winked.

"Just a short one, Hels." He followed Hels up to

the house, half tar paper, half boards that had been thrown together. He stood in the doorway, looking down over the roof tops of the village to the mill stacks and the lake while Hels went inside.

Not such a bad place, he'd told Celie, and it wasn't.

Hels came back and poured some of the colorless liquid into a tin cup.

"Whoa, Hels, I gotta work all night, don't forget." A warm stream flowed into him. He felt better already. He had another drink with Hels.

"Pretty good moon, eh, Joe?"

"Surest thing." This was the life: independent, outdoors trapping, a little drink to warm you up. All women were like Celie. They wanted to get into town, but they had to go where their men lived . . . surest thing! Joe was sleepy. He got up from the stoop.

"S'long, Hels. I'll be up to steal those white rats of yours one of these days." He went back to his house. It must be time for dinner.

As he came through the kitchen, there was no sign of a meal. Celie was ironing some dresses for Rose Marie.

"What about dinner?" asked Joe, a little thickly.

Celie looked at him indignantly.

"Joe Linsen, it's three o'clock and I've seen you sitting up there on Hels Helsen's stoop having a drink with him."

Joe went into the bedroom whistling, without making any reply. That was the way to get Celie going . . . surest thing!

"Joe, shh, Rose Marie's just gotten off."

Joe threw himself across the bed. The house was no place for him in the daytime. It was for women. Worn out with his day of doing nothing, Joe fell asleep.

Celie went down to the store for groceries. She was angry with Joe as she had never been before; angry and frightened. This was where love got you in the end. She didn't love Joe anymore, anyway. That was all over. She was like the girl in *The Love Trap* story that ran in the papers.

She went into the big barny store feeling that it was a refuge. Maybe she could get a job here again. She could leave Rose Marie with her mother pretty soon. She'd work here and save every cent of her money and get away . . . anywhere, to Clarion, to Chicago, maybe. That was what she'd planned once; why hadn't she done it?

"Oh, hello," she said to Mrs. Munsen. "Fine, she's growing so. Thirteen pounds and four ounces. Curly, I guess, at least it looks like it now. Oh, Joe's fine. He's filing on the night shift."

She bought her groceries and went down to the meat counter. With Mrs. Munsen and Thelma Konki she was a little on her guard when she came to the store. She knew they looked at her clothes to see whether she was still wearing her old ones and always told her that the place was so changed she wouldn't know where to lay her hand on things.

Mr. Quinn's face lighted when he saw her.

" 'Lo, Celie, girl," he said with his Swedish accent.

"One pound of wieners, butch," she said, smiling, "and some sauerkraut; you know, enough."

"How 'bout a little chicken, Celie? Dem wieners don't get you fat. You look kinda tired, Cele. Maybe you take bein' married too hard?" No one else was at the meat counter except Nellie Hann's little boy, and the pain was bad in his back. He could take time to stop and talk with Celie Linsen.

"Oh, no, butch." Unaccountable tears filled her eyes suddenly.

"Ach, Celie, I didn't mean to make you cry, ish!" Old Quinn was so upset his kindly wrinkled face reddened.

"You step out more, Celie, you don't want to be an old woman before you be a young girl. I miss the way you used to run around in here. Mind now, you child, you walk out of here like you used to, real spry. An' come in and get a chicken for Sunday. I make you a special, eh, Cele?"

Celie took her packages and hurried out of the store. Her heels pounded on the board floor the quick brisk rhythm they used to make. Old Quinn watched her go. Something was wrong with Celie Linsen. Such a pretty girl . . . she'd settle down like the rest. Old Quinn was not a mill worker. He'd been a camp cook for years. He had learned sympathy along with his woman's work, or maybe it was that great grandmother that had had learning and been a teacher back in the old country.

"Hey, butch, three quarts milk and Ma says two was sour last time so she wants two fer nothin', d'ye hear?"

Old Quinn turned wearily toward the ice box. He was almost too old to remember how he came to stay in the Point. He hated the daily rabble of children who shouted their orders to him and got him so mixed up. Celie Henderson was like a cool drink of water. She made him think of the old country when he was a young man and a fool.

He'd come over to America with ten other young fellows on a contract with the iron mines, on the other side of the peninsula. That was too hard for him. He drifted over to the mills. Work was too hard there, too. His heart wasn't just right. Then the cook in the camp was killed in a fight. Old Quinn took his place back in 1910, he still remembered the date, and here he was. Old Quinn coughed. He'd go to see the doctor tonight, maybe. That pain . . .

Celie was glad to hurry out of the store. She had forgotten to bring a compact with her, but she knew her eyes were red. Once, Celie would never have left the house without a compact, without making sure her lips were a bright scarlet. She didn't have so much time to think about herself, now.

How could old Quinn know, she wondered. The mill whistle blew while she was on her way home. Men came up the hill like troops of an army. Lights blinked on in the box-like houses. It was still light, but there was light to burn. There was Selma Lichtenberg busy in her kitchen. As she passed her mother's house she could see Christina by her stove. Christina had gone on living right there. She had twelve boarders, now. She was a little more silent, a little more grim, but otherwise just the same. "Oh, I work awhile," was all she said when Celie urged her to live with them. "Old people by themselves, young people together, that's the best way."

As Celie passed Hensen's, Mrs. Hensen was getting an armful of wood from the woodpile.

" 'Lo, Celie, I see you go by and I tried to make you hear me. I wanted you should stop in an' have coffee with. You can, tomorrow, can?"

"Thanks, Mrs. Hensen," said Celie.

The whole town was in action. The pumps at the corners had a group waiting to fill their pails. Suppers were on the stoves in the little houses. The men were home. There was plenty of work in the mill, plenty of youth in the village. The bustle of life in the three streets of the Point was louder than the sough of the trees beyond the town or the melancholy swish of Superior. It caught Celie in its rhythm and quickened her feet.

She wondered if Joe were still asleep. She ran into the house through the kitchen. It was still and full of soft shadows in the dusky light. In the parlor, Rose Marie was sleeping on the davenport. She went into the little bedroom. Joe still lay crossways on the bed.

"Joe . . ." She bent over him. He was sleeping

spread-eagled, his boots had pulled the spread into a knot. The pillow was damp by his mouth. In his exhaustion, he had slobbered like a baby.

Celie had held her hate tight to her. She had planned to herself all afternoon how she would leave him and make her way by herself. Seeing him there, asleep, the hate ebbed away from her. She tried to keep it.

"Joe, wake up, you're spoiling the spread." She spoke crossly. "Joe!" She bent over him. His tousled black head, his shoulders, his lips parted a little against the damp pillow, moved her. "Joe!" She kissed his lips. Her fingers pushed back his hair. There was alcohol on his breath, but Celie was not Ole Henderson's child for nothing. A strange new feeling for him rose in her. Celie Linsen had left her adolescence behind. A girl grows into a woman early in the country of the sticks.

Joe raised his head, bewildered.

"What time is it, Cele?" He had forgotten the miserable, wasted day he had put in, his resentment against Celie. Like a child, all that was yesterday. Men stay children a long while up north.

Celie rushed out to the kitchen to heat up the hash she had made for noon. She pushed the coffee over to the hottest place on the stove. She cut thick slices of bread and spread them with butter for Joe's lunch pail.

"You'll be late, Joe," she called in to him.

"Oh, no, I won't. You watch your old man!" Their voices rang in the house with a lilt to them. Rose Marie woke and cried. Celie hurried Joe off and sat down to feed her. The kitchen was warm and bright. The wood in the range crackled. Men labored for that wood, women grew old while they labored, but the wood in the end supported them, the wood of the tall trees.

Rose Marie nursed quietly, drawing in not bitterness, but strength, tonight. Celie Linsen kicked off her high-heeled pumps that hurt a little. It felt good to stretch her stockinged feet out to the oven ledge. There was a darn halfway up her stocking and a fresh run. Celie looked past it. She was thinking about Joe. She put Rose Marie to sleep on their bed and laid down beside her. It was lonesome without Joe.

About midnight, Celie woke. Something was wrong. She turned the lights on in the room. For fifteen months she had lain by Joe's long, hard body. His shoulder against her own had meant security. Without him, the woods came too close to the house. She heard the un-real cry of the foxes. A rattle-trap car back-fired far down the street. She went over to the window and peeked out at the side of the shade. Over on the bluffs at Farley's place, the lights streamed out. For the first time since young Farley had taken her out, Celie had no envy in her. They and the life they lived were remote from her. Hers was here in this little house and down in the mill where Joe was. She was wide awake. She stepped into her pumps and went out to the kitchen.

The house was too still. She wanted to keep doing something. She went hurriedly, timidly out to the woodshed and came back with an armful of wood. She opened the drafts and added new fuel. The black stove was company. She washed the dishes in the sink, and turned to the pile of washing under the table. She might as well do it up now as anytime.

When she went outdoors with her pan of washed clothes, she was no longer timid. It was only the house, alone, that crowded down on her. She hung the clothes on the line. A cool wind blew them out full, blew through her hair and against her face. She felt gay as she hadn't felt since Ole died. It was growing lighter. There were still stars in the sky, very pale, very far away. The moon was already fading. At the bottom of the town, by the lake, rose the four stacks of the mill. Red smoke and sometimes a spark shot out of them into the sky.

Celie remembered how Christina had said, "I like it when the mill runs nights. It don't seem so lonely, then." Suddenly Celie knew what her mother meant. Christina had always seemed so old to her. It was queer to be feeling the same things she did.

Celie thought she heard music over towards Farley's place, but she didn't care. She went inside. It was three o'clock. Joe'd be laying off pretty soon. She decided to put the sauerkraut on to cook and make a cake. After all, it was Joe's heavy meal.

As the whistle for the day-shift screamed out in the gray dawn, Celie took her pail and went down to the pump. She was a little tired now. Norm Lichtenberg came by and pumped for her.

"You're up pretty early, Cele."

"Why not, Joe's filing on the night shift."

Joe came up the hill, tired with the unaccustomed tension of the night's work. He had never been tired like this out in the woods. The fine line between his eyes was drawn there again upon his forehead. There was no kick in going home in the morning, either, the way there was in the evening. Celie'd be just getting up. Joe stooped under the line of clothes in the yard and went in through the kitchen. The table was set. The hearty smell of sauerkraut and wieners came to him from the stove. Rose Marie was in her high chair and Celie was feeding her cereal. Joe hung up his things.

"Hello," he had remembered again. He wasn't sure how Celie would greet him.

"Dinner's ready, Joe. I'm running a night shift, too, only I don't know how to change Rose Marie over." She giggled. "Do you think moonlight would be as good as sun for her, Joe?"

Joe stopped washing his hands. "You mean, Cele, you've been up all night and you're going to bed after dinner, too?"

Celie was wiping Rose Marie's mouth. "Of course. What's the difference when you sleep?"

Mrs. Nurmi, who lived next door, stood at her kitchen window.

"I never knew Celie Linsen to get her wash out sooner'n me before," she told her daughter sorrowfully. "However did she do it?"

2

THAT October was warm in the Point. Clear, sunny days came and went without the slightest change in purpose or desire. There was no room for purpose or even any desire in the ripe quiet that held the world. Each day hung like a single fruit on a tree, perfect, awaiting a wind to bear it down. But there was no wind. The lake was glass, blue glass with a green bottom. The gangly maple outside Celie's kitchen window was scarlet again, with yellow leaves on the off side, a red cloak lined with yellow. The milkweed stalks along the fence of the fox farm held out full white pods for the first touch of wind. The low-lying hills across the town were a smoldering line of purple smoke.

Celie got up at three that afternoon to feed the baby. Afterwards, she took her out on the grass on a blanket. Joe was still asleep in the house. Celie walked around on tiptoe. He'd be up soon and they'd have a four o'clock breakfast. They were used to the night shift now, but the days were too good to miss. They went to bed early to have a piece of the afternoon left.

Celie spread newspapers out on the kitchen table and emptied the coffee grounds of last night's coffee. She had been too sleepy to wash the pot last night. Joe bought a paper now and then. He liked the feeling of carrying it home. Sometimes he read it in front of the stove in the evenings and looked at the "men wanted" in the Clarion ads. It was called the *Mill and Mine, A Clarion Daily.*

Celie sometimes looked at the recipes and the cartoons and the daily pattern. She read about the house-party at the Farleys' place and the news of sales in Clarion. Today she looked idly over the headlines. The type was larger than usual and blacker. A word here and there leaped up at her from the page. "Crash" and "Stocks" and "Wall Street." Celie glanced at the paper's date, October 30th, 1929—that was yesterday's. She read on to catch the drift of it all. The coffee grounds ran rivulets over the type.

Joe came out from the bedroom. He was dressed, but his hair was tousled.

"What you doing, Cele, tellin' your fortune in coffee grounds?"

"No, Joe, look, they must've had an awful time in New York."

"Yeah, big panic in Wall Street," explained Joe, authoritatively, as the man of the house.

"What about, Joe?"

"Oh, those wealthy guys buy stocks, shares in things, you know, and keep 'em till the price goes up . . . like eggs, Cele, and then sell. Well, sometimes, they buy without having any money on the chance that the things they buy'll get higher, only they get less and then they lose, see?"

"Mmm-hmm," said Celie, still reading between the coffee grounds.

"Well, that's all there is to it. Everything went way down, I guess, and them millionaires and all lost a young fortune. It's tough, but I guess those millionaires can afford it. I guess they could lose quite a bit and still not have to work on the night shift or move out of New York. Maybe this is one time we have the laugh on them, all them capitalists, eh, Cele? We haven't any money so it can't affect us if the whole bottom drops out the way they were saying it did down at the mill."

It didn't affect them, anyway, her and Joe and Rose Marie. Celie rolled up the paper with the coffee grounds and stuffed it in the stove as though by so doing she disposed of the crash in Wall Street. Then she rinsed the pot and made fresh coffee.

"D'ye want bacon, Joe?"

"No, let's go up and see my traps before work, shall we, Cele?"

"All right. I wish we could take Rose Marie, Joe. The woods are so pretty and she never gets to see them much."

"Well, take her along, if you don't think she'll mind the jiggles. That road's mostly old corduroy, y'know."

"Rose Marie wouldn't mind. Look at her, Joe, isn't she a cute one?"

Rose Marie was waving bare feet in the air. She was six months old.

"Y'know, Celie, why that baby is so happy all the time? 'Cause we began her out in the sun over at Mead, you know."

Celie flushed, but she smiled back shyly. "Maybe, Joe."

They had come a long way.

3

A DULL gray light covered the Point. It was dusk by four o'clock, now. A raw November wind swept down from the north, whipping the lake to foam and splashing it well over the old dock. The wind blew dust into the eyes of the little boys shooting crap in front of the store and tugged at the empty sleeve of old Kronki, loafing on the store steps. He had compensation from the company for that arm. He chewed contentedly and watched the wind blow the heavy door of the store out of Mrs. Nurmi's hand.

Leaves must be thick in the woods with this wind at 'em. Cold, soon, and blizzards out in the woods, but it'd be warm in the bunk house. The wind blew his empty sleeve out full. He reached over with his left hand and tucked the end of the sleeve into the opening of his jumper.

All the doors of the company houses were shut

against the cold. The thrifty had nailed up storm windows and most of the Swedes and Germans built storm sheds over the doors. Base burners were lugged in from the woodshed and set up in the parlor. Winter had begun in the Point. The town huddled bleakly on the shore of the lake. The cold wind stripped off the last zinnia blossoms from Christina Henderson's garden and tore the scarlet cloak from the maple outside Celie Linsen's window.

Mrs. Nurmi came by Celie as she was taking down clothes in the yard. Mrs. Nurmi's round, red face looked out snugly under her shawl.

" 'Twon't seem half so cold when snow comes," she called out. "Gets to your bones now."

Celie smiled but made no answer. Snow and another winter in the Point! Through the summer and fall she had forgotten how it would be. She carried her clothes into the kitchen and hung them back of the stove. She lifted the cover on the saucepan. The rice was boiling. She could make the gravy now.

They had gotten up before three and Joe had gone off to see his traps. He'd put out more now and was having a run of luck with them. Celie saw each trap as one thing more to keep them in the Point, to make Joe like it better. She set the table listlessly. She was always tired these days. She looked scrawny, Christina told her. Joe said it was a help to be on the night shift 'cause it was easier to get up in the afternoons than black mornings, but it was a topsy-turvy way to live. Sleeping in the daytime wasn't the same. Celie felt that she went to bed tired and woke up still tired.

Living this way, she got her work done up in half the time it took in the day. No one came in; Selma or Christina or Nellie Hann. Even the first part of the evening, the women stayed home with their men. Pearl, Hels Helsen's woman, used to come and hold Rose Marie sometimes or bring a piece of venison or a bottle of beer. Celie couldn't go to the women's *kaffeekalaser;* she missed that, too. She went to the store as soon as she woke up. That was the excitement of the day, but she had to hurry back or Joe'd be late for work. It was black outside the window; nothing to stop and watch the way there was in the daytime, only sounds to scare you. The wind pushing against the loose pane, the foxes' baying, a late car down on the lower road, and in between, a heavy, black stillness. She and Joe were shut in a world of their own; only Joe saw the other men on the night shift, she was shut in alone so much. It had been fun at first. Celie had had the feeling that it wouldn't last long, that it was just for a while. But one night followed another all through October and now it was the middle of November.

The woodshed door banged and the hinges squeaked complainingly. Joe came into the kitchen.

" 'Lo," said Celie, pouring gravy over a mound of rice on Joe's plate.

"Gosh, Cele, Norm Lichtenberg got his buck yesterday, a big one, and Stumpf got his and Hels, I guess,

154

got a couple. He said yes when I asked him and winked. That oughta be good for two. I don't know what's the matter. I don't have any luck just goin' out an hour or so in the morning or just before work. Guess I'll hunt a whole day and then lay off a night."

Celie dropped the cover to the saucepan with a clatter.

"Joe Linsen, don't you dare!" Her voice scared her. She hadn't known it would come out like that. But the voice went on while she stood aside and listened.

"You're as bad as your father. You can't get ahead if you do things like that. You never think of taking a day to look for a job away from here, but you can lose a night's pay easy to get rested up after hunting." Scorn flashed from Celie's eyes. She choked a little over her words.

Joe's face reddened. He sat down to the table and started eating. Celie poured the coffee with elaborate care. Well, she might as well say it as think it, she told herself.

"Tell you what, Cele." Joe wasn't angry. Celie was surprised, but then it was only because he was so crazy for his hunting. "I'll work tonight and go hunting first thing in the morning and we'll take tomorrow night off and go into Clarion to a show, how's that? Fair enough?" He was delighted with his own inspiration. "Pete Metz, he files in the daytime. He'd jump at an extra penny for one night. I'll stop in and see Farley on my way to work."

"You're awful free with your money, Joe."

"Money ain't everything, Cele."

After Joe went out, Cele rushed to clear the dishes. She was excited at doing something different, at the thought of going in to Clarion. She almost forgot the fear that had been in the back of her mind all week. Now, as she went in to get Rose Marie, it was with her again. Not like that other time, when she had felt guilty because of it and scared. Celie had never been sick in all her life and that other time, the thought of being hurt when the baby came made a tight feeling come in her throat so she had to swallow quickly. She never could bring herself to talk about it, even to Selma or Christina. She had tried to tell Joe how scared she was, only it didn't seem quite fair. Women kept still about those things.

This time, she could grow big under everyone's eyes. They couldn't say anything. This time, she knew all about it. It wouldn't be something unknown and terrible. It wasn't as bad as women let on to each other, only, today, all those months it took stretched ahead endlessly. She was tired. With another baby to do for, she would always be tired.

Rose Marie cried again. She was hungry; the doctor said to come up to the clinic and he'd tell her how to wean her.

"Don't cry, baby, poor baby, honey, Celie's baby," Celie murmured awkwardly. Mostly, she did things for Rose Marie silently. Words like you talked to a baby came slowly. You felt a little silly when you heard yourself. Maybe a little of the coffee milk would be all right. Celie carried Rose Marie out to the kitchen table. With one hand, she poured the milk from the pitcher into a saucepan and heated it over the stove. It was thin enough, you could see, but she added a little water from the teakettle. When the milk was warm she sat down by the stove and fed Rose Marie with a spoon.

At first, Rose Marie cried between spoonfuls, then she grew quiet. It was easy to wean a baby, only it took a lot of time feeding her with a spoon. Celie held the baby over her shoulder and patted her back.

Oh, it wouldn't be so bad having another baby. Maybe it would be a boy like Joe wanted. She wouldn't need very many new things, anyway, that is, if Rose Marie had outgrown them by then. Sure it would be nice having a new baby. She wondered how Mrs. Suess felt each time she had another. Her Christopher was the ninth, and Mrs. Braumbaugh had six and Mrs. Slechter must have ten. She remembered how they'd all felt sorry for Selma, though. Celie rocked Rose Marie, bending backward and forward in the straight kitchen chair.

Nice to be just Celie Henderson again. She hadn't known, then, how it would be when you were married. Celie looked more than eighteen. Twenty-four, even, with the wistful turn to her mouth.

It was growing dark outside now. The wind rattled the windows and blew the curtains gently. Celie put Rose Marie in bed and pulled the shades down. There was a shower on Una Biehl tonight. Christina was going to come up and sit while she went.

Celie pulled off her sweater and skirt and set about dressing. There was something accustomed about the business of slipping into a dress, fixing the belt, twisting the hair into place that comforted her and made her world more natural. Freshly reddened lips had no wistful line to them. Oh, well, Celie shrugged at her reflection in the mirror and a half smile showed in the glass. She wouldn't be very big before January. Maybe, with a coat on, the women'd never guess before February.

"Cele!"

"Why, Joe, aren't you going to work?"

Joe laughed. The very sound warmed Celie and drew the fear out of her.

"I stopped in to see Farley on my way down, and, you know, Cele, he isn't a bad sort. He said, 'What d'ye say you take me hunting an' I'll give you a night off.' Well, say! And, Cele, he said his wife'd like you to come out there while we're gone, just to visit and keep her company. We'll go first thing in the morning. He's goin' to meet me at the mill." Joe was in high spirits. "An' what's more, Cele, it's snowing . . . like a flour sifter. Oughta be a cinch to track a deer, tomorrow."

"Joe, imagine him giving you the time!"

"What's it to him? Says he wants to go 'fore his Uncle comes up or he won't think he's sticking to business. I never liked him before because he was so gone on you, but he's all right. Well, I had to come up to tell you, Cele. I told him I wanted to go back up to the house before work an' he said, 'Sure, take your time.' "

Joe went off, slamming the door behind him. Celie opened it again and stood in the doorway. The steady drop of white snowflakes covered the meanness of the Point. The night was warmer than the day. The atmosphere was softly mysterious. Celie stepped out a minute and let the snow fall gently on her hair. It fell on her lashes and tickled her nose. There was no sound of the wind or the lake tonight. It was good to be here in the circle of the lighted houses.

Christina came into sight, trudging steadily up the street, a solid, stubby figure in the moving snow.

"That's a great way to keep your house warm," she commented without greeting.

"I know," laughed Celie, "but it isn't cold out."

Celie followed Christina into the kitchen.

"This is the greatest way you live. Now you mean the baby thinks it's day and stays awake part of the night?"

Celie nodded. "Yes, I bring her out in the kitchen and let her play with a spoon or something . . . she loves the egg-beater . . . until she gets sleepy. I've bathed her already so you don't need to do that."

Christina took off her coat and the crocheted cap she wore. The cap was a halfway step between the shawl of the old country and the hats Celie wore. She laid out her balls of rags.

"I thought I'd braid you a rug for your bedroom, Celie, all rose and white. Now you run along."

Celie pulled on her hat at Joe's shaving mirror by the sink and slipped into the old lapin jacket which could still muster an air of smartness in the world.

" 'Bye, Mamma." Each woman thought silently how like old times it was, Celie going off all dressed up and calling back, " 'Bye, Mamma." But Celie was never aware of such shades of feeling in those old days. She hurried down the street toward the Biehls'. On the way, she stopped for Selma.

"Gee, you look swell, Selma. When'd you get that coat?"

"Oh, this fall. Didn't you see it in the catalogue? It was 97054 and you could get it in green, brown or black."

"I'm glad you got black; you won't get tired of it so soon. I need a new coat. Joe and me are going to Clarion tomorrow night, maybe. I guess I'll look around then." There was a touch of importance in the tone.

"I wish we could go to town, this Saturday. I'll talk to Norm, but he hates to drive in a snow storm. Say, I guess this is a real surprise on Una."

Outside house number 31, they met other women and girls.

"Christina said she'd stay with Rose Marie; Joe's workin' nights, now," Celie explained to Mrs. Wilhelm. There was noisy whispering and giggles.

160

"You knock, go on. Shh!" One of the women knocked loudly. Una opened the door. She was a short, light-haired girl.

"Oh, you!" cried out Selma. "You're all dressed up. How'd you know?"

"She's the smart one . . . ach, Una, they won't catch you yet." They trooped into the house, filling its box-like parlor and dining room to overflowing. Una sat down by the dining room table expectantly. Talk languished. Una was pink-cheeked and embarrassed. The women whispered together on the couch back by the wall. Then Selma and Celie came in from the kitchen, tugging a clothes-basket full of presents.

"Ach, you got the bassinet a-ready!" yelled Mrs. Suess. The women burst into high laughter. The fun was on. In through the doorway, on the kitchen table stood four cakes, made by the best cooks in the Point, three pies, a plate of doughnuts. The smell of coffee, strong, fragrant, heartening, filled the small rooms. Joe Biehl, Una's brother, called down,

"Gee, Mom, I can't sleep for smelling coffee, kin I have some an' some cake?"

"You come down and get one cup and then don't you let me hear another word out of'n you," called back Mrs. Biehl good-humoredly.

"Ma, Ma," the voice was at the top of the stairs, whispering, "my trousers is back of the stove; throw 'em up, will you?"

The women in the front rooms shrieked with laughter.

"Give 'im an apron," one of the girls called out. Mrs. Biehl cut a generous slice of cake and poured a cup of coffee. Then she took them upstairs where Joe squatted in his union suit.

After the shower was over, the women crowded around the dining room table. Mrs. Arvid dealt the battered decks of cards for a game of hearts.

"You got her, my goodness, Sadie, you got her again." Mrs. Lindermulder's massive elbow jabbed into the fat over Mrs. Hensen's ribs. Mrs. Hensen blushed beet red as she turned up the queen of spades. The women's laughter carried far down the street through the silence of white, falling snow. The chickens huddled in the shed by the dining room wall stirred uneasily and scolded in their sleep.

At twelve, the younger women served refreshments: a piece of pie and a slice of cake to a plate, coffee, and maybe a doughnut.

"Your ma make these fried cakes, Cele?"

"Yes, but they're not quite as short as usual," deprecated Celie.

"Then I'll have one," decided Mrs. Peters, reaching out a fat hand for one. "You know, the doctor, he says I have diabetes, the sugar kind, an' I gotta cut out sugar . . . say!" Mrs. Peters bit into the fried cake and laughed. The other women laughed with her.

"You gotta watch your figger, though, Mary!"

"Me!" Mrs. Peters shook all over with Falstaffian mirth.

"This'll be good for the hunting tomorrow, Joe says." Celie and Selma were walking back up the street.

"Well, s'long," Celie said at Selma's door. "You let me know if I can do anything for you in town tomorrow night."

Celie was in high spirits. It didn't seem so long ago since she'd been having a shower on her, only a little over a year, it was. The snow was over the tops of her galoshes now. It'd be four feet deep by morning. Funny, the way there didn't seem to be any sky at all, just soft, falling snow when you looked up. Celie ran in through the shed door. She stopped suddenly in the kitchen. Something was wrong. The fire was going hard. Two kettles of water were pushed on the front lids. The baby's bathtub was out on the table and a litter of towels, the baby's shirt, a pile of diapers warming in the open oven.

"That you, Cele?" Christina came out of the other room. "Run down and get the doctor, Cele. Rose Marie's had two convulsions. I thought sure she'd die 'fore you ever got here. She's quiet, now, you hurry down there."

Celie was gone in a flash; a sudden, cold terror, different from anything she had ever known, at her throat and in her legs. Maybe Rosie'd die like the Blatz baby . . . oh, God!" she whispered as she ran. She stumbled up the steps of the doctor's house and knocked on the door. Maybe he wasn't there, maybe he had been drinking the way he did sometimes. She could hear movement in the house.

"Yes, walk in and I'll be right there." The doctor's voice had a different tone from the voices in the Point. Celie opened the door into the doctor's living room. She had never been there before. Even now she looked around curiously. The books way up to the ceiling, comfortable chairs, a table strewed with magazines . . . it was the curtains that came together and covered the windows all over that made it so different from the houses in the Point. Celie sat down on the edge of the doctor's big chair. Her knees trembled. She twisted her hands in her lap. Sometime, she and Joe'd have a room like this, not so many books, more pictures on the wall, but like this.

"Why, Celie Henderson, what's wrong, girl?" Even here in his board house in the Point, the doctor looked apart from the place. That very difference comforted Celie.

"Rose Marie, Doc. She's had convulsions and is going to die maybe."

"Not so fast, Cele, babies don't die so easily. Is she quiet now?"

"Yes, Mamma said she was when I got home, but please hurry."

The doctor's car shot up the street to the last house.

Cele sat silent in the seat by the doctor. Christina met them in the kitchen.

"I guess the baby be all right, now. She's slept a half hour." Satisfaction fitted well on her grim features. It was a triumph not to need the doctor. The doctor went in to see the baby. Celie followed him.

The room that admitted only the bed, the table with the baby's basket, the make-shift dressing table crowded close together was suddenly a strange place. Its very strangeness filled Celie with fear. Rose Marie slept, looking a little peaked. Her hands were clenched in blue-veined fists. The doctor held one tiny wrist, listened to her heart.

"She's all right now, Cele, but she's not gaining very fast. I thought I told you to come up and we'd start weaning her."

"I did, Doc, by myself. I didn't seem to have hardly any milk today, and she cried so I gave her some of the coffee milk. She liked it."

"Coffee milk?" The doctor's face twisted quizzically.

"Yes, you know, the milk we have for our coffee, only I put water in it."

The doctor's full, tired face broke into a smile. "Oh, Cele, it isn't as simple as that. That's what made the baby sick. You have to start in very carefully and measure the milk and boil it, child."

Celie breathed more easily. "She won't die then? She's all right, now?" She looked so young, standing beside Christina still dressed for the party, the doctor asked irrelevantly, "How old are you, Celie?"

"Eighteen."

The doctor nodded. "You get some paper and I'll write out just what you give her."

After the doctor went, taking Christina with him, Celie sat down on the bed by the baby. She didn't dare leave her out of her sight. She wouldn't leave her even to go to Clarion tomorrow. All the rest of her life she would stay by her. Celie fell asleep in her clothes, curled on the foot of the bed.

At five, Joe came off the night shift. He stopped in at the house. He wasn't tired tonight. He even felt good. He knew which way they'd go; follow the tracks out past the fresh cutting and then go in a ways on that old log road. When he came into the kitchen, the fire was out. The house was cold. He went into the bedroom. Celie was still asleep on the bed. She stirred and opened her eyes.

"Hello, sleepyhead." Joe grinned.

"Oh, Joe, Rose Marie's been sick, had convulsions and everything."

"Gosh, Cele, is she all right now?" Joe went over to the basket and looked down on the baby. "Whatever do you s'pose got into the little devil?"

"Oh, Joe, I fed her wrong. I was trying to wean her and I didn't do it right. I had to get the doctor."

Joe put his arm around her. "You poor kid, Cele, I'll

tell Farley his wife better come over here while we're gone."

"Oh, no, Joe, I can take the baby over there, she's all right again, and I kinda want to see that house. Joe, I fell asleep and didn't get anything ready to eat for you."

"That's all right, Cele. What d'ye take me for?"

"And, Joe, I'm going to have another baby." It came out without Celie's thinking beforehand.

"No, Cele!" Joe was taken back. Celie's head nodded, but she felt better, closer to Joe. "Gee, Cele, that's tough."

"Didn't you want it, Joe? Maybe it'll be a boy."

"Well, when it gets here, I guess we will, only we were getting along all right with just Rose Marie."

"What did you expect, Joe?"

Joe flushed a little. "I guess so, Cele."

They didn't talk things over, Celie and Joe. They were shy in the face of such frankness. Joe felt out of place. He felt Celie expected something of him. He was eager to get off to the woods. He went over and got his gun in the corner back of the dressing table. He looked at Celie quickly to see how she was taking it. Rose Marie's fretful cry broke in. Celie sprang to take her up. Joe patted Celie's shoulder.

"I gotta get going, kid. 'Member, we're going in to town tonight and see a show like old times."

Celie heard him picking up his things in the shed.

The door banged and the querulous whine of the hinges sounded after it. Rose Marie filled Celie's mind.

"Want to watch Celie fix your milk, baby?" There were always things to do, just when you got to worrying or thinking. She'd have to stir the formula all the time. Milk burns so easy.

4

WHEN Celie found herself standing with Rose Marie in her arms in front of the side door to Farley's place, she was suddenly shy. Maybe she ought to have parked the old Ford down by their garage. She got out her compact and powdered her nose again. It was difficult with Rose Marie on one arm.

Urna Hait opened the door. Celie and she had been in school together, but they were very formal now. Urna wore a green uniform and a cap on her head. Celie was Mrs. Joe Linsen. These things made a difference.

"Is Mrs. Farley in?" asked Celie.

"Mercy, she ain't out of bed yet," answered Urna Hait, reprovingly. Celie was a trifle abashed. She had done up her work and it was still only nine-thirty. A swift mental picture of ladies in the movies receiving callers in bed passed through her mind.

"Will you tell her Mrs. Linsen is here, if she's awake, that is," said Celie, the more firmly because of Urna Hait. Urna clattered in through the swinging door to the dining room. Celie had never seen a swinging door in a house before. In a few minutes, Urna reappeared.

"Mis' Farley says to come up an' I'm to take her breakfast to her." Celie followed Urna into the other part of the house. She had looked through the windows of the big house on the bluffs when it stood vacant and cupped her hands around her eyes, calling out with the other children, "There's the stairs," or "Lookee, they've got a table big's the one at the boardin' house." The big house had been left furnished just as it was when the owner of the mill had gone into bankruptcy and shot himself there in the living room, fifteen years ago. Celie looked quickly around this room as she went up the stairs, at the big leather chairs and the stone fire-place. It was all like being in a movie. She hoped Rose Marie would sleep so she could get a good chance to see things. At the top of the stairs, Urna Hait supported the tray against the door-jamb with one hand and turned the knob with the other. Mrs. Farley was in bed, just like a movie-star. She called out cheerfully,

"Hello, Mrs. Linsen; sit down while I get outside of this breakfast."

Celie had a jumbled impression of the turquoise blue negligee with fluffy lace ruffles at the neck and arms, of silver-lined mules under the bed, of green furniture and lavender curtains at the windows.

"I'm always up so early with Joe filing on the night shift, I didn't stop to think how early it was. Joe said Mr. Farley said you'd like me to come over." Celie laid the baby on the window seat and started unwrapping her.

"Oh, you brought the baby out in all this snow." Her voice sounded so surprised. Celie answered bluntly,

"What else would I do with her in the daytime? I don't have any Urna Hait." She was a little abashed at the remark when she had made it.

"Of course, dumb me; put her over on the chaise longue and put the pillows around her. She's a cunning thing."

Celie spread out the pads she had brought and fixed her in the long chair that looked like the movies. Her eyes noted the little baby pillows and the cigarettes on the table by it.

"My sister has a kid about her age, not as pretty though, has her aunty Char's nose." Mrs. Farley laughed. Celie smiled, too. She wasn't so snobby, really. "Have a cup of coffee and a cigarette. Urna brought two cups." Celie felt herself all thumbs as she reached across the bed for the cup. She noticed Mrs. Farley's red finger nails and the big diamond ring.

"Thank you," she said and felt she was play-acting.

"Your name is Celie, isn't it? Duckie came back from here and told me you were the only thing worth looking at up here." When Mrs. Farley smiled, her teeth were uneven, Celie noticed critically, but she had large black eyes and her hair was a pretty red.

"His aunt wrote me to come down and be a maid."

Celie didn't know why she said it. Mrs. Farley lit a cigarette and laughed.

"You're not *very* proud, are you? My goodness, I thought you'd burn us up that day in the store." She was good-natured, Celie thought. "You ought to have come down to Detroit, though, and gotten a job. This is a hell of a place to live. Cigarette?"

"Thanks." Celie had only smoked a few times. The girls in the Point didn't mostly. She lighted it awkwardly. "Isn't it the worst dump you ever saw?" Mrs. Farley had struck a common note.

"Dump! Say, I've died three times over this year up here. Gosh!"

"It's pretty swell out here, though," said Celie.

"That's what got me up here, but you oughta hear the wind around these windows. In Detroit, we were on the fifteenth floor, but you could open the windows and hear the cars on Woodward Avenue. Give me a two-room flat down there any day instead of this."

"That's the way I feel," said Celie. "Gee! I want to get away from here." The sentence came out with such intensity, Mrs. Farley looked at her a second.

"Two souls with one swell thought," she commented. She was used to saying things to make people laugh. Sometimes she had put in a few wise-cracks between her songs at the Tricorne. Folks always told her she ought to be on the stage.

"Call me Charlotte, will you, Celie?" Arthur was a dummy he couldn't see this girl had ideas, Charlotte

171

thought to herself. But Arthur was dumb about a lot of things. She watched her over her cigarette. Charlotte Farley was shrewd in her way. Celie was a pretty thing; she could have gotten a long way if she had played the old man. "Well, what'll we do all day?" Charlotte blew the smoke into rings. "The answer is, nothing." She laughed.

Celie was slowly growing into the atmosphere of the room, like a chameleon. She drank in everything through all her senses; the colors, the gayety of the taffeta-flounced dressing table, the bedspread to match, the warm air of the room that was so different from the fierce heat of the base burner, Charlotte's perfume that hung delicately in the air. She sank further down in the little boudoir chair and crossed her ankles. She was suddenly at home.

"Anyway, I might get dressed." Charlotte got lazily out of bed and opened a door into a white and lavender bathroom. It was like a show window of the plumbing store in Clarion to Celie but her eyes showed no surprise.

"I'll feed Rose Marie while you're taking your bath, only I got to heat her bottle."

"Sure, come on in and heat it in the wash basin. The water in the taps is always boiling." Celie moved around feeling like someone else. Charlotte sang in the shower in a throaty voice that slurred her words together. Celie took up Rose Marie and sat down in the chaise longue to feed her. "She like music?" called Charlotte and sang the favorite Tricorne blues. Celie was happier than she had been in months. Some craving was satisfied. Joe faded out of her mind. She fed Rose Marie absent-mindedly. She hummed along with Charlotte without thinking much about it. Charlotte's voice ran on into "Sleepy Valley." Celie sang out. Her voice was clear and high against Charlotte's husky, vibrant tones. It rounded the ends of the lines like the full tones of a bell. Charlotte turned off the shower with "Singing in the Rain." Celie finished Rose Marie's bottle singing it, too. "Say, your voice isn't half bad," commented Charlotte, sitting down at the taffeta-flounced dressing table. "Not much style, but good tone. You ought to have come down to the Tricorne while I was there. I might have got you in on a number. You could have lived in the pent-house with Sally and me. Not that anyone would know it was a pent-house, but that's what we called it."

"Gee," said Celie wistfully.

"It's great stuff. I don't know why I ever came off up here." Celie finished with Rose Marie. "Here, put her on that puff on the floor," directed Charlotte.

Celie spread out the lavender puff and put Rose Marie on it. She did look sweet in her best white dress with the pink sweater Christina had made her.

"She smiles a lot now," Celie said to Charlotte, suddenly wanting her to admire her.

"Hi, baby." Charlotte waved her lipstick at her in the mirror. "Have another smoke?" Charlotte crossed to the closet. "Say, you know, I bet you could wear this

173

dark blue thing of mine." Charlotte was generous by sudden impulse. She looked over at Celie in her green silk. Her sharp eyes took only a moment to sum it all up. It was cheap but it had an air to it. "Here, try this on. I'm through with it, it's too tight." Celie forgot to be proud in her eagerness. She put on the dark wool dress with its deep white collar and cuffs. Instinctively, she modeled it, one hand on hip as she turned in front of the long glass in the bathroom door.

"Keep it, I'm sick of it," said Charlotte, getting into a vivid blue knit dress.

"Thank you," said Celie shyly.

"Lord, I wonder why I bother to get dressed up here at all." Charlotte flopped on the bed again and yawned. "That damned snow makes me cuckoo." Celie was still glowing from seeing the reflection of herself in the mirror. The dark dress made her hair look lighter, she told herself secretly. "It's a little big through the waist for you, but you can take it in."

"I guess I won't bother." Celie stopped short, aghast at herself. Charlotte's friendliness and the room had warmed her so she had been on the point of telling her even that. Charlotte noticed the sudden pause.

"Don't tell me you're going to have another baby, for heaven's sake?" she asked sharply. Celie flushed and nodded. "Say, you're a fool. Why do you have 'em? You'll be like all the rest of the women up here. I sh'd think one would teach you something."

"Oh, well, I don't mind, really."

"Well, you catch me getting into a jam like that," muttered Charlotte, smoothing her hair. "That's no way to help your husband along—having a lot of kids."

Celie sat silent. She realized of a sudden that Joe had dropped completely out of her mind for the first time since that day at Mead. She watched Rose Marie trying to turn over on the puff and thought if only it weren't for the baby and Joe she could get ahead, know people that lived the way Charlotte Farley did.

"You're just a kid yourself, aren't you? I bet you aren't more than twenty-one, are you?" asked Charlotte.

"I'm eighteen," said Celie, feeling like a child beside Charlotte.

"Oh, my God!" said Charlotte.

"We're going to Clarion tonight to a show." Celie wanted to prove that they went places and did things. She said it casually as though they did it every night or so. "Why don't you and Arthur come, too?"

"Don't care if we do. Something to break the monotony, anyway. We can all go in our car 'cause it's closed."

For Celie, the rest of the day was shadowed by the thought of the night's trip. Life had altered since morning. It was as much wider than the life of the Point as the big house on the bluffs was than the cramped box-like house next to the fox farm. Celie herself, walking down the carpeted stairs to lunch, felt like a different person. She caught sight of herself in the mirror over the mantel. It must be somebody else sitting there having a picture salad with a real night club singer from Detroit.

When Joe and Arthur started back they were in high spirits. Joe had had the first shot at a deer, but he had let Farley fire the second shot and tie his license tag on him. Farley had promised him ten dollars for it, but Joe laughed.

"Maybe you can do me a turn. I don't want to file saws on the night shift all year."

"Don't blame you, let's have a drink on it," young Farley answered, expansively offering him his silver flask he used to carry in the orchestra at the Tricorne. "You know, you'd make a good foreman, I bet. I'll put you in before spring."

Joe thought how proud Celie would be, how they would buy a new car. Those Plymouths were sweet jobs. He hadn't been so dumb, after all, sticking on here. Celie couldn't see ahead any. Young Farley was feeling pretty good, but he could remind him of it, anyway.

By four-thirty, it was dark in the corners of the long living room at Farley's. The falling flakes, smaller now, but falling steadily, were almost imperceptible outside the windows. There was a fire in the fireplace and the big lamp on the heavy library table spread a wide patch of yellow light, but Celie felt uneasy. She remembered the story of Hilton killing himself here. The very heaviness of the big club chairs oppressed her.

"Let's go out and meet them. If I could leave Rose Marie with Urna, I know which way they'll come," Celie said to Charlotte.

"O.K. It's cold out, I bet."

They walked out into the winter's dark along the track. Celie in her old lapin jacket and her best opera pumps inside her galoshes. Charlotte in a big racoon coat but with opera pumps of lizard inside her galoshes.

" 'Tisn't as cold as it was, but there's more wind," commented Celie in a manner not unlike Ole Henderson's.

"It's all fierce to me. Glad they're getting some of this snow in Detroit."

"Gee, do you hear that lake?" Celie had to turn to catch her breath against the wind. Above them, the tops of the tall trees rattled against each other. The wind called to all that was wild in the dusk. The voices of the two figures plodding along on the tracks were lost in the deep roar of the lake. The thick dusk steadily blotted out their forms as fast as they advanced and made them part of the swaying shadows of the woods.

"I s'pose they'll be dead bunnies when they get back and want to call off the Clarion trip," snorted Charlotte.

"Joe promised me we'd go. That was the last thing he said. It'll be fun going in together. There, look, isn't that them?"

"Duckie'll drop over to see me playing the big woodswoman."

5

W HEN they came out of the movie in Clarion, it was still snowing.

"There's a swell place to get red-hots across the street," said Celie.

"Come on." Young Farley took her arm and they ran across the street. Charlotte was finding Joe Linsen an amusing change from Arthur. They sat on the high stools of Hacula's place. Celie laughed for sheer high spirits. This was living; going places and knowing people like Charlotte.

"Char, didn't you like the dress she wore in the big scene?" she called past young Farley.

"And could he love?" Char rolled her eyes. "You've lost me, darling." She waved her hand mockingly at Farley.

"After your husband got a big buck, too!" scoffed Joe.

Joe walked over to the front to get a light. He looked out the window uneasily.

"Come on, we better take the wieners along. It's beginning to drift," he called back to them.

They piled into the bright blue Ford.

"Wow! what a night!" Farley lowered the window and reached around to wipe the windshield.

"Just like a corn-popper; want me to drive, boy?"

"Maybe you better, if you know the road blind. I can't tell where it goes in this blizzard." Joe got out and took Farley's place. Charlotte began singing. Cele and Farley joined in. Joe sat up straight in the seat, his head thrust a little forward. Occasionally the car swerved. He swore softly.

"Say, no kidding, I don't know whether we can make it or not. Look at that!" The four stared through the snowy windshield.

"Can't see a thing and don't know that there's anything there to see, thanks," said Charlotte, "only if there's any chance of getting stuck, I'm going back."

"We've only come a mile and a half from town and I can't see any track ahead. What do you say, shall we go back?"

"Turn her around, I say," said Farley, "Clarion for me."

"Any place where it's warm," chimed in Charlotte.

Celie said nothing for a minute. She was trying to peer through the snowy windshield. Snow lay everywhere, draping the stumps and fenceposts out of all recognition. It sparkled in the path of the machine's headlights.

"Oh, Joe, I've got to get back to Rose Marie. Mamma couldn't come over, you know, and I got that little Wilhelm girl."

"She's all right, Cele. Mrs. Wilhelm'll probably go over. What on earth could happen to her?" Joe reassured her.

All the fun of the evening dropped away from her. Celie sat up as straight as she could on Arthur Farley's knees. Her face was tense in its earnestness. "Joe, really, I got to get back. I don't know, but I just can't leave her all night."

"Well, we'll drive you back to the hotel and then start out. Maybe Cele'll change her mind by then," said Joe.

"Oh, Joe, it's drifting worse all the time. I never should have come." Tears stood in Celie's eyes.

Charlotte reached for the door handle. "Didn't we just pass a house on the left hand side?"

"Yeah, 'bout two rods back," said Joe.

"Well, Duckie and I'll walk back that far and you go on. Celie'll have hysterics if you don't get there."

They piled out. "It's a bad night, all right," commented Farley. "Sure you'll make it, Joe?"

"Well, we can turn back. Maybe you'll see us yet. Sure you can walk to that house?"

"You bet, come on, Char."

Celie paid little attention to anything. She was in a fever to get off. An unaccountable feeling of guilt rushed over her.

"Celie, you're a fool, honest. Nothing can happen to Rose Marie."

"I know, Joe, but I have to get home; please, don't you see?"

Joe set his mouth and drove. "Keep wiping her, Cele, that windshield wiper don't do any more good than a fly-swatter." They drove in silence. Joe tried to talk once or twice. "Don't you think Char's nice, really, Cele?"

An hour before Cele would have talked excitedly about young Farley's wife, now she only answered "Mmm-hmm." She cleaned a place on her side of the windshield and looked out into the night until her eyes smarted, but the snow covered it over again.

"Feel it under the wheels, feel her pull, Cele?"

Celie thought of Rose Marie trying to turn over on the puff in Charlotte's room. She would never leave her with a kid again. The Wilhelm girl wasn't more than thirteen. What if Rose Marie should have convulsions again? Worry was new to Celie. It made its way uncomfortably into her self-centered young mind and left its mark.

"Damn it! We're way off the road again." The car sputtered and the wheels turned without traction. Joe backed and tried it again. The slipping sound of the wheels, turning without advancing struck fear in Celie's heart. Again they backed and drove at the white drifting snow top speed. The wheels took a hold. The car went ahead.

"Do you, you do think we'll make it all right, Joe?"

"Oh, I guess so. May take us till morning, but we'll get there."

Now that he was in for it, this sort of a ride exhilarated Joe. Something in him responded to the excitement of it. This country couldn't get the best of him, not by a long shot. He knew this road. It curved here

. . . no, it didn't either. They must have passed the place. They must be ten miles on their way, anyway. Funny thing they couldn't see the fence along the Blind River. It came in here, some place. The road was down grade. That helped to ease the weight of snow against the wheels. It was halfway to the top of the radiator some places right in the road, now. The snow whirled more slowly against the windshield.

"It's slacking, Joe. Now aren't you glad we came?"

"Sure, but it ain't stopped drifting any." A gust of wind whirled the snow across the path of the car and banged against the side. It came in around the door and windows and up through the floor in a fine white spray. Celie pulled her legs up under her. The car plunged through a drift; the snow flew up like a white cloud around them. They could hear it pelt against the top.

"God, Cele, I don't know where I'm going, we may come out spank against a fence, I'm so mixed up. Anyway, we must've come fifteen miles. It's taken us long enough; it's quarter to two already and we left Clarion by eleven-thirty."

A sharp, clanging noise began . . .

"There goes the chain on the back wheel, Cele." Joe stopped and got out. He was gone too long, it seemed to Cele. She could see nothing. The snow whirled so close around the windows of the car. She shivered.

"Joe, Joe!" Fear made her voice more shrill. "Joe!" She was screaming now.

"Here I am, Cele." Joe opened the door. "But I can't

fix it; there's a piece of it gone." He threw the chain on the floor of the car. When he tried to sit down, the skirts of his overcoat were frozen stiff. "Take a hold, and bend it, Cele, will you?" Celie grasped the frozen hem on both sides. By main force, they bent it so Joe could sit on the seat.

"You'll get all wet, Joe."

"Can't be helped. Wish I hadn't got all dressed up and put on these no-good city things. If I had my old Soo woolens, I wouldn't even feel it."

"Oh, Joe, hurry, don't stand here." Joe started the engine. The car chugged and coughed.

"Bad starting on the up-grade like this." He backed and came ahead full speed like a battering ram. "There she goes, Cele." Cele felt herself leaning forward, half lifting her weight to her knees trying to help the car. "No use, Cele, look at that snow, banked up as solid as a wall." The car chugged up the grade, straight into the snow.

"Oh, Joe, give her gas. She won't make it . . . quick, Joe!"

"I've got my foot right down to the floor, silly." The engine struggled, missed a beat, gasped, died. The snow was even with the radiator in front. The night was suddenly quiet, broken only by the dull battering of the wind against the toy car stuck there in the snow. Inside the toy car, Joe whistled, "Well, that's all of that. If you hadn't been such a damned ass, we'd be in Clarion instead of parked here for the night."

Celie did not notice that Joe swore at her. "Joe, can't you shovel the car out? Don't just sit here . . ."

"What in hell's name good would it do?"

Suddenly Celie started crying. "Oh, Joe, Rose Marie . . . I've got to get there."

"Shut up, honey." Joe pulled her over to him. "We can't be more'n five miles from there. Maybe we can walk it." He opened the door on his side. The cold air rushed into the car, the snow whirled around them like so much confetti. "Are you strong, kid?"

"You bet, Joe." Celie had stopped crying. She opened the door on her side and got out. The snow was up above her waist in the drift. Her legs in their chiffon stockings felt bathed in ice. The wind blew through the lapin jacket as though through paper. Celie wallowed and plunged. Joe staggered through the drift, feeling his way around the car.

"All right, Cele?" He helped her out of the drift. The snow wasn't so high ahead. They plowed through it, keeping a hold of each other. The snow still sifted down so steadily they could see no more than a foot ahead. The wind blew a moving sheet of snow across in front of them and gathered the top snow into soft merciless ripples. That wind had risen in the greater forests of upper Canada and borne down across Superior, gathering power and wrath as it traveled. It had lashed the ice-cakes far up on the shore and churned the waves to a froth in a fierce, heathen joy. It could still terrify the petty humans who built their homes on this north point.

Celie was winded. She panted and choked. There was a sharp pain in her side. Joe helped her forward, half carrying her. Suddenly he stumbled.

"We're off again, Cele. That's a tree stump. We better get back before it's too late to find the car."

Celie was fighting for breath. The wind blew straight at her. She hid her face in Joe's wet coat for a second.

"Come on, we're going back to that car and be lucky to get there." Celie said nothing. She was chilled through. Her legs were too heavy to lift through the drifts. "Hold on to my coat, Cele." They groped and staggered back. Already the wind and snow had covered over their footprints. Celie followed blindly. There was no brim on her beret to keep the whirling snow out of her eyes. Her fingers held numbly to Joe's coat. "There, by God, we made it, Cele." They stumbled into the car and slammed the door against the snow. Celie could not stop shivering. Her teeth chattered. Joe pulled her over on his knees and stretched his coat around her. "You'll freeze to death, honey, if you don't." Celie was too tired to protest. Her wet legs ached dully. She put the fingers of one hand in her mouth to keep her teeth from chattering. Joe was cold, too. "Let's have a cigarette, Cele, that'll help." He lighted one for her. She held it between shaky fingers.

"It smells warm, Joe," she offered. Joe managed a short laugh.

"Well, we've got seven, kid, to last between now and morning and it's two o'clock. That oughta do us."

"Joe, do you think we'll freeze to death?" Celie said after a moment.

"Not on your life. We'll keep pinching each other." Their breath floated white in the cold air. Joe held Celie tight. "Look here, Cele, you put on this coat around your legs. I'll keep warm walking. I'm going to look around here a little."

"Joe, don't you dare leave me!"

Joe stood outside the car door for a minute. Celie rapped sharply on the pane. "Joe, I won't be left alone, I tell you."

Joe opened the door and got in again. "It wouldn't do any good; too much danger of my being lost and then where would we be? I couldn't tell where we are if you hanged me for it. Guess we'll stick it out here till morning, Cele."

They sat silent except that Celie's shivering was audible. Joe broke out suddenly, "Don't you dare tell anyone we got stuck in the snow, Celie. All the boys'll give me the laugh."

"How could you help it, Joe? It was all my fault."

"Aw, I ought to have known it'd drift out here on the plains. We'd be likely to get stuck up here."

"Will we have to wait till the plow comes, Joe?"

"I don't know, Cele. In the morning we can see where we are."

Celie slept a little with her head against the inner side of Joe's coat. She was too cold to sleep long. "Is it nearly morning, Joe?"

"You only slept about ten minutes, Cele. Here, have a cigarette to warm up with." Two red points were cheering in the dark. Joe shivered convulsively.

"Joe, you're freezing, too."

"Don't be silly, I was just shifting around a little," Joe answered crossly. "Go on to sleep again."

"I'm afraid of freezing to death, Joe, and not waking up."

"I'll wake you up. It won't be long now, Cele, it's stopped snowing, mostly."

About four in the morning, the wind died down, but the stillness deepened the cold. Celie fell asleep again. Joe took off his coat and spread the dry part of it over her. He tried to hold his breath now and again to stop his own convulsive shaking. He began to worry, himself, about freezing to death. Lumberjacks going back to camp after a good binge sometimes lay down in the snow and froze to death. In a car, this way, though, it was more protected, only it couldn't be much colder. A little wind blew against the car still, but not enough to raise the snow much. He believed he could make out his way now. He woke Celie.

"Cele, honey, listen, it's stopped blowing so I can follow my own tracks back and I'm going to see where we are. You wrap up warm with this. I'll keep warm walking."

In the light from the dash Celie looked pale and tired. "Joe, you won't get lost, sure?"

"Not on your life, Cele, anyway, you can follow my tracks now."

Joe started out in a straight line from the car, keeping as long as he could in the path of the car's headlights. He was so cold even walking didn't help. He moved along stiffly, falling whenever he didn't lift his feet high enough in the drifts. He stopped and looked back. Not very easy to make out his tracks. He felt a little sleepy himself. He yawned and fell to shivering again. He tried to hug himself with his arms. Then he saw a light, a tiny glow not much more than the point of a cigarette, up on the near side of the road. Joe wallowed through the snow toward it. If he'd had his own car he'd have had his snow shoes along. This city stuff wasn't meant for him.

The glimmer of light held steady, only it took so long to get to it. He must have been gone a good hour now. It was getting lighter over on that side, that was east then and the Point lay over in there. The black dark had changed to a dirty green dark. The light belonged to a house, a kind of shack. The shack puzzled Joe. He knew every building for fifteen miles on all sides of the Point, he prided himself. The only thing it could be was a shack put up by some city fellows out hunting. As he got closer to it, Joe recognized it as a shack Hans Nordgren, the game warden, used sometimes, a fellow Joe and the young fellows in the Point didn't stick around much. The warden was always changing his shack. He lived nearer the Point, Joe had thought, down by Sullivan's, but Joe couldn't have found it in the blizzard even if he had known it.

Celie was wide awake the minute that Joe was out of sight. The eerie desolation settled down on her. Anyway, no wild animals could get through the car windows. Celie sat up, her feet tucked under her. Her hand touched the metal of the window-frame: it was so cold it burned. Her fingers ached; they were the worst. Her whole body felt half its usual size, it was so shriveled with cold. Her feet had gone to sleep. The needle pricks made her feel alive, anyway . . . what if Gretchen Wilhelm hadn't covered Rose Marie up? She didn't tell her about pinning the blanket. Maybe Rose Marie was cold. Celie had stopped thinking about herself. Nothing mattered if only she got back to Rose Marie.

Poor little Rosie; she was such a happy baby, like Joe said. She didn't cry hardly at all. She was shy, though, she wouldn't let anybody hold her 'cept Joe and her. How could she have gone off and left her all evening with that Wilhelm girl that probably didn't know anything, anyway? She'd been so crazy to see a show she'd almost forgotten about her. Something went deep into Celie's consciousness that would always be part of it. She would never again be able to forget Rose Marie completely. If only she got back and found her safe!

The dirty-green darkness gave way to a thin, gray light. Black trees stood up along the road. The wind had blown all the snow out of them. They looked gaunt and cold. The fences were buried far out of sight along with yesterday's world. In all the smooth sweep of white snow the only track was the line of Joe's foot-holes. Celie watched the farthest point in the road.

Maybe this was to serve her right for not wanting the new baby. "Oh, Lord, I want the baby, I do, really," she breathed jerkily through her shivering. It would be warm in June when the baby came. The thought, somehow, cheered her.

The game warden came back with Joe. Joe was warm now after a drink of whisky and with a dry woolen jumper of the warden's on his back. He thought to himself of the two beaver pelts he had drying at home. Old Nordgren'd send him up for them quick enough if he got wind of 'em.

"Say, it's some easier this way!" Joe said.

"You kin tell it's cold to have a crust like this a-ready." Nordgren went ahead. His snow shoes left intricate markings in the snow. Joe followed. He was sleepy, coming out again into the cold. Damn it, if he'd only known Nordgren's shack was there!

Nordgren carried Celie back most of the way. Joe tried, but he made slower time than the warden.

"Not often I get such a chance, Linsen," laughed Nordgren.

Celie was uncomfortable on his back. Her ankles burned where his warm hands covered them. She was too numb to think how funny it was to be carried along pickaback on Hans Nordgren's shoulders. Suddenly she clutched his jumper.

"Mr. Nordgren, do you have a phone?"

"Sure, Mike, I got a phone an' got more'n that. I got a faun some of them city hunters shot down and said they thought it was a buck. I fined 'em for it an' brought it home; what else to do with it? I had me a steak last night. Say, it was tender. I cook one for you."

When Celie got the doctor's office at the Point, the doctor himself answered the phone. He would go over and tell Christina about the baby if she didn't have it already. He was sure it was all right. The county plow had started out as soon as the wind stopped. There was no need to worry. As Celie hung up the phone she remembered the last time she had sent a message through the doctor's office to Christina was to tell her she and Joe were married.

Celie lay down on Hans Nordgren's bunk. Hans and Joe sat by the stove talking. It was two in the afternoon when she woke up. She went back to the car on snow shoes. She could laugh again now and smile at Nordgren so the old Swede's heart warmed in him. He went with them down to the highway.

"You be lucky an your car ain' froze up." Ahead, they could see the plow, like some giant bug, fanning the deep snow into clouds above the top of the driver's box. Behind it, toward the Point, stretched a narrow road between the snow banks, just large enough for a car to pass.

"When I come up here, twenty years ago, an' we got snowed up, say! we stayed snowed up," said Hans

Nordgren. "Now, the Point might's well be one of those suburbs." He laughed at his witticism, and waved them off.

"Oh, Joe, drive fast, I can't wait to see Rose Marie," Celie said as soon as the car started.

"Oughta make seventy on this boulevard here." Joe pressed the accelerator to the floor. The bright blue car of Farley's streaked over the white road. Joe smiled with satisfaction as the speedometer climbed. "Seventy-two, that's what you call goin', eh, Cele?"

Already Celie and Joe had no memory of the cold terror of the night. It was splintered as fine as the particles of snow that sparkled ahead in the sun.

6

FOR a week in January snow fell in the Point. Monday, it fell steadily. Tuesday, a feeble sun languished until noon, but by afternoon had disappeared again behind the low white sky. Thursday, it grew colder and the *Clarion Daily* predicted clear weather, but snow came down instead, dry, white, soft, falling into every least crack and crevice. The angular peaks of the company houses became rounded white thatch, the sidewalks were footpaths between white walls, the bareness was covered, even the meanness turned picturesque.

To the wife of young Farley in the big house on the bluffs, the snow brought boredom and restlessness. She roamed around the house, applied new polish to her nails, smoked one cigarette after another, and twisted the knobs on the big radio by the living-room windows. Once she got the Tricorne in Detroit, but the static turned the rhythms to fire-crackers and crowded out the sound. She looked out of the windows across the lake. It was all an endless white. She turned her back on the windows and knew that she was tired of Arthur. The adventure had played out, that was all, and she was through. It was Friday that she went up to pack her things.

To Celie Linsen in the house by the fox-farm, the snow crowding against her windows that Friday night blocked out the world. Joe had gone to work. She was content to be in the warm, lighted kitchen with Rose Marie splashing and blowing in her bathtub on the table. She took two diapers from the warming oven and dried Rose Marie's wet chubby body in them. She held her up in the air and Rose Marie reached out for the swinging electric bulb.

"Baby honey, will you go in the movies when you grow up? And live in a grand house in Hollywood?"

She held her on her knees and dressed her. A kind of pleasure came to her from the clean, warm clothes. She pulled the blue gingham romper down over the baby's head. Rose Marie made gurgling sounds as the starched ruffle on the collar tickled her fat neck. "You beat any baby-ads in the magazines I ever saw; now,

193

sit up in that chair and watch Celie make a cake and don't throw things 'cause she won't pick 'em up."

Celie moved about the kitchen, singing. She was full of energy and happy for the moment. She went out to the woodshed to get her bowl of eggs and stopped to look out the door. The falling snow made the darkness seem lighter. The white ground seemed to throw up a light of its own. Celie thought of the road a quarter of a mile from Hans Nordgren's shack. She slammed the door and tipped the chopping block against it. It was good to go back to the bright kitchen and Rose Marie.

Young Farley had no time to watch the snow that Friday afternoon. He sat at his desk in the superintendent's office and re-read the letter in front of him for the second time.

"It will be necessary to drop out the night shift completely. There is no improvement in business. There is nothing that I can point to in your management as showing any direct money value. Some of them here are beginning to get critical. Nash and Jones and Mc-Nalty are coming up with me Saturday to look things over. Better plan to throw 'em a party at the house. Tell Charlotte to give 'em the works . . ."

Young Farley frowned. He hadn't liked this job in the first place. Now they were coming up to find fault with him, were they? Through the opaque glass in the office door he saw the stubby silhouette of Stumpf, the walking boss.

"Come in," he called.

"I wasn't waitin' any," commented Stumpf who found the young city fellow in the office a trial to his idea of the fitness of things. He never failed to show his superiority to him. "I hear ye told the boys to cut way to the edge of the Markheim road. Well, the boys gen'lly gets their orders through me an' the day for stealin' anybody else's timber is went, least any of the Markheims'. 'Course it's nothin' to me an' I ain't carin' what you do, but you're over the boundary there, an' you'll have a law-suit on your hands 'at'll be a purty 'un." Without waiting for comment, Stumpf opened the door and clumped out.

Young Farley's growing sense of inferiority to the job in front of him added yet another degree. He didn't know enough about this job and he wasn't kidding the men any. He hadn't been too sure about that boundary when he gave the order. When Lorenson, the foreman, came in, Arthur Farley braced himself. Lorenson knocked and waited for an answer. He was a mild dispositioned Swede who always seemed respectful.

"Mr. Farley, I came to tell you I got a job over in Menominee in the knitting mills. You see, that yard job takes it out of ye"—his tone was apologetic—"an' my wife's people live over there an' they got the job for me, so I'll be leaving if it's all right with you."

Young Farley smiled. He felt almost grateful to Lorenson for his attitude. Here was an opening for Joe Linsen now that the night shift was going off. He would hate to fire him some way. Besides, Linsen would be loyal to him, not like Stumpf.

"Well, Lorenson, that's all right. We're sorry to lose you, but it is a hard job down there, out in all weather . . ." Young Farley's dramatic sense came to the fore; it prompted his gesture as he put out his hand to shake the astonished Swede's. "Here, Lorenson, have a cigar."

Tim Lorenson went out of the company offices smoking a cigar, a sheepish look on his face.

Joe Linsen filing on the night shift, Friday night, was restless, too, but not because of the snow. It was still hard to get down to this tinker's job, to become accustomed to the grating noise of the file, the glare of the drop lights. His eyes tired, watching the up and down zig-zags of the big saw teeth. What if Farley should make him yard foreman! He hadn't even dared tell it to Celie. The little half-crazy Finn, Yerki, who filed with him looked over at him and grinned an empty, toothless grin.

"Sleepy, huh?" he jibed.

Joe grunted and shrugged his shoulders.

Charlotte Farley left her suitcase packed the next morning, but she snapped the lid and pushed it under the bed. When the old boys took the sleeper back to Detroit, little Charlotte would be on it, too.

She didn't mind the drab, frozen village today, knowing that tomorrow she would step off the train in

Detroit. She even joked with the queer old duck of a butcher.

"Make those steaks thick, butch, two or three inches at least; they're for big beef boys."

"Don't often cut 'em tik like that," murmured old Quinn admiringly. He liked ladies who ordered quality meats instead of soup-bone or wieners.

Charlotte was in so good a humor she laughed at the old lumberjack with the arm gone, bobbing his head to wipe his nose against his shoulder. She liked the admiring glances from the lumberjacks in the company pool room and smiled at the fat Austrian woman who glued her eyes on Charlotte's silk ankles as she passed. She could hear herself back in Detroit telling how she was Mrs. Heaven to the town God forgot. Just as she turned the car off toward the stone posts that marked the road to the big house, she thought of Celie Linsen. She looked quite smart when she got a decent dress on her. Poor little thing, she'd go on having a baby every other year and never get away from this dump. Funny, Joe wasn't half bad. She bet he could dance; good-looking enough to be in the movies, getting fan mail, but not the kind you bet on to make a pile. On a sudden impulse, young Mrs. Farley turned the car about and drove up to the end of town.

She knocked at the door that stood so abruptly at the top of the three steps. She had to wait some minutes, then Joe came. He was taken back to find her there. He stood, embarrassed in his old red and green bathrobe, his union suit showing beneath it, his hair down over his face.

Charlotte Farley laughed. "I forgot all about your being on the night shift and came around to ask you to come over to dinner. We're having kind of a dinner party because the old man and his buddies are coming up from Detroit. It seems they're kind of grouchy and the idea is to give 'em a real party."

"I'll be working, that's the only thing, but Celie, maybe she could go. Come in an' I'll call her."

Charlotte looked around the little room curiously, but it was not unlike the cramped parlour of the upstairs apartment in Detroit she had known herself before the palmy days of the Tricorne.

In the bedroom, Celie argued fiercely with Joe. "You should see the negligee she has, Joe. I can't go out like this with my nightgown showing."

"Well, you can't keep her waiting all day, either."

In sudden desperation, Celie grabbed the shiny, blue rayon bedspread from the foot of the bed and draped it around her. The crude, bright blue was becoming to her. She stepped into her cold leather pumps. Her old bedroom slippers were too far from the silver mules under Charlotte's bed. She came into the parlor, wearing her improvised negligee.

"Hello."

"Say, I'm sorry I got you up. I forgot this was night for you, but I wondered if you could come over to a dinner party I'm giving."

Celie's eyes sparkled. The words dinner party sounded so grand. "Why, I'd like to. I wish Joe could come."

"I'll ask Duckie; maybe he can fix it up." Charlotte hesitated, a little embarrassed. "You looked so good in that blue wool dress, I . . . you could wear a dinner dress I have. It's kind of a funny purple, makes me look sallow. I'll send it over to you."

When she had gone, Celie went back to bed, but not to sleep.

"Joe, imagine her inviting us!"

"Why not?" inquired Joe, under blankets. "Maybe I'll be a foreman of this whole place yet."

Saturday night, snow still fell, but life flourished in the Point. It was pay night, for one thing. Sam Andres walked up the street with his envelope. He had already subtracted one dollar for himself, the rest, after the money for rent and the store bill and the doctor's fee and the mutual benefit were subtracted by the company bookkeeper, the whole five dollars of it, went to Anna Andres. He begrudged her this, tonight. She had been cold to him lately and she'd run into Clarion twice that he knew of and had a new coat he didn't know where she got it from. If she was double-crossing him, she could just get out from under his roof. He went into the house, four below Linsens'.

Anna Andres was a big woman with classic, regular features; a look of complete peace lay on them although it had nothing to do with the few thoughts and petulant animal nature behind it. She looked up as Sam came in without speaking. Her eyes rested on him while he took out his envelope and put it on the shelf over the sink as usual.

"Hush your crying, damn you," she said to the baby creeping around the stove, but her voice had no unusual vehemence. Anna Andres had learned swear words when she learned English. "And you get that water I told you, quick." A lanky boy came out from the sitting room and took the pail from the shed. A girl who was dark and short like Sam poured coffee into the thick cups on the table. "Well, you kin eat now. I'm going out to Farleys to help that Urna wait table," Anna Andres announced. "She's having doings."

"You keep your ears open an' hear if they do any talking about a cut. Some of the boys at the yard said the timekeeper told Sven Melby when he kicked about his envelope, that next year at this time he'd be lucky if he got half that."

"Did he say how a person could live?" asked Anna Andres grimly.

"Naw, they don't think of that, them city guys."

Four houses above, at Linsens', life bubbled merrily. Christina had come over and was feeding Rose Marie her breakfast while Celie dressed in the bedroom.

"Mamma, wait till you see this." Celie came out to the kitchen in the old dinner gown of Charlotte's. It was a dull purple that fitted tightly about the bodice and

200

hips and flared in back to the floor. The dress was held together at the neck by gleaming straps and fell off at the shoulders. Celie's light hair and fair skin against the lurid purple color gave her a childlike look.

Christina grunted. "It's too bad Ole can't see you. He liked all them actressy clothes." There was a pause. "But he never thought much of that young Farley or even his uncle. I don't like your getting in with them, Cele."

Cele laughed. She wished she had slippers to match or silver ones instead of wearing the old green ones. But the color might have been worse.

"How you goin' to get over there?" queried Christina.

"Oh, I'll walk. I'll put on my galoshes and hold the skirt up."

"I sh'd think they could come for you."

"Oh, well, I don't mind." Celie was too elated to worry about such details. She was breathless as she ran down the middle of the road. She couldn't stop to walk. The falling snow turned the worn off fur of her collar into soft ermine. Snow gathered on the brim of her hat like a fantastic wreath. The falling snow shut out the village as completely as Celie's thoughts shut it from her mind. She was wide awake even though she hadn't slept much yesterday. It was just like a newspaper serial not having dinner till seven and being dressed up in a dress that touched the floor and felt as though it would fall off your shoulders. This was the sort of thing she'd always wanted to do. It was funny to stay right in the

Point and be doing these things. Maybe after all, Joe could work up in the mill and some day Charlotte and Arthur would move to Detroit and they'd take her and Joe with them and they'd live there. She wished there were going to be other people there. She had seen the big shots. They weren't much. They always came to the store and talked about too much over-head and waste and profits falling off. She knew old Farley. He always came through the store and grinned at the girls. But, anyway, it was a dinner party, it was going some place. She could see the milky streak the Farleys' porch light cut through the snow. She wished Joe could have come and driven her up under the driveway roof in style.

Urna opened the door and showed Celie upstairs.

"Let me see you, Cele," Char called out from her room. Celie went in, dropping her jacket on the bed, the way they did in movies.

"Not bad, not bad at all; in fact, too good for the old goats downstairs. Here, let me do your lips for you. You get it too thick."

Celie held her lips firm while Charlotte touched them up. She stole a glance at herself in Charlotte's mirror. She felt shy with herself, but excited.

"That dress is too formal if anyone should ask you, but what's that to us?"

They went down the wide stairs to the living room. The four men at the other end rose as they came. Celie held herself very straight as she walked across the long heavy room. Mr. McNalty rose a little heavily by

202

reason of his 200 pounds, Mr. Farley pulled himself out of the big chair by its arms, Mr. Jones rubbed his chin and took off his half-glasses. They had come for business. McNalty and Jones had doubts about Farley putting his nephew in there. It had been accomplished with many drinks; the inquiry would be accomplished likewise, with more drinks and Charlotte's shrewdness.

"Celie, you know Arthur's uncle, and this is Mr. McNalty . . ." Charlotte introduced them with a sarcastic droop to her lips.

They had drinks and a big tray of crackers covered over with sharp, fishy-smelling paste. Celie took one and wanted to spit it out quickly, but she swallowed it and listened to Mr. McNalty talk about the rough ride up on the sleeper. The drinks were strong and too tart. She liked beer better. She was so hungry she had to have another of the horrid little crackers.

They went in to dinner in the big room that was paneled with curly maple. The wallpaper above the high wainscoting had picture trees but lacked the wasteful stumps and underground tangle of Michigan woods. Candles on the table threw points of light into the wallpaper forest. The table was long and oval, a spacious expanse after the kitchen table that Celie set each day.

"Old Hilton sure knew how to do things, didn't he? Look at these dishes an' this dining room, and all . . . and then killed himself."

"He didn't wait for a real crash either," put in Jones.

"Stop your talk about crashes and listen to this one."

Char commented, imperiously. She knew how to sympathize with men, how to win them around, but best of all, how to boss them. Charlotte was pretty and had a way with her. She liked being hostess at a dinner party, even for three old men. Having Celie was a wild impulse, but Char was glad she invited her. She was like a kid at a party.

Three old codgers feeling sore about their losses. Charlotte felt she was through with Arthur and the double-chinned old man, his uncle. No reason why she should bother with them and for that reason she laughed readily and often. She listened to the story of old McNalty's operation and what Nash paid for his shares of General Motors. Once in a while, she looked over at Celie Linsen, a new person in the dull purple dress. Celie was looking at old Farley with serious eyes. Arthur Farley, on Celie's other side, leaned over.

"Say, Celie, this is Joe's last time on the night shift. He's taking Lorenson's place, Monday, as yard foreman." Celie forgot that she had been hating the way old Farley's eyelids hung over his eyes.

"Arthur, really? And maybe we can have another house with a bathroom and an extra bedroom?"

Arthur laughed. "Ask the old man there."

"Can we, Mr. Farley? You see with the baby, it's kind of crowded."

Old Farley took another drink. Why did Char get a married girl to dinner who would have to be worrying about her house all the time, but pretty in a cold Swede way, she was. "Sure, give her Lorenson's house, Art."

Celie glowed the rest of the evening. The evening grew long and dull. Black cigars filled the air with smoke. Things blurred in front of Celie's eyes and she wondered if she were tight. Only the French Canadians and some of the Austrian women ever got drunk in the Point. The camp followers, of course, but they didn't count. Celie's shoulders drooped a little; she was tired, her eyes smarted from the smoke. But maybe they would change their minds about Joe being foreman or giving them a new house if they didn't like her. She sat up straight again.

Old Farley came over to the end of the leather couch and put his arm around her. Celie Linsen pulled away from it, but smiled. He was a bold old man, fat and wrinkled, not like Ole her father. A wave of missing Ole Henderson went through her. Ole was as solid as . . . as the woods. She'd never thought very much about him before, except when he died. He was never afraid of his job on the pond and lots of men wouldn't dare take it. There never was any fear in him or near him. That was why he gave you such a secure, safe feeling. She missed it when she went up to see Christina. Christina was full of worries and gloomy fears. A picture of Ole came to her mind, hearty and solid, smoking his pipe after dinner.

She looked at the others and Charlotte singing with the radio to McNalty. Arthur would look like the rest, some day, like his uncle, maybe. They were all different from Ole and Joe, they didn't belong here, nor were they part of the place like Ole; they made her think, suddenly, of that man who had shot himself in this very room. Nothing would ever have made Ole do that, or Joe.

"You'll have to come in to Clarion and have dinner with me next time I come, eh?" Old Farley tightened his arm around her. "Say, Art, maybe we better keep this girl's husband on the night shift. Maybe that's a good place for him," he called across the room. Celie shrank a little from his joking.

"Too late, Farley, there ain't goin' to be any more night shift. An' we'll either have to give a cut or run four days a week," Jones, who had drunk less than the rest, called back. Jones looked across at young Farley with contempt, piano player—no mill boss he was.

"Lay off business till morning," Char broke in. "I'll sing for you." Her husky voice, scarcely singing, rose through the smoke-filled room. She would go back to the Tricorne and be singing again. She'd learned her lesson, now, maybe, unless she found a man, sometime, like that ignorant Swede, Joe Linsen, Celie had. He could keep a woman, she bet, but that kind liked his Swedish Celie, too, who'd have him a baby a year . . . nothing in it, any of it, not for her. Charlotte's voice that was scarcely music, crooned just off key, "Happy days are here again."

Anna Andres, putting away silver in the dining room, listened to the talk. That littlest brat of hers needed codliver oil like the doctor said; what did that man from Detroit mean about four days' work a week?

The heads of the Lake Superior Lumber Company, up from Detroit on business, took the three o'clock sleeper from Clarion. As usual, they had left the investigation they had come for unfinished. Charlotte's husky crooning had not been interrupted. Arthur drove them to Clarion in the company car, glad to get rid of them. Back at the house, Charlotte Farley put her suitcase in the bright blue Ford. She must take care not to pass them on the road. She drove through the empty street of the Point. What a hole to get herself stuck in. Poor Cele, but then, she was dumb, or she wouldn't stay here.

The long week of the snow was over. It was clear and the stars were out when Joe Linsen came up from work.

Part IV

THE Monday after the dinner party at Farleys', Joe and Celie went back on the day shift. They didn't mind getting up in the black early morning, knowing it would be daylight in another hour. Everything Celie did that morning took on a new color and excitement. She stirred up a cake by the kitchen window with the sun coming in on the bowl and the yellow batter and flashing along the whirling edges of the egg-beater. She took her pan of washing out to hang on the line and looked over to see Mrs. Nurmi in her kitchen window. Everything was easier to do, knowing that all the other women in the Point were busy, too. She wheeled Rosie down to the store in the afternoon, sliding along the icy walks like one of the children in the Point. She had a visit with Nellie Hann and Mrs. Bernsen over by Mrs. Munsen's counter, and stopped in at the Post Office even though she didn't expect any mail. It was almost like being born a baby again into a new world. With the electricity on, the light was the same yellow glare all night; now, in the daytime, the light changed, shifting its brightness around to the bedroom window in the afternoon. It seemed to Celie that the lavender-blue twilight came just for her. She sat by the window in the sitting room holding Rosie until it was almost black outside. Then she switched on the light and went out to get supper.

Joe came up from the mill-yard whistling. He'd stopped in at the store on his way home and bought some cigarettes and a newspaper. He'd been working outdoors all day and his face was red with the cold. Some of the fresh frosty air clung to his jumper and wool cap as he hung them up on the back of the kitchen door. They had supper and Joe sat down afterwards to read the paper while Celie did the dishes. They were oddly self-conscious this first evening off the night shift. Their remarks took on significance beyond the ordinary.

"You know, Joe, I believe Rose Marie understands we're both back on the day shift, 'cause she went right to sleep tonight just as though it was daytime," Celie said.

"You feel more like doing things around the house in the evening than you do when you get back from work in the morning. I'll get some lumber and fix those shelves for you tomorrow night."

"Joe, we could walk down and see Selma and Norm, or go over to see Mamma." They felt rich in the things they could do now that they were living like normal people again.

"It's not bad just to stay home an evening," Joe said over his pipe. "I might try the radio; you couldn't get anything but recipes and advertising when you'd turn on the radio in the morning, 'member?" Joe went in to the radio. He moved the knob around just to hear the multiplicity of sounds that filled the air. "Know what that is, Cele? That's coming from a dance place in Los Angeles, California."

"You seem to have more time, or it's more yours or

something at night," Celie said, hanging up her dish-cloth. "I mean, if it was daytime, I'd think I ought to be doing something, but at night, naturally, you just sit around. Let's go in the sitting room, Joe, just for fun. We never use it the way Ole and Mamma used to."

They went into the living room. Joe sat down in the one big chair. Celie curled on the couch. "You know, I'll kind of hate to leave this house, Cele," Joe said.

"I like it, too, but we really ought to take a better house with you having a better job."

"And is it a better job? Say! it's something like it, Cele, a regular man's job. You should see me. I have a big chart and I go 'round and check in all the lumber. I bet there's fifty million foot down there in the yard this minute . . ."

Celie listened woman-wise. Joe liked his job again. She was planning about the new baby. She only half heard the words, but she heard the heartiness and confidence in his tone. They told her more than the amount of lumber.

Joe filled his pipe. "Celie, aren't you glad we didn't go off away some place and get a new job just before I got this chance?"

Woman-wise, Celie answered, "I don't know, Joe, you might have a better one some place, by now. I'm not any crazier about the place than I ever was."

"Why, Cele, where could I go where I'd be on intimate terms, you might say, with the head of the place, like I am here with Art Farley?"

Celie could not put it into words, but she remembered the feeling of insecurity she had had that night out at Farley's, about Art and all of them. Christina said Ole never had much use for them. Celie thought how nice Art was to Joe. She leaned back and forgot her uneasy feeling. Selma Lichtenberg would have given a lot to go out there for dinner.

"What d'ye say, Cele, we go to bed early tonight just to see how it feels to sleep at night without the Nurmis making whoopee all the time."

They went into the little bedroom. It was more isolated from the Point at night, with the darkness around its window. There was nothing beyond the dimensions of their room.

"Imagine loving you at night again, Cele?"

"I hated the nightshift, really, and I couldn't bake worth a cent at night," said Celie. Their voices sank to a murmur, an endearment, silence. Then they, too, slept, a childlike sleep as deep as Rose Marie's.

2

THE next afternoon, Celie dressed Rose Marie in her best. She herself put on the dark wool dress and arranged her hair with infinite pains. She went quickly past Mrs. Nieberg's front windows. Mrs. Nieberg had invited her to have coffee, but Celie wanted to see Charlotte. She wanted to live in the glamorous world that Charlotte knew. It was more exciting to talk to her than to read a serial story.

Rose Marie was growing too heavy to carry. She borrowed the Nurmi boy's sled and put her in a box on top. It was heavy pulling where the snow was soft. Celie had to stop for breath by the big stone posts that marked the road to Farleys'.

Going out here was like having a secret from all the Point. That dinner party . . . Celie's mind had kept away from it. It was the only dinner party she had ever known, but it was not good to think of. Even Charlotte had seemed to laugh too loudly. Celie had been glad to get home, but Char was different alone.

Celie picked up the rope of the sled and started on. Coming toward her in the road was the tall, loose-jointed figure of Joe's father. He was always untalkative on the street, always intent upon some pursuit of his own. As they came together, Celie smiled, coolly.

" 'Lo, Lin."

But today, Lin Linsen stopped. "Hello, Celie, that's a heavy drag you got."

"It's all right," Celie answered impatiently.

"What you headed out this way for?" Lin picked Rose Marie out of the sled as he asked it.

"Oh, Lin, I just got her tucked all in," Celie broke out.

"A grandfather's got to see his grandchild when he

kin," Lin answered mildly. He looked at Celie with his bright, quick gaze. He knew she didn't take to him. That was all right; no woman could understand a man wanting to live by himself and cook his own victuals; it made her mad. Linsen was fond of children. Most of the small boys of the town knew their way to his shack. He settled Rose Marie in his arm.

"Damn funny thing Joe should have a girl first," he grunted.

Celie pouted a little. "Lin, put her in or she'll get cold."

"Where you goin'? I'll walk along with you and carry her for you."

"Oh, no, I'm going out to see Mrs. Farley." Celie said it importantly. She didn't want him to come along; he always looked so backwoods.

He started ahead. There was nothing for Celie to do but fall in step with him.

" 'Course you know she's cleared out," said Lin Linsen slowly, as he walked along. Celie was silent in angry amazement.

"How would you know all about it?"

He shrugged. Lin Linsen had a mean humor in him. "I was just out here seein' if I could get a steady order from them for fish this summer an' I seen the young fella; he oughta know."

Celie stood still irresolutely. She hated Lin Linsen. She couldn't stand it to have Char gone. She plowed the snow with her foot. If she kept on Lin would come all the way with her.

As though he knew he had goaded her far enough, Lin put the baby back in her improvised seat on the sled, tucking her in as carefully as any woman could.

"She wasn't much from what I see of her, Cele," he said as he stood up.

What would he know, Lin Linsen that everybody called a hermit. Celie's anger boiled in her at him and Joe for having him for a father. "I didn't know you knew her so well," she snapped, her eyes flashing.

Lin looked at her placidly, his own eyes as calm as Superior in the sun. He'd always thought it was queer Joe married Celie. Joe was like himself, not the kind for a husband. But Celie was pretty when she got mad. Lin shrugged again.

"I didn't think she'd last much longer than that; city women don't up here; too lonesome for 'em. The young fella was plenty cut up, though, when I see him just now. Guess she skipped out on him." Lin had a malicious bent for gossip in his nature. He looked at Celie.

All the anger and animation had gone from her. Her face was cold and pinched in the late winter light.

"You ought nota stand here, Celie," said Lin more gently.

Celie glanced at the big wooden house ahead without speaking. It loomed up dark and lonely against the gray-white sky. Lin followed her glance.

"He's gonna shut it up, he told me. I guess he don't

know where he's at. 'S no place for him, anyhow, trying to run a sawmill; maybe he'll follow her down where he b'longs."

A sudden desire worked up through Celie's stunned thoughts. She wanted to see young Farley. She didn't know what she would say to him, but she would know when she saw him. They mustn't close up this house and go away; it was too lonely here without the lights in the windows. It seemed to Celie that there were no houses in the Point but this and her own. If they went . . . maybe Art could find a place for Joe in Detroit.

"Lin, you go on; I'm fine now, I'm going to take my time walking back." Cele bent over to fix Rosie's blanket again.

Lin watched her, seeing her more clearly than Joe ever would. Lin knew the lake, all her sudden, fickle moods and wiles. The knowledge had gone deep into him without his thinking of it, making him as intuitive as any woman. You couldn't change the lake; it taught you that; same way with people. Lin had left Celie and Joe alone when he saw how Celie felt. He missed Joe, but Joe'd be out on the lake again; he couldn't keep away. Hels told him Joe had traps again. When a man was first married he stuck around home, but after he got used to it, he was the same as before.

"Well, I'll cut down over here, I guess. It's shorter to the lake. 'By, littl'un," he said to Rosie, and turned across the field.

Celie watched him go, his loosely built figure with

its careless stride. She tried not to see how his shoulders swung back like Joe's. Then she picked up the rope of the sled and started on toward the big house. She wanted to hear from Art himself about Char.

Up through the gray-white light came the five-thirty whistle, shrill, relentless, inevitable as the deepening dusk. Celie hesitated. From this point on the bluff, she seemed almost even with the tops of the mill-stacks. The low sheds with their big windows were lighted as though for a carnival. The lights twinkled through the dusk at her and at the dark house beyond.

Celie turned around. Her impulse died at the sound, pushed out by the things the whistle made imperative. Joe would be up from the mill. Supper would be late as it was. Involuntarily, as though without choice, she fell into the rhythm of the mill whistle, she who had never lived a day beyond its sound, whose very birth had fallen between some certain two of its shrill commands. She'd forgotten how late it was when she started.

The way back was twice as long. The soft snow clogged the runners of the sled. It was colder and more bleak, knowing that Charlotte had gone, spurning the town like a dress she was through with.

Celie reached the big stone posts at the end of the mile long drive just as Joe came up from the mill. He was hungry tonight and in a hurry to eat and be off with Hels to look at traps. He was startled to come on Celie here instead of home. It offended his sense of the fitness of things to have her out so late. He spoke more roughly than he felt. His voice sounded to Celie too nearly like Lin's.

"What are you doing here, Cele?"

She lifted her head. Some sudden whim moved her to anger him.

"Oh, I thought I might see Art Farley." It was a little girl impulse. Celie hadn't played with Joe since they were married. She could see his face even in the half-dusk redden and grow stern. That was all she wanted. Her own voice softened. "Here, Joe, you pull Rosie; she got so heavy."

Without a word, Joe took the sled-rope and strode ahead. Celie followed. He went too fast for her to keep up with him. Each lighted house they passed gleamed out a reproach to her. Her own house was dark. She'd banked the kitchen fire, though; it wouldn't take long to get supper.

At the door of the house, Celie caught up to Joe. She took Rose Marie up from the sled without looking at him and started into the house.

"I'll have supper ready in a minute, Joe," she called back.

Celie stirred up the fire before she put Rose Marie down. She pushed the tea kettle forward to heat for her bottle. She had never hurried faster. She fed the baby and left her still dressed on the bed. Then she flew to getting supper, guiltily, feeling the unwritten law of the mill town upon her; that a woman have supper ready when her man comes home. She tried to think of Christina's ever not being there when Ole came.

The fried pork sizzled in the spider. It was too late for baked potatoes. She pared recklessly thick slices into a boiling kettle of water. She made fresh coffee. It was funny Joe didn't come in. When supper was on the table, Celie went out to the shed door.

"Joe, Joe . . ." There was no sign of him.

Billy Nurmi was chopping wood in his shed. He called out to Celie, "Joe went up to Helsen's 'n' I guess they must've went out to the woods 'cause I see 'em come down by here and head over by the tracks."

Celie made no answer. She came back in the house. Joe was mad at what she said. He'd gone off without eating. She shoved the coffee back on the stove. Then she went into the living room and sat down on the couch. It was cold in there and the woodbox was empty. Anyway, there wasn't any good to sit in the living room alone. She went into the bedroom aimlessly. Joe was mad at her. Maybe he thought she wanted to see Art because she was still crazy about him. She moved around the bedroom, picking up things, hanging up Joe's shirt he had left on the chair. She pinned a sweater over the bright bulb so it wouldn't wake the baby. She went back to the kitchen.

She hadn't meant to eat, but she was hungry with the food all there in front of her. It was the new baby that made her hungry. The food was tasteless, but she helped herself to the pork and gravy. It was easier to think, doing something. Joe shouldn't have been mad. He should have known she didn't care anything for Art Farley anymore. She wondered again about Char. She might have told her she was going. She wondered if Art would leave, too. He ought to follow Char and see if she wouldn't come back.

Suddenly the pork was salty and crisp. An assurance rose within her, proud, heartening. Joe would go after her if she should ever leave. That was why he got mad today because he thought she'd really been to see Art. Celie put the supper in the warming oven to keep. A curious smile curved Celie's lips as she turned to wash her dishes.

Joe Linsen and Hels Helsen tramped through the woods, single-file, Hels ahead. They had visited their last trap. They were on their way back. It was getting dark in the woods, safer than going in the day time. Joe'd have enough beaver skins to make Celie a real coat, pretty soon, if it weren't for the law against it. They could put 'em in a trunk and wait a while. After today, he wouldn't even tell her about 'em. Hels' feet held to the path without effort. Joe got off a little. His thoughts kept going back to Celie and Arthur Farley so he couldn't keep his mind on the path. He took a short cut over a bank of snow to the right.

"Hi, Hels," he waved his flashlight at him and fell headlong over the snowbank.

Hels gave a sound like a derisive laugh, but it hid itself under an asthmatic cough.

"Laugh, damn you," Joe called, picking himself up. Then he stooped over again. "Hels, look here." Joe's voice sank almost to a whisper.

"Ain't learned to walk yet, eh?" Hels' voice moved nearer.

"Feel down here, Hels." Hels stooped and put his hand down through the snow. Joe stepped back and gave the whole snowbank a kick with his boot. Masses of snow slid to the ground with a slipping sound, exposing an angular branching frame-work. Hels kicked at the bank farther down. His boot made a dull sound.

"A deer," said Hels shortly; "look at the antlers."

"Must be a big one, Hels, 'cause I can't budge it." Hels grasped the end of the branch near him. He braced himself and pulled.

"Christ!" exclaimed Hels, "two of 'em . . . horns stuck." Together they tugged and lifted at the heads and shoulders of two large stags locked together by their antlers. Shown only by the flashes from Joe's torch the dead beasts loomed up, distorted and menacing still. The men grunted and gave up trying to separate them. The bodies fell with a thud, but the grip of the intricately linked antlers still held.

"Must've been some fight to get 'emselves locked together so tight they couldn't get apart," said Joe.

"Starved to death, prob'ly," said Hels. "I've heard of it, but I never seen it before. Must've been here since early Fall. Lookit, coyotes been at the hind-quarters. Been more damage done if there hadn't been so much snow." The two men walked around the spot, half-stumbling in the dark, held by the sight of the two dead stags.

"I gotta come back and get them heads another time. Twelve point and fourteen point buck heads'll be easy to sell to someone from below the straits," said Joe.

They started off through the woods, silent awhile. "Pretty ugly fellows in the mating season, I guess," Joe added thoughtfully.

"Sure, Knut Karlson was near killed by one in rutting time last year. Missed his shot and had to play dead to save himself." Their thick boots made dull, padded sounds as they pushed along the trail. Joe could see the two stags, heads lowered, eyes glittering, antlers locked, crashing into the trees in their struggle; couldn't even get their heads down to drink. He wondered how long it took them to die.

"Lucky for the stags the rutting season is only once a year."

Hels grunted. Joe was setting a good pace and Hels' age told on his wind a little. Joe's thoughts went on. He grinned to himself; he had often thought in sunny times of Cele as a doe.

He turned his head toward Hels. "Guess it's open season always for men, eh, Hels?"

Hels didn't hear. Joe eased his pace a little. Something about a winter night that made you hungry.

3

AGAIN the big house on the bluffs was closed—
just as it stood. Dust gathered alike on the heavy
chairs and the thin glass goblets. No one thought to
draw the shades and the day's sun and the night's dark
passed uninterrupted over the wall paper forest. The
colors faded a little more in the bright light, watching
the bare branches beyond the windows put forth new
buds. Upstairs, in one of the closets, there were some
silver mules and a negligee that had been left behind.
A drop of Nuit de Noel stood in the deep red perfume
bottle on the dressing table. But the big house that had
taken old Hilton's last penny twenty years ago was
built like his fortune of wood, and wood does not last
forever. Already the porch railings had begun to rot
and Einar Erickson, the old Norwegian caretaker, put
his foot through the bottom of the back steps one day
when he made rounds.

Young Farley went to board at Christina Henderson's. Christina was glad to have him. With the cut
coming, Hans and Sam and the four new boys she had
couldn't pay as much for board as they used to.

He saw Joe and Celie when they stopped in at
Christina's of an evening. Joe and Farley talked together about lumber and the men at the mill. Celie
would come in from the kitchen with some beer and
fresh bread spread thick with butter. Joe said you
couldn't tell Christina's beer from Ole's, and Christina

would sit by the table and knit with a smile on her thin lips. It was the end of March and Celie could feel the baby kicking in her as she sat there with them. She picked up the newspaper and held it up for fear they might see her dress move. Once again, Celie's thin face with the high cheekbones had filled out. She was a little florid these days.

One night they were all at Christina's for supper. Christina was in the kitchen, dishing up. She made Celie sit down at the table.

"I heard from Charlotte today," young Farley said. "She's in love with a guy in Detroit. She's going to go to New York with him. She says if it lasts, maybe she'll want a divorce." It was the first time Farley had mentioned his wife since she left.

"You oughta be able to get it easy enough," muttered Joe. He couldn't make Arthur out. Celie looked up startled. She wondered if Arthur didn't care any more, he said it so lightly.

Then Christina brought in more rice fritters and they talked of other things.

4

THE cut came into effect the last of March and the mill shut down three days a week. Joe worked five because there was so much lumber in the yard, but that wouldn't last. The official notice of the change was tacked on the front door of the store the day of Mrs.

Wilhelm's party. The women were glad to get together that afternoon to talk it over. This party was different from the others Celie had known. It lacked the excitement of a shower; the women were jolly, but the talk had a certain heaviness about it. Wilhelms were moving.

"Well, things don't look so good in the Point, with the cut an' all, an' the mill shutting down three days a week. You can't tell, it might shut down all time," explained Mrs. Wilhelm, while the others looked troubled as they drank their coffee. They were all bewildered. The cut was bad enough, they could stand that if everybody got it. It was shutting down the mill that was the worst.

"Your man's lucky to have another job to go to," said Mrs. Meldahl, enviously.

"Lorenson got it for him . . . over in the knitting mills at Menominee. Pete says he don't believe he'll like it like the sawmill, but I tell him, it'll be safer than here with things like they are."

Each woman was busied with her own thoughts. "I 'member this' the way they did at Mead; first run part time an' then close down tight," said Mrs. Finkel. At the mention of Mead, a shiver went through Celie. It was as though she heard the wind passing over the deserted town. An edge of fear came into her eyes. She crumbled her piece of cake without eating it.

"Nurmis is movin', did you know that, Cele?"

"No," said Celie, "they're so noisy I don't know what we'll do without them."

"He got a job runnin' the elevator in the new bank building in Clarion."

Christina made a tck in her throat. "That's a man's job for you," she said tartly. She missed Ole these days. She hardly knew what to make of things without him to explain them. But this was a mill town for you. It would shut down, she knew it—no optimist, Christina Henderson. She had lived too close to the stern rigors of winter nine months a year. Soon there wouldn't be anybody to board. She knit her fears into the sweater for Celie's new baby.

There were silences instead of the usual steady chatter. The women wanted to talk, but they were cautious of each other. Each wanted to know first whether the others had secret resources to fall back on.

"You got relatives in Wisconsin, didn't I hear you say, once, Mrs. Biehl?" Mrs. Lindermoulder asked.

"Just Otto's half-sister, an' I guess they ain't doing too well," Mrs. Biehl answered hastily.

Wisconsin was dairy country, good steady work and always enough to eat if you owned your own farm. The Biehls had been talking of buying land over there, near the Dells, for ten years now. They even had their money saved up, but Mrs. Biehl's goiter operation took it all. She thought of this as she drank her coffee.

"They might better not have had the night shift this winter an' run full time in the days, Norm says," remarked Selma Lichtenberg.

"I guess they didn't know themselves. It just happened 'cause business is bad everywhere, now," said Mary Bates whose husband was chief accountant in the office.

"Mill towns peter out no matter how business is," said Christina. "Ole always said the timber wouldn't last more'n fifteen years at the most."

"That would have been time to get the boys grown, anyway," said Mrs. Suess, a trifle wistfully. Mrs. Wilhelm filled the cups with coffee.

"Say, I can tell you something! I asked for more of that quick-dry green enamel over at the store yesterday to finish my bedroom suite, an' Mr. Simpson said he was all out. When you goin' to have more in, I asked him, an' he said the company give 'm orders when he was out of anythin' 'cept groceries not to order again."

"Oh, for the Land' sakes! That looks bad, don't it?"

"It means the store is like to close down on us someday. We should have invited Mis' Simpson or Mis' Munsen tonight an' we could have got it from her."

"They were always talking about not carrying so much stock when I was there, though," said Celie. She could not imagine the store closed up.

"An' John was over to the doctor's today for croup medicine," said Mrs. Biehl, "an' he said he seen a sign up by the doc's desk 'at said a cut in fees to meet, you know, the cut in what we get. Babies was cut down to fifteen dollars. Celie, you'll be savin' five dollars on yours. And, Selma, that ought to make you get to work." The women laughed.

"I always say you can stand any place when it's going," said Mrs. Hensen, "but I hate a place that's closed down part time."

"An' don't you hate a man underfoot the days he ain't workin'? Sundays is all right cause you don't try to do much, but when you're tryin' to bake or sew or some-thin'!" Mrs. Wilhelm and Mrs. Hensen nodded in agreement.

"Joe'd be off to the woods. I wouldn't even see him," said Celie, thinking aloud.

"I wonder what they're goin' to do about painting the houses this year," said Selma. "Mr. DesMains promised us they'd do it this spring, for sure. I s'pose they won't do it, now they're so hard up."

"They'll have a bunch of rotting lumber on their hands if they don't," said Mrs. Bernsen. "Up here, the snow lies against 'em so long, they oughta paint 'em every spring, 'cause they don't put it on thick enough to do any good."

"I was thinkin' how pretty it'd be if they could paint the houses all white instead of gray," Selma went on.

"I don't know, but what I'd as soon have 'em leave 'em alone as raise the rent any. I'll tell you sixteen dollars a month makes a hole in your check." An atmosphere of uneasiness was in the air.

"Well, your cake's as light as ever, Mina," said Christina to Mrs Wilhelm.

"Say, you shoulda seen me mixing it up on the sink board instead of on the Hoover cabinet. I was as bad as a mouse without a hole." The women looked out through the open door into the kitchen. There was an empty space next to the window where Mrs. Wilhelm's Hoover cabinet had always stood. "Pete crated it last night."

A silence fell upon them again and widened to hold each woman's thoughts.

"This is a good house, Celie; I'd think you'd ask for it. It's not so far out as yours," Mrs. Wilhelm suggested.

"I would like it," Celie answered without animation.

"We got a real nice house in Menominee," continued Mrs. Wilhelm; "it's down near the tracks but it's got a porch and laundry tubs, Mrs. Lorenson wrote me."

Houses were a delicate subject in the Point. Different houses had advantages over others, but even the best had no laundry tubs.

"Well, Mina, I'm glad you're going if it's to better yourself, but it'll be lonely lookin' out my kitchen window, Mondays and not seeing your wash out."

Celie pushed back her chair. "I've got to go, too. Good-by, Mrs. Wilhelm. I hope you like it there." An unexpected thickness made it hard to say the words. Celie's eyes stung as though she would cry.

"I'd like to stay long enough to see your baby, Cele. 'Membe now, I'm bettin' it'll be a boy." Mrs. Wilhelm kissed her.

Christina followed Celie. They walked up the street silently.

"Mamma, you don't think the town'll really close up, do you?"

"I don't know, Cele, you can't ever tell about mill towns. I wouldn't think right off." At the corner, Christina turned towards her street. "It sure helps to have Farley boardin' with me."

"What does he say about it, Mamma?"

"I don't ask him, but he don't look too cheerful. My! that's a cold wind." The women parted and Celie went on up to the last house.

"Thanks, Mary." She counted out twenty cents from the kitchen shelf to pay the Wilhelm girl. She took Rose Marie out of the high chair and put her on the floor. Rose Marie pulled herself up by the table leg and made her way around the kitchen by means of the furniture.

"Ah . . . h? Ah . . . h?" The baby queried proudly, but Celie was looking moodily at the kitchen calendar. It was the twenty-seventh of March. It wouldn't be long now, if the baby was born on the first of June. She couldn't shake off the uneasy fear in her mind that the afternoon had planted there. Something in their voices, the older women's, Mrs. Wilhelm and Christina and Mrs. Bernsen, chilled her. Celie pulled the shade at the window. There was still some light in the sky, but it was a cold, gray light. She added a stick of wood to the fire. Then she turned on the radio; the jingle of jazz shut out the boisterous blowing of the wind outside the house, the clatter of the bare branches in the woods, the lake splashing up over its big bowl.

5

THE first of April, Celie watched the Nurmis move out and a feeling of desolation grew in her. The Nurmis were Finns. She and Mrs. Nurmi never visited back and forth, but they lived so close by they had grown into her life. She missed the rattle of the Nurmis' old car, the sound of Mrs. Nurmi throwing up her window to call to the children. She knew the records they played over and over, and, though she had never been in their house, she knew the scroll top of the white iron bed that was pushed against the window on her side of the house.

Now they had gone without even locking their door, as though they were leaving something worthless behind. It banged and rattled so, Joe had gone over and nailed it shut. Celie had tried not to look out of the windows facing the Nurmis' at first, but it was useless, she had come to live by the weather outside her windows. The very change from day to day affected her feelings. She did not mind being big and unwieldy so much when the March wind hurled itself shrieking between the houses, as though the world suffered with her. It was easier still when the maple tree showed fat buds along its bare branches.

She looked out of the window toward the fox farm as she made breakfast and did the dishes, bathed the baby, and set the table for dinner. But she used the window toward Nurmis' when she made the bed in their bedroom, or put Rose Marie to sleep, or changed her dress for the afternoon. And then, one morning, the Nurmis' empty house with the door nailed shut mattered no longer. Celie looked across at the curtainless window through the deserted house and saw the sun, streaming through from the other side, make a pattern on the board floor. Against the outside wall of the house, where the tarpaper had been nailed to keep the snow from the lower clapboards, the ground was washed clean of snow. A few blades of witch grass showed bright green. Above the roof line of the Nurmis' house stretched a clear blue sky. Spring had slipped in between the houses and down the streets of the Point.

It was Sunday morning toward the middle of April. Joe, on his side of the bed, was still sleeping, a long ridge under the bedclothes. Celie came back from the kitchen with Rose Marie's bottle and sat down on her side of the bed toward the Nurmis' window. She fed Rose Marie with the warm spring sun on her, warm even through her nightgown. She set the empty bottle on the window sill that was gilded and touched with red along its outer edge. Joe's regular breathing seemed to deepen the stillness in the little room. Rose Marie blinked at the sun with bright eyes. One cheek was deeper pink where she had lain against the pillow, and her hair curled damply above the neck of her sleeper. Celie kissed her and held her close. Today, she felt no dread of the future, no feeling of desolation. She had forgotten for a minute her bigness and that her feet would ache at night.

"Go wake Daddy, Rose Marie, tell him it's a swell day an' we're going out for a picnic." Celie made Rose Marie pounce on Joe's black head.

"Pull his hair, baby, pull hard." Joe woke and grabbed Rose Marie as Celie held her above him. He tickled her till she gurgled and crowed with glee. "Creepy-mouse, creepy-mouse . . . cree . . . p," played Celie along the top of the quilt. Rose Marie toppled off of Joe's chest and lay in an ecstasy of baby laughter.

"What's this about a picnic?" said Joe. Gee, Celie was pretty. She was the only woman he'd ever seen that could be pretty when she was going to have a baby, Joe thought.

"Wake up, Joe, it's warm enough and we're going out for a picnic!"

"Suits me," Joe said aloud.

He's in a good humor, Celie thought to herself, she would talk to him about getting a job away. "Joe, you bathe Rose Marie while I get breakfast, please, for once."

"If she breaks, it ain't my fault, though, Cele!"

Celie rushed around the kitchen singing. Joe whistled in the bedroom. Rose Marie jabbered at the sun. By eleven, they were packed in the old car.

"Which way, Cele? Down by the lake or out Clarion way?"

"No, let's drive awhile; let's pretend we're leaving the Point for good."

Joe lit his pipe. He'd known that Celie'd be at him again to leave. Maybe he ought to look around again. Gee, it was good to get out. Joe never worried long and today was too fresh and bright to bother about anything. He threw his hat in the back seat and loosened the knot of his tie, couldn't even have the collar tight around his neck today.

" 'Member, Joe, this time last year there was snow on the ground? It started the day Rose Marie was born."

"I remember, all right, riding home in the limey, half scared to death about you."

"An' you brought me some arbutus."

"I didn't think you cared much about it."

"Why, Joe Linsen!"

"You didn't say anything when I put it on the dressing table."

"Well!"

"It's just like old times riding along in the flivver, isn't it, Cele?"

"Only we have Rose Marie along."

"She's a good scout; she won't tell, will you, Rosie?" Joe bent over and kissed Celie. "Gee, Cele, you can blush just as good as ever."

Celie laughed. "You crazy thing, Joe!"

Kronki and old Quinn, the butcher, sat smoking on the boarding house steps. Quinn waved as they passed. The Austrians and Catholic Swedes and French Canadians were coming from Mass. They streamed along the edge of the road, dressed in their best clothes, the women proudly, the men uncomfortable and embarrassed in their white shirts and best ties. They called out at the car. Celie and Joe waved.

"There's Nora Maloney taking up with Tony Ruski, Joe. She ought to do better than that."

"Tony's all right, Cele. He's a good worker, one of my best men. I see him sneak behind a pile of lumber and steal a smoke now and then, but he's careful. I pretend not to see him." Joe was proud of his new job. He was conscious that the men liked him. He liked them, too.

"H'lo, Sam, Hans. That's Sandy, Cele, I was tellin' you about; said his wife was down sick and he couldn't come to work. Say, I told him, you mustn't beat up on her so hard, and he laughed and went back to work without any trouble."

They had passed Crazy Bill's and Ma Talbot's house. The road stretched ahead of them, brown and clean of snow. It was too early to be sandy yet. In the ditches off to the side, there were streaks of snow, but the hilly ridge ahead was brown and gray, delicately touched with green.

"Have to get our old boat out soon, Cele; look at the lake!"

The deep, piercing blue water lapped gently against the white sand. Far off it spread, as far as the eye could see.

"There's Dad, see him, Cele? I thought he'd be out." A tiny rowboat bobbed in the water. They could just make out the bent figure in the middle. The car rattled along the road. Rose Marie had fallen asleep. They forgot to talk. Celie watched the green of the tamaracks back from the lake and the red barked alders. Joe looked at the water running free in the creeks and wondered how the trout would bite. It was early yet for many cars. The road and the April world was theirs.

When they came to the crossroads, Joe slowed down. One was the main road to Clarion, the other was a corduroy road the State had taken over for a tourist route. Back in the beginning, it had been an Indian trail connecting the copper country with the eastern side of the peninsula. It lay through the hardwoods, past the coveted Markheim territory that was virgin timber.

"Which way, Cele?"

"Oh, let's take the new road, Joe. We haven't been on it since last summer."

"I hear the State's not going to do any work on it this year; costs too much and ain't enough people get up here to use it," said Joe.

But Celie was looking dreamily at the narrow blue ribbon of lake that still showed below the hill. The new road turned sharply south, crossed over rattlesnake ridge and then dipped down between the woods.

"Gee, I like it out here, don't you, Joe?"

"Now you're shouting, girl."

"Look, Joe, see the sun up there on that rounded stone; let's eat up there."

They seemed to be climbing straight into the blue sky itself. The big bowlders at the side were gray, but the smaller rocks ahead gleamed white under the bright sun. Joe carried Rose Marie and the lunch basket. Celie followed with an old quilt.

"Joe, feel! The sun's really warm."

"Watch out you don't get sunburnt, Cele. Take it easy. It's pretty steep."

Celie stopped a minute to rest. Joe went on. She watched him climbing with easy steps. Now he was at the brow of the hill. The cloudless blue of the sky filled in around him, outlining his crisp, wavy hair, his broad shoulders, Rose Marie's head bobbing over his arm. Celie liked the way his shoulders swung back a little from his belt. . . . It was good to get out of the house and away from the village. They wouldn't meet anyone up here. She didn't care how her old pink dress looked. She forgot that she was big, even.

There was snow where the big bowlders made shady caves with the ground, but out in the open the ground was soft. Spring was early this year.

Joe came back for her. "I could carry you up, too, Cele."

"Joe, don't you dare!"

Joe picked her up and carried her the few rods to the

top. He laid her down on the quilt by Rose Marie. Celie lay in the sun for a minute. Joe stretched out on a rock with his pipe in his mouth. Rose Marie chewed the bright pieces of yarn that tied the quilt, unnoticed. A bird sang near them, swinging on a red willow sprout, a prolonged, trilling note. The green needles of a jack pine close to Joe's bowlder glistened in the sun.

"Want to eat, Joe?"

"No, let's just lie here. Gee, it seems a long time since last summer. I bet we're 'bout the first people down this road this spring."

"D'ye s'pose there'll ever be enough people up here so they'll keep both roads open all winter, Joe?"

"Not with cuts, and places being shut down like they are."

Celie looked across over the low-lying hills, colored now with splotches of red, the dark green of the firs and the new spring green, where a month ago it had been a bleak waste of snow. No trace of a dwelling, even the brown string-like road was out of sight from here. A new bird note broke the stillness, sweet and thin and high above them.

"Joe, look!" Celie whispered excitedly, "quick!" Rose Marie was standing by herself on the quilt, tottering a little on unsteady legs. Then she took a step, and another, and fell face downward into Celie's lap. "She walked, all by herself, Joe; did you see her?"

"Sure I did." Joe grinned. "She's not so slow."

"Oh, baby." Celie squeezed her and set her up on the

240

quilt. "You can have your milk right off, just for that."

They ate their lunch hungrily.

"Gee, what a day!" Joe stretched out on the quilt, as he finished, with his head on Celie's lap.

"Did you hear the Bernsens are moving out?"

"Yeah, I heard about it."

Celie hesitated. Joe got on his guard so if she said anything about leaving. She twisted Rose Marie's hair while she talked. "Mrs. Finkel says this is the way they did at Mead; close down part time and then just shut up tight."

Joe grunted. "They've got twice as big an operation here as they had at Mead."

"Oh, Joe, aren't we ever going to get away from here?" Celie couldn't look at him. She looked away again over the rocky ridge and the cut-over land. Even in April, it was bleak. The frozen silence of winter still lurked in the shadowy places.

Joe puffed at his pipe. "Gosh, Cele, can't you ever enjoy a day without thrashing around about what we're going to do next? I thought when I got to be foreman you'd be satisfied."

"But, Joe, what if the mill closes down, you can't go on being a foreman."

"Oh, this won't last, Cele, folks gotta have lumber, don't they? An' if I go some place and say I've been foreman a month it ain't goin' to do me half the good it would if I went and said I'd been foreman a couple of years. Don't worry, Cele, we'll get ahead."

Celie was silent, but the gayety of the day was gone. "It's getting cold here, Joe."

They picked up their things and went back down to the road.

"Wanta drive on a ways, Cele? Look at Rose Marie. She's asleep a-ready." They covered her up in the back seat. Celie rode along, watching the curves of the old log road without seeing them. She was thinking how it would feel to be leaving for good. How free she'd feel of the scare that had lain on her since that afternoon at Wilhelms' when the women were all talking. The mill could close up tight and it wouldn't matter to them. She'd have the women over to her house for coffee and they'd all envy her secretly. No place could be worse than the Point. It was all right now in the spring, but when it got cold and the deep snow came . . . This year she'd be in a town where they'd have a furnace, maybe. Anyway, you could get to the stores or a movie any time you wanted, and there'd be trains going out more than once a day . . . Suppose they were going now; everything but the furniture packed in behind. They'd have to drive and drive way down over the straits, maybe they'd end up in Detroit. They wouldn't ever be coming this way again; this is the last time they'd see a wood road. Celie's mouth had a half smile. They were leaving now—for good.

They were going through the best timber. The tall somber trees subdued the April sun. Light without warmth fell on the road. They rounded a double curve.

Joe whistled. In front of the car, squarely blocking the road, stood a giant ice cake that had broken off from the great ice mass covering the cliff. Long icicles still hung from the rocky ledge, waiting to drop. Remnants of the deep snow drift that had covered the road still filled the ruts. The road was narrow and shadowed by the tall timber. No heat had penetrated. A clammy chill pervaded the ice-blocked pass.

"What d'ye know about that? We couldn't get by if we wanted to." Joe got out to have a closer look. He did not notice Celie.

"Joe . . ." She gave a piercing scream so sharp, so filled with fear it might well have split the barrier of ice.

Joe's throat contracted. He ran back to the car. "Celie, what happened?"

Celie turned away from him. Her face was a greenish white. He tried to take hold of her hands. She beat at him with icy fists. Joe got into the car and put his arm firmly around her shoulder. She sat rigid, shivering.

"Celie, stop it. Tell me what's the matter." Fear made his own voice rough. He shook her. Suddenly she crumpled weakly against him, sobbing out loud.

"Why, Cele, girl . . ." Joe moved out from under the wheel into her seat and held her tightly. Her sobs grew quieter. Joe's fright for her turned suddenly into anger. "Cele, what in hell's the matter with you?"

"Joe, it's like you said, look; we couldn't get out if

we wanted to." Celie laughed, a thin, harsh laugh that ended in a dry sob.

"For God's sake, Cele, sit up, and we'll get out of here." Joe turned the car around with difficulty in the narrow road. All the time, Celie kept her eyes fixed on the ice block, as though fascinated. In that short time, the light had drawn farther away. The barrier was translucent, streaked with pale blue and the green shadows from the fir trees.

Joe drove rapidly back over the road. Every now and then, he looked at Celie's white set face. She was still a little limp when he helped her into the house and pulled the big chair into the kitchen for her. He carried Rose Marie into her crib, still asleep. Celie hadn't spoken all the way home. The house was cold. Joe hurriedly lighted a fire in the kitchen stove. The wood crackling noisily woke Rose Marie. She stirred and cried.

"I'm all right now, Joe, I can feed her." Celie spoke dully. Joe watched her anxiously. Her eyes were a cold blue, the paleness of her face made it seem old and drawn. As she turned sideways, her pregnant body looked misshapen.

That night cold weather came again to the Point, holding spring off until May. The bright green witch grass by the Nurmis' house turned yellow with frost.

Part V

CELIE LINSEN'S baby was born at midday, the warmest week in June. Summer heat came with a rush that week, opening the windows and doors of the box-like houses, sending up the radishes and green onion tops in Christina Henderson's garden patch, drawing the children of the Point down to play on the grass-covered dock and the sandy beach of the lake. Celie's baby was a boy. Celie smiled when they told her.

"Aren't you glad, now, Joe?" she asked when he came in to see her. Joe bent and kissed her.

Celie turned over to sleep. Efficient Mrs. Maloney pulled the cracked green shade.

"I like it up," Celie murmured.

Celie was up in a week. The doctor scolded when he came and found her making Rose Marie's formula in the kitchen. Christina looked grimly pleased. Celie was no weak one like Mrs. Finkel's daughter who never did a stroke of work for three weeks after. Celie named the new baby Joseph Ole Linsen, but the second week they were calling him Jole.

Celie had no time to think, these days. Her world was contained in the tiny house at the top of the town. Rose Marie could navigate the three rooms now and crawl under the bed or under the stove with equal ease. Meals and washings and feedings; Celie moved from one thing to another all day long. When the Bernsens moved, she meant to go down to see them off, but it was Jole's feeding time and she forgot it until too late. Every three hours, through the day, she sat by the window facing Nurmis' and nursed Jole. It was good to sit down and rest her feet, good to have a little baby again to hold against her. She looked out the window and down the street, but her thoughts were here in her own house. Lots of things she had minded once didn't bother her any more; being tied at home so much, the full feeling of her breasts, the way her hands got red from so much washing, even wearing her old opera pumps that were loose and out of shape, but so comfortable. She sat in the sunny window, half dozing, sharing in the baby's animal content. When Jole finished nursing, she took him out by the stoop and settled him in the baby carriage Mrs. Wilhelm left behind when she moved. She pulled the top farther down over his eyes and left him. Already, the sun was turning the baby's pink feet a shade darker. She turned back into the house.

"Hello, Celie." Selma Lichtenberg came around to the back door. She had a new dress on and green kid sandals. She had gone to Clarion this spring and had a permanent, Celie noticed a little enviously. Celie herself was acutely aware of her old pumps and the cotton dress she had not gotten around to take in again after Jole was born. Her hair had grown long and it was easier to pin it up than to keep it curled, even if it did make her look older.

"Oh, he's sweet, Celie, gee." Selma bent over Jole admiringly.

"You ought to see him in that dress you gave him.

He's too cute. We took him down to Christina's Sunday in it," Celie said.

"Did you go in?" Selma bent down to knock the sand out of her shoes.

"No, we just stopped outside and drove back home, why?"

"Well, Cele, you know it's good luck to have a new baby lie on your bed, if it's the first house he's ever been in and I wondered if you'd bring Jole down." Selma looked up wistfully. "Isn't it funny I don't have a baby, Cele?"

The two girls went into the house. Celie set up the ironing board and ironed while Selma held Rose Marie. Celie's hands, shaking out Joe's shirt and pressing the iron firmly over it, were growing strangely like Christina's. They were young hands, but capable with strength in the large jointed fingers.

"You bet I will, Selma, but I'll have to bring Rose Marie, too. Maybe that'll bring you double luck." She stood in the doorway a minute, watching Selma down the street. She went back to her ironing feeling rich and older and wiser than Selma Lichtenberg. She was conscious of the clean smell of freshly ironed clothes mingled with the breath of the June day.

Celie was just putting up the board when Christina came in. She was bareheaded and the light breeze had loosened a strand of hair from her tight knot. She looked tired, Celie thought. Celie was so used to Christina's plain features, her faded blue eyes, her reddened leathery skin, she seldom thought of any changes coming to her. But today she noticed Christina's shoulders drooped. She walked as though she were tired.

"Celie, you got enough dinner today so you can have young Farley here? I been over nursing Verneau's baby an' I gotta go back there without stopping to get dinner."

"Why can't she take care of her own baby?" The inborn contempt of the Swede for the lower strata of French Canadians in the town was in Celie's voice.

"They're down sick, too," Christina answered simply.

"What's the matter with them?"

"Same old thing every June, summer complaint."

"Has the doc been to see them?"

"He's been on a drink, I guess, but there ain't nothin' to do, anyway, 'cept physic 'em and put 'em to bed. I left word for him to come down soon's he could."

"Here, Mamma, have a cup of coffee. I'm glad I didn't throw it out, now." Celie poured a cup of the strong coffee and cut a slice of cake. Christina took them silently. There was no need for thanks. Celie was her daughter.

"You got your cake a mite too short," she said as she finished it. "I'll just take a look at Jole." Christina tiptoed heavily toward the bedroom.

"Rose Marie's in there, Mamma. Jole's outside."

"These June days are risky, Cele. You be sure he's covered up well or he'll get cold in his bowels like the Verneau baby. I've felt chilly myself all day."

Celie was excited at the prospect of Arthur Farley for dinner. She hadn't seen him lately. Joe had gotten in the habit of getting the groceries on his way back from work. Celie couldn't get away easily. Art had never been there for a meal before. Instead of the fish soup and baked potatoes and pie that she had planned, she ought to have a salad, Celie thought, but that took lettuce and Joe said lettuce was silly. Celie fed Rose Marie early and got her off to bed. Jole was all right until one. Then she went in to change her dress and comb her hair. She had done it over twice when the mill whistle blew.

Joe and Farley came into the house together. Farley had picked Joe up on the way.

"Thanks, Celie, for taking me in," Farley said and sat down with Joe in the living room. They talked about radios. Celie was out in the kitchen, dishing up, but she wondered impatiently why they didn't talk about the mill or Joe's job. Men were so queer the way they wasted their opportunities. Joe moved the table out into the living room for her. Celie had it set with lace paper doilies. She was a little embarrassed serving dinner to Arthur Farley. She sat still while he and Joe were talking. Once or twice she looked up quickly and found Arthur's eyes on her. Finally she burst in,

"Art, what do you think about that house of Lorenson's? Could we move into it, like your uncle said?"

Young Farley frowned a little. He ran his hand over his hair. "Well, Celie, I'll tell you, you're going to get it, of course, but just now while the mill is kinda upset with these part-time days, I think it would be better to stay where you are."

Celie's face fell. Things weren't going well at the mill, then. She sat silent and depressed. It was worse to have Art say it than the women or Joe.

There was a silence, then young Farley said abruptly, "Well, I'm leaving today." Joe and Celie stared at him. Celie set the bread plate down so sharply a slice fell off on the tablecloth.

"For good, you mean?" Joe finally asked.

"I hope to tell you it's for good. I'll never get caught again in a hole like this; I'm heading right back to Detroit." He lit a cigarette and threw the match across on top of the living room stove. Celie's eyes followed the match. Arthur was through with the Point, now. That was all it meant to him.

"Who's going to run the mill?" Joe asked.

Young Farley shrugged. "The old man'll find someone fast enough; it's nothing to me."

Celie left her pie untasted. She went out to the kitchen to pour more coffee. She or Joe, they must ask him about a job in Detroit. He couldn't just go like that.

"Well, 'by, you folks; if you ever come to the big city give me a ring." He laughed as he said it, as though he knew they never would. The joking left a scar across Celie's mind. Young Farley shook hands with Celie. "Maybe, I'll see Char in Detroit. She's at the Tricorne again, I hear." He said it easily. "Joe, I'll give you a lift down to the mill."

"I've got to go get Jole," Celie murmured almost to herself. She couldn't stay there any longer. She went out to the yard, without waiting to see them go.

Jole was sleeping warmly in the sun. Her hands trembled as she picked him up. She hid her face against him. When she came in, she saw Arthur getting in behind the wheel. The bright sun on the windshield flashed against the mirror he had given them for a wedding present. It flashed in Celie's eyes and blinded her for an instant. She sat down by the kitchen window to nurse Jole. It was early for his feeding, but she wanted to hold him against her, to push off that cold feeling of desolation. As long as Arthur had been in the Point, there had always been a hold on the world below the straits.

She sat silently a long time after Jole had finished nursing. She forgot about the dinner dishes stacked on the table. She was pretending to herself; suppose Arthur Farley had asked her to go away with him! She wouldn't go; she couldn't ever leave Joe, she would tell him, and then he would tell her he couldn't go without her . . . it hurt her that it was only pretending.

Celie put Jole in his basket. Then she went back and picked up the dishes. Her hands moved slowly. Now, without Jole to hold, the feeling of loneliness came over her in a full tide. Charlotte had gone, Arthur was going. The camps would let out. Joe must see now; he'd have to get a new job some place.

Celie was glad when Rose Marie woke up. She had been uneasy in the quiet house. It prisoned her strangely. Moved by some impulse to get away from her own house, she put both children in the car and drove out the road between the two stone posts to Farleys'. No, it wasn't Farleys' any more, it was Hilton's Folly again.

The sun rested warmly on the wide porch overlooking the bluffs. She spread out a quilt for Rose Marie and carried Jole's basket up against the house. It was lovely out here. Celie could see the intense blue of the lake. All the trees were green now. The grass around the Hilton place was different from the grass plots in the Point. The separate blades didn't show, it all looked woven together like a carpet; the clover in it made a flower pattern. Celie walked slowly around the long veranda with Rose Marie. Once, she stopped by a window and cupped her hands against the pane. The long room shaded by the porch looked dark and ghostly.

It seemed queer that she had ever been in there to a dinner party wearing a purple velvet evening gown. "See, Rosie, see the china cupboard!" She held Rose Marie up to the window. "It's better outside, isn't it, baby?" They went back to the quilt in the sun. Celie sat down beside Rose Marie. It was good to sit still. She forgot the things to do at home. Gee, the lake was pretty in the sun. The old Celie woke in her. Maybe they could leave the children with Selma and go canoeing tonight.

2

JUST before the heat went out of the sun, and the deep blue of the lake cooled, Celie bundled the babies back into the car. Jole was asleep, but Rose Marie sat up straight. She grasped the wheel tight in her sturdy fists, and looked at Celie with roguish blue eyes. Celie put her hands over the chubby little ones and turned the car out of Farleys' driveway. Rose Marie was beginning to be company.

The house on the bluffs was no place to stay when it got late. Then, it was better to be on the street, watching the men pouring out of the mill, streaming up the hill. Celie had a sudden desire to be in the store again. It was always so busy from five o'clock on. Men stopped on their way home to buy cigarettes or tobacco, children came in for something "ma forgot to put on the list." Celie parked the car out in front and left Jole sleeping. She carried Rose Marie in with her. She could buy a can of baking powder as an excuse; hers was most gone anyway. She hadn't been down so late since they went back on the day shift.

The store was always brightly lighted. The mill had light to burn; they should worry about light bills. Celie remembered how the lights sometimes flashed in your eyes when you were up on the ladder getting cans from the top shelf. It was gay; so many new things; new bolts of materials, new baby clothes that hadn't got shrunk in the wash, new brooms, new wash tubs and ironing boards and bright tin pails. Rosie liked it. She reached for everything she saw. The store was busy tonight. A group of women stood talking to Mrs. Munsen on the dry goods and toilet article side. Celie walked by them.

"H'lo, Celie, what you going to do if the mill closes up?" asked Mrs. Munsen.

Celie was startled. She let Rose Marie sit on the glass case.

"I don't know. Do you think it really will, soon?"

"Well, young Farley cleared out today. You heard that, didn't you?"

"Yea," said Celie Linsen slowly. "I heard that." It was warm in the store. She opened Rose Marie's sweater.

"I hope them men over there don't start nothin': they've been in here an hour or more talkin'!" Mrs. Munsen jerked her head toward the group standing back where they sold men's boots and socks. "Nine or ten of them, mostly Austrians and Polaks, they are."

"I left Jole out in the car; I gotta be going," Celie said and went back out without buying her baking powder. All the warm assurance of the day had been drained out of her. She drove up the hill just as the mill whistle blew. Up the hill came the men. The town was in action again.

If the mill should close, there would be none of that. Folks would move away. Those that stayed would idle around. No mill whistle to tell when to dish up. People wouldn't have any money . . . But, that couldn't happen, Celie told herself. Why, the mill had been running in the Point since before she was born. It couldn't stop short like that. Celie looked at the houses along her street, bare, shabby boxes, but cozy enough if you knew the inside of them, each chimney streaming supper smoke. The town was ugly now in early summer, the piles of tin cans and rubbish heaped against each woodshed were swollen and scattered out to the street. She felt, rather than thought, of the hungry people living under those roofs . . . too many to let the mill close down.

Celie stopped at Selma's to lay Jole on Selma's bed for luck.

"Sure, we can stay with the children, you and Joe go ahead," Selma said. Celie hurried back to the car. It was late for Jole to be out.

"Say, Celie, ain't it awful if the mill closes down?" Selma followed out to the street. "They say Art Farley left on the train, that he didn't even take his car with him. Buddy Hefflin was telling me down at the store."

"I wouldn't believe what he told me," said Celie; "he used to be full of stories every time I got up near his cage when I was in the store." She started the car. She didn't want to hear anything more.

She hurried with Rose Marie's cereal and nursed Jole only a bare fifteen minutes. She had them both in bed before Joe came home. Joe was late nights. All the men in the yard checked in to him every night. When the whistle blew, he had to take his lists up to the office and file them. Joe might get to be a big man in the mill some day, unless it really did close for good, Celie thought to herself.

She stood by the stove, cooking hash for supper. You couldn't turn it till the crust browned, just so. And, suddenly, Celie's mind turned again to the thought of Arthur's going. It was still there, like some cavity in a tooth that the tongue cannot keep from touching. The hash scorched a little. Celie slid her knife deftly underneath. She was just turning it out on the platter when Joe came in. She looked up quickly. Joe stood there hanging his jumper on the back of the door. She had a swift lifting of spirit. Joe was back. He filled the kitchen again. Celie felt that the mill couldn't close. Things didn't change with Joe.

"Cele"—Joe was blowing through his pipe to test it—"you're not still gone on him, are you?"

Celie looked at him, wondering. "Why, Joe, it didn't mean a thing to me, his going."

Joe looked at her steadily. The look in Joe's eyes took Celie back to that day in Mead. She had never thought since of all that happened there without wondering shamefacedly how she had come to do it. She had even wondered once or twice whether she loved Joe, but now, suddenly, she was sure.

"Guess I'll go in and look at the kids." There had been too many words already. Joe went into the bedroom. Celie put everything on the table. She sat down without waiting for Joe and helped herself. She felt strangely comforted.

"Say, Joe, there won't be none left for you if you don't come quick."

Joe came. He ate silently until his plate was empty.

Celie forgot to worry about the mill closing, forgot even to mention it.

"Say, Joe, I thought maybe you'd like to take the canoe out, tonight. I stopped in at Selma's and she and Norm can come up and stay with the children."

"Darn tootin'! Cele."

Just as Celie finished wiping the dishes, there was a knock at the kitchen door. Hels Helsen's woman, Pearl, stood in the doorway. She was an Indian half-breed; no one knew where Hels had found her, a thick shapeless figure of a woman with greasy black hair and small eyes.

"I come down sit by you," she grunted in her heavy voice.

"Sure, Pearl, what's the matter; Hels been drinking too much firewater?" Joe asked, laughing.

Pearl shook her head. "Dem white fox, you know? De bitch die. Hels, he ain't safe yet."

"Gee, that's a bad break. He was showing them to me just the other day. What happened to her?"

Pearl's short, thick shoulders shrugged. A light of unholy satisfaction gleamed for a second in her narrow slit eyes.

Joe kept his canoe in the cellar hole of an old power house down near the lake. The cellar hole was half grown up with weeds. It was eerie and smelled damply of plaster. Joe climbed down in and hoisted the canoe to the edge. Celie caught it at the stern end and held it steady till Joe could come around and lift it over. She helped him load it on his head and then went ahead with the flashlight and paddle so he could see where to go.

"There she is, Cele!" They had done it so many times before they got the canoe into the water with few words. It was a mysterious business. Nobody knew where they hid the canoe. They moved stealthily. Joe was never talkative on the lake.

The water lapped the bottom of the canoe. The sand grated lightly. Celie got in the canoe. Joe gave her a hand to steady her. It was a big, hard hand that was always warm; Celie's was cold. Joe shoved off and leaped in. The canoe shot out into the dark water.

"Not bad, eh, Cele?" Joe said in a low, contented voice.

"It's nice, Joe," Celie answered.

"You picked the right night, moon'n everything; looks kinda rainy though."

Joe's paddle made no sound as he sent the canoe swiftly through the water. Everywhere was the soft darkness and endless space.

"Kinda gives you a kick to be out on Superior, doesn't it, Celie?"

"You bet, Joe," said Celie. She closed her eyes and hugged her body warmly.

"Cold, kid?"

"No, but it isn't hot yet on the lake."

Joe skirted the shore of the Point, telling the shore by the black line the trees on the bluff cut against the sky. Celie had no fear in a canoe with Joe. He had taken her out on Superior since she was fourteen. Once a storm came up and she was frightened. Joe had thundered at her, "Sit down, you baby!" and he had brought her home safely. Celie had never been frightened since.

"Wind's coming up, Cele, hear it?"

From the trees on the bluffs came a restless, rustling sigh. The wind stirred the lake to a hiss as it washed over the sandy beach. From the trees on the bluffs came a lingering moan; no anger, no vengeance in the moan, only sadness. So the winds had moaned before the four stacks of the mill were built, so they would moan after they were gone.

"Celie, 'member we went canoeing the other time after Farley left?"

"Joe, I didn't even think of that."

"I did," said Joe, but it was too dark for Celie to see his face.

"Joe, it doesn't matter, does it?" Celie asked out of a long silence.

"Nope," answered Joe, gruffly.

They were too deep in the sound of their own voices to hear the wind as it rose again, sobbed softly over the few twisted veterans of the white pine days and died yet more softly away in a gentle sigh. It was summer, but the resignation of winter still lingered in the voice of the wind.

Celie slid down on the floor of the canoe. She could feel the slap and sway of the water against her body as though there were no canoe-shell between. She could see Joe sitting up at the end, part of the darkness of the trees on the bluff behind him, the movement of his arm part of the movement of the wind and water. Joe turned the canoe around with powerful strokes of his paddle. Once, the water, meeting the paddle broadside, made a gurgling, splashing noise that sounded loudly in the night. The canoe headed back and shot quickly for the shore by the old pier.

"Gee, it rests you more than a rocking chair," said Celie.

"We ought to bring Rosie out pretty soon, don't you think, Cele; I want her to learn to like a canoe."

"When it gets hot. Say, Joe, do you think that they really will shut down the mill this summer?"

Joe puffed at his pipe before answering, then he said briefly, "They can't shut down the lake, anyway."

When Celie and Joe drove into the yard, Norm Lichtenberg was watching for them at the door.

"Say, Cele, the doc, he just stopped by an' said Christina's down sick."

Celie couldn't believe it for a minute. Christina was

never sick. Then she said, "Where, Norm? Is she over home?"

"Yeah, we'll stay here an' you and Joe go on over."

Celie swallowed hard to keep back the cold fear at her throat. Sickness was mysterious and terrifying. There was no evading it. But Ole had just died less than a year ago, Christina couldn't go the same year. She had worked too hard, taking care of those no-good Verneau kids, that was all. She'd get well when she was once rested.

"Don't get so scared, Celie," Joe said on the way over. "Christina's strong; she'll pull through."

Celie ran upstairs in Christina's house. It seemed strange to her, like someone else's house. At the top of the steep stairs, she met the doctor. His face was very sober. His solemn expression made Celie apprehensive.

"Pretty sick, Celie."

"What is it, Doc, is it flu?"

"I can't be sure, Celie, till the mail comes in to-morrow noon with the report from Lansing," he said in a low, worried voice.

Celie went into the bedroom. Christina turned her head toward the door. Her face had a dull, heavy look. She did not know Celie. Her dry lips made muttering, incoherent sounds.

"Mamma?" Celie went in and stood by the bed. Mrs. Maloney was in the room. She put her fingers to her lips.

"She ain't right in her mind, Celie," she whispered loudly.

Celie had never seen Christina sick. She looked almost made of wood. The usually sharp eyes were listless. As Celie watched, a tremor passed through the long, gaunt frame under the blanket. Her face was inexpressibly tired and old. Celie felt sharply that Christina would not get well. No tears came to her eyes, but an unutterable loneliness seized her, a selfish, desolate feeling. Christina was going, too. The doctor came in and told her to wait downstairs awhile.

Celie went down to the familiar-strange living room with the red plaster walls and the heavy lace curtains. In through the dining room was the table, spread as it always was in the old days. Christina's ferns flourished greenly by the window. The cuckoo clock hung above the sideboard. Mrs. Suess and Mrs. Biehl sat solemnly on the couch, doing nothing, only sitting, their faces long with anxiety. Joe sat in the rocking chair by the radio. Even the heavy air of the room could not quite change the free set of his shoulders. His hair was still blown back by the wind on the lake. Celie went on through to the kitchen. She had nothing to get, but the kitchen seemed to prove that Christina could not really be sick. It was too full of her. There was oatmeal in the top of the double-boiler on the stove. Somebody, Mrs. Maloney, probably, had kept the fire going. Joe followed her out.

"Celie, I'll run up and see to the kids. You stay here

an' don't worry." He pressed her shoulder gently. "She'll be all right, Cele, think what a constitution she has." Cele only shook her head. "Look, Cele, why don't you fix some coffee for the doc? He'll be up all night. S'long, Cele." Celie stood still. Joe had gone. Ole was gone, the Farleys, now Christina . . . Slowly, Celie got out the coffee. Christina always boiled hers up with an egg. It helped a little to move around among Christina's things, to feel in the broken bowl back in the corner of the cupboard for the egg, to get a piece of cheesecloth in the table drawer to stop the spout of the coffee pot the way only Christina did. She was glad she had made it when the doctor came down. He lighted a cigarette and stood smoking silently a minute.

"We'll do all we can for her, Celie."

"The coffee'll be ready in a minute, Doc," Celie said quietly. Nothing Doc could say mattered, really. Christina was dying. She knew.

"I've got some more people sick, Celie. I'll take a cup and then I'll go, but I'll be back soon."

"Doc, I can't see how Christina could come down so sick, all in a minute, like. It was only yesterday she stopped in at our house," Celie said wonderingly.

"I guess, Celie, she's been sick on her feet for a week or more; didn't say anything about it, just kept dragging around nursing that Verneau trash." The doctor got into his coat as though it were an effort. "That's always the way; good money thrown after bad." He went out the door.

As soon as the door closed, the two women in the living room came out to the kitchen.

"Celie, you poor kid," Mrs. Suess began, "you know what? The Verneau baby died this afternoon and they say Mis' Verneau's dying there now." Her desire to tell the news triumphed over the sympathy in her voice.

Mrs. Biehl broke in: "They've taken Hans Swinson into Clarion to the hospital with the same thing. He works with Verneau, you know."

"Gettin' the flu here top of the mill shutting down 'n' all is an awful thing," mourned Mrs. Suess. She shook her head sorrowfully. Her round red face looked oddly old in spite of the curly bobbed hair that framed it.

"I didn't know the Verneau baby died," Celie said. She got cups for the women and filled them with coffee. "I guess I'll go up and send Mis' Maloney down."

Celie stood in the passageway a second and looked in. Christina lay motionless, but her low muttering continued. She picked at the bedclothes oddly. Mrs. Maloney sat stolidly by the bed, never taking her eyes away from her. Mrs. Maloney was a tall, thin Irish woman who had started nursing in the Catholic hospital at Clarion. She had been dismissed summarily by the sisters when she was discovered coming in the back way at four in the morning. Since then, she had married Maloney, the sheriff in the Point, and introduced the new babies of the Point into the world. She herself boasted she had some jokes that would make a woman laugh fit to start her labor pains. She went across to the doorway when she saw Celie there. She was never one to walk on tiptoe; now her flat feet jarred the room.

"Celie, he can say what he wants to about not being able to tell yet, but it's typhoid if I know anything about it." Celie was vague about the word, but it filled her with new dread.

"She's awful sick, Mis' Maloney, isn't she?" Mrs. Maloney nodded. "You go down and get some coffee, Mis' Maloney; I'll stay here."

Celie sat down on the chair by the bed. She looked at Christina. Her usually thin face looked somehow thicker. Her eyes opened on Celie dully. All resemblance between the faces of the mother and daughter was gone. That was what a mill town did for you, Celie thought; it killed Ole off and now Christina. Someday, if they didn't get away, it would take Joe and she would go on living here alone, like Christina, getting to look like her. Celie reached out shyly and took Christina's hand. It was hot and dry. It burned her own cold one. Here was Christina sick and her and Joe out in a canoe all that time. That was the way when Ole died; she was down by the lake swimming. Just when she was having a good time, something always happened.

Mrs. Maloney came back up with a basin of water and towels. "The doctor said to keep sponging her off, Cele."

"Let me do it, please," Celie said.

Mrs. Maloney went back downstairs. Celie sponged Christina's body gently. The skin looked so old it startled her. She stared at the sagging wrinkles on Christina's light breasts, at her thin legs. Celie had never thought how Christina's body must look under the high-necked gray and blue print dresses she always wore; how her legs would look under the white cotton stockings. Celie pulled Christina's nightgown carefully down over her again and covered her with the quilts.

Now and then, she made out words in Christina's delirium: "Ole" and "mill" and "old country." Once she heard her name and the sound of it went through her like a shock. The sight of Christina's body stayed in Celie's mind. She leaned over Christina tenderly. A terrible sadness filled her for Christina, for herself who would some day look like that. She looked at the firm white flesh of her own arms. She felt a twinge of greedy joy. She was young! When Mrs. Maloney came back in the room, Celie was still thoughtful.

"You know, Mis' Maloney, life's sad, isn't it?" It was a new discovery.

Mrs. Maloney's mouth twisted sarcastically, "Oh, I tell you, Cele, it's one swell vaudeville."

Celie felt almost rested when she came back from feeding Joe the next morning. She drove the car slowly along the crossroad between her street and Christina's. The day was so bright, hot sun fell on all the peaked roofs. The yards swarmed with children; all the doors of the little houses were open and the voices of the women in the houses drifted out to the street. At the foot of the town, beyond the four stacks of the mill, stretched the endless, bright blue of Superior. Celie had changed her sweater and skirt to a sleeveless cotton dress. The change refreshed her. It was summer again after the long winter and timid spring. Christina would be better this morning. People didn't die on a day like this. All the dread of the night before had left Celie's mind. As she went up the walk to the house, she felt she was living there again. Ole would come in for dinner; Joe would take her in to a show in Clarion after supper.

But in the house, her assurance left her. The bright July day was shut securely out by the hook of the screen door. Mrs. Maloney and the doctor were both upstairs. Christina still lay in a stupor. The shades had been pulled against the sun and only a bright line from under the shades fell in a crimson bar on the worn crocheted rug. Celie came across to the bed.

"H'lo, Celie," said Mrs. Maloney, who showed no sign of not having slept. The doctor looked worn out.

"Celie, I want to talk to you a minute," the doctor said. They went out to the passageway between the two rooms. "Celie, the report on the specimen came back from Lansing; they brought it up direct from Clarion. It's typhoid, Celie, brought in by that Verneau outfit, but after all the summer complaint that's around . . ." His eyes shifted before Celie's frightened gaze. "I

269

should have sent a specimen in on Verneaus last week." The admission cost him effort. Celie said nothing. "You and Mrs. Maloney come downstairs and I'll give you the typhoid shots. Four more cases in the Point, this morning. I'm going to give the whole tribe the shots." Contempt for the people in the isolated community he had come to live in got into his words and the bitter line of his mouth, perhaps, some contempt for himself, as well.

"But Mamma, she's worse, eh Doc?" Celie burst out. What did typhoid in the village mean to her? It was Christina she cared about.

He shook his head. "I'm afraid, Celie. I'm . . ." He turned without finishing his sentence. Why should he be sorry; what was there for any of them in this miserable end of the earth? Better if typhoid carried the whole pack of them off. He went on downstairs.

Celie had the little magic pin-prick the doctor said would keep her from getting sick, then she went back up to sit there. Christina's eyes seemed to rest on her, but she couldn't be sure. Celie put out her hand and smoothed back the scraggly gray hair. "Poor Mamma," she murmured awkwardly. In the still little room, walled off from the summer world outside, things were different from last night, someway, less real. She looked at the gaunt, tired face on the pillow and tried to make it belong to her mother. "Poor Mamma," Celie said again, patting her head gently, but the woman on the bed seemed a stranger; someone she was used to seeing only at the store.

Celie was glad when it was time to feed Jole. She left Christina to Mrs. Maloney and drove back home. It was good to get out of the hushed house. At the pump by Tim Olsen's there was a knot of people talking together. Celie scarcely saw them, this morning. She was in a queer world remote from the affairs of the Point.

Selma met her at the door. "Oh, Celie, isn't it awful! Norm came up to tell me; there's typhoid all over the Point. He stayed here while I went down to get vaccinated. And everybody at the mill had to take it, too. That settled Norm. He says we can't get out of here too soon to suit him."

"Tell Norm to talk to Joe, will you, Selma? Gee, think of living here till you get old, and then dying here!"

"Catch me doing it!" Selma answered confidently.

Christina lived through the week. Each day found her a little more weary of her body, still looking out at her room with dull unseeing eyes. Saturday afternoon, Celie went across the passageway to her own old room to sleep a little. All week she had been by Christina's bed except when she went home to feed Jole. Today Jole cried when she finished nursing him. The doctor said she must get some rest or she'd have to wean him.

Celie lay down on the cot-bed Christina had moved in when she had rented the room. She looked at the

271

familiar ceiling. There was the crack that ran almost from the window to the door. There was the place where the roof had leaked. The room seemed empty without her things in it. She used to cut out movie stars' pictures and pin them up. Not much time to do that any more; that was long ago, before Jole or Rosie were born, even before she was married.

Celie fell asleep, her arm crooked under her head . . . They were leaving the Point. Everything was packed now. The house looked empty with the curtains gone. She almost hated to go off and leave it. "Here, Joe," she lifted Jole up for Joe who was already in the car to take him. They were going to Detroit . . .

"Celie, I hate to wake you, but you won't never forgive me if I don't." Mrs. Maloney took a hold of her arm to rouse her. Celie opened her eyes. "Christina died, Celie, I didn't even have time to call you. I went to look at her 'cause I thought she shivered and she was clean gone."

Celie stared uncomprehending. Then she remembered. She'd been dreaming again about leaving. She was here just the same as before; no, not quite the same; Mamma had gone now and left her behind.

"I want to see her," Celie said.

3

CHRISTINA HENDERSON was buried on Monday in the cemetery beyond the fox farm. It was a small space between the road and the fringe of the hardwoods; there were not many crosses in the cemetery. The people were young in the Point, sometimes a whole year went by without a death.

Next to the graves of Ole and Christina was a small mound to mark the body of the Pederson's tenth baby. On the other side was the grave of the lumberjack who froze to death walking in to camp last winter. Nobody knew his name, only Jake.

The funeral was over. It had been a big funeral, even larger than Ole's. Everyone in the Point knew Christina Henderson. The Swedish minister who had married Joe and Celie came out to say a prayer over Christina. Father DeVaux, the traveling priest for the Catholic mission, came too. Everybody said it was a shame the doctor never came. They did not see his car driving rapidly by on the lower road, nor the stern face he turned toward the edge of the woods by the cemetery.

The women looked at Celie curiously, wondering how she would take it. She stood there by Joe, with one hand holding Rose Marie's. "Her face was pale," Selma told Nellie Hann, afterwards.

"Yes, but she never had what you'd call a bright complexion," Nellie reminded her.

The little crowd pressed around her in wordless sympathy. Some of the older women touched her as they left. Mrs. Maloney held Jole out in the car. There was no caretaker for the cemetery in the Point. Folks buried their own dead. Joe picked up his shovel and looked at Celie uncertainly. She nodded silently. He laid each shovelful of sandy soil down gently over the coffin that he and Norm Lichtenberg had built themselves. Celie helped to fit the sod over the top. The coarse witch grass, mingled with mullen stalks and plantain weeds, went on growing as before, with this new burden beneath them.

"I wish we could buy a monument, Joe, a big white one," Celie said wistfully. "Mamma was saving for one for Ole, you know."

"I thought Ole'd like it better if I brought a little fir tree, Cele, and planted it there, maybe a white pine; that'd last."

"Yes, only I'd like the stone, too," Celie insisted. They walked slowly out to the fence. Joe carried his shovel in one hand and Rose Marie on his shoulder.

"I'm glad they both died in the summer, Joe, when it's warm," Celie whispered. She put her hand tight to her lips. Selma and Norm were waiting in the road by the car. She didn't want them to see her cry.

"Don't you want me to stay with you awhile, Cele?" Selma asked when they came to their house.

"Oh, no, Selma, thanks. I got lots to do. I haven't washed yet this week and the house hasn't been cleaned." So Selma and Norm went on with Mrs. Maloney. Joe and Celie and Rose Marie and Jole went into the house.

The small square room was stiffly in order. In the kitchen the clothes-bars were covered with clean clothes.

"Oh, Joe, look! Mis' Biehl and Mis' Suess must've done the washing an' everything." Celie walked through the house. There was nothing left to do. And then Rose Marie cried and woke Jole. It was time to feed the babies.

"I'll feed Rosie, Cele, you go ahead and nurse Jole. Poor little kids," Joe said, but he looked over at Celie.

4

THE week after Christina died, Celie kept herself at home. She was tired, more tired than before Jole was born. After her work was done, she lay down on the bed and slept until Rose Marie woke. She couldn't seem to get rested.

The women were good about stopping in to see her. They came to talk of Christina, but the news of the town was uppermost in their minds. Celie didn't always listen when they talked.

"Hans Swinson died even though they took him in to Clarion, Cele," they told her, "and Mrs. Swinson's goin' to sue the comp'ny. You could too if she collects."

"It couldn't do any good," answered Celie.

Some of the women were bitter about the doctor.

"They say if he'da been on the job and sent them speci-
mens in on Verneaus when they first took sick, Christina
wouldn'ta got it," Mrs. O'Malley told her. Celie went
on washing Rose Marie's hands without answering.
Christina was dead now. She couldn't make it seem
true, but it was. She told herself over and over every
day. What good was there to talk? Some line around
Celie's mouth was like Christina's. She had come to understand a little why Christina was always so quiet.

Saturday noon, Celie sat outside on the top step to
wait for Joe. Last week at this time, Christina was still
living, Celie told herself. She didn't die till afternoon.
It was hard to think of her dead, a clear warm day like
this. The trees where the woods began were kind of a
blue-green. You couldn't tell where the sky and lake
met, they were all of a piece. Living up at the end of
town without any real neighbors, you got to notice those
things more. The faint whistle of the train came to her
over the roofs of the town. The limey whistle was
really louder than the Clarion train. You could just
make out the thin curl of smoke way around the edge
of the lake. It seemed to hang in the sky like a cloud
without moving. The train came into sight around the
bend. Watching it, Celie didn't see the men tramping
out from the woods until they were even with the
house. Forty or more. Celie looked around, startled.
Of course, the camps were breaking up like Art Farley

said they would. The lumberjacks must have been paid off today.

The men looked alike at first; rough-looking, in their heavy boots, plaid shirts and stagged pants. Funny, the way they always tied their stuff up in a bandanna on the end of a stick; no, there was one with a regular soldier's pack. One man's beard came half-way to his belt. Three of them walked together, the rest straggled all over the road. One man walked alone a ways behind the rest. In the middle, was a young fellow with straw-colored hair, he looked like a Swede. Not many Swedes out in the camps, Joe said.

Queer the way they didn't talk to each other, just tramped along. Some of them would catch that train back to Clarion, some would hike it in. She wondered if there were any more left in the woods; the camps ran slack in the summer time, though. They stared at her all the way past. One man poked the man next to him in the ribs and jerked his head toward Celie. She caught his eyes. He looked down at the road in confusion and stumbled. She was the first woman they had seen in a couple of months, maybe.

They passed, their heads and shoulders bobbing up and down with their uneven paces. They got down to the pump at the corner, then even with Wilhelm's old house. The red bandanna of the last man in the group jerked crazily above the corner of Wilhelm's roof. Celie's end of the road seemed quieter than before. The trees beyond Helsen's stood up more silently than ever. The blue-green clump of woods seemed lonely.

. . . No noise of saws or whistling, no sound of cursing or the thud of logs, thrown one against the other to drown out the sound of the wind in the woods any more. Woodchucks would be at the old freight cars for the salt of men's hands still on the board tables and bunks. Coyote and lynx cats would come close to the clearing. Deer would venture down to the cutover land near the camp . . .

Celie sat with her chin on her hand. She had been lonesome all week. A dull sense of loss was still with her. Seeing the lumberjacks tramp past only deepened her feeling. She stared down the street unseeingly. There was a place inside her where she could think about things and feel them over again. She had only just found it. It shut out everyone but Christina and Ole and the Farleys and sometimes Joe. She was glad when both children were asleep and she could sit still and find herself there.

Joe came up the street. He saw Celie before she saw him. Moping again. It had been hard on Cele losing Ole and then Christina. It was going to be hard to tell her about the mill. She'd been so wrapped up in Christina's death she seemed to have forgotten the talk about the mill closing. He'd been just as glad.

" 'Lo, Cele," he called out.

"Oh, Joe, I was waiting for you."

278

They sat down at the kitchen table. Joe poured brown-sugar syrup on his pancakes.

"Celie, the mill's closing down today." His eyes watched the lip of the pitcher for the last drop of syrup while he said it.

Celie sat still, watching Joe's face. She had never thought Joe could look like that. Even when she told him about Rosie coming he didn't look that way; ashamed, almost. This thing she hadn't quite believed could happen was here. It had almost happened. "Joe, are you sure?" She asked it in a low, startled voice.

"Yeah, old man Farley told me. He's been up here running the mill since Art left. I guess he didn't know Art had skinned out when he came. Anyway, there's a notice on the door of the store and down at the mill."

"What'll we do, Joe?" Celie asked after a bewildered pause.

Joe looked over at her. She was taking it better than he thought she would. She'd always wanted to get away 'cause she was scared of the mill shutting down. "Norm and I are going into Clarion this afternoon to look for a job." He'd saved this to tell her if she cried or anything. Celie was getting sensible, though, ever since that time on the new road when they came on the ice cake. Only she was awful quiet. "Of course, there's a lot of lumber in the yard. They'll keep me as long as there's a stick left, not so much pay, I guess, but it'll be something."

279

"When are you starting for Clarion; you'll want your dessert in a hurry." Celie's eyes were curiously hard.

"I've had enough. We thought we'd go right after dinner. Norm's going to take his car."

"When did you know it? About the mill closing, I mean?"

Joe looked out the window. "Oh, I've had an idea about it, everybody yapping about it so hard, but I didn't believe it'd really happen, this year, anyway." Joe mumbled his words. He hadn't thought it would close up tight . . . all that lumber in the yard . . . folks still needed lumber, that was the way he looked at it. And it wouldn't in ordinary times, it was like old Farley said, the depression . . .

"You see, Celie, the depression's knocked the lumber business for a loop." Joe brought the words out eagerly. It seemed to explain why his guess was wrong; it kind of accounted for the mill, too.

It was the first time Celie had heard the word depression. It was a big word. She was uncertain about its meaning. But she could feel it: something the way she had felt when those lumberjacks went by this noon, the way when Art Farley left . . .

"You know, Cele, due to the flop in Wall Street. Boy! we're lucky not to be caught like them big money-eyed guys, in a regular blind alley. I was telling Norm that." Joe's voice gained confidence. He'd felt pretty bad when Farley told him for sure about the mill.

Celie's mind followed slowly: depression—Wall

Street—those headlines in the paper that day; they were all bound up together. She hadn't seen a paper for ever so long, to read it, that is. She got up abruptly and started clearing the table. Joe sat a minute longer, finishing his cigarette, then he went into the bedroom to get dressed.

"Don't wake Rosie, Joe."

Celie pumped water on the dishes. The cold water made greasy streaks over the syrupy plates. She felt like crying, more than when Christina died, but she went on washing dishes instead. She was wiping up the nickel parts of the stove, the curlycue letters that spelled Royal Oak on the oven door when Joe came back out. He always looked a little strange in his best blue serge. She dried her hands and fixed his tie.

"You oughta shine your shoes up, Joe."

He hadn't worn his best suit since the night they got stuck in the road. When she pressed the trousers there wasn't much crease left to follow by. She'd gotten the one on the left leg a little crooked, but it wouldn't show when he walked.

Joe always seemed to like his suit when he got it on, Celie thought. When they lived in Clarion and he had a city job, he'd wear city suits all the time. Gee, it'd be nice. Her spirits rose.

"Well, s'long, Cele, maybe I'll have a job in a bank when I get back."

"D'ye think you can get one, Joe? You know that other time you looked . . ."

"I know, but I didn't look so hard, really. I had a good job here an' I couldn't see throwing it up unless it was for more money. Tell you, Cele, maybe I'll look around a little for a house, too. It'll have to have a yard around it though." Joe's voice was confident. A little shiver of excitement went through Celie.

" 'By, Joe." She kissed him, as wives kiss husbands going off to get a new job; hopefully, proudly, with only the least touch of misgiving in their minds.

Selma came up to sit with Celie after lunch. It was hot in the house. They took the children out on the steps where the sight of the woods across from Helsen's made them feel cooler.

"When are you going to pack up your mother's house, Celie?" Selma asked.

"I don't know, I thought I'd wait till we know where we're going to live."

Selma nodded. "Gee, I hope we live near each other in Clarion. Imagine living where you can walk downtown and back before supper!"

"I can wheel the babies down easy."

"Maybe we might get one of those two-family houses and you live on one floor and we on the other."

"Joe'n I'd have to have the downstairs 'cause of the children."

"You'll have a lot of furniture with Christina's, too, won't you?"

"I could furnish four bedrooms," said Celie, slowly. She hadn't thought of Christina's things as belonging to her before. She thought of Christina's dining room suite. She'd always liked that, and the cuckoo clock she used to be afraid of when she was little. Her mind came back to the present.

"I wonder if everyone will move away right off?" Celie wondered aloud.

"Sure, I guess. What is there to keep 'em with the mill closed up? Norm was telling me he went out with Guy Bates to give the order to the lumber camps an' some of them jacks were so dumb they couldn't take it in, at first. A couple of 'em don't even speak American. He had to tell 'em there wouldn't be any more meals there and make motions of eating and then shake his head before they could get it. Gee, it musta been funny. He 'n' Bill waited to see 'em start in and when they was looking over the camp to see what there was worth the comp'ny's hauling in, they found the one old jack with white hair sitting out back of the saw filer's hut. He could talk American all right, but he just wouldn't believe 'em. Norm kept telling him and he kept looking around and saying, 'Plenty of lumber here; I ain't working in no mill.' Norm says he was a scream, half cuckoo, prob'ly. Finally they had to come back without him. If he don't come in a couple of days they'll go back for him."

Celie took Jole up to nurse him. "I wonder what Joe's father'll do? Maybe he can get work for the fish market in Clarion in the summer."

"He's lived alone, anyway, since Joe an' you got married, hasn't he?"

"He'll probably go on the same way. There's houses enough." Celie looked down the street over the gray peaked roofs of the houses and thought of them empty. "He could even have a house with a bathroom if he wanted." Celie put Jole to sleep in the carriage Mrs. Wilhelm had left behind. She sat on the corner of the stoop and kept one slender foot in a cracked patent leather opera pump on the spring to make it jiggle.

"The first thing I'll need to buy when I get to Clarion is a new pair of pumps," Celie said.

"They say folks in Clarion don't use mail order catalogues hardly at all," Selma commented.

"Look, there's Mrs. Flauberg coming up here to visit. I'll go in an' put the coffee pot on," Celie said.

Mrs. Flauberg was nearly Christina's age. She was a tall Swedish woman with black hair pulled back into a tight knot. Her lawn dress with caps of organdie at the shoulder made her long arms appear longer. The billowing organdie collar curved around a long thin neck.

" 'Lo, Celie, I been meaning to get up to see you ever since Christina died." She sat down on the step. "Gracious, there's so many things happening here all at once, you don't know what to worry over most. Mrs. Maloney was telling me today, the danger from typhoid's over, anyway."

"It better be," Selma laughed. "Them shots made my arm sore for three days."

284

"Well, I hope Mis' Swinson collects on the comp'ny. She's been to Clarion 'n' got a real lawyer. You couldn't do that, Celie, 'cause you weren't what you could call dependent on your ma."

Celie was still shy at the mention of Christina. She said nothing.

"And d'you know what Mis' Maloney told me to-day, that the doc's leaving tomorrow. He's through like the rest of us. I'd think he'd be willing to after lettin' the Verneaus spread typhoid around."

"I guess there won't be any more babies in the Point then!" Selma said, laughing.

"Oh, yes, there's always babies. I lived in a town where there wasn't any doctor when Fred was born. The town'll go on the county nurse, that's all. A doctor doesn't do so much, anyway." Mrs. Flauberg sniffed. "My man took care of me."

Celie went in to get the coffee ready.

"Look, Cele," Selma called in through the screen door, "I bet that's the lumberjack I was telling you about wouldn't leave when the rest did."

Down the dusty road from the woods came the stubby figure of an old man. He shuffled along uncertainly. He carried an old felt hat in his hand. On his head, he wore a bandanna knotted at the corners. Celie came to the screen door to see him. "Aw, I'm going to give him a cup of coffee," she said impulsively.

"Hey, there," Selma called out to him. "D'ye want

some coffee?" She giggled. "He probably only drinks moon, Cele."

The old man stopped still in the road, hesitating. Then he came across to the steps. There was no expression in his stolid face. He sat down on the path where Rose Marie was digging in the dirt. Selma called out to her in alarm,

"Here, Rosie, come here, baby," but the little girl forgot to dig, looking at the man with the funny hat on his head. Celie came back with a tin cup of coffee and a piece of cake. She felt kind of foolish now. When she got near him, she saw how dirty his hands were. He smelled of sweat and grime worse than Hels Helsen. The heavy woolen jumper he wore even in July was ragged and patched. He grunted as he took the cup and cake. He blew noisily on the coffee while Rose Marie watched. He drank it in gulps and ate the cake even to the crumbs that had fallen on the front of his jumper. Selma and Mrs. Flauberg and Celie watched him in silence. Celie stood close by Rose Marie.

When he finished, he got up from the ground. Celie noticed how blue his eyes were, like Rose Marie's. He picked up his hat and fished some half-wilted stalks of fireweed out of the crown.

"Here, girlie." He gave them to Rose Marie who clutched them delightedly, making pleased exclamations to Celie. The old man turned and tramped down the road, wobbling a little from one side of the road to another.

Celie tried to take the flowers from Rose Marie. "Dirty flowers, Rosie." She made a sound of disgust in her throat, but Rose Marie held on to them and started to cry. "Oh, all right, then; I guess he just picked them." As she looked at them, she remembered suddenly the same purple pink flowers growing in the old root cellar that day in Mead. She got up quickly.

"Come on in and drink your coffee," she said to Selma and Mrs. Flauberg. Rose Marie sat waving the flowers and crowing.

"Don't it beat all, the way kids'll take a notion to something like that, just that old fireweed!" said Mrs. Flauberg.

They were drinking their second cups of coffee when the five-thirty mill whistle blew. The shrill sound cut across the life of the Point like the sharp edge of a saw. The three women in the last company house were silent. Celie set down her cup, because her hand shook a little. The sound ceased as suddenly as it had begun, leaving no echo behind it. It had been, it was gone, an impertinent futile scream, louder only for a second than the deeper, everlasting sounds of the wind and the trees and the waters of Lake Superior.

"Don't seem's though it wouldn't keep on every morning, noon and night the way it always has done," said Mrs. Flauberg finally.

"Look, Cele, it made Jole cry. Can I go get him?" Celie nodded.

5

SELMA helped Celie put the children to bed. Then they went back to sit on the step. The trees beyond Helsen's were black now; the lake was indistinct but the sky above them was light. Streaks of white light played over the sky, ribbing it as the wind ribs the sand.

"It's almost light enough to read out here." Selma's voice was softer than usual, drawing some cadence from the soft night air. Celie sat sidewise on the step, her head back, her eyes on the moving streaks of the Northern Lights. They were silent a long time.

"If we weren't going to move into town, I mean if the mill were going and all, and we stayed right here, Selma, I don't believe I'd move down to Mamma's. I like it up here by the woods. It's lonesome, but it's kind of still and peaceful."

"But you'd have a separate dining room and a bathroom and an upstairs there," Selma answered incredulously. The house you had in the Point was a large factor in determining social status.

"I know, but you get more view up here."

The wavering white lights across the sky changed to pale green and yellow. They brushed lightly over the stars like a peacock's tail. A soft radiance fell on the long low sheds of the mill. The sky was white just back of the four black smokestacks. Celie felt less tired tonight. She drew a long breath as though to take strength from the wide-spaced night. Her shoulders relaxed against the side of the door.

"Celie, see those lights down by the lake? I bet those are Norm's lights," Selma said excitedly. They watched. The lights came along the lake to the store and turned up toward them. The boys were home.

Celie went hurriedly inside to heat up supper. She couldn't meet them there at the door. She would know the minute she saw Joe whether he had a job or not. She couldn't stand to know so suddenly. She would rather hear the news slowly.

She opened the draft on the stove. All the time her ears were listening intently for every word Joe and Norm said to Selma. She heard them come in the house and fled, on a sudden impulse, to the woodshed for cream. She forgot that it was in on the window sill. Joe was a long time coming out to her, Celie thought, heating the meat gravy to pour over the rice.

"Where's Cele?" she heard him ask finally. Celie heard him come out to the kitchen. She kept her eyes on the little bubbles forming in the gravy.

"Hello, Joe," she called carelessly; "tell Norm and Selma to come sit down." Her voice was high and brittle with fear; her hands were cold, even the one holding the handle of the hot saucepan.

"But, Norm, however did you know they wanted someone?"

Then Norm had a job, Celie told herself. What about Joe? She served the four plates and put them in front of each one. She hadn't looked at him yet. She tasted the rice first and raised her eyes to Joe's.

After all, she couldn't tell. He was eating hungrily. His hair needed brushing back a little. He had pulled the knot of his tie loose from his collar and unfastened the top button, the way he did. Whether he had found a job or not, he looked just the same. Celie took courage.

"Did you boys have any luck?" she asked.

"Say, that's the hardest work I've done since the night shift, Cele. I bet I was in the office of every plant and mill and railroad station in Clarion," Joe said.

Celie waited.

"Every place, they had the same story. 'We're laying off!' or 'We've cut everybody in half, as it is!' Only one place, the coal yards for the Blue Ribbon Coal Co. they said to come back next month; maybe they'd need a night watchman. That'd be like going on the night shift again. I didn't think much of that. That's a regular old man's job anyway. I'd rather stay on here."

It was a long speech for Joe. Celie couldn't eat any more.

"So you didn't find anything?" she asked in a husky voice.

"No," said Joe, "no, Celie, I didn't."

"Oh, Celie, Norm got a job for a florist, running their delivery truck; and he's going to wear a uniform all the time." Selma's voice was excited.

"I've got to start in Monday, so we'll have to find us a house Sunday."

"You were lucky, Norm," Celie said without enthusiasm.

"Joe really saw the sign first. We were driving into town and Joe says, 'There's a sign, driver wanted'; I told him he oughta take it."

"You were the driver, weren't you?" Joe asked and laughed.

Joe doesn't really want to get away. He'd just as soon stay on here where he doesn't have to hustle around, Celie thought bitterly.

"I'll tell you, Joe, I'll be down there where I can keep an eye out for you right along. I'll find a job for you before winter."

Celie was glad when Selma and Norm went. She sank down on the step after they drove off. She felt she had spent all day here. The peace of the night, the faraway magic of the Northern Lights didn't touch her. A bitter contempt, stirred up by fear, filled her. Joe sat down on a lower step and took out his pipe. They were silent for a while.

"Celie, I'm sorry; there weren't any jobs worth having. Every place you went people were talking about the depression."

"You mean you didn't want to get away! You could have taken the job Norm took till you got something better. You never wanted to get a job, you like it here!"

She accused him bitterly. Joe tried to break in, but Celie went on.

"Oh, it doesn't matter what you say, you're just like your father; you'll never get anywhere. Only it's a pity you're married." Her eyes found a tip of a pine tree that stuck up above the black clump. It had a single, sharp point.

Joe was silent so long Celie looked at him quickly. In the greenish light, Joe's face was strangely white. She couldn't see his eyes clearly; they were dark spots in the pale skin. She leaned closer to him.

"Joe, answer me; you knew all the time the mill would close; that I wanted to get away from this hole and you never meant to move!" Her face was close to his. She could see every expression; the stubborn, moody look of his eyes, the line of his mouth. She could see that she hurt him, but he was a weak good-for-nothing; she wanted to hurt him. Everyone would move away and leave them, her and Joe, in the half-empty village with tumble-down houses around them; the children would run wild over the place, she'd have babies without any doctor. Joe had promised her they'd go. When they went together before they were married, Joe always talked about getting a radio job. He'd forgotten about that. She used the radio he'd discarded out in the shed to set things on.

"Joe Linsen, you lied to me!" She brought it out white-hot, fed on her fear of loneliness, of being left behind. She had said it now. It stood out in the night, sharp as the tip of that far pine tree. The very knowledge that she could hurt him cooled her anger. It gave her a kind of power. She felt that she was stronger than Joe. She looked at him pityingly. He didn't answer. "Joe," her voice changed. In the eerie light, her face was an odd mixture of fragility and cruel strength.

Suddenly, into the tense atmosphere between Joe and Celie, into every house of the Point, came for the second time that night the strident clamor of the mill whistle.

Celie started and clutched Joe's sleeve. Once, it blew a short blast; then two, then three. "Joe, it's the fire-alarm!" Celie whispered.

"Cele, you stay up here where you're safe. You can watch from up here. If there's any danger, I'll come and get you."

Joe had gone, half running, and half sliding down the hill. Celie heard doors bang and autos start. Hels Helsen came by on heavy, padding feet. As she watched a new light flashed into the sky, hot as the fading greenish lights were cold, a gigantic, orange light, topped with grayish white clouds of smoke. It was fire, all right. It was back of the mill, one of the lumber piles, maybe. If one started, they'd all go; the whole town would go. She and Joe would have to leave. Celie felt a sudden wicked joy.

The reflection of the flame lighted the town. She could hear men shouting. She saw the little old-fashioned fire engine being dragged by men down to the mill. Even as she looked the hot, greedy, orange flames were choked with black smoke. Celie watched breathlessly.

Rose Marie cried at the strange noises. Celie wrapped a blanket around her and brought her out to watch the fire.

It wasn't gaining. It was dying down. The town wasn't going to go up in one glorious fire that would wipe it all out and make them leave. It would fall through, like everything else, just peter out. As the burst of colored flame died down it was too dark to see more than the big outlines of the village. Celie took Rose Marie into the house.

It was four in the morning before Joe came home. Celie had fallen asleep on top of the bed. She woke at the whine of the screen door. Joe's face was black and streaked with sweat. His shirt was gone and his tie. The trousers to his city suit were burned in jagged holes. Celie sat up in bed.

"Joe, what ever happened? Are you all right?"

"Oh, some of them damned fool Austrians and Polaks were so mad at the mill closing down they got together and tried to set fire to the place. They thought it'd be a swell idea to begin with the dry lumber; that's the most valuable to the comp'ny, an' they started with that little shack I keep my check sheets in and all, 'cause it's in the middle of them piles. Well, I got there and unlocked it and got the old fire extinguisher out somehow. We had a fight, but keeping the water on the other piles we got it out. Somebody'll have to watch it all night, but I don't think there's much of any danger." He chuckled. "I guess old man Farley thinks this is pretty wild country. Sam Andres, you know, the big tall Pole? Well, he come up next to Farley and shook his fist at him. He swore he'd kill him if he closed down the mill and made his kids go hungry, and then they both worked on the same hose. Lord, I'm tired." Joe threw himself across the bed.

"Gee, Joe, why didn't you let the whole place burn? I hoped it would."

Joe looked at her, curiously. "Gosh, Cele, I don't know what to think of you! That's the best hardwood you can get any place. Anyway, don't you know I'm foreman down in the yard?"

"Not anymore you aren't."

"Say, get this, Cele, I'm foreman till the last stick is sold out of there." He thumped his pillow and turned over on the bed.

She'd better go lock the screen door. When she came back, Joe was asleep. Celie stood and looked at him a minute. He shouldn't have gone to bed without washing his face. It'd be dried on in the morning.

She unlaced his city shoes and peeled off his rayon socks without waking him, then she covered him over with the quilt. Funny, the way he could make her feel small. She went over and pulled the covers up around Jole and Rosie. The air off the lake was cool in the morning. She got into bed beside Joe.

CONSULADO GENERAL DE ESPAÑA EN LOS
ESTADOS UNIDOS DE AMÉRICA (Los Ángeles)

N.I.F: S2812241D

UNI DESCRIPCION	DTO	IMPORTE
1 Costes complemetarios		100,00

TOTAL TICKET...   100,00
ENTREGADO CONTADO.   100,00
CAMBIO...   0,00
IMPORTE EN USD

21/06/2007 - 08:25:09 Num:07241010001231
GRACIAS POR SU VISITA
LE ATENDIO MP

Part VI

THE mill at the Point had been closed over a month. Old Mike Farley had gone back to Detroit. The Carlson House and the village of the Point were things of the past to him. The big company store had sold off its remaining stock to Frank Simpson, who opened a store in the front room of his house. Rats ran freely through the old company boarding house. Padlocks guarded the doors of the mill. In the mill-yard three streets of piled lumber-houses stood seasoning.

The main street of the town presented a solid front of vacant, staring windows and slowly rotting timber to the four smokeless stacks above the top of the mill. The last movie bill was still tacked up in front of the movie house, but the dust and rain of two months had powdered and blistered the picture faces. From a town of eight hundred souls when the camps were running full, the Point had sunk to thirty families, scattered up the three streets of the town.

The big house on the bluffs stood patiently surrounded by yellowing hay. There had been an effort to sell the place as a summer residence, but the prospective buyer wrote back that the abandoned mill town at its elbow was too great an eyesore to overlook.

The *Clarion Daily* printed an obituary to the town as "another of those lumber towns we must see pass, left high and dry by the financial depression in the business world." Selma Lichtenberg cut it out and sent it to Celie, writing underneath, "Look who's on the map now!" Celie saved it in Christina's Swedish Bible.

"The depression must be an awful thing in the cities," she commented to Joe.

The *Clarion Daily* could not know the reckless idleness of the Point or the life that flourished there; that Mrs. Hacula had a new baby, that the oldest Hacula girl and Mrs. Flauberg's boy were planning to be married, or that the old lumberjack who'd been the last to leave the woods, wandered back again and died on his hike into camp. Joe Linsen found him when he went to look at his traps. Hels Helsen had gotten a new white fox bitch from Alaska.

There was neither night nor day shift in the Point, yet Celie and Joe were busy. Joe and his father had a standing order with a market in Clarion for all the fish they could catch. Hans Nordgren said there was a chance Joe might be appointed a State trapper. Joe's eyes gleamed, but he thought he'd wait till he got it before he told Celie.

Celie and Joe moved down to Christina's house, after all. Jole and Rose Marie could have a room to themselves, and there was a good vegetable garden out back. But Celie missed her house next to the fox farm. This was Christina's house, still. Celie felt she must do everything as Christina had done it. There were too many empty houses out the windows. The one on each side was deserted, till Mrs. O'Malley moved in on one side. Celie missed the woods across the road and the gangly maple tree outside the kitchen window. But she went with Joe whenever she could.

Sometimes, she felt the deep quiet of the village like a weight in her body. She was depressed and lonely as she never had been before. She would stop from her sweeping and rush in and pick Jole up out of his basket to hug him.

One day Joe was off all day and the rain fell steadily between her house and the Bernsens' empty windows. She took Rose Marie and Jole on the bed with her and pulled the blanket up over their heads to drown out the melancholy sound of rain on the roof. One night, when Joe was up helping Helsen with a sick fox, Celie dressed up in the purple velvet dress she had worn at Farleys' and paraded up and down in front of her mirror, acting. She laughed at the mirrored reflection.

"Yes, Mr. Linsen and myself spent several months north of the straits on business, at a place just outside of Clarion. Clarion, itself, is only a small dump, not a place anyone would care to live in." She frowned in the mirror and deprecated the town with an airy wave of her hand.

Suddenly, in the midst of it, the play-acting ran out. Celie ripped off the purple dress and threw it on the closet shelf in a heap.

She missed Christina and Ole here in their house. One day she had a queer sense of missing herself, the Celie who used to live up in the room Rosie and Jole had, who used to go rushing out in the morning for fear of being late at the store. She was different now, she felt, and the thought sent her to the mirror to look at herself closely. She looked more than twenty, more like twenty-five, she told herself. Then she put a bright spot of rouge on each cheekbone and did her hair over before she went down to get supper.

She went through Christina's trunks and packed away her clothes until she could bring herself to give them away. In among the things Christina had brought from Sweden, Celie found her wedding picture. She looked at it a long time. Christina looked back at her with merry eyes. Soft loops of fair hair lay under the coquettish lace cap. Celie noticed the firm throat above the collar of the dress. She remembered Christina's neck with the deep hollows and her wrinkled, sagging breasts. There was only the faintest suggestion of the Christina Celie knew in the picture. Celie set the picture on top of the sideboard. She showed it to Joe when he came home to dinner.

"Christina looks so young here, doesn't she, Joe?" She hung over the picture wistfully.

"Sure, an' Ole looks pretty proud of her."

"I wish she hadn't had it so hard."

"Why, I don't think she did have. It always seemed to me that Ole and Christina had a good time. I used to look at 'em when I first boarded here, Cele, and think what a swell couple they were."

Celie cleared the table in thoughtful silence.

"They always lived off up here, Joe. Christina always

worked herself to death. I'll never forget how tired she looked when she died."

"Ole always liked it up here. There wasn't a man in the town people thought more of, an' they were independent, Celie. They would be if they were still living here. Lots of people their ages're on the dole, getting enough to live on, handed out to 'em by charity, in the cities. You wouldn't catch Ole takin' charity."

" 'Course, but I mean some people have gotten along, Joe, and made money and had servants an' all. I wish Christina and Ole could have . . ."

Joe got out his pipe. You couldn't talk to women.

"Say, Cele, d'you want to ride out with me this afternoon while I chop some wood? Stumpf says anybody that's a mind to can have the wood that's left after the first cutting. I thought maybe I could get a cord or two to sell in Clarion for ready money. We could take Hels' old truck to cart it in."

"Sure, Joe, you bet, I'll hurry with the dishes."

Celie rode with Joe on the front seat of the truck. Rose Marie sat between them. Jole's basket, covered with mosquito netting, rode securely in the back.

"Look, Joe, maybe we could move that maple down to our house, d'ye think?" Celie asked as they went past their old house.

Joe looked at it calculatingly. "Sure, I don't know why not; where'd you put it?"

"By the corner of the porch, Joe, an' then it would be nice and shady when it got big."

Joe drove silently. Women were changeable, all right. Here Celie was planning on waiting for a tree to grow big enough to shade the porch when the next minute she talked about nothing but getting away.

They drove slowly by the cemetery. The mullen stalks had grown way above the crude wooden crosses.

"That little tree's doing good, isn't it, Cele?"

Then the hardwoods began. On either side of the road, stretched the shaded tangles of underbrush, the brown boles of the fir trees, the white and yellow gray of the birches, the deeper gray of the beech and maple trees.

"Look, Joe, the leaves are turning, already." A single branch among the green leaves of a maple tree hung like a scarlet flag out over the road.

"The mill owns all this in here. I s'pose when it starts up again, they'll clear it."

"D'ye think it ever will start up again, Joe?"

"I don't know why not, they can't get their money out till they do. You know, Cele, if we ever get some money ahead, I might buy up this piece of hardwoods."

They rode along silently again. Celie had never thought of buying woods. She had to think about it. It would be fun to know all these trees belonged to you, though.

" 'Course, I don't ever suppose we will have enough money. I bet that piece of woods runs to something close to a thousand dollars, but that's the way folks get rich, not taking drivers' jobs in Clarion."

Joe's mind dismissed the subject. His thoughts centered on Snake Creek that came down through the woods. But Celie's mind held to it. Maybe Joe was right. Christina had a hundred dollars in the bank in Clarion. There was a little book to show it. Maybe they could add to it, a little at a time. Celie, woman-wise, was happier with a concrete goal. Joe drove the truck in over the bumpy log road half a mile or more. Celie had to get in back to hold Jole's basket steady.

"There we are!"

Celie got out and Joe put Jole's basket on the flat top of an old white pine stump. In the clearing there were yellow leaves already. The sun fell warmly on the discarded leafy tops of trees and fir boughs thrown out of the way. There was plenty of wood carelessly left behind, free for the taking. Rose Marie's "Daddy, Daddy" sounded loudly in the stillness. The air was pungent with the smell of balsam and pine, and the autumn scent of dying leaves and rotting stumps. Joe found the top of a tree thick enough through for firewood and pulled it into the clear space. The sound of his ax stirred echoes through the woods.

Celie picked up acorns for Rosie. "Say, Joe, you know what?"

Joe stopped impatiently. "No, what?"

"I bet we could get orders for wreaths in at Clarion,

Christmas wreaths. You could get me the stuff, and I could make 'em."

Joe went back to his work. Celie sat down on the ground to try it. Rosie sat close by watching and jabbering.

"See, Rosie, we'll use these boughs with the brown things on an' I bet they'll sell like everything."

Joe worked every day for a week. He was off for the woods by five. When Joe had something to do, he needed no mill whistle or time clock to drive him. Each night he came home with fir boughs for Celie, pick-up wood for their own woodshed and the solid sticks for selling in Clarion. Nellie Hann's husband and the Hacula boys and Frank Simpson took his advice and went out to gather their wood for the winter. "Too thin picking to make it pay to sell in Clarion, Joe," Arvid Hacula told him.

"Well, I got plenty of time," said Joe.

An idle lawlessness pervaded the town. Maloney, the sheriff, knew the Haculas and the Saboniches were making moon, but when they warned him they didn't want any interference, he said, "I'm no sheriff, any more; I'm in the fishing business." The policy of live and let live controlled the life of the Point.

Saturday morning, after Joe had been carting wood for a week, Joe and Celie, with Rosie and Jole crowded into the front seat of the truck, two cords of firewood piled behind them, drove in to Clarion. Joe would sell his wood and see about orders for wreaths, then they would go to Selma and Norm's for dinner.

Celie wore the dark wool dress of Charlotte Farley's. She had gloves in her purse to put on in Clarion. Her opera pumps were shined so the cracks across the toes scarcely showed. Rosie wore the pink silk dress and bonnet that Christina had given her last Easter. Jole wore his best bonnet. But Joe wore his plaid shirt and Soo woolens tucked into his heavy boots. "I'm in the lumber business, Cele," he told her when she brought out his city suit with the one pair of trousers.

It was exciting driving in to town, down through the residence part to the street with the stores and the big bank building. The lumber and coal yards were down by the lake near the coppery red ore docks.

"D'ye want to get off up town, Cele, so people don't see you riding on a truck?"

"No, I want to see if you can sell it first." Celie sat on the truck in the dirty yard of the Consumers Coal, Ice and Wood Co. The sound of coal sliding into the wagons scared Jole so he cried, but Rosie stood up to watch. Joe came out with a man from the office. They looked at the wood and talked.

"Couldn't do it any lower," Celie heard Joe say. The man wrote in a notebook. He and Joe went into the office again. Then Joe got in by the wheel.

"Will he buy it, Joe?" Celie whispered excitedly.

307

"Darn right," said Joe. He backed the truck up to an open shed and started unloading.

"Here, Joe, I can help." Celie jumped down and went around to the end of the truck.

"Say, get back in there. What d'ye take me for, a damned Austrian?" Celie climbed back up, somehow pleased.

They drove away from the yard with the empty truck. "Here, Cele, here's five dollars. You take Rosie and do some shopping. Buy yourself a new pair of shoes or something," said Joe importantly.

Celie smiled happily as she tucked the bill into her purse. There were some things in the Five and Dime she wanted. The shoes could wait, though. They had to save money, her and Joe.

Joe drove to the florist's and showed them Celie's wreaths. She didn't make them quite right. They must be tied this way. The man showed Joe how. Then they'd take them. They'd pay fifty cents a wreath for the big ones, twenty-five cents for the little ones. Joe wouldn't believe it. Celie was a smart girl, the kind that helped her man ahead, more than fretting all the time. He hadn't always been sure of Cele, but he might have known; she was Christina and Ole Henderson's daughter. He picked her up on the corner of Main and Sunset streets, by the Clarion Savings Bank. She was coming out of the big swinging door with Rosie as he drove up. Gee, she was a kippy looking one, Joe thought to himself admiringly and forgot to wonder why she came out of the bank.

They drove to Selma's new address. They had a time finding it. It was a two-room flat above a grocery store. It had no front entrance, Celie noticed. Selma was at the door at the top of the dark flight of stairs.

"My, Celie, it's good to see you. I haven't spoken to another woman since I've been here. I've never been so lonesome." She hugged the babies eagerly. "Norm and I want to get up to the Point Sunday."

"Look, Cele, let me show you, look at the bathroom and a washtub right here under the drainboard. We've got a bed that pulls out of here, and a place to shake your dust pan, even." Celie followed Selma around and admired the two rooms and bath.

"How does Norm like it, Selma?" Joe asked.

"Well, he likes it fine, only right after he got the job, a man walked in an' offered to do it for fifteen dollars a week, so Norm had to say he'd do it for that to keep his job. And rent here is dear; we pay twenty-two for this flat," Selma said a little proudly. "Maybe we're going to sell our car 'cause we can use the greenhouse delivery truck Sundays."

"Oh, Cele, I forgot to show you the little ice box, built right in the wall, and the ice comes up on the dumb-waiter. 'Course it isn't electric, but it's a lot better than the root cellar we had in the Point." Celie looked in at the scanty contents of the ice box and decided against staying.

"Well, Selma, we got to go, but we'll expect you and Norm tomorrow for dinner." Selma accepted with alacrity.

"Say, Cele, I keep thinking of you and how blue it must make you, off up there with all the empty houses. Norm's going to keep his eye open for you, Joe."

Joe and Celie drove away on the truck with Jole and Rosie squeezed in between them.

"You didn't want to stay to eat, Celie?" Joe asked as they drove away.

"No, she didn't have only barely enough for themselves. I thought we could buy some wieners and have a picnic on the way home, Joe."

They drove back out the Clarion road toward the Point. Rosie chewed graham crackers contentedly. Jole was asleep. Celie was quiet, thinking about Selma's flat. Her own five rooms seemed spacious, with the front door opening right out doors. From their bedroom windows they could see the lake. All the rents in the Point were only five dollars a month, now, since the mill closed up.

The road was dusty. The mid-afternoon heat of September lay hot on Rosie's curly hair as she leaned against Celie. Celie could feel it through her wool dress. The road curved sharply; that was Deadman's Curve, and then the plains where they got stuck last winter. The road seemed familiar, as though it belonged to her and Joe. She remembered coming over it so many times; the time she drove to Clarion with Art Farley; the morning after she and Joe were married and she was kinda scared to go back. . . .

The road followed close to Superior. The lake looked hazy today in the early fall heat. There was Mead stretched lazily out in the sun.

"I'm getting hungry, Cele. What d'ye say we stop here?" Joe asked, looking straight at Celie.

Cele hesitated. "Oh, Joe, I don't want to stop there, ever since . . ."

"What's the matter? You ain't sorry for that day, are you, Cele?"

"No," answered Celie slowly, "no, I'm not." She raised her chin a trifle. "Only, it seems a long time ago, doesn't it?"

They got out of the truck. Joe carried the baby's basket. Celie carried the bag of lunch they had brought. Joe strode ahead to the tumbledown house with a wooden trellis hanging by one scantling to the side of the porch.

"There."

They sat down on the grass to eat their lunch.

"That wasn't so bad for one day, was it, Cele?" Celie shook her head. "You know, Cele, there's lots of ways of making a living without a reg'lar job. I don't want you to worry just cause the mill's shut down. We'll manage, all right. 'Course, I don't know how soon we can get away from the Point, but . . ."

"I guess I can stand it awhile," Celie said. "I'd hate to be crowded in some place like Selma is."

Both the children were asleep. Joe and Celie had the world to themselves. Not another living being breathed within miles of them. Another winter's wind had blown away the ghosts of the old town. The spring's rain, the summer's sun had cleansed and sweetened every tumbledown dwelling. Out beyond the town lay the lake.

Joe stretched out in the warm grass and laid his head down in Celie's lap. He looked up in her face. "Gee, Cele, you're swell." Celie looked down at him, a little sadly.

Joe hadn't changed the way she had. He was just the same; there was no changing him. He wouldn't go very far, maybe, but he was hers, anyway. Celie looked across the grassy street. There was the fireweed, violety pink masses of it, growing out beyond the root cellar, beyond the old houses to the line of woods. She'd hated it, that other time, she'd tried to take it out of Rosie's hand the other day, because it made her think of this place, but she kind of liked it today. It was pretty enough for a garden, almost, and sturdy to grow in that burned out ground.

Joe had fallen asleep, too, the easy way he did. He'd wake in a few minutes and be rested and want to go. Celie pushed back his hair from his sunburned forehead. Her eyes followed the waving stalks of the fireweed down to the narrow blue ribbon of lake. The stillness of the place, interrupted by a dozen insect sounds, made her strangely alert. She was glad to sit still and think things over inside herself.

Ever since Joe came back from fighting the fire, she had known they were not going to get away from the Point. She hadn't really let herself think about it, though, until now. She and Joe would always live there. She would grow old the way Christina had, but they would be independent like Christina and Ole; Joe would always make a living. She would always have to work hard; there would be more babies and she would look tired like Christina did, but it wouldn't matter, so much.

Rosie and Jole would go away. She would bring them up with that idea. They'd make a success down across the straits and come back and wonder how she ever stood it up here. It was all right; plenty of things were left to her, after all; seeing Rosie and Jole grow up and make their way, watching Joe leave the house and come back again, his head thrown back a little and his arms swinging so loose, the way they did, from his shoulders; knowing him every year better, his body and his thoughts even when he didn't talk, and his words.

"S'long, Cele," when he went out. "Celie, Celie?" questioning when he came in. He never called her "ma" the way some men called their wives.

A couple more months and it would be cold, snow again that blocked off the roads from the world, but today it was warm. Celie wriggled her shoulders a little and felt the warmth deep in her. She gave over thinking in the sheer, lazy content of the day. Whatever fears Celie had for the future, she shut her lips tightly upon, like Christina. They would manage all right, she and Joe.

A light wind sighed over the deserted mill town. It whispered among the stalks of the fireweed and sobbed softly in the top of a tall white pine.

Follies is published by Theatre Communications Group, Inc.,
355 Lexington Ave., New York, NY 10017–6603.

This publication is made possible in part with public funds from
the New York State Council on the Arts, a State Agency.

TCG books are exclusively distributed to the book trade by Consortium
Book Sales and Distribution, 1045 Westgate Dr., St. Paul, MN 55114.

LIBRARY OF CONGRESS CATALOGING-IN-PUBLICATION DATA

Sondheim, Stephen
[Follies. Libretto]
Follies / by Stephen Sondheim and James Goldman.— 1st ed.
p. cm.
ISBN 1-55936-196-4 (pbk. : alk. paper)
1. Musicals—Librettos. I. Goldman, James. II. Title.
ML50.S705 F65 2001
782.1'4'0268—dc21   00-068276

First TCG edition, November 2001

Cover image by Wim Hardeman, copyright © 2001 by Raoulfilm, Inc.
Text design and composition by Lisa Govan

PRODUCTION HISTORY

Follies was originally presented on April 4, 1971, by Harold Prince in association with Ruth Mitchell at the Winter Garden Theatre in New York City. It was directed by Harold Prince and Michael Bennett. Scenic production was by Boris Aronson, with costumes by Florence Klotz, lighting by Tharon Musser, choreography by Michael Bennett, orchestrations by Jonathan Tunick, musical direction by Harold Hastings and dance music arrangements by John Berkman. The cast was as follows:

MAJORDOMO	Dick Laressa
SALLY DURANT PLUMMER	Dorothy Collins
YOUNG SALLY	Marti Rolph
CHRISTINE DONOVAN	Ethel Barrymore Colt
WILLY WHEELER	Fred Kelly
STELLA DEEMS	Mary McCarty
MAX DEEMS	John J. Martin
HEIDI SCHILLER	Justine Johnston
CHAUFFEUR	John Grigas
MEREDITH LANE	Sheila Smith
ROSCOE	Michael Bartlett
DEEDEE WEST	Helen Blount
HATTIE WALKER	Ethel Shutta
EMILY WHITMAN	Marcie Stringer
THEODORE WHITMAN	Charles Welch
VINCENT	Victor Griffin
VANESSA	Jayne Turner

YOUNG VINCENT	Michael Misita
YOUNG VANESSA	Graciela Daniele
SOLANGE LAFITTE	Fifi D'Orsay
CARLOTTA CAMPION	Yvonne De Carlo
PHYLLIS ROGERS STONE	Alexis Smith
BENJAMIN STONE	John McMartin
YOUNG PHYLLIS	Virginia Sandifur
YOUNG BEN	Kurt Peterson
BUDDY PLUMMER	Gene Nelson
YOUNG BUDDY	Harvey Evans
DIMITRI WEISMANN	Arnold Moss
YOUNG STELLA	Julie Pars
YOUNG HEIDI	Victoria Mallory
KEVIN	Ralph Nelson
PARTY MUSICIANS	Taft Jordan, Aaron Bell, Charles Spics, Robert Curtis
SHOWGIRLS	Suzanne Briggs, Trudy Carson, Kathie Dalton, Ursula Maschmeyer, Linda Perkins, Margot Travers
SINGERS AND DANCERS	Graciela Daniele, Mary Jane Houdina, Sonja Lekova, Rita O'Connor, Julie Pars, Suzanne Rogers, Roy Barry, Steve Boockvor, Michael Misita, Joseph Nelson, Ralph Nelson, Ken Urmston, Donald Weissmuller

The singers and dancers appeared as guests, waiters, waitresses, photographers, chorus girls, chorus boys, etc.

Follies opened on July 21, 1987, at the Shaftesbury Theatre, London. It was produced by Cameron Mackintosh and directed by Mike Ockrent. It was designed by Maria Björnson with lighting design by Mark Henderson, sound design by Andrew Bruce, choreography by Bob Avian, orchestrations by Jonathan Tunick, musical direction by Martin Koch and dance music arrangements by Chris Walker. The cast was as follows:

STAGE MANAGER	Roy Sone
RONNIE COHEN	Ronnie Price
DIMITRI WEISMANN	Leonard Sachs
CARLOTTA CAMPION	Dolores Gray
STELLA DEEMS	Lynda Baron
HEIDI SCHILLER	Adele Leigh
SOLANGE LAFITTE	Maria Charles
HATTIE WALKER	Margaret Courtenay
BILLIE WHITMAN	Pearl Carr
WALLY WHITMAN	Teddy Johnson
SALLY DURANT PLUMMER	Julia McKenzie
BUDDY PLUMMER	David Healy
PHYLLIS ROGERS STONE	Diana Rigg
BEN STONE	Daniel Massey
ROSCOE	Paul Bentley
YOUNG PHYLLIS	Gillian Bevan
YOUNG SALLY	Deborah Poplett
YOUNG BEN	Simon Green
YOUNG BUDDY	Evan Pappas
CHRISTINE DONOVAN	Josephine Gordon

DEEDEE WEST	Dorothy Vernon
MEREDITH LANE	Jill Martin
MAX BLANCK	Bruce Graham
YOUNG HEIDI	Michelle Todd
MARGIE	Sally Ann Triplett
PARTY GUESTS, WAITERS, FOLLIES BOYS AND STAGEHANDS	Luke Baxter, Peppi Borza, Brad Graham, Stephen Lübmann, Raymond Marlowe, Roy Sone, Roger Sutton, Julian Wild
THE FOLLIES GIRLS	Lisa Henson, Margaret Houston, Vanessa Leagh Hicks, Jennifer Scott Malden, Siobhan O'Kane, Dawn Spence, Catherine Terry

Follies opened on April 5, 2001, at New York City's Roundabout Theatre Company (Todd Haimes, Artistic Director; Ellen Richard, Managing Director). It was directed by Matthew Warchus. Set design was by Mark Thompson, with costume design by Theoni V. Aldrege, lighting design by Hugh Vanstone, sound design by Jonathan Deans, choreography by Kathleen Marshall, orchestrations by Jonathan Tunick, musical direction by Eric Stern with John Miller and dance music arrangements by John Berkman and David Chase. The cast was as follows:

DIMITRI WEISMANN	Louis Zorich
SALLY DURANT PLUMMER	Judith Ivey
PHYLLIS ROGERS STONE	Blythe Danner
BENJAMIN STONE	Gregory Harrison
BUDDY PLUMMER	Treat Williams
ROSCOE	Larry Raiken
DEEDEE WEST	Dorothy Stanley
HATTIE WALKER	Betty Garrett
SOLANGE LAFITTE	Jane White
EMILY WHITMAN	Marge Champion
THEODORE WHITMAN	Donald Saddler
SANDRA CRANE	Nancy Ringham
STELLA DEEMS	Carol Woods
SAM DEEMS	Peter Cormican
CARLOTTA CAMPION	Polly Bergen
HEIDI SCHILLER	Joan Roberts
YOUNG SALLY	Lauren Ward
YOUNG PHYLLIS	Erin Dilly

YOUNG BUDDY	Joey Sorge
YOUNG BEN	Richard Roland
YOUNG HEIDI	Brooke Sunny Moriber
YOUNG DEEDEE	Roxane Barlow
YOUNG EMILY	Carole Bentley
YOUNG CARLOTTA	Sally Mae Dunn
YOUNG SANDRA	Dottie Earle
YOUNG SOLANGE	Jacqueline Hendy
YOUNG HATTIE	Kelli O'Hara
YOUNG STELLA	Allyson Tucker
YOUNG THEODORE	Rod McCune
KEVIN	Stephen Campanella
BUDDY'S BLUES GIRLS	Roxane Barlow,
("Margie," "Sally")	Jessica Leigh Brown
SHOWGIRLS	Jessica Leigh Brown, Colleen Dunn,
	Amy Heggins, Wendy Waring
ENSEMBLE	Roxane Barlow, Carole Bentley,
	Jessica Leigh Brown, Stephen Campanella,
	Colleen Dunn, Sally Mae Dunn, Dottie Earle,
	Aldrin Gonzalez, Amy Heggins, Jacqueline Hendy,
	Rod McCune, Kelli O'Hara, T. Oliver Reid,
	Alex Sanchez, Allyson Tucker, Matt Wall,
	Wendy Waring

CHARACTERS

Dimitri Weismann

"The Weismann Girls"
Sally Durant Plummer
Young Sally
Phyllis Rogers Stone
Young Phyllis
Carlotta Campion
Young Carlotta
Hattie Walker
Young Hattie
Stella Deems
Young Stella
Solange LaFitte
Young Solange
Heidi Schiller
Young Heidi
Emily Whitman
Young Emily
Sandra Crane
Young Sandra
Deedee West
Young Deedee

Benjamin Stone
Young Ben
Buddy Plummer
Young Buddy
Roscoe
Sam Deems
Young Theodore
Kevin, a waiter
Ladies and Gentlemen
    of the Ensemble

SCENE

A party on the stage of the Weismann Theatre

TIME

Tonight

MUSICAL NUMBERS

Beautiful Girls	*Roscoe and Company*
Don't Look at Me	*Sally and Ben*
Waiting for the Girls Upstairs	*Buddy, Ben, Phyllis, Sally, Young Buddy, Young Ben, Young Phyllis and Young Sally*
Rain on the Roof	*The Whitmans*
Ah, Paris!	*Solange*
Broadway Baby	*Hattie*
The Road You Didn't Take	*Ben*
Bolero d'Amour	*Danced by Vincent and Vanessa*
In Buddy's Eyes	*Sally*
Who's That Woman?	*Stella and Company*
I'm Still Here	*Carlotta*
Too Many Mornings	*Ben and Sally*
The Right Girl	*Buddy*
One More Kiss	*Heidi and Young Heidi*
Could I Leave You?	*Phyllis*

Loveland

THE FOLLY OF LOVE

Loveland	*Company*

THE FOLLY OF YOUTH

You're Gonna Love
Tomorrow/Love Will
See Us Through

*Young Ben and
Young Phyllis
Young Buddy and
Young Sally*

BUDDY'S FOLLY

The God-Why-Don't-
You-Love-Me Blues

Buddy, "Margie" and "Sally"

SALLY'S FOLLY

Losing My Mind

Sally

PHYLLIS'S FOLLY

The Story of Lucy and Jessie

Phyllis and Company

BEN'S FOLLY

Live, Laugh, Love

Ben and Company

ACT I

The theatre curtain is an old asbestos fire curtain, covered with dust, unused for years. There is the sound of soft tympani, like thunder from a long time ago. Slowly the curtain starts to rise.

Music begins; soft, slow, strange. The stage is dark and mysterious. Standing center is the one and only Dimitri Weismann, flashlight in hand, surveying the remnants of his once famous theatre.

From the shadows behind him he hears the eerie sound of footsteps hurrying along the metal gantry. He swings his flashlight up into the darkness; nothing there. Silence. Then from the dark auditorium rises the ghostly sound of audience applause. The applause fades; silence again.

Now the muffled sound of an argument coming from above the auditorium ceiling; then the sound of a slamming door. Weismann shines the flashlight into the depths of the stage, walks toward a metal staircase at the back wall and starts to climb it.

The music swells to a climax when suddenly revealed on the gantry center stage is a Showgirl. She stands motionless. She is tall, slim and beautiful. She is unseen by Weismann as he passes her and exits through a dressing-room door.

Slowly she comes to life, as if she were a ghost who had been waiting in the theatre for years in anticipation. She moves as showgirls did—but slower, almost drifting. From darkness, out of nowhere, comes another Showgirl, like the first, then another.

Then the heavy door upstage right slides open and a shaft of light spills onto the stage, revealing a lone figure tentatively entering the old theatre. It is Sally Durant Plummer. She is blond, petite, sweet-faced and, at forty-nine, still remarkably like the girl she was thirty years ago.

SALLY *(To Weismann's Assistant silhouetted at the entrance)*: Thank you, that's so sweet. I know I'm early, I wanted to be first.

(The ghostly Showgirls, unseen by Sally, gaze on the new arrival with strange curiosity.)

I just couldn't wait. I haven't seen New York in thirty years and all my friends.

(Weismann's Assistant stays silhouetted in the doorway as Sally moves downstage.)

I'm Sally Durant Plummer. You can't imagine how glamorous it was or what it meant to be a Weismann Girl. The way it felt to come onstage, all those eyes looking at you . . . It's going to be a lovely party. I'm so glad I came.

(As the ghostly Showgirls move inquisitively toward Sally, the slow, strange music swells, strikes an expectant chord and cuts to bright, light-hearted pastiche tunes of the 1920s and 1930s as . . .

The guests arrive. The stage is suddenly filled with color and energy, as couple after couple, ranging in age from their fifties to their eighties, move about excitedly.

In the midst of the excitement, Ben Stone and Phyllis Rogers Stone enter. Phyllis is a tall and queenly woman, stylish and intelligent. Her fine-boned face is probably more beautiful now than it was thirty years ago. Her husband Ben is tall, trim, distinguished; a successful and authoritative man.

They move downstage, wryly taking in the scene.

PHYLLIS: Lord, will you look at it.

BEN: Another theatre comes down. What kind of loving wife are you to drag me here?

PHYLLIS: I wanted to come back, Ben. One last look at where it all began. I wanted something when I came here thirty years ago but I forgot to write it down and God knows what it was.

BEN: Well, I'm glad you're glad to be here: that makes one of us.

PHYLLIS: Oh Ben, I love the way you hate it when I'm happy and you're not.

(She turns, mingles with the other guests. More guests arrive, among them Buddy Plummer. In his early fifties, he's appealing, lively, outgoing and, like the other principals, he is dealing with a lot of thoughts and feelings he can't express.)

BUDDY *(Smiling to a guest)*: My wife . . . she took the early plane. You haven't seen her, have you? Blond, cute as hell, about so high.

(The guest shakes his head. Buddy, still smiling, turns to another guest.)

It's crazy—all the traveling I do, I can't get used to flying. Once I met this fellow out in Denver—Salt Lake City. Anyway, he's in the airport bar and is he stoned. He's scared of planes, he tells me, so I say, "Look, fella, if it's that bad, miss the flight." "I can't," the guy says, "I'm the pilot."

3

(Buddy laughs, shoulder-slapping the other guests. The music rises. There is sudden excitement. Standing in a spotlight, motionless, is Dimitri Weismann. Now we can see him clearly. He is an acerbic, charming, energetic man. He must be eighty, but looks no more than sixty-five.)

WEISMANN: So many of you came. Amazing. Welcome to our first—and last—reunion. It's 1971; time marches on. Though I've aged in thirty years, let me assure you I am still Dimitri Weismann. Every year between the Great Wars, I produced a Follies in this theatre. Since then, this house has been a home to ballet, rep, movies, blue movies and, now, in a final burst of glory, it's to be a parking lot. Before it goes, I felt an urge to see you one last time . . . a final chance to glamorize the old days, stumble through a song or two and lie about ourselves a little. I have, as you can see, spared no expense. Still, there's a band, free food and drink, and the inevitable Roscoe, here as always to bring on the Weismann Girls. So take one last look at your girls. They won't be coming down these stairs again. Maestro, if you please!

(All the former Follies girls move to the wings, the band starts to vamp and Roscoe, an elderly tenor in top hat, white tie and tails, appears high on a stairway. He strikes a majestic pose, and in an absolutely glorious voice begins to sing:)

ROSCOE:
       Hats off,
       Here they come, those
       Beautiful girls.
       That's what
       You've been waiting for.

       Nature never fashioned
       A flower so fair.

No rose can compare—
Nothing respectable
Half so delectable.

Cheer them
In their glory,
Diamonds and pearls,
Dazzling jewels
By the score.

This is what beauty can be,
Beauty celestial, the best, you'll agree:
All for you,
These beautiful girls!

(Roscoe steps back. The music soars up as the full orchestra takes over.

Spotlights strike Deedee West, posed as she was thirty years ago, about to make her grand entrance down the Follies stairs. She wears, all the women do, a sash on which her Follies year appears in gold. She smiles and starts down.

One by one, all the women follow. Some are grand and sure, some are flustered or self-conscious, some amused, some very serious. The years on their sashes range from 1918 to 1941, and it feels as if an entire era were coming down the stairs.

Once down, the women parade across the stage just as they did all those years before. As they move across the stage, everybody sings:)

ALL:

Careful,
Here's the home of
Beautiful girls,
Where your
Reason is undone.

5

Beauty
Can't be hindered
From taking its toll.
You may lose control.
Faced with these Loreleis,
What man can moralize?

Caution,
On your guard with
Beautiful girls,
Flawless charmers every one.
This is how Samson was shorn:
Each in her style a Delilah reborn,
Each a gem,
A beautiful diadem
Of beautiful—welcome them—

ROSCOE:
These beautiful—

ALL:
Girls!

*(The line of women across the stage breaks up the instant the
singing ends. There are shouted greetings and squeals, hugs
and kisses. Waiters move about with trays of drinks. Sally,
dazzled by the wonder of it all, is standing, smiling, taking
it all in. She doesn't see Buddy until he comes up to her.)*

BUDDY: Hi honey.
SALLY: Oh Buddy, you did come. Did I look all right?
BUDDY: Like you're twenty-one again. I mean it. Just look at
you. How was your flight? You watch the movie?
SALLY: Don't be angry with me Buddy. I had to be here.
BUDDY: It's okay; we'll work it out.
SALLY: I wanted to so much.

BUDDY: I know, I know you did . . .

SALLY: Oh, look; there's Stella Deems. I've got to talk to her.

(Sally heads toward Stella as Buddy drifts into the party. Hattie Walker approaches Ben, autograph book in hand. Phyllis joins them.)

HATTIE *(Shows the autograph book to Ben)*: Mr. Stone, would you mind? For my grandson.

BEN: Nonsense, I'd be delighted. What's your grandson's name?

HATTIE: Jerome. He's eleven, but he reads all your speeches.

BEN: A misspent youth. I spent mine in the local music hall. It had a broken fire door and I saw every show that came to town. You wore a white dress cut to here. I didn't hear a note you sang. *(Handing book back)* Next time you find him reading, send him out to look for broken doors.

HATTIE: Mr. Stone, you sure know how to make a girl feel good.

(Hattie walks away.)

PHYLLIS: My God, you're charming.

BEN: You should see me when you're not around.

PHYLLIS *(Referring to Solange LaFitte, who is dressed outrageously, talking energetically to Weismann)*: They might have told us it was a costume party.

SOLANGE: Mitya, mon cher, it's me—Solange LaFitte. You know what I've been doing since my style went out of style? I sell more perfume than Chanel. *(Takes bottle from her evening bag)* "Caveman" by Solange. For men who have an air about them. Vulgar, but my darling, it will change your life. *(Posing)* I ask you, is it possible to look like this at sixty-nine?

WEISMANN: It must be magic.

SOLANGE *(Taking out another bottle)*: "Magic" by Solange.

(She strolls away with Weismann as we find Emily and Theodore Whitman in animated conversation with Sandra Crane.)

THEODORE: We bought an Arthur Murray franchise.

EMILY: Smartest thing we ever did.

THEODORE: We teach dance for a living.

(They do a nifty dance step.)

EMILY: We're still a team.

(They dance away as Sally moves in with Stella and Sam Deems.)

STELLA: . . . We had a hard time letting go. We kept on working all through '42. Then one day—we were doing daytime radio in Philly—and Sam, he turned to me and said, "Stella, baby, this is a load of crap." The mike was open. Fifty thousand housewives heard the news.

SAM: The next day, we were on the way to Florida. She helps me in the store.

STELLA: I do all my singing in the tub. It's the cat's pajamas. Great seeing you again . . .

SALLY: Sally.

STELLA: Right.

(Sally turns to face the audience and sings softly:)

SALLY:
> Ta-da!
> Now, folks, we bring you,
> Di-rect from Phoenix,
> Live and in person,
> Sally Durant!
> Here she is at last,
> Twinkle in her eye—

PHYLLIS: Sally?

(Young Phyllis and Young Sally enter, unseen by Phyllis and Sally.)

YOUNG PHYLLIS: Sally! Sally, come on, will you? That's our call.

YOUNG SALLY: Oh God, my hook's undone.

YOUNG PHYLLIS: Let me.

YOUNG SALLY: Okay, okay.

(They giggle and throw their arms around each other.)

PHYLLIS: Sally . . . it is you, isn't it?

SALLY: Phyllis! You came, you're here. Just look at you. I want to hug you, but I can't. You're like a queen or something.

PHYLLIS: Well, if you can't, I can.

(They embrace as Young Phyllis and Young Sally break apart.)

YOUNG PHYLLIS: Hurry, hurry.

(Young Phyllis and Young Sally exit.)

PHYLLIS: Sally, you look just as cute as ever.

SALLY: Me? I've got a tummy and my hair's too dyed. Who cares? New York's all changed. This afternoon when I walked past 44th and Third—why, Phyl, it wasn't there.

PHYLLIS: What wasn't?

SALLY: Our apartment, where we lived. Don't you remember? Five flights up. I did the cleaning and you cooked: baked beans and peanut butter sandwiches.

PHYLLIS: You never made the beds.

SALLY: I still don't, sometimes. And that awful bathtub in the kitchen . . .

PHYLLIS: You know, I think I loved it.

SALLY: You were homesick and you cried a lot, but we had fun.

PHYLLIS: You married Buddy, didn't you?

SALLY *(Nodding)*: You married Ben. I know. I read about you in the magazines. I even saw your living room in *Vogue.* It's all white. Is Ben still in Washington?

PHYLLIS: He's out of politics. He's president of a foundation now. Here in New York.

SALLY: He's here now? Here tonight?

PHYLLIS: Yes, he'll be so happy to see you.

(They go off into the crowd. Elsewhere in the party, Buddy spies Ben.)

BUDDY: Well, whaddaya know? Hey, Ben. Ben Stone.

BEN: Buddy.

BUDDY: You look great.

BEN: Don't let appearances deceive you.

(They hug.)

BUDDY: Not a chance. I've missed you, Ben.

BEN: You know how many years it's been.

BUDDY: Don't count. I wasn't sure you'd come.

BEN: Blame Phyllis.

(Young Ben and Young Buddy enter, Ben and Buddy can't see them.)

YOUNG BUDDY: I got you a terrific date tonight.

YOUNG BEN: I can't, Buddy. I've got to study.

YOUNG BUDDY: Aw, come on, Ben. It's all fixed up. She's Sally's roommate.

YOUNG BEN: I don't know.

YOUNG BUDDY: Her name is Phyllis something.

YOUNG BEN: What's she like?

YOUNG BUDDY: Nice girl. She's lonely. Do the kid a favor. Whatcha got to lose?

(Young Ben and Young Buddy fade away.)

BUDDY: I always knew you'd make it big.

BEN: I've had a lot of luck.

BUDDY: Me, too. I mean, you grow up hearing it's the little things that count, turns out it's true. I come home from a trip, see Sally, and I'm glad to see her. No big deal, no fireworks. I'm sentimental on my second drink. You ever play around?

BEN: I gave all that up years ago.

BUDDY: Same here. Not like the old days, is it? Law school, who could study? I'd have made some lousy lawyer. No regrets; right, Ben?

(Carlotta Campion enters and calls to Ben:)

CARLOTTA: Ben Stone!

BEN: No regrets.

(Ben turns to Carlotta as Buddy drifts off into the party.)

BEN: Well, it's not much of a ball to be the belle of, but congratulations anyway. That outfit is a triumph of restraint.

CARLOTTA: I always liked the way you talk. I haven't seen your picture in the papers lately.

BEN: Thanks, the same to you.

CARLOTTA: You ought to watch more television. I've got a series of my own.

SALLY *(Watching from a distance)*: Ben?

(Young Sally enters as Carlotta goes back to the party.)

YOUNG SALLY: Ben. Ben Stone, I want a reason. Look at me, damn it. You turn around and look at me!

SALLY *(Quietly)*: Ben, it's me.

(The memory fades as Sally, working up her courage to confront Ben, starts to sing:)

> Now, folks, we bring you,
> Di-rect from Phoenix,
> Live and in person,
> Sally Durant!
> Here she is at last,
> Twinkle in her eye,
> Hot off the press,
> Strictly a mess,
> Nevertheless . . .

(Smiling nervously.)

Hi, Ben.

(Then, before he can respond:)

> No, don't look at me—
> Please, not just yet.
> Why am I here? This is crazy!
> No, don't look at me—
> I know that face,
> You're trying to place
> The name . . .
> Say something, Ben, anything.
>
> No, don't talk to me.
> Ben, I forget:
> What were we like, it's so hazy!
> Look at these people,
> Aren't they eerie?
> Look at this party,
> Isn't it dreary?
> I'm so glad I came.

(Music continues under the following:)

BEN *(Looking at her)*: Can I look now?

(She nods, smiling nervously.)

Yes, it's possible. You might be Sally. Did you fall asleep
at Toscanini broadcasts? *(She nods)* Did you eat Baby
Ruths for breakfast?

SALLY: I still do sometimes. Oh, Ben, you're just the way I knew
you'd be. You make me feel like I was nineteen and the
four of us were going on the town.

SALLY AND BEN *(Singing)*:
So—
Just look at us . . .

SALLY:
Fat . . .

BEN:
Turning gray . . .

SALLY AND BEN:
Still playing games,
Acting crazy.

SALLY:
Isn't it awful?

BEN:
God, how depressing—

SALLY AND BEN:
Me, I'm a hundred,
You, you're a blessing—
I'm so glad I came!

BEN: What we need is a drink.

(The music ends. Sally and Ben walk off together. A spot-light comes up on Carlotta, deep in conversation with Sandra. The orchestra begins to play "One More Kiss.")

CARLOTTA: I never get to talk. I take a plane, go to a party, every guy I meet says, "Boy, oh boy, a real live movie actress; tell me all about yourself." I get as far as: "I was born in Idaho," and he starts telling me the story of *his* life. Not just his troubles: he unloads the whole thing, ups and downs. Mostly, he just wants to talk. Sometimes, he wants a place to put his head a while. Other times, he wants the works: some nights, he gets it.

(Focus shifts to Hattie and Deedee.)

HATTIE: . . . Yes, yes, I know. It's always sad to lose a husband. I've lost five. You wouldn't think it now, to look at me. I've always married crazy boys. They raced around in motor cars and aeroplanes. They lived too fast, but while they lived, my goodness, it was something.

*(Heidi Schiller enters alone, listening to the strains of "One More Kiss." On a platform above her, Young Heidi appears. For a moment Heidi and Young Heidi are both listening to the music.
Weismann enters.)*

HEIDI: Mitya, listen. That's my waltz they're playing. You remember?
WEISMANN: Heidi, could I possibly forget?
HEIDI: Franz Lehar wrote it for me in Vienna. I was having cof-fee in my drawing room. In ran Franz and straight to the piano: "Liebchen, it's for you." Or was it Oscar Strauss? *(Pauses)* Facts never interest me. What matters is the song.

(They exit together. Focus shifts to Phyllis and Buddy.)

PHYLLIS: Oh, Buddy, no; I didn't really do that, did I?

BUDDY: Cross my heart. In Central Park. You and Sally both dove in. We dared you to.

PHYLLIS: God, it's so good to see you—and what fun it was to do things. Ben and I don't do things anymore—we say them. Life is like a soundtrack, words with all the action missing. Why, we've even got a chauffeur who's articulate.

BUDDY: Some life you've got. Me, I'm in oil these days. Sounds big but it isn't. I'm a salesman and we sell these rigs and drills. I'm good at selling. Takes me on the road a lot, but I like meeting people, going places; keeps the juices flowing. *(Pauses)* Phyl, look around you. Stage door, call board. God, the time we clocked here, me and Ben. The place was always packed with guys and flowers, waiting for the girls to come down.

YOUNG BUDDY'S VOICE *(Sings)*:
    Hey, up there . . .

BUDDY: I even carved my name here some place.

YOUNG BUDDY'S VOICE *(Sings)*:
    Way up there . . .

YOUNG BUDDY AND YOUNG BEN'S VOICES *(Sing)*:
    Whaddaya say, up there?

BUDDY: Just being back together here, the four of us, I feel all the things I used to feel. Like it was yesterday.

PHYLLIS: Oh, Buddy, that was 1941; that's thirty years ago.

(Ben and Sally join them.)

BEN: Corsages, Sally? Are you sure about that?

SALLY: Every night, you'd bring them.
BUDDY: Bought them from the lady on the corner.
PHYLLIS: Yesterday's gardenias.
SALLY: And then we'd go and dance all night at Tommy's.
BUDDY: Tony's.
BEN: Tony's. Well, my God.

(Buddy sings up to the flies:)

BUDDY:

> Hey, up there!
> Way up there!
> Whaddaya say, up there?

I see it all. It's like a movie in my head that plays and plays.
It isn't just the bad things I remember. It's the whole show.

> Waiting around for the girls upstairs
> After the curtain came down,
> Money in my pocket to spend.
> "Honey, could you maybe get a friend for my friend?"

BEN:

> Hearing the sound of the girls above
> Dressing to go on the town,

BUDDY:

> Clicking heels on steel and cement,

BEN:

> Picking up the giggles floating down through the vent,

BUDDY AND BEN:

> Goddamnedest hours that I ever spent
> Were waiting for the girls
> Upstairs.

BUDDY:

    Hey, up there!
    Way up there!
    Whaddaya say, up there?

BEN:

    That's where the keys hung and
    That's were you picked up your mail.

BUDDY:

    I remember:
    Me and Ben,
    Me and Ben,
    We'd come around at ten,
    Me and Ben,
    And hang around the wings
    Watching things
    With what-the-hell-was-his-name,
    You know, the old guy . . .
    Max! I remember . . .

    Anyway,
    There we'd stay
    Until the curtain fell.
    And when the curtain fell,
    Then all hell broke:
    Girls on the run
    And scenery flying,
    Doors slamming left and right.

BEN:

    Girls in their un-
    Dies, blushing but trying
    Not to duck out of sight.

BUDDY AND BEN:

> Girls by the hun-
> Dreds waving and crying,
> "See you tomorrow night!"
> Girls looking frazzled and girls looking great,
> Girls in a frenzy to get a date,
> Girls like a madhouse and two of them late . . .
> And who had to wait?
> And wait . . .
> And wait . . .
> And . . .

PHYLLIS:

> Waiting around for the boys downstairs,
> Stalling as long as we dare.
> Which dress from my wardrobe of two?
> One of them was borrowed and the other was blue.

SALLY:

> Holding our ground for the boys below,
> Fussing around with our hair,

PHYLLIS:

> Giggling, wriggling out of our tights.

SALLY:

> Chattering and clattering down all of those flights—

SALLY AND PHYLLIS:

> God, I'd forgotten there ever were nights
> Of waiting for the boys
> Downstairs.

BUDDY:

> You up there!

SALLY:
>Down in a minute!

BEN:
>You two up there!

PHYLLIS:
>Just keep your shirts on!

BUDDY AND BEN:
>Aren't you through up there?

SALLY AND PHYLLIS:
>Heard you the first time!

>*(Young Buddy, Young Ben, Young Sally and Young Phyllis enter.)*

BUDDY AND BEN,
>YOUNG BUDDY AND
>YOUNG BEN:

Look, are you coming or
Aren't you coming 'cause
Look, if we're going, we
Gotta get going 'cause
Look, they won't hold us
A table at ringside all
Night!

SALLY AND PHYLLIS,
>YOUNG SALLY AND
>YOUNG PHYLLIS:

Coming, we're coming, will
You hold your horses, we're
Coming, we're ready, be
There in a jiffy, we're
Coming, we're coming. All
Right!

YOUNG SALLY:
>Hi . . .

YOUNG BEN:
>Girls . . .

YOUNG PHYLLIS:
>Ben . . .

YOUNG BUDDY:
   Sally . . .

YOUNG SALLY:
   Boy, we're beat.

YOUNG BUDDY:
   You look neat.

YOUNG PHYLLIS:
   We saw you in the wings.

YOUNG BEN:
   How are things?

YOUNG PHYLLIS:
   Did someone pass you in?

YOUNG BUDDY:
   Slipped a fin
   To what-the-hell-is-his-name,
   You know, the doorman.

YOUNG PHYLLIS:
   Al?

YOUNG BUDDY:
   No.

YOUNG SALLY:
   Big?

YOUNG BEN:
   Fat.

YOUNG PHYLLIS:
   Young?

YOUNG BUDDY:
Bald.

YOUNG SALLY:
Harry!

YOUNG BEN:
Yeah.

YOUNG SALLY:
Okey-doaks.

YOUNG BUDDY:
Come on, folks.

YOUNG PHYLLIS:
And where we gonna go?

YOUNG BEN:
A little joint I know—

YOUNG SALLY:
What?

YOUNG BUDDY:
Great new show there.

YOUNG PHYLLIS:
Hey, I thought you said tonight'd be Tony's—

YOUNG BUDDY:
This joint is just as grand.

YOUNG SALLY:
We girls got dressed for dancing at Tony's—

YOUNG BEN:
>This joint is in demand.

YOUNG SALLY AND YOUNG PHYLLIS:
>Ta-ta, good-bye, you'll find us at Tony's—

YOUNG BUDDY AND YOUNG BEN:
>Wait till you hear the band!

YOUNG SALLY AND YOUNG PHYLLIS:	YOUNG BUDDY AND YOUNG BEN:
You told us Tony's, That we'd go to Tony's.	I told you Tony's? I never said Tony's.

SALLY AND PHYLLIS, YOUNG SALLY AND YOUNG PHYLLIS:	BUDDY AND BEN, YOUNG BUDDY AND YOUNG BEN:
Then Ben mentioned Tony's.	
Well, someone said Tony's. There's dancing at Tony's— All right, then, we'll go!	When's Ben mentioned Tony's? It's ritzy at Tony's— All right, then, we'll go!

(And, as suddenly as they appeared, the memories are gone. Ben, Phyllis, Buddy and Sally stand quite still for a moment, caught by the remembered joy of being young. Then, as the music pulses on, they snap back to the present, look at one another, then away, all deeply shaken by the immediacy of the past and by regret for what's been lost and wasted. Angrily at first, they turn toward us and sing:)

BUDDY:
>Waiting around for the girls upstairs,
>Weren't we chuckleheads then?

BEN:

> Very young and very old hat—
> Everybody has to go through stages like that.

SALLY, PHYLLIS, BUDDY AND BEN:

> Waiting around for the girls upstairs—
> Thank you but never again.
> Life was fun but, oh, so intense.
> Everything was possible and nothing made sense
> Back there when one of the major events
> Was waiting for the girls,
> Waiting for the girls,
> Waiting for the girls,
> Upstairs.

(Blackout.

> *In the darkness we hear the sound of ghostly applause, gradually increasing in volume, as though the theatre were reawakening. Showgirl ghosts look on as the Whitmans, Solange and Hattie appear in separate pools of light. They relive their old Follies solos: "Rain on the Roof," "Ah, Paris!" and "Broadway Baby":)*

EMILY AND THEODORE:

> Listen to the rain on the roof go
> Pit-pitty-pat
> Pit-pitty-pat-pitty,
> Sit, kitty cat,
> We won't get home for hours.
> Relax and
> Listen to the rain on the roof go
> Plunk-planka-plink
> Plunk-planka-plink-planka,
> Let's have a drink
> And shelter from the showers.

Rain, rain, don't go away,
Fill up the sky.
Rain through the night,
We'll stay
Cozy and dry.

Listen to the rain on the roof go
Pit-pitty-pat
(They kiss)
Plunk-a-plink
(Kiss)
Plank
(Kiss)
Pity that
It's not a hurricane.
Listen—plink—to the
(Kiss, kiss)
Lovely rain.

SOLANGE:

New York has neon, Berlin has bars,
But ah! Paris! *(Pronounced "Paree!")*
Shanghai has silk and Madrid guitars,
But ah! Paris!
In Cairo you find bizarre bazaars,
In London: pip! pip! you sip tea.
But when it comes to love,
None of the above
Compares, *compris*?
So if it's making love
That you're thinking of,
Ah ah ah ah ah ah ah ah ah! Paris!

I have seen the ruins of Rome,
I've been in the igloos of Nome.
I have gone to Moscow, it's very gay—

Well, anyway,
On the first of May!
I have seen Rangoon and Soho,
And I like them more than so-so.
But when there's a moon,
Good-bye, Rangoon—
Hello, Montmartre, hello!

Peking has rickshaws, New Orleans jazz,
But ah! Paris!
Beirut has sunshine—that's all it has,
But ah! Paris!
Constantinople has Turkish baths *(Pronounced "bazz")*
And Athens that lovely debris.
Carlsbad may have a spa,
But for *ooh-la-la*,
You come with me!
Carlsbad is where you're cured
After you have toured
Ah ah ah ah ah ah ah ah ah! Paris!

HATTIE:

I'm just a
Broadway baby.
Walking off my tired feet.
Pounding Forty-second Street
To be in a show.
Broadway baby,
Learning how to sing and dance,
Waiting for that one big chance
To be in a show.

Gee,
I'd like to be
On some marquee,
All twinkling lights,

A spark
To pierce the dark
From Battery Park
Way up to Washington Heights.
Some day, maybe,
All my dreams will be repaid:
Heck, I'd even play the maid
To be in a show.

Say, Mr. Producer,
I'm talking to you, sir:
I don't need a lot,
Only what I got,
Plus a tube of greasepaint
And a follow-spot!

I'm just a Broadway baby,
Slaving at the five-and-ten,
Dreaming of the great day when
I'll be in a show.
Broadway baby,
Making rounds all afternoon,
Eating at a greasy spoon
To save on my dough.

At
My tiny flat
There's just my cat,
A bed and a chair.
Still
I'll stick it till
I'm on a bill
All over Times Square.

Some day maybe,
If I stick it long enough

I may get to strut my stuff
Working for a nice man
Like a Ziegfeld or a Weismann

HATTIE, SOLANGE, EMILY AND THEODORE:
In a great big
Broadway show!

(The memory is shattered by a noisy return of the party guests. A Photographer enters with Weismann. All the old Follies performers gather for a group photograph.)

PHOTOGRAPHER: All right, here we go: 5, 4, 3, 2, 1.

(The camera flashes, capturing the entire group in one extravagant, theatrical pose. There is a ghostly moment of silence. Then, as the group breaks up:)

WEISMANN: Are there any hungry actors in the house? Follow me.
EMILY WHITMAN: Mr. Weismann did not discover us. George M. Cohan beat him to it. Right, dear?
THEODORE WHITMAN: Right.
SOLANGE: Chevalier himself discovered me.
HATTIE: In bed, I'll bet.

(They drift off. The only two people left on stage are Ben and Sally.)

SALLY: Oh, Ben, your life must be so thrilling. All the famous people and the parties.
BEN: Oh, yes. The diplomats love telling dirty stories and the writers brag about their picture deals, and all the opera singers talk about is food.
SALLY: Honestly?
BEN: Would I lie to you? No, it's a good life really. After all, success is being good at doing what you want to do. Know what you want and do it, that's the secret.

(He sings:)

BEN:

> You're either a poet
> Or you're a lover
> Or you're the famous
> Benjamin Stone.
> You take one road,
> You try one door,
> There isn't time for any more.
> One's life consists of either/or.
> One has regrets
> Which one forgets,
> And as the years go on,
>
> The road you didn't take
> Hardly comes to mind,
> Does it?
> The door you didn't try,
> Where could it have led?
> The choice you didn't make
> Never was defined,
> Was it?
> Dreams you didn't dare
> Are dead.
> Were they ever there?
> Who said?
> I don't remember,
> I don't remember
> At all.

(Ben stops, stands still, remembering, as the music continues under and the lights reveal Young Ben and Young Buddy walking along. Young Ben is dressed up for a date.)

YOUNG BUDDY *(Handing a set of keys to Young Ben)*: Here
you go. Keys to the old jalopy.

YOUNG BEN: Thanks.

YOUNG BUDDY *(Taking out his wallet)*: You need a couple of
bucks?

YOUNG BEN: I'm fine.

YOUNG BUDDY: Come on, it's only money, what's it matter?

YOUNG BEN: You wouldn't know.

BEN:

> The books I'll never read
> Wouldn't change a thing,
> Would they?
> The girls I'll never know
> I'm too tired for.
> The lives I'll never lead
> Couldn't make me sing,
> Could they? Could they? Could they?
> Chances that you miss,
> Ignore.
> Ignorance is bliss—
> What's more,
> You won't remember,
> You won't remember
> At all,
> Not at all.

(Young Phyllis appears.)

YOUNG BEN: Borrowed money, borrowed car. Some day I'm
going to have the biggest goddamn limousine.

YOUNG PHYLLIS: We've got each other, Ben. What difference
does it make?

YOUNG BEN: All the difference.

BEN:

You yearn for the women,
Long for the money,
Envy the famous
Benjamin Stones.
You take your road,
The decades fly,
The yearnings fade, the longings die.
You learn to bid them all good-bye.
And oh, the peace,
The blessed peace . . .
At last you come to know:

The roads you never take
Go through rocky ground,
Don't they?
The choices that you make
Aren't all that grim.
The worlds you never see
Still will be around,
Won't they?
The Ben I'll never be,
Who remembers him?

SALLY: I remember him. I even think I loved him once.

(Ben and Sally move off as lights come up on Buddy and Phyllis together on the gantry. Below them, on the stage, a few couples begin social dancing.)

BUDDY: Well, there they go, my Sally and your Ben. They make a lovely couple, don't they? You have any kids, Phyl?
PHYLLIS: None at all. Ben put it off, and then it was too late.
BUDDY: We've got two: Tom and Tim. Sally picked the names out. They're in San Francisco now and she gets lonely for them, so she calls them on the phone and fights. She's

fought with everyone she knows. Phyl, all I want is Sally
back the way she used to be. I want the girl I married.

PHYLLIS: That's impossible, but never mind.

BUDDY: I begged her not to come tonight. It's happening again,
the way I knew it would.

PHYLLIS: What is?

BUDDY: She's still in love with Ben.

PHYLLIS: I used to wonder but I never knew for sure. Times
change. It might have mattered once.

*(Young Ben and Young Phyllis emerge from the dancing
couples. Phyllis sees them, Buddy doesn't. Phyllis, caught
by surprise at the sweetness of her memory, watches.)*

YOUNG PHYLLIS: Ben, I don't need a ring like this, it cost too
much.

YOUNG BEN: It's nothing, Phyl; just half a carat. Give me time.
The day will come I'll walk you into Tiffany's and buy the
store.

YOUNG PHYLLIS: You'll never give me anything as beautiful as
this.

YOUNG BEN: You'll make a good wife, Phyl.

YOUNG PHYLLIS: Good isn't good enough. I need to grow, I
know that, and I will. I'll study and I'll read and walk my
feet off in the Metropolitan Museum. You'll be so proud
of me.

PHYLLIS: Oh my God . . .

BUDDY: What is it?

PHYLLIS: Bargains, Buddy. One makes bargains with one's life.
That's what maturity amounts to. When we're young,
there is no limit to the roles we hope to play—star, mother,
hostess, hausfrau—all rolled into one. I learned to choose,
to constantly select; as if each day were a painting and I
had to get the colors right. We're careful of our colors, Ben
and I, and what we've made is beautiful. I had a lover
once. His name was Jack, I think. He played the drums

and had long hair and no command of language. He was everything Ben wasn't, and we'd while away the afternoons with Gallo wine and one another, listening to the pop hits and the news. I thought it answered everything, but these things pass and I have sixty thousand dollars worth of Georgian silver in my dining room.

BUDDY: What happened to you Phyl?

PHYLLIS: I went my own damn way and don't make waves.

(Phyllis strides away from Buddy, who also leaves slowly in the opposite direction.

The social dancing evolves into the Danse d'Amore, during which the Young and Old Whitmans echo each other's steps.

As the dance finishes, focus moves to Sally and Ben.)

SALLY: . . . And Ben, I used to think a lot about the future; what I'd do or where I'd be or what if this or that dream never happened. All the things I thought made life worth living, they don't seem to matter much. I wanted a career once, but the Follies closed and nothing happened and you know what? I was fine. I wanted children and I had two gorgeous boys who did what boys do: they grew up and moved away. I miss them, but they're not the answer.

BEN: What is?

SALLY: Buddy. He's what makes life worth living.

(She sings:)

> Life is slow but it seems exciting
> 'Cause Buddy's there.
> Gourmet cooking and letter-writing
> And knowing Buddy's there.
> Every morning—don't faint—
> I tend the flowers. Can you believe it?
> Every weekend I paint

For umpteen hours.
And yes, I miss a lot
Living like a shut-in.
No, I haven't got
Cooks and cars and diamonds.
Yes, my clothes are not
Paris fashions, but in
Buddy's eyes,
I'm young, I'm beautiful.
In Buddy's eyes
I don't get older.
So life is ducky
And time goes flying
And I'm so lucky
I feel like crying,
And—

(Her voice catches as Young Ben and Young Sally appear.)

YOUNG SALLY *(Hurt and angry)*: No, Ben. Not now, not tonight, not ever.

YOUNG BEN: You don't mean that, Sally.

YOUNG SALLY: You—you give a ring to her and mess around with me. You can't play with people's feelings, not with mine.

YOUNG BEN: I want you, you want me, you know it.

YOUNG SALLY *(Passionately)*: Oh, God, Ben . . .

(They go into each other's arms, then drift off.)

SALLY:

In Buddy's eyes,
I'm young, I'm beautiful.
In Buddy's eyes
I can't get older.
I'm still the princess,

Still the prize.
In Buddy's eyes,
I'm young, I'm beautiful.
In Buddy's arms,
On Buddy's shoulder,
I won't get older.
Nothing dies.
And all I ever dreamed I'd be,
The best I ever thought of me,
Is every minute there to see
In Buddy's eyes.

*(The band strikes up a tune. Ben and Sally start to dance.
Phyllis moves briskly to Ben and taps him on the shoulder.)*

PHYLLIS: Ben, get me a refill, would you?

(Ben nods, moves off.)

Sally, wait. Don't go. *(Conversational)* Let's dish. Tell me
everything. You ever miss New York? Where did you get
your dress? What's the weather out in Phoenix? How do
you like my husband?
SALLY: Ben? I've always liked him, you know that.
PHYLLIS: You find him changed?
SALLY: Not really, not down deep.
PHYLLIS: I rarely dip beneath the surface. Buddy thinks you're
still in love with him.
SALLY: That man . . . he gets so jealous sometimes.
PHYLLIS: What of? That's the enigma of the week.
SALLY *(Squeezing Phyllis's arm)*: I'm sorry, I don't want to fight
with you, Phyl. I don't have to.
PHYLLIS: Would you care to expand on that?

*(There is a loud noise of girlish shrieks from offstage.
Everyone enters, led by Weismann.)*

STELLA *(Moving downstage with Sandra and Deedee)*: I'm not
    making an ass of myself alone. If I do the Mirror Number,
    we all do the Mirror Number. You, too, Phyllis.
SALLY: Oh, come on, Phyl. Join the fun. *(Does a tap step)* See?
    There's nothing to it, it's a snap.
PHYLLIS: If you can do it, I can do it.
DEEDEE: I wish my kids could see me now.
SANDRA: Would you believe it? I have stage fright.
CARLOTTA: I haven't danced in thirty years.
STELLA: Well, heaven help us.
    (To the bandleader) Hit it, baby.

(She sings:)

> Who's that woman? I know her well,
> All decked out head to toe.
> She lives life like a carousel:
> Beau after beau after beau.
> Nightly, daily,
> Always laughing gaily,
> Seems I see her everywhere I go.
> Oh—
>
> Who's that woman?
> I know I know that woman,
> So clever, but ever so sad.
> Love, she said, was a fad.
> The kind of love that she couldn't make fun of
> She'd have none of.
>
> Who's that woman,
> That cheery, weary woman
> Who's dressing for yet one more spree?
> Each day I see her pass
> In my looking glass—
> Lord, lord, lord, that woman is me!

SALLY, PHYLLIS, STELLA, DEEDEE, SANDRA AND CARLOTTA:
Mirror, mirror, on the wall,
Who's the saddest gal in town?
Who's been riding for a fall?
Whose Lothario let her down?
Mirror, mirror, answer me:
Who is she who plays the clown?
Is she out each night till three?
Does she laugh with too much glee?
On reflection, she'd agree.
Mirror, mirror,
Mirror, mirror,
Mirror, mirror . . .

(The women are joined by their young selves. The sound of tap shoes, lots of them, in perfect precision, pick up the beat.)

STELLA:	SALLY, PHYLLIS, DEEDEE, SANDRA, CARLOTTA AND THEIR YOUNG SELVES:
Who's that woman?	Mirror, mirror, on the wall,
I mean I've seen that woman	
Who's joking but choking	Who's the saddest gal in town?
Back tears.	
All those glittering years	Who's been riding for a fall?
She thought that	
Love was a matter of,	Love was a matter of,
"Hi, there!"	"Hi, there!"
"Kiss me!" "Bye, there!"	"Kiss me!" "Bye, there!"
Who's that woman,	Mirror, mirror, answer me.
That cheery, weary woman,	
Who's dressing for yet one	Who is she who plays the clown?
More spree?	
The vision's getting blurred.	
Isn't that absurd?	

Lord, lord, lord!	Lord, lord, lord!
Lord, lord, lord, lord, lord!	
That woman is me.	
	Mirror, mirror!
That woman is me.	
	Mirror, mirror!
That woman is me!	Mirror, mirror!
	Mirror!

(The guests break into loud applause. As it starts to die down:)

STELLA *(Winded)*: Wasn't that a blast? I love life, you know that. I've got my troubles and I take my lumps, we've got no kids, we never made much money and a lot of folks I love are dead, but on the whole and everything considered . . . Where was I? What the hell, I talk too much.

(Excited chatter rises as:)

SALLY *(Breathless, bubbling)*: Oh, Buddy, did you see me?
BUDDY: Kid, I couldn't take my eyes off you.
PHYLLIS: Well, Ben? Was I ravishing? You haven't said.
BEN: I'm speechless. How on earth did you remember?
PHYLLIS: I don't know. Unless it's muscle memory. It's curious, the things our bodies won't forget.
BEN: It sure is.

(Ben walks away from her. She follows as:)

BUDDY: It's been some party, hasn't it. How's Ben?
SALLY: I don't think Phyllis makes him happy. I see sadness in his eyes.
BUDDY: I'll bet you do.
SALLY: What's that supposed to mean?
BUDDY *(Swallowing his anger)*: Look, Sally, I've been thinking. I'm away too much. Why don't I tell them at the office that

I'm finished on the road. We could go out more, have some fun. I know I let you down sometimes, but I'll try harder. Honestly, I will. Come on, kid, let's go home.

SALLY: I wouldn't leave here for the world.

PHYLLIS: Ben?

BEN: Now's not a good time, Phyl.

PHYLLIS: That's right, turn off. My God, we haven't had an honest talk since '41. You think the Japs'll win the war?

BEN: I'm in no mood for honest talks.

PHYLLIS: I am. When did you love me last? Was it ten years ago or never? Do you ever contemplate divorce? Or suicide? Why don't you play around? Or do you? Have you cried much lately? Are you ever savaged by regret? Does one more day with me seem insupportable? Or are you dead?

BEN: I have my moments.

BUDDY: We've had a good life, kid.

SALLY: Since when?

BUDDY: Don't talk like that. What do you want from me? No matter what I do, it's never good enough. I come home feeling great and touch you and you look at me like I've been living in some sewer.

SALLY: Haven't you? You've always got a woman someplace. Oh, I know. You leave things in your pockets so I'll know.

BUDDY: She lives in Dallas and her name is—

SALLY: I don't want to hear it.

BUDDY: Margie! Margie—that's her name. She works at Neiman's and she's got a little house. It's quiet, we'll just sit and talk for hours. And she cooks for me and sews my buttons on and when we go to bed, it's like she thought I was some kind of miracle. She's twenty-nine and pretty and you know what my luck is? My luck is I love you. *(Strides angrily away)*

PHYLLIS: God, the way I wanted you when we were dating. Why did you want me? What was I? Just some chorus girl who lost it in a rumble seat? Don't you remember? You were there. Son of a bitch, I'm going to cry. *(No tears)*

BEN: You wore a gray dress and the zipper stuck, and all you did was sob about your mother and how she'd feel if she knew. You were terrific.

PHYLLIS: Listen, Ben. I've spent years wanting to be old. Imagine that. I couldn't wait till we were old enough so nothing mattered anymore. I've still got time for something in my life. I want another chance. I'm still young and I'm talking to the walls. Where are you?

BEN: Right where you are, and it's yes to all your questions. Yes, I loved you once and, yes, I play around and, yes, I have regrets and, God yes, one more day with you— *(He storms off)*

PHYLLIS *(Reaches for a drink from a passing waiter)*: I'll take that. You have a nice face. I don't suppose you play the drums.

(Phyllis follows the waiter off. Carlotta and Weismann are sitting engrossed in conversation.)

CARLOTTA: . . . So, Mitya, here's what it comes down to. Movies, Vegas, television: I'm a triple threat. I've done them all. But none of that compares to this. There's nothing like the shows we did here. Don't you miss it?

WEISMANN: Me? I always know when things are over. After this, I did some plays; then that was over. So I married once or twice and that was over. Now I've got an art collection, but sooner or later . . .

CARLOTTA: Tell me about it.

(She sings:)

> Good times and bum times,
> I've seen them all and, my dear,
> I'm still here.
> Plush velvet sometimes,
> Sometimes just pretzels and beer,
> But I'm here.

I've stuffed the dailies
In my shoes,
Strummed ukuleles,
Sung the blues,
Seen all my dreams disappear,
But I'm here.

I've slept in shanties, guest of the W.P.A.,
But I'm here.
Danced in my scanties,
Three bucks a night was the pay,
But I'm here.
I've stood on bread lines
With the best,
Watched while the headlines
Did the rest.
In the Depression was I depressed?
Nowhere near.
I met a big financier,
And I'm here.

I've been through Gandhi,
Windsor and Wally's affair,
And I'm here.
Amos 'n' Andy,
Mah-jongg and platinum hair,
And I'm here.
I got through *Abie's
Irish Rose,*
Five Dionne babies,
Major Bowes,
Had heebie-jeebies
For Beebe's
Bathysphere.
I lived through Shirley Temple
And I'm here.

I've gotten through Herbert and J. Edgar Hoover—
Gee, that was fun and a half.
When you've been through Herbert and J. Edgar
    Hoover,
Anything else is a laugh.

I've been through Reno,
I've been through Beverly Hills,
And I'm here.
Reefers and vino,
Rest cures, religion and pills,
But I'm here.
Been called a pinko
Commie tool,
Got through it stinko
By my pool.
I should have gone to an acting school,
That seems clear.
Still, someone said, "She's sincere,"
So I'm here.

Black sable one day,
Next day it goes into hock,
But I'm here.
Top billing Monday,
Tuesday you're touring in stock,
But I'm here.

First you're another
Sloe-eyed vamp,
Then someone's mother,
Then you're camp.
Then you career from career
To career.
I'm almost through my memoirs,
And I'm here.

I've gotten through, "Hey, lady, aren't you whoozis?
Wow! What a looker you were."
Or, better yet, "Sorry, I thought you were whoozis.
Whatever happened to her?"

Good times and bum times,
I've seen them all and, my dear,
I'm still here.
Plush velvet sometimes,
Sometimes just pretzels and beer,
But I'm here.
I've run the gamut
A to Z.
Three cheers and dammit,
C'est la vie.
I got through all of last year,
And I'm here.
Lord knows, at least I was there,
And I'm here!
Look who's here!
I'm still here!

(Lights rise on Ben and Sally talking and . . .)

BEN: Sally, truth to tell, the one impulsive thing I ever did was
marry Phyllis. We must have loved each other very much.
And these days? Why does she stay with me, for God's
sake? She despises me, you know.
SALLY: How do you bear it? Me, I read a lot—just trashy stuff,
to pass the time—and the amount of junk about love people write . . . When I loved you and you loved me . . . I
drift off sometimes. I just close my eyes and let it come.

(Ben closes his eyes.)

You feel anything?

BEN: Not much.

(Young Ben and Young Sally appear. He's bare to the waist, she wears a slip. They kiss each other passionately.)

YOUNG SALLY: I love you, Ben. I always will. You're the only one. I couldn't live without you, Ben. I'd kill myself.

BEN: I made love to a girl this afternoon. I do that now and then; it happens. After it was over, guess what? I began to cry. I would give—what have I got?—my soul's of little value, but I'd give it to be twenty-five again.

SALLY: It's not too late. It never is.

BEN: It's my life and I've lived it wrong.

SALLY: I know. I've always known.

SALLY AND YOUNG SALLY: Oh my sweet Ben.

YOUNG SALLY: I don't mind giving up the stage, and Buddy doesn't love me, not like you do. I can wait until the war is over.

BEN: Did I love you, Sally? Was it real?

SALLY AND YOUNG SALLY: I'll write you letters and I'll knit you socks. I'll go half crazy from the waiting but I'll stand it somehow. I can wait forever just so long as at the end of it there's you.

(Young Sally slips into Ben's arms. Sally moves into Young Ben's. Both couples mirror each other's movements. Ben sings to Young Sally:)

BEN:

> Too many mornings,
> Waking and pretending I reach for you.
> Thousands of mornings,
> Dreaming of my girl . . .
>
> All that time wasted,
> Merely passing through,

Time I could have spent,
So content
Wasting time with you.

Too many mornings,
Wishing that the room might be filled with you,
Morning to morning,
Turning into days.
All the days
That I thought would never end,
All the nights
With another day to spend,
All those times
I'd look up to see
Sally standing at the door,
Sally moving to the bed,
Sally resting in my arms
With her head against my head.

(Young Ben and Young Sally leave their partners and slip back into each other's arms.)

SALLY *(Speaks)*: If you don't kiss me, Ben, I think I'm going to die.

(Sally sings:)

How I planned:
What I'd wear tonight and
When should I get here,
How should I find you,
Where I'd stand,
What I'd say in case you
Didn't remember,
How I'd remind you—
You remembered,

And my fears were wrong!
Was it ever real?
Did I ever love you this much?
Did we ever feel
So happy then?

BEN: SALLY:
It was always real

                                 I should have worn green.
And I've always loved you   I wore green the last time,
    this much.
We can always feel

                                 The time I
This happy . . .   Was happy . . .

SALLY AND BEN:
Too many mornings
Wasted in pretending I reach for you,
How many mornings
Are there still to come?

How much time can we hope that there will be?
Not much time, but it's time enough for me,
If there's time to look up and see
Sally standing at the door,
Sally moving to the bed,
Sally resting in your/my arms,
With your head against my head.

(Sally falls into Ben's arms. The couples are in identical
embraces. They kiss.
    Curtain.)

ACT II

The entr'acte music ends.

    The curtain rises. Sally, Ben, Young Sally and Young Ben are exactly as we left them, but now Buddy and Young Buddy are observing them from a distance. The final bars of music fade away, the embrace ends.

BEN: I want you, Sally.

SALLY: Ben, I know you do.

BEN: I want you now. This minute. Come on, let's get out of here.

SALLY: Just one thing, Ben. We're getting married, aren't we? I mean, this time you're going to marry me.

YOUNG SALLY: You love me, Ben. Let's get married now. She can't love you like I do.

BEN: Oh my God, what am I doing?

YOUNG BEN: Just give me time.

YOUNG SALLY: There isn't any time. You're shipping out.

SALLY: We'll be so happy.

YOUNG SALLY: What if you don't come back?

YOUNG BEN: Lawyers don't get shot.

YOUNG SALLY: Ben, marry me.

BEN AND YOUNG BEN: Sally, listen.
SALLY: I'll make you the best wife.
YOUNG SALLY: Now, if you really love me.
YOUNG BEN: Love you, yes, I love you.
YOUNG SALLY: Then why not?
BEN: Sally, listen to me. Stop . . .
YOUNG BEN: I have to leave.
BEN: Please, we have to talk . . .
SALLY *(Kissing Ben)*: Silly Ben. It's all right.
YOUNG SALLY: I want a reason.
YOUNG BEN: Quit pressing me.
SALLY: I'll get my wrap and we can leave.
YOUNG SALLY: Look at me, dammit!

(Young Ben exits.)

BEN: Sally, wait.
SALLY: I'm so happy.

(Sally exits.)

YOUNG SALLY: You turn around and look at me.

(Ben and Young Sally exit in opposite directions. Young Buddy moves downstage.)

YOUNG BUDDY: No!

(Buddy moves downstage, mirroring his young self.)

BUDDY: What the hell do I see in her for Chrissake? I knew all that was going on. *(Turns on his young self)* Why the hell did I marry her?

(Young Buddy walks away slowly. Buddy sings:)

The right girl—yeah!
The right girl,
She makes you feel like a million bucks
Instead of—what?—like a rented tux.

The right girl—yeah!
The right girl,
She's with you, no matter how you feel,
You're not the good guy, you're not the heel.
You're not the dreamboat that sank—you're real
When you got—
The right girl—yeah!
And I got—

(He has no words for what he's got. Instead, he bursts into an angry dance, leaping down stairs, twisting, tapping without tap shoes all the fury and regret he feels. Then, without preparation, the music changes and the anger's gone and he sings:)

Hey, Margie, I'm back, babe.
Come help me unpack, babe.
Hey, Margie, hey, bright girl,
I'm home.

What's new, babe? You miss me?
You smell good, come kiss me.
Hey, Margie, you wanna go dancing?
I'm home.

Des Moines was rotten and the deal fell through.
I pushed, babe.
I'm bushed, babe.
I needed you to tell my troubles to—
The heck, babe—
Let's neck, babe.

Hey, Margie,
You wanna go dancing?
You wanna go driving? Or something?
Okay, babe,
Whatever you say, babe—
You wanna stay home!
You wanna stay home!

(He holds an imagined Margie in his arms and dances with her tenderly; then:)

Hey, Margie, it's day, babe,
My flight goes—no, stay, babe,
You know how you cry, babe—
Stay home.

Be good, now, we'll speak, babe,
It might be next week, babe—
Hey, Margie—good-bye, babe—
I gotta go home.

(The angry music of the opening returns.)

The right girl—yeah!
The right girl,
She sees you're nothing and thinks you're king,
She knows you got other songs to sing.
You still could be—hell, well, anything
When you got—yeah!
The right girl—
And I got . . .

(The music becomes tender again.)

Hey, Margie, I'm back, babe.
Come help me unpack, babe.

Hey, Margie, hey, bright girl,
I'm home.
You miss me? I knew it.
Hey, Margie, I blew it—
I don't love the right girl.

Ah, shit . . .

(Final chord. Sally enters.)

SALLY: Buddy.

BUDDY: Sally . . . The mess, the moods, the spells you get, in bed for days without a word. Or else you're crying, God, the tears around our place—or flying out to Tom or Tim and camping at their doorstep just to fight. It's crazy and—we're finished, kid; that's all she wrote. It's over.

SALLY: Don't feel bad, darling. You'll be better off without me and I'm going to be just fine. You see, Ben wants to marry me. He asked me if I'd marry him and naturally I said I would.

BUDDY: Marry you? You're either drunk or crazy and I don't care which.

SALLY: He took me in his arms and kissed me. I know every word he said.

BUDDY *(In a rage)*: I've spent my whole life making things the way you want them and no matter what we do or where we go or what we've got, it isn't what you want. It used to drive me nuts. Not anymore. So you wake up hung over or you wake up in the funny farm, it's all the goddamn same to me.

(Buddy storms off.)

SALLY: He held me and the band was playing. I'm getting married and I'm going to live forever with the man I love. Oh, dear Lord, isn't it a wonder?

(Lights fade. They come up on Ben and Carlotta. She is laughing, soft and throaty. He sits near her, tense, desperate and fairly drunk.)

BEN: Just meet me later. I don't want to be alone, that's all.

CARLOTTA: You're married; you can play around. I'm in between; I never cheat on guys I'm living with.

BEN: I only want to talk.

CARLOTTA: Come on, come on now; you're a big boy.

BEN: Right you are. I'll tell you fascinating tales of my adventures, make you laugh.

CARLOTTA: It's nothing; you'll feel better in the morning.

BEN: Take me home and hold me—Jesus, please.

CARLOTTA: We had some fun once; it was just a thing. That's all you meant to me, Ben, just a thing. *(She gently touches his hair)* The guy I'm living with, he's just a thing, too. But he's twenty-six. I like him. I liked you. Next year I'll like some other guy. Men are so sweet.

(Focus shifts to another area of the stage where a couple is necking. Soon we see that the couple is Phyllis and Kevin, the waiter she spoke with earlier. He is kissing her neck.)

PHYLLIS *(Looking at nothing)*: I used to wish I had a son. I was going to call him Eddie, and I used to go to shops to look for things for him to wear. I'd see a nightshirt on the counter, pick it up and hold it in my hands—young man, you're getting me all wet.

KEVIN: Now, that's a hell of a remark.

PHYLLIS: I don't know what we're doing here.

KEVIN *(Feelings hurt)*: This wasn't my idea. You started it.

PHYLLIS: All right, all right; you've been assaulted by a crazy lady. Where's a drink?

KEVIN: I'll get you one.

PHYLLIS: Come here. *(He hesitates)* The moon's gone down; you're safe. *(As he brings her a drink)* Now that we've been introduced; tell me: do you find me attractive?

KEVIN: I dunno—Yeah, I do. It beats me.

PHYLLIS: Thanks. Do you sleep around a lot?

KEVIN: Sure, all the time.

PHYLLIS: Do you find, in your experience, does that make sex less pleasurable?

KEVIN: Does what?

PHYLLIS: Not loving anyone.

KEVIN: Hell, I dunno. I never think about it.

PHYLLIS *(Her face starts to fall apart)*: That's a neat trick.

KEVIN: Hey, lady, what's the matter?

PHYLLIS: If I knew, I'd have it fixed.

(Phyllis turns away from Kevin, who leaves her as the lights fade.

Elsewhere, a spotlight picks up Heidi, who sits lost in reverie. She sings "One More Kiss." Midway, Young Heidi appears, and the song becomes a duet, an old voice and a young one, entwined.)

HEIDI:

> One more kiss before we part,
> One more kiss and—farewell,
> Never shall we meet again,
> Just a kiss and then
> We break the spell.
>
> One more kiss to melt the heart,
> One more glimpse of the past,

HEIDI AND YOUNG HEIDI:

> One more souvenir of bliss,
> Knowing well that this
> One must be the last.

Dreams are a sweet mistake.
All dreamers must awake.

YOUNG HEIDI:
On, then, with the dance,
No backward glance
Or my heart will break.
Never look back.

HEIDI: Never look back. One more kiss before we part. All things beautiful must die Lover, give me . . .	YOUNG HEIDI: Ah . . . ah . . . Not with tears or a sigh. All things beautiful must die Now that our love is done,

HEIDI AND YOUNG HEIDI:
. . . One
More kiss and—good-bye.

(Lights fade on Heidi and Young Heidi as they walk away. Lights come up on Phyllis as she approaches Ben.)

PHYLLIS: Well, don't you look moody.
BEN: I've been thinking.
PHYLLIS: That makes two of us. Ben, do you know, according to statistics, I can't expect to die for thirty years. That's one long time and I've been analyzing what my options are. Hell, even on the gallows, there are choices: you can take it like a man or cry a lot. What's there for me? It all comes down to this: I won't go back to what we've had, not one more day of it.
BEN: How right you are. I don't know how I've stood it all these years. The only thing I want from you is a divorce.

PHYLLIS: Get him: puppy love at fifty-three. I see you both in your bikinis, honeymooning at Boca Raton. She'll be a hit at the foundation in her tap shoes.

BEN: Hell, I've never been in love with Sally, not in any way that matters. There's no one in my life; there's nothing. That's what's killing me.

PHYLLIS: I'm nothing. That's not much.

BEN: God, I see lovers on the street—it's real, it's going on out there and I can't reach it. Someone's got to love me and I don't care if it doesn't last a month, I don't care if I'm ludicrous or who she is or what she's like.

PHYLLIS: You haven't got a clue what love is. I should have left you years ago.

BEN: Leave me now. That's all I want. Just pack a bag and disappear.

(Phyllis sings:)

PHYLLIS:

Leave you? Leave you?
How could I leave you?
How could I go it alone?
Could I wave the years away
With a quick good-bye?
How do you wipe tears away
When your eyes are dry?

Sweetheart, lover,
Could I recover,
Give up the joys I have known?
Not to fetch your pills again
Every day at five,
Not to give those dinners for ten
Elderly men
From the U.N.—
How could I survive?

Could I leave you
And your shelves of the world's best books
And the evenings of martyred looks,
Cryptic sighs,
Sullen glares from those injured eyes?
Leave the quips with a sting, jokes with a sneer,
Passionless lovemaking once a year?
Leave the lies ill concealed
And the wounds never healed
And the games not worth winning
And—wait, I'm just beginning!

What, leave you, leave you,
How could I leave you?
What would I do on my own?
Putting thoughts of you aside
In the south of France,
Would I think of suicide?
Darling, shall we dance?

Could I live through the pain
On a terrace in Spain?
Would it pass? It would pass.
Could I bury my rage
With a boy half your age
In the grass? Bet your ass.
But I've done that already—or didn't you know, love?
Tell me, how could I leave when I left long ago, love?

Could I leave you?
No, the point is, could you leave me?
Well, I guess you could leave me the house,
Leave me the flat,
Leave me the Braques and Chagalls and all that.
You could leave me the stocks for sentiment's sake
And ninety percent of the money you make,

And the rugs
And the cooks—
Darling, you keep the drugs,
Angel, you keep the books,
Honey, I'll take the grand,
Sugar, you keep the spinet
And all of our friends and
Just wait a goddamn minute!

Oh, leave you? Leave you?
How could I leave you?
Sweetheart, I have to confess:
Could I leave you?
Yes.
Will I leave you?
Will *I* leave *you*?
Guess!

BEN: My hands, they won't stop shaking.

(Young Ben and Young Phyllis appear.)

YOUNG BEN: You'll make a good wife, Phyl.

YOUNG PHYLLIS: I'll try. Oh, Ben, I'll try so hard. I'm not much now, I know that, but I'll study and I'll read and I'll walk my feet off in the Metropolitan Museum.

PHYLLIS: I tried so hard. I studied and I read. I thought I wasn't much—I was terrific. And I walked my goddamn feet off. *(Turning to Young Phyllis)* What happened to you, Phyl?

YOUNG PHYLLIS: I love you, Ben.

BEN *(To Young Ben)*: She did—and what did you give her?

YOUNG BEN: Someday I'll have the biggest goddamn limousine.

BEN *(To Young Ben with loathing)*: You were so smart.

PHYLLIS *(To Young Phyllis)*: Where did you go?

YOUNG PHYLLIS: We've got each other, Ben. What difference does it make?

BEN *(To Young Ben)*: You had it all and you threw it away.

(Buddy enters, steaming.)

BUDDY: You bastard.
BEN *(Wrenching himself into the present)*: What?
BUDDY: You fourteen-carat bastard.

(Young Buddy enters.)

YOUNG BUDDY: You're my best friend, best I ever had, Ben.
BEN *(To Buddy)*: What's all this about?
BUDDY: You know damn well what this is about.
YOUNG BUDDY: You wouldn't screw around with Sally. Take
    her dancing maybe but that's all, right?
BEN: I don't understand.
BUDDY: Yes, you do.
YOUNG BUDDY: That's all—right, Ben?
YOUNG BEN: She's a sweet kid but that's where it stops.
BUDDY: What did you do to her?
YOUNG BUDDY: You're a goddamn liar.
YOUNG BEN: Screw you.
SALLY *(Appearing with Young Sally; to Ben)*: It's getting late,
    Ben. We should go.
PHYLLIS *(To Ben)*: You're not in love with Sally. Boy, you take
    the cake.
SALLY: Have you told Phyl yet?
BEN: But I never said I loved you, did I?
YOUNG SALLY: Now, if you really love me.
YOUNG BEN: Love you, yes I love you.
YOUNG SALLY: Then why not?
BEN: I'm sorry. I never meant to hurt you, but, Sally, it was fin-
    ished years ago.
YOUNG BUDDY *(To Young Sally)*: You really love me, don't
    you, kid?
YOUNG SALLY: With all my heart, Buddy . . .

BUDDY *(To Young Sally)*: That's a lie.

SALLY: Please, Ben, I'd like to go now.

BUDDY *(To Sally)*: Ben ran out and I was there. That's all it was.

YOUNG SALLY *(To Young Ben)*: I want a reason. Am I cheap? Is that it? I'm not good enough.

YOUNG BEN: Think what you goddamn please.

YOUNG SALLY: Don't leave me, Ben.

SALLY *(Turning on Young Sally)*: You fool!

YOUNG PHYLLIS: I want a baby, Ben.

SALLY *(To Young Sally)*: You could have had him, but you played it wrong.

YOUNG PHYLLIS *(To Young Ben)*: Ben, can't we have one, can't we try?

(Sally and Buddy speak simultaneously.)

SALLY *(To Young Sally)*: You had him crazy for you but you let him up your skirts too soon!

BUDDY *(To Young Buddy)*: You took her back. She two-timed you and you married her.

(Phyllis and Ben speak simultaneously.)

PHYLLIS *(To Ben)*: I now see right through you. Hollow, that's what you are. You're an empty place.

BEN *(To Young Ben)*: You never loved her. Why'd you marry her? Because it made sense? Is that all for chrissake?

(All four speak simultaneously, each of them turning on their past self with mounting rage as if they mean to do physical violence to the memories.)

Smart. You knew what you were doing: both eyes open. You can't spend your life with someone you don't love. It's crazy. You unfeeling bastard on the make. Look what you've done to me!

BUDDY *(To Young Buddy)*: She never loved you and you knew it. In your guts you damn well knew it. What did you expect for chrissakes? Married to a girl like that. You pissed my life away that's what you did to me.

PHYLLIS *(To Young Phyllis)*: He never loved you and you knew it. Deep down you knew. You thought he'd change if you loved him enough. You silly bitch, you fool. You threw my life away!

SALLY *(To Young Sally)*: The only man I ever wanted, and you lost him for me. Everything, you lost me everything. You tramp. You left me here with nothing. I could kill you. I could die!

(All eight at once. It's now senseless, and frightening.)

YOUNG BUDDY *(To Young Sally)*: Baby I love you so much. The moon, I'll buy it for you. Everything you ever wanted, baby, that's what Buddy's going to get for you.

YOUNG SALLY *(To Young Buddy)*: Honey, you're the only one. The things you do to me. The way you make me feel. I love it, Buddy. Geez, I love you.

YOUNG PHYLLIS *(To Young Ben)*: Dearest, oh my dearest Ben, I'll be so good for you, you'll be so happy. I'll be everything you ever wanted, just for you.

YOUNG BEN *(To Young Phyllis)*: Darling, to the top. That's where we're going: straight up and the view from there, the view is something.

BUDDY *(To Young Buddy)*: I could have had a great life all along. I had the wrong wife, that was all. You've screwed me and I'll get you for it!

SALLY *(To Young Sally)*: I'll pay you back, that's what I'll do. For all the things I never had. You're gonna pay!

PHYLLIS *(To Young Phyllis)*: I've had no life—I haven't lived. You can't do what you've done to me and get away with it!

BEN *(To Young Ben)*: You killed me—I've been dead for thirty years. It's all your work—you did it!

(As the madness of the confrontation hits its peak, heavenly music is heard and we find ourselves transported to Loveland: a Ziegfeld extravaganza, complete with costumed Chorus and a bevy of Showgirls. The Chorus sings as the eight protagonists are swallowed up in the celebration:)

CHORUS:

> Time stops, hearts are young,
> Only serenades are sung
> In Loveland,
> Where everybody lives to love.

> Raindrops never rain,
> Every road is Lover's Lane
> In Loveland,
> Where everybody loves to live.

> See that sunny sun and honeymoon,
> There where seven hundred days hath June.

> Sweetheart, take my hand,
> Let us find that wondrous land
> Called Loveland, Loveland, Loveland . . .

FIRST SHOWGIRL:

> L is for the Long Long road ahead
> That leads all lovers to the landscape of their dreams.

CHORUS:

> Loveland,
> Where everybody lives to love.

SECOND SHOWGIRL:

> O is for the Overwhelming Optimism
> Only lovers know, or so it seems.

CHORUS:
> Loveland,
> Where everybody loves to live.

THIRD SHOWGIRL:
> V is for the Various Vicissitudes they'll weather,
> Because it's also for the vow they made together.

CHORUS:
> Loveland, Loveland . . .

FOURTH SHOWGIRL:
> E is for the Endless Expectations
> Lovers elevate so often to extremes.

CHORUS:
> Loveland, Loveland . . .

FIFTH SHOWGIRL:
> L is for the Lies that get perfected,
> A is for the Aims that go awry.

CHORUS:
> Loveland,
> Where everybody lives to love.

SIXTH SHOWGIRL:
> N is for the Needs that get neglected,
> D is for the Doubts that never die.

CHORUS:
> Loveland,
> Where everybody loves to live.
>
> Lovers pine and sigh but never part.
> Time is measured by a beating heart.

Bells ring, fountains splash,
Folks use kisses 'stead of cash
In Loveland, Loveland . . .

Love, Love, Loveland . . .
Love, Love, Loveland . . .
Love!

(The Young Lovers sing:)

YOUNG BEN:
"What will tomorrow bring?"
The pundits query.

YOUNG PHYLLIS:
Will it be cheery?

YOUNG BEN:
Will it be sad?

YOUNG PHYLLIS:
Will it be birds in spring
Or hara-kiri?

YOUNG BEN:
Don't worry, dearie.

YOUNG PHYLLIS:
Don't worry, lad.

YOUNG BEN:
I'll have our future
Suit your
Whim,
Blue chip preferred.

YOUNG PHYLLIS:
Putting it in a
Syno-

Nym,
Perfect's the word.

YOUNG BEN AND YOUNG PHYLLIS:
We're in this thing together,
Aren'tcha glad?
Each day from now will be
The best day you ever had.

YOUNG BEN:
You're gonna love tomorrow.

YOUNG PHYLLIS:
Mm-hm.

YOUNG BEN:
You're gonna be with me.

YOUNG PHYLLIS:
Mm-hm.

YOUNG BEN:
You're gonna love tomorrow,
I'm giving you my personal guarantee.

YOUNG PHYLLIS:
Say toodle-oo to sorrow.

YOUNG BEN:
Mm-hm.

YOUNG PHYLLIS:
And fare-thee-well, ennui.

YOUNG BEN:
Bye-bye.

YOUNG PHYLLIS:
> You're gonna love tomorrow,
> As long as your tomorrow is spent with me.

YOUNG BEN AND YOUNG PHYLLIS:
> Today was perfectly perfect,
> You say.
> Well, don't go away,
> 'Cause if you think you liked today,
>
> You're gonna *love* tomorrow.
> Mm-hm.
> You stick around and see.

YOUNG PHYLLIS:
> Mm-hm.

YOUNG BEN AND YOUNG PHYLLIS:
> And if you love tomorrow,
> Then think of how it's gonna be:
> Tomorrow's what you're gonna have a lifetime of
> With me!

(Young Phyllis and Young Ben dance gaily off as Young Buddy and Young Sally dance on, hand in hand, and sing:)

YOUNG BUDDY:
> Sally, dear,
> Now that we're
> Man and wife,
> I will do
> Wonders to
> Make your life
> Soul-stirring
> And free of care.

YOUNG SALLY:

> If we fight
> (And we might),
> I'll concede.
> Furthermore,
> Dear, should your
> Ego need
> Bolstering,
> I'll do my share.

YOUNG BUDDY:

> But though I'll do my utmost
> To see you never frown,

YOUNG SALLY:

> And though I'll try to cut most
> Of our expenses down,

YOUNG BUDDY:

> I've some traits, I warn you,
> To which you'll have objections.

YOUNG SALLY:

> I, too, have a cornu-
> Copia of imperfections.
>
> I may burn the toast.

YOUNG BUDDY:

> Oh, well,
> I may make a rotten host.

YOUNG SALLY:

> Do tell.

YOUNG BUDDY AND YOUNG SALLY:

> But no matter what goes wrong,
> Love will see us through
> Till something better comes along.

YOUNG BUDDY:
>   I may vex your folks.

YOUNG SALLY:
>   Okay.
>   I may interrupt your jokes.

YOUNG BUDDY:
>   You may.

YOUNG BUDDY AND YOUNG SALLY:
>   But if I come on too strong,
>   Love will see us through
>   Till something better comes along.

YOUNG BUDDY:
>   I may play cards all night
>   And come home at three.

YOUNG SALLY:
>   Just leave a light
>   On the porch for me.

YOUNG BUDDY AND YOUNG SALLY:
>   Well, nobody's perfect!

YOUNG SALLY:
>   I may trump your ace.

YOUNG BUDDY:
>   Please do.
>   I may clutter up the place.

YOUNG SALLY:
>   Me, too.

YOUNG BUDDY AND YOUNG SALLY:
> But the minute we embrace
> To love's old sweet song,
> Dear, that will see us through
> Till something better comes along.

(Young Ben and Young Phyllis reenter.)

YOUNG SALLY:
> Hi.

YOUNG BEN:
> Girls.

YOUNG PHYLLIS:
> Ben.

YOUNG BUDDY:
> Sally.

YOUNG BEN:
You're gonna love tomorrow

YOUNG SALLY:
I may burn the toast.

YOUNG PHYLLIS:
Mm-hm,

YOUNG BUDDY:
Oh, well,
I may make a rotten host.

YOUNG BEN:
You're gonna be with me.

YOUNG SALLY:
Do tell.

YOUNG PHYLLIS:
Mm-hm.

YOUNG BEN:

You're gonna love tomorrow
I'm giving you my personal
Guarantee.

YOUNG BUDDY AND
YOUNG SALLY:
But no matter what goes wrong,
Love will see us through
Till something better comes
Along.

YOUNG PHYLLIS:
Say toodle-oo to sorrow.

YOUNG BEN:
Mm-hm.

YOUNG PHYLLIS:
And fare-thee-well, ennui.

YOUNG BEN:
Bye-bye.

YOUNG PHYLLIS:

You're gonna love tomorrow,
As long as your tomorrow is
Spent with me.

YOUNG BEN AND
   YOUNG PHYLLIS:
Today was perfectly perfect,
You say.

Well, don't go away,
'Cause if you think you liked
Today,

YOUNG BUDDY:
I may vex your folks.

YOUNG SALLY:
Okay.
I may interrupt your jokes.

YOUNG BUDDY:

You may.

YOUNG BUDDY AND
   YOUNG SALLY:
But if I come on too strong,
Love will see us through
Till something better comes
Along.

YOUNG BUDDY:

I may play cards all night
And come home at three.

YOUNG SALLY:
Just leave a light
On the porch for me!

YOUNG BUDDY AND
   YOUNG SALLY:
Well, nobody's perfect!

| | YOUNG SALLY: |
| You're gonna love tomorrow. | I may trump your ace. |

	YOUNG BUDDY:
Mm-hm.	Please do.
	I may clutter up the place.
You stick around and see.	

| | YOUNG SALLY: |
| Mm-hm. | Me, too. |

	YOUNG BUDDY AND
	YOUNG SALLY:
And if you love tomorrow,	But the minute we embrace
Then think of how it's	To love's old sweet song,
Gonna be.	
Tomorrow's what you're	Dear, that will see us through
Gonna have,	Till something,
And Monday's what you're	Love will help us hew
Gonna have,	To something,
And love is what you're	Love will have to do
Gonna have	Till something
A lifetime of	Better comes
With me!	Along!

(A show curtain drops in downstage as the number ends. Buddy pops his head through the curtain, grins at us engagingly and sings:)

BUDDY:

Hello, folks, we're into the Follies!
First, though, folks, we'll pause for a mo'.
No, no, folks, you'll still get your jollies—
It's just I got a problem that I think you should know.
See, I've been very perturbed of late, very upset,
Very betwixt and between.

The things that I want, I don't seem to get.
The things that I get—you know what I mean?

*(He steps through the curtain into full view. He is in his
Follies costume now: plaid baggy pants, garish jacket and a
shiny derby hat.)*

I've got those
"God-why-don't-you-love-me-oh-you-do-I'll-see-you-
    later"
Blues,
That
"Long-as-you-ignore-me-you're-the-only-thing-that-
    matters"
Feeling,
That
"If-I'm-good-enough-for-you-you're-not-good-enough-
    and-thank-you-for-the-present-but-what's-wrong-`
    with-it?" stuff,
Those
"Don't-come-any-closer-'cause-you-know-how-much-
    I-love-you"
Feelings,
Those
"Tell-me-that-you-love-me-oh-you-did-I-gotta-run-
    now"
Blues.

*(A Chorus Girl comes flouncing on, as a caricature of his
beloved Margie.)*

Margie! Oh, Margie!
She says she really loves me.

"MARGIE":
    I love you,

71

BUDDY:
> —She says.
> She says she really cares.

"MARGIE":
> I care. I care.

BUDDY:
> She says that I'm her hero.

"MARGIE":
> My hero.

BUDDY:
> —She says.
> I'm perfect, she swears.

"MARGIE":
> You're perfect, goddammit.

BUDDY:
> She says that if we parted,

"MARGIE":
> If we parted—?

BUDDY:
> —She says,
> She says that she'd be sick.

"MARGIE":
> Bleah.

BUDDY:
> She says she's mine forever—

"MARGIE":
> Forever.

BUDDY:
—She says.
I gotta get outta here quick!

I've got those
"Whisper-how-I'm-better-than-I-think-but-what-do-
    you-know?"
Blues,
That
"Why-do-you-keep-telling-me-I-stink-when-I-adore-
    you"
Feeling,
That
"Say-I'm-all-the-world-to-you-you're-out-of-your-mind-
    I-know-there's-someone-else-and-I-could-kiss-your-
    behind,"
Those
"You-say-I'm-terrific-but-your-taste-was-always-
    rotten"
Feelings,
Those
"Go-away-I-need-you,"
"Come-to-me-I'll-kill-you,"
"Darling-I'll-do-anything-to-keep-you-with-me-till-you-
    tell-me-that-you-love-me-oh-you-did-now-beat-it-
    will-you?"
Blues!

*(Another Chorus Girl, this time a cartoon of Sally, hip-
swings her way onstage.)*

Sally! Oh, Sally!
She says she loves another—

"SALLY":
Another—

73

BUDDY:

    —She says,
    A fella she prefers.

"SALLY":

    Furs. Furs.

BUDDY:

    She says that he's her idol.

"SALLY":

    Idolidolidolidol—

BUDDY:

    —She says.
    Ideal, she avers.

"SALLY":

    You deal . . . "avers"?

BUDDY:

    She says that anybody—

"SALLY":

    Buddy—Bleah!—

BUDDY:

    —She says,
    Would suit her more than I.

"SALLY":

    Aye, aye, aye.

BUDDY:

    She says that I'm a washout—

"SALLY" *(Mouthed)*:
    A washout—

BUDDY:
    —She says,
    I love her so much, I could die!
"SALLY" *(Spoken)*: Get outta here!

    (Buddy tears around the stage trying to catch her. "Margie"
    returns from the wings.)

    Ooh. Ooh.
    Go 'way! Go 'way!
    Ah! Ah!

    (There is a collision involving all three of them and, when
    they untangle themselves, they sing:)

BUDDY:
    I've got those

BUDDY, "MARGIE" AND "SALLY":
    "God-why-don't-you-love-me-oh-you-do-I'll-see-you-
        later"
    Blues—

"MARGIE" AND "SALLY":
    Bla-bla-blues—!

BUDDY, "MARGIE" AND "SALLY":
    That
    "Long-as-you-ignore-me-you're-the-only-thing-that-
        matters"
    Feeling—

"MARGIE" AND "SALLY":
    Feeling—!

BUDDY:
    That
    "If-I'm-good-enough-for-you-you're-not-good-
        enough"—

"MARGIE" AND "SALLY":
    Woo—!

BUDDY:
    And "Thank-you-for-the-present-but-what's-wrong-
        with-it?" stuff,

"MARGIE" AND "SALLY":
    Oh—!

BUDDY:
    Those
    "Don't-come-any-closer-'cause-you-know-how-much-
        I-love-you"
    Feelings,

"MARGIE" AND "SALLY":
    Bla-bla-blues—!

BUDDY: "MARGIE" AND "SALLY":
Those
"If-you-will-then-I-can't,
If-you-don't-then-I-gotta,
Give-it-to-me-I-don't-want-it,
If-you-won't-I-gotta-have-it,
High-low-wrong-right-
Yes-no-black-white,
God-why-don't-you-love-me-
    oh-you-do-I'll-see-you-later"   "Fast-slow-kiss-fight-
                                          Stay-go-up-tight"

BUDDY, "MARGIE" AND "SALLY":
Blues!

(The number ends as they chase one another offstage. The lights dim down, the show curtain parts just enough to form a graceful frame, and standing there is Sally. She is costumed in a clinging, beaded silver gown, as if she were a screen seductress from the 1930s. Standing very still, she sings:)

SALLY:
The sun comes up,
I think about you.
The coffee cup,
I think about you.
I want you so,
It's like I'm losing my mind.

The morning ends,
I think about you.
I talk to friends,
I think about you.
And do they know?
It's like losing my mind.

All afternoon,
Doing every little chore,
The thought of you stays bright.
Sometimes I stand
In the middle of the floor,
Not going left,
Not going right.

I dim the lights
And think about you,
Spend sleepless nights

To think about you.
You said you loved me,
Or were you just being kind?
Or am I losing my mind?

I want you so,
It's like losing my mind.
Does no one know?
It's like losing my mind.

All afternoon,
Doing every little chore,
The thought of you stays bright.
Sometimes I stand
In the middle of the floor,
Not going left,
Not going right.

I dim the lights
And think about you,
Spend sleepless nights
To think about you.
You said you loved me,
Or were you just being kind?
Or am I losing my mind?

(The lights dim. We can just see Sally's face in the pinpoint spotlight as the curtain gently closes. There is a jazzy blare of trumpets, the lights abruptly rise, and Phyllis struts onstage wearing a short, fringe-skirted, bright red dress that exposes long and shapely legs. She throws a knowing grin at us and sings, as a gaggle of Chorus Boys enter to back her up:)

PHYLLIS:
　　Here's a little story that should make you cry,
　　About two unhappy dames.

Let us call them Lucy "X" and Jessie "Y,"
Which are not their real names.
Now Lucy has the purity
Along with the unsurety
That comes with being only twenty-one.
Jessie has maturity
And plenty of security.
Whatever you can do with them she's done.
Given their advantages,
You may ask why
The two ladies have such grief.
This is my belief,
In brief:

Lucy is juicy
But terribly drab.
Jessie is dressy
But cold as a slab.
Lucy wants to be dressy,
Jessie wants to be juicy
Lucy wants to be Jessie,
And Jessie Lucy.
You see,
Jessie is racy
But hard as a rock.
Lucy is lacy
But dull as a smock.
Jessie wants to be lacy,
Lucy wants to be Jessie.
That's the sorrowful précis.
It's very messy.

Poor sad souls,
Itching to be switching roles.
Lucy wants to do what Jessie does,
Jessie wants to be what Lucy was.

Lucy's a lassie
You pat on the head.
Jessie is classy
But virtually dead.
Lucy wants to be classy,
Jessie wants to be Lassie.
If Lucy and Jessie could only combine,
I could tell you someone
Who would finally feel just fine!

CHORUS BOYS:

Now if you see Lucy "X,"
Youthful, truthful Lucy "X,"
Let her know she's better than she suspects.
Now if you see Jessie "Y,"
Faded, jaded Jessie "Y,"
Tell her that she's sweller than apple pie.
Juicy Lucy,
Dressy Jessie,
Tell them that they ought to get together quick,
'Cause getting it together is the whole trick!

(She exits with the Chorus Boys and is replaced with a line of Chorus Girls as a curtain drops behind them. They sing:)

CHORUS:

Here he comes,
Mister Whiz.
Sound the drums,
Here he is.

Raconteur,
Bon vivant.
Tell us, sir,
What we want
To know:

The modus operandi
A dandy
Should use
When he is feeling low.

*(The curtain rises, revealing Ben in a smoking jacket,
looking pleased with himself and surrounded by other
Chorus Girls and Boys. He sings:)*

BEN:

When the winds are blowing,

CHORUS:

Yes?

BEN:

That's the time to smile.

CHORUS:

Oh?

BEN:

Learn how to laugh,
Learn how to love, learn how to live,
That's my style.
When the rent is owing . . .

CHORUS:

Yes?

BEN:

What's the use of tears?

CHORUS:

Oh?

BEN:

I'd rather laugh,
I'd rather love,
I'd rather live
In arrears.

Some fellows sweat
To get to be millionaires,
Some have a sport
They're devotees of.
Some like to be the champs
At saving postage stamps,
Me, I like to live,
Me, I like to laugh,
Me, I like to love.

Some like to sink
And think in their easy chairs
Of all the things
They've risen above.
Some like to be profound
By reading Proust and Pound.
Me, I like to live,
Me, I like to laugh,
Me, I like to love.

Success is swell
And success is sweet,
But every height has a drop.
The less achievement,
The less defeat.
What's the point of shovin'
Your way to the top?
Live 'n' laugh 'n' love 'n'
 You're never a flop.
 So when the walls are crumbling . . .

CHORUS:

Yes?

BEN:

Don't give up the ship.

CHORUS:

No.

BEN:

Learn how to laugh,
Learn how to love,
Learn how to live,
That's my tip.
When I hear the rumbling,

CHORUS:

Yes?

BEN:

Do I lose my grip?

CHORUS:

No!

BEN:

I have to laugh,
I have to love,
I have to live.
That's my trip.

BEN AND CHORUS:

When the wind is blowing,
That's all the time to smile . . .

(They dance.)

When the rent is owing,
Never lose your style . . .

(Ben dances nimbly and does some fancy work with a hat and cane, à la Fred Astaire.)

BEN:

Some get a boot
From shooting off cablegrams
Or buzzing bells
To summon the staff.
Some climbers get their kicks
From social politics.
Me, I like to live,
Me, I like to love,
Me, I like to . . .

(He forgets the lyric. He calls for it from the conductor, who barks it to him; Ben recovers his poise.)

Some break their asses
Passing their bar exams,
Lay out their lives
Like lines on a graph . . .
One day they're diplomats—
Well, bully and congrats!
Me, I like to live,
Me, I like to love,
Me, I . . .

(He goes completely blank. Then he sings, shouting desperately:)

Me, I like—me, I love—me.
I DON'T LOVE ME!

(The Chorus line keeps dancing. Ben turns, shouts at one Chorus Girl after another as the amplified voices of the offstage party guests get louder and louder:)

BEN: Look at me. I'm nothing. Can't you see it? I'm a fraud. It's all a trick. You couldn't love me. No one could. You'd be a fool to trust me. All I'll do is hurt you, tell you lies. Her zipper stuck and I kept saying: "Phyl, I love you . . . I love you . . ."

CHORUS:
Success is swell
And success is sweet,
But every height has a
  drop.
The less achievement
The less defeat.
What's the point of
  shovin'
Your way to the top?

(The cacophony is all but deafening. Then sudden silence. All but Ben stand motionless. We can scarcely hear Ben as he screams:)

Phyllis!

(A flash of light and deafening sound as everything breaks apart and disassembles insanely. Bits and pieces of other songs shatter through. The Chorus line, although broken up, is still dancing, as if in a nightmare. The noise reaches a peak of madness before slowly starting to recede. Softer, softer . . . leaving Ben kneeling on the stage as a solitary ghostly Showgirl drifts by.)

(Cries out, shaken) Phyllis!
PHYLLIS: I'm here, Ben. I'm right here.
BEN: I need you, Phyl.
PHYLLIS: I know.

BEN: I've always been afraid of you. You see straight through me, I've always thought, It isn't possible: it can't be me she loves.

PHYLLIS *(Handing him his jacket)*: Come on, let's get our coats.

(They move to one side as Sally enters; Buddy follows.)

BUDDY: Hey, kid, it's me.

SALLY: I left the dishes in the sink. I left them there, I was in such a hurry and there is no Ben for me, not ever, anyplace.

BUDDY: There never was, and that's the truth.

SALLY *(Breaking down)*: I'm forty-nine years old, that's all I am. What am I going to do?

(Guests in overcoats and evening wraps begin to cross the stage, exiting.)

DEEDEE: You know what? We should do this every year.

SANDRA: Are you insane?

EMILY: There's still time for a nightcap.

SOLANGE: No, no, no. I need my beauty sleep.

HATTIE: I'll say you do.

SAM *(To Carlotta and Stella)*: Ladies? One for the road?

CARLOTTA: Why stop at one? The party's never over, not while I'm around. Right, Stella?

STELLA: Honey, you're an inspiration to me.

(They exit.)

HEIDI *(Gazing fondly at the theatre)*: Ah, Mitya, don't you hate to see it go?

WEISMANN: If nothing else, I know when things are over.

(They exit as the two couples come together and awkwardly face each other.

Emerging from the shadows, the young selves approach their older counterparts.)

BEN *(To Sally)*: There's no way I can make amends. I feel—
SALLY: Don't say it. I'm all right. *(To Phyllis)* You take good
    care of him.
PHYLLIS: I'll do my best.
BUDDY: So long, Ben.
BEN: Next time you're back in town—
BUDDY: Sure, sure. And if you're ever out in Phoenix—

(Silence. They have nothing left to say.
    The young selves watch as Ben and Phyllis, and Buddy
    and Sally slowly exit.)

YOUNG BUDDY:
    Hey, up there . . .

YOUNG BEN:
    Way up there . . .

YOUNG BEN AND YOUNG BUDDY:
    Whaddaya say up there!

YOUNG SALLY: Hi . . .
YOUNG BEN: Girls . . .
YOUNG PHYLLIS: Ben . . .
YOUNG BUDDY: Sally . . .

(The door closes. The stage goes black.)

CURTAIN

For the theatre, **JAMES GOLDMAN** has written *The Lion in Winter*, *They Might Be Giants* (London), *Blood, Sweat and Stanley Poole* (with William Goldman), *Tolstoy* (London), *Follies* (with Stephen Sondheim) and the musical *A Family Affair* for which he also wrote the lyrics with John Kander.

His other lyrics include ballads for the films *Robin and Marian* and *The Lion in Winter*. He received an Academy Award and Best Screenplay Awards from the Writers Guilds of America and Great Britain for *The Lion in Winter*.

His other films include *Nicholas and Alexandra*, *They Might Be Giants* and *White Nights*. His novels are *Waldorf*, *The Man from Greek and Roman*, *Myself As Witness* and *Fulton County*.

For television, he has written *Evening Primrose* (with Stephen Sondheim), *Oliver Twist*, *Anna Karenina* and the mini-series *Anastasia*.

At the time of his death in October 1998, Mr. Goldman had completed the screenplay of *Tolstoy* and the book and lyrics for the musical *The Celebrated, Scandalous, Heroic Misadventures of Tom Jones* (music by Larry Grossman), which will receive a workshop production in June 2001.

STEPHEN SONDHEIM wrote the music and lyrics for *Passion* (1994), *Assassins* (1991), *Into the Woods* (1987), *Sunday in the Park with George* (1984), *Merrily We Roll Along* (1981), *Sweeney Todd* (1979), *Pacific Overtures* (1976), *The Frogs* (1974), *A Little Night Music* (1973), *Follies* (1971, revised in London, 1987 and in New York, 2001), *Company* (1970), *Anyone Can Whistle* (1964) and *A Funny Thing Happened on the Way to the Forum* (1962), as well as lyrics for *West Side Story* (1957), *Gypsy* (1959), *Do I Hear a Waltz?* (1965) and additional lyrics for *Candide* (1973). *Side by Side by Sondheim* (1976), *Marry Me a Little* (1981), *You're Gonna Love Tomorrow* (1983) and *Putting It Together* (1992, 2000) are anthologies of his work.

For film, he composed the scores of *Stavisky* (1974) and *Reds* (1981) and songs for *Dick Tracy* (Academy Award, 1990). He also wrote songs for the television production *Evening Primrose* (1966), co-authored the film *The Last of Sheila* (1973) and the play *Getting Away with Murder* (1996), and provided incidental music for the plays *The Girls of Summer* (1956), *Invitation to a March* (1961) and *Twigs* (1971).

He won Tony Awards for Best Score for a Musical for *Passion, Into the Woods, Sweeney Todd, A Little Night Music, Follies* (1971) and *Company*: all of these shows won the New York Drama Critics Circle Award, as did *Pacific Overtures* and *Sunday in the Park with George*, the latter also receiving the Pulitzer Prize for Drama (1985).

Mr. Sondheim was born in 1930 and raised in New York City. He graduated from Williams College, winning the Hutch-

inson Prize for Music Composition, after which he studied theory and composition with Milton Babbitt.

He is on the Council of the Dramatists Guild, the national association of playwrights, composers and lyricists, having served as its president from 1973 to 1981, and in 1983 was elected to the American Academy of Arts and Letters. In 1990 he was appointed the first Visiting Professor of Contemporary Theatre at Oxford University, and in 1993 was a recipient of the Kennedy Center Honors.